A Story of Stories

A Story of Stories

The Texas Border Barrio Life
&
Writings of Doña Ramona González

CRISTINA DEVEREAUX RAMÍREZ

Foreword by NORMA ELIA CANTÚ
Translations by NEIL J. DEVEREAUX

Tinta Books | Trinity University Press | *San Antonio*

Published by Tinta Books, an imprint of
Trinity University Press
San Antonio, Texas 78212

Book design by BookMatters, Berkeley
Cover design by Rebecca Lown

Cover art courtesy of the El Paso High School Library Archives

ISBN 978-1-59534-996-5 paper
ISBN 978-1-59534-997-2 e-book

Trinity University Press strives to produce its books using methods and
materials in an environmentally sensitive manner. We favor working
with manufacturers that practice sustainable management of all
natural resources, produce paper using recycled stock, and manage
forests with the best possible practices for people, biodiversity, and
sustainability. The press is a member of the Green Press Initiative, a
nonprofit program dedicated to supporting publishers in their efforts
to reduce their impacts on endangered forests, climate change, and
forest-dependent communities.

The paper used in this publication meets the minimum requirements
of the American National Standard for Information Sciences—
Permanence of Paper for Printed Library Materials, ANSI 39.48–1992.

CIP data on file at the Library of Congress

28 27 26 25 24 | 5 4 3 2 1

To doña Ramona González's children, grandchildren, and future generations. May they know the matriarchal history *de nuestra familia. Esto es su herencia.*

I also dedicate this book to all the women / *todas las mujeres*—mothers, daughters, sisters, aunts, grandmothers / *madres, hijas, hermanas, tías, y abuelas* of El Paso, Texas—past, present, and future. May this book inspire you to tell your or your family's story.

This is the story, set somewhere between the hot sun of the Mexican sky and the desert sands of Texas, of two families' search for a better life. Crossing the border was the first step in a journey that would break many barriers.

—NORMA G. HERNÁNDEZ, "Our Story: Then and Now,
Los González Rodriquez"

Generally, almost all writers have a code, as they say, a secret code or one of holding back or pointing out events. I write about barrio people, their customs, and their poverty.

—RAMONA GONZÁLEZ, "Por vida de estas santas cruces,
yo viví en estos barrios"

Contents

Foreword, by Norma Elia Cantú   xi
   Words and Stories / Stories and Words
   The Magic of *A Story of Stories:*
   The Texas Border Barrio Life and Writings of Doña Ramona González

Introduction   1
   Abuela, sí estás aquí / Grandmother, Yes, You Are Here

Memorias ancestrales / Ancestral Rememberings   18

Un cuento de cuentos / A Story of Stories   30

Chihuahuita, *el barrio de mi corazón*   62

Cuentos del barrio / Stories from the Barrio, Part I
   "*Por vida de estas santas cruces yo viví en estos barrios*" /
   "By the Life of These Holy Crosses, I Lived in These Barrios"   88

González Grocery, *el alma del barrio*   185

Cuentos del barrio / Stories from the Barrio, Part II
    "*Mi tiendita*" / "My Little Store"   201

Barrio Literacy: Doña Ramona's Poems and Fables for Children   279

Notes   289
Works Cited   295
Image Credits   303
Acknowledgments   305

Foreword

Words and Stories / Stories and Words

The Magic of *A Story of Stories: The Texas Border Barrio Life and Writings of Doña Ramona González*

NORMA ELIA CANTÚ

For a long time, I used the name Ramoncita as my password for my AOL email account. I don't know where the reference originated. I didn't know anyone by that name, although there was a Ramoncita Esparza who hosted radio programs on the Mexican radio station we listened to when I was a child in Laredo, Texas. Reading Cristina Ramírez's story of her grandmother, I was struck by the fact that the grandmother was named Ramoncita. Perhaps she was speaking to me those many years ago and time collapsed and here I am now, writing a foreword to a book about her. Perhaps. Magic? Perhaps.

I'd like to think so.

When I accepted the invitation to write this foreword for *A Story of Stories: The Texas Border Barrio Life and Writings of Doña Ramona González,* I had not read the manuscript, but I recalled fondly the conversations I'd had with Cristina Ramírez about her grandmother. Ramírez's passion for getting her grandmother's story out in the world resonated with my own work. As a Chicana folklorist, I am always interested in learning about those voices that have been ignored or forgotten, usually women's, the voices that remain silent. Moreover, as a writer of what I call autobioethnography, and as a collaborator with other Latinas on a *testimonio* project more than twenty years ago, I was very much interested in the story of how the granddaughter came to the story of her grandmother's writing life.

Ramírez had submitted a query to a book series I edit, but without receiving feedback from the press, she didn't pursue it further. I had been copied on the letter, so years later, and upon reading her piece about Juana Belén Gutiérrez de Mendoza for *Revolutionary Women of Texas and Mexico*,[1] I reached out and inquired if the book had gone anywhere. Lo and behold, in the reply email, Ramírez informed me that she had a contract with Trinity University Press. I had seen her *Mestiza Rhetorics: An Anthology of Mexicana Activism in the Spanish-Language Press, 1887–1922*,[2] and so I knew she would be meticulously working to bring her grandmother to the light. Ramírez had already participated in a digital project at the University of Houston, resulting in the Ramona González Papers now being archived with the Recovering the US Hispanic Literary Heritage Digital Collections.

Every book has a life story, and this is a rich one! The various stories woven into the fabric of this book resonate with me on many levels. I, too, had a close relationship with my grandmother, although I was not yet a college student, as Cristina was, when I sat with my grandmother listening to stories and sharing alone time. The stories Ramoncita tells echo the stories my grandmother would tell to keep me and my siblings connected to our culture and fearful of straying too far from the house, especially after sundown. Perhaps all of us have magical grandmothers whose hidden stories remain just that—hidden. How many more Ramoncitas must have gone to their graves without letting anyone know of their dreams and aspirations, that they harbored thoughts of being a writer?

Perhaps many.

As the title suggests, this book is a story of stories. The nonconforming tale of a tale can be called a testimonio or what I would venture to coin a genealogical story. The collection of stories, the autobiographical elements through which we learn about the devoted granddaughter, constitute an awakening, a coming to consciousness. Ramírez lovingly tells the story of discovering the legacy of her grandmother Ramona; she tells the story of doña Ramona González herself, of finding that her grandmother had published stories with the most influential Chicano writers of her time, like Rudolfo Anaya and Estela Portillo Trambley. *A Story of Stories* is a journey through a family's history that originated in Mexico and crossed the border into El Paso, Texas, guided by a granddaughter who tells a story of it all. The narrative unfolds amid the author's own coming to story. Ramírez tells of the poems and stories that her grandmother bequeathed and that exist as a testament to the granddaughter's tenacity in bringing them to light. In the retelling, Ramírez reclaims a voice for her grandmother; she lives again, and her stories keep her alive.

Ramírez, who seeks to vindicate her grandmother's exclusion from the historical record and the neglect of her legacy as a writer, as a Chicana, retells the story of a generation of women who were integral to the Movimiento Chicano. Their imaginations fueled the literary production of today. I imagine the other Ramonas of the 1960s and 1970s also faced the über-*macho* tenor that greatly ignored women. If they were allowed to speak at all, they were silenced time and again and relegated to the margins. In publishing Ramoncita's lost writings, Ramírez vindicates one such forgotten writer. She generously forgives the exclusion and near oblivion of such voices in the movimiento's publications and in the canon-setting anthologies of the time, attributing it to Ramona's lack of formal higher education. I suspect that there was an inherent sexist position vis-à-vis Chicanas who were writing and publishing at the time.

I take this opportunity to highly recommend this book and to thank Ramírez for her work on such an important recovery project. I thank her for straying from her usual historical work and delving into a personal and intimate subject to tell the story of how her grandmother existed and thrived in the shadows. Who better than her granddaughter to recover and highlight the marvelous work of this forgotten participant in the movimiento?

As I draw to a close, I want to reiterate the significance of the work we find between the covers of this book. Reading it, we are inspired to talk to our elders and to those near(er) their final journey. In this story of looking for a grandmother, her memories, and her life's mission, Ramírez is the consummate historian. She has added her voice to our Texas history in a work that reads like a PBS documentary but is much more poetic and deep.

I imagine Ramoncita sitting by the window, contemplating the world, dreaming up poems and stories, and writing to make this a better place for her grandchildren, for La Raza. Perhaps she smiles and thinks, yes, her work and her struggles were worth it. As Gloria Anzaldúa urged us to do, she did work that mattered and *valió la pena*. It was worth the pain. May this book go out into the world with a blessing and a white dove to guide it home to readers' hearts.

Introduction

Abuela, sí estás aquí
Grandmother, Yes, You Are Here

i am the product of all the ancestors getting together
and deciding these stories need to be told
—RUPI KAUR, *the sun and her flowers*

Literacy practices, oral traditions, and storytelling frame the way we identify, create, and interpret our worlds. These ways of knowing are passed on to family—storytelling at the dinner table, in the intimacy of the living room, and at the bedside. Doña Ramona González, my maternal grandmother, knew the power of words and wrote down her memories and thoughts for the benefit of future generations. Doña Ramona's *legado*, or legacy—for her family and for the community that can now enjoy her writings—emphasizes the passing of cultural literacy from one generation to the next.[1] Nearly fifteen years before I learned of my grandmother's writings, I attempted to capture my comprehension of her literacy transmission in the poem "Abuela." In 2001, six years after doña Ramona's death in 1995—the poem was published in the El Paso literary journal *Border Senses*.[2] Little did I know that my words foretold of *un gran plato servido con palabras* (a grand plate served with words), one that my family would one day uncover.

ABUELA

The fragile days I spent
With you
Have broken into a million pieces.
No estás aquí.

I can hear your *cuentos y dichos*
In my mind
Like echoes through a canyon.
The memories mix with the smell
Of *guiso y calabazas.*
Your wisdom is the first sign of
Spring on a winter afternoon.
It too resides in me.

Before, I would not let the wisdom in,
I thought it to be old-fashioned
Like a song that no one sings anymore.

Abuela, me has dejado un gran plato
Servido con palabras
De tu juventud.

Abuela, I feel you now,
Como el sol en las espaldas
De una mujer sin blusa,
I embrace you now,
Like a child embraces her mother
For the last time.
Abuela, sí estás aquí.

The poem's last line, "*Abuela, sí estás aquí,*" reflects the tangible quality of my grandmother's writings that are now in our possession. While this line acknowledges her influence in the present moment, I ask, "Where is *aquí*—the *here?*" As an extension of ourselves, the practice of writing, in poems, essays, short stories, and more, gives our conscious selves a permanence in the material realm. Doña Ramona's words anchor the thematic foundation of her writings and life's work, which by her wisdom were preserved. This collection of her selected writings tells of the treasure, *el tesoro*, she left our family and you, her contemporary reader.[3]

Me acuerdo / I remember

In 1991, as a young college student, I moved in with my eighty-five-year-old grandmother to attend the University of Texas at El Paso. I followed the traditional Mexican American custom of the younger generation caring for their elders and moved in with her. I took the small single room in the back of her duplex apartment in an old barrio. El Paso High School, with its neoclassical columns reaching the building's impressively tall façade, was visible from the front steps. Doña Ramona had graduated from that flagship public high school nearly seventy years earlier, in 1925. Every morning in the Chihuahuan desert, the building still stands out with the sun glistening off the light brown Greco-Roman façade as if it were a kingdom in the sky. In contrast, the apartment where we lived, only blocks away, was nothing fancy: old furniture, an unkept yard, and a productive rosebush that my grandmother cherished. During my college years, I didn't live on campus or with my friends. I never wanted to do so. And I don't believe I missed anything as a result of that decision. Instead, my life was all the richer for choosing to live with my grandmother.

For five years my grandmother and I lived together in an intimate fashion. More than a quarter century since her death, I can still picture her sitting quietly at the morning-sun-drenched nook of her dining table, her slightly hunched frame casting a soft shadow over her simple breakfast of *café con pan*. At other times she would lean into a game of solitaire, which she played incessantly. I felt what many young people might feel toward their grandparents: a mixture of deep love cloaked in curiosity about their lives and times they lived in. My grandmother's eighty-nine years spanned a period of sweeping technological advances and social change in America, including two world wars and a Great Depression. I wondered what would it have been like to live through the Depression or to have lived on the international border in such close proximity to the Mexican Revolution? Living in an age of emergent technologies and conveniences, which she sometimes didn't even care to understand, my Mexican American grandmother came from what seemed a very different time and place. She was wonderfully mysterious. At the same time, that quality of otherworldliness drew people to her—she was playful, mischievous, with a sense of humor.

Sometimes my grandmother and I sat in silence, me eating and her playing solitaire. Other times we talked. A cross-border language rooted in daily *pláticas*, or talks, sustained our relationship. Central to Mexican culture and family life, *pláticas* are the basis of information and knowledge exchange. They are an enriching form of bridging the generations and keeping families close. Eating lunch together one afternoon, Ramona pointed to the covered typewriter sitting on the cluttered desk in the dining room. In a calm, almost melancholy voice, she said, "Cuando era mucho más joven, me encantaba escribir." (When I was much younger, I loved to write). Leaning in to open the desk drawer, she pulled out a thin literary journal with a brown paper cover. She opened it and pointed to her name in the table of contents. Setting the book on the table, she returned to her solitaire hand. In silence, I browsed the contents of the yellowing copy of what was a special edition of the journal *El Grito, Chicanas en la literatura y el arte.* I noted the year of publication, 1973, and that she had published five short stories in Spanish. I don't recall much after browsing the contents, but this occasion marked the moment I learned that my grandmother was a writer and had published some of her writings. I would later learn that *El Grito* was one of the most significant Chicano literary journals of her time.

Through her daily actions, my grandmother revealed the *mezcla* (blending) of her beliefs and values. She practiced the customs of Mexican *curanderas*, women spiritualists and healers. Her freshly prepared food, seasoned with fresh *verdolagas* (purslane) picked from her backyard, could cure many ailments. Using certain herbs, she practiced rituals marking the passage of time and seasonal changes. At times when my energy was low, she'd confess, "Te estoy quitando un poco de tu energía; tienes demasiada" (I am taking a bit of your energy; you have more than enough). Always approachable in conversations with others, she would ask family members or visitors about their personal lives. If they engaged her, she stopped her card game, reshuffled the cards, and laid them out to divine their fortune. A queen or king of hearts represented a love interest; a jack of diamonds, an impending stroke of luck. The joker represented unpredictable or complicated times ahead. My brothers, cousins, and even my college companions were enthralled by her fortune-telling skills. These practices signaled her practicing a form of *curanderismo.*

On my twenty-first birthday, I invited several college friends to our small apartment. I was nervous about what they would think of my grandmother. She was then in her mid-eighties. I feared she would dampen the mood, or worse, embarrass me. I could not have been more wrong. After some birthday cake and ice cream, my friends—a mix of students from the United States, Europe, and Mexico—serenaded me with "Las mañanitas," the traditional Mexican birthday song. I saw my grandmother crying as they sang. She may have felt they were singing to her. Wiser today, I believe they were.

Later that evening, my grandmother asked Tina, a Swedish ex-change student, for her hand. "Dame tu mano," she said. Without hesitating, Tina extended her hand. My grandmother slowly turned her hand over, palm up, and gently brushed her palm and fingers. I panicked, imagining my friends would think my grandmother was silly, perhaps even a sorceress. After a few quiet moments, doña Ramona murmured, "Muy interesante."

Attempting to lock eyes with her impromptu fortune teller, Tina asked, "What is it? What do you see?" My grandmother peered into Tina's future via the palm of her hand and studied the lines zigzag-ging across her hand and fingers. "You are a strong and dedicated person. You have much travel ahead and you will win many awards. People love you and pray for you." (Tina did indeed go on to win many track and field competitions around the world.) After she had divined Tina's future, the others queued up to have my grandmother read their palms and fortunes, too! We continued to chitchat, but in some ways, they forgot about me. The plan of my birthday party faded into the night. Instead, the chatter centered on what my grandmother had told them. My friends remained that night until my grandmother had touched each of their hands and read their futures.

In her final years, my grandmother rarely left her small apartment. We ended each day together. I always sat in the same place at the dining table. Looking to my right, I saw my grandmother seated in her green recliner leaning toward the dim lamplight, holding a magnifying glass and reading a book. No radio or television noise interfered with these quiet evening hours. Always addressing me in Spanish, in a soft yet firm voice, she would ask, "¿Qué tal tu día, mija?" (How was your day, dear?). I would answer with stories about the day, interesting lectures or boys that I had met. Every evening around 9 p.m., she announced, "Tengo mucho sueño. Me retiro temprano." (I'm very tired. I'm retir-ing early.) Rising from her chair and turning slowly to walk down the hallway, she left me alone in the faint reading light. Seeing her empty chair, I pondered the brevity of life. Moments later I heard the shuffling of her feet, the knock of her wooden cane on the wall that led her to her bed, and the soft click of her door shutting for the night.

La escritora / The Writer

Doña Ramona González (1906–1995), as she was called by people in her beloved barrio, was a native of El Paso, a Tejana, a writer, and my *abuela*. She wrote history and creative literary genres such as fables and poems. Her stories and poetry, which are recovered here, bring the reader up close to people from her youth, *la gente de su barrio*. González spent the first dozen years of her life in Chihuahuita, a border community wedged along the Rio Grande between Ciudad Juárez, Mexico, and El Paso. The people and desert mountain geography of this unique community would become her literary muse. After graduating from El Paso High School in 1925, she hoped to attend the Texas College of Mines, now the University of Texas at El Paso, to learn the skills of journalism and writing. For a young woman from the barrio, however, this dream of writing would be deferred.

The daughter of Mexican immigrants, Ascención Rodríguez and Jesús Chafino, González was a vivacious, optimistic, and self-driven young woman. My *tía* (aunt) Norma, now in her nineties, describes her mother in her early twenties. "Ramona was a beauty. She had a perky nose, large dark eyes set in a round face framed by black, lustrous, curly hair. She was tall and slim with a light complexion. However, she was shy." My grandmother came into young adulthood in a time when women, especially Mexican American women, did not attend college. They were expected to marry, stay home, and raise a family. She dutifully performed these obligations, but she had other dreams—most of all, to be a writer. In her early sixties she began to record the stories of her youth. Her writings capture the early decades of the twentieth century during a wave of Mexican American

Ramona González on the steps
of her home on Durazno Street,
El Paso, Texas, ca. 1920.

migration into El Paso's barrios due to the post-revolution upheaval
and associated poverty in Mexico.

Ramona González's story begins as a second-generation child from
a large family, with a determined immigrant mother who journeyed
north from Chihuahua, Mexico, in search of a better future—the
quintessential American immigration story. González and her family
lived in various locations in El Paso during her lifetime: Segundo
Barrio, the Lincoln Park community, Missouri Street, and Cliff Drive.
The experience of growing up in the vicinity of the US–Mexico
border, interacting with and living among countless Mexicans and
Mexican Americans, shaped her identity and formed the cornerstone
of those she would write about.

Later in life, after fulfilling her family duties, González started to

```
               A La Niña

Niña, no llores, no llores,
El tiempo es para mejor pasar.
Niña, sonríe, niña sonríe
Que el tiempo pronto se va.

Niña, eres dulzura, eres dulzura,
Atesórala como una virtud.
Que nadie se lleve ese almíbar,
Que es de tu vida, la Primavera.

Niña, eres el perfume, el perfume
Eres el aroma sinigual
De la gardenia y de la rosa,
y los azares del oloroso naranjal.

Conserva las lágrimas,
Guarda tu dulzura,
Esparce el perfume
Por el caminopor donde vas.
```

Original, handwritten version
of the poem "La niña."

write. Even then, she wrote in semisecrecy. Our family suspects she began writing in the mid-1950s. Years later, in 1973, she published five short stories from her border barrio writings in *El Grito* alongside key Chicano authors of her time, among them Tomás Rivera, Rudolfo Anaya, Rolando Hinojosa, and Estela Portillo Trambley.[4] After this seminal publication, González continued to write. Possibly due to her lack of educational pedigree, she failed in her follow-up attempts to publish the remainder of her narratives centering on life in the El Paso barrios. As long as these writings lingered unpublished in the undiscovered archive, there remained a hidden border voice and a gap in El Paso's literary history.

While my family's stories are woven through this book, I believe the discovery and publication of her writings were expressly intended for me. I shared the last five years of González's life with her, forging an unbreakable bond through meals, stories, and time—she, an eighty-five-year-old *anciana;* me, a *jovencita,* at twenty years of age. Yet we managed to share an understanding that went beyond our age difference. Reading my grandmother's poems and children's stories, I imagine that she is addressing me.

TO THE LITTLE GIRL[5]

Little girl, do not cry, do not cry,
Time is for something better than just for getting by.
Little girl, smile, little girl, smile
For time soon flees away.

Little girl you are sweetness, you are sweetness,
Treasure it like a virtue.
Let no one take from you that nectar,
That is the springtime of your life.

Child, you are perfume, perfume,
You are the aroma beyond compare
From the gardenia and from the rose,
And the blossoms of the fragrant orange grove.

Conserve your tears,
Keep your sweetness,
Spread the perfume
Along the pathway that you go.

Through such writings as "A la niña" (To the Little Girl) I believe she wrote me, her granddaughter, into her *cuento de cuentos.* As an intergenerational bilingual writing project, this book about my grandmother binds our words, worlds, and writings. Throughout these pages, a *trenza,* a braid of words, ideas, and paths chosen by those who came before me, shapes the history and writings that appear here.

Una trenza de palabras / A Braid of Words

When I was a young girl, in the morning before school, my mother styled my hair into a *trenza,* or braid, a traditional Mexican woman's hairstyle. She wrapped the *trenza* to the back of my head and at times wove ribbons through it. For Mexican Americans, the trenza hearkens to its origins from pre-Columbian times and represents generations of stories told by their ancestors. As a hairstyle, the trenza symbolizes pride and beauty, holding loose hair strands in place while creating a visual pattern of interconnectedness. It represents my personal method of archiving and documenting the writings of my grandmother. Each strand tells the story of a passing on of cultural, linguistic, and family literacies across generations.

Chicano/a writers and scholars have used the trenza metaphor to give life to theory and research processes that emphasize cultural connections to their work. Scholar Sandra Quiñones, for example, uses the concept as a metaphorical and analytical tool for understanding the experiences and perspectives of Latina teachers.[6] I extend the use of that metaphor in this project to illustrate the action of *trenzando,* the action of weaving together my family's words. My words, alongside those of my grandmother, interwoven with the translations of my father, represent *una trenza uniendo tres generaciones de voces,* a braid uniting three generations of voices. The legacy of this *trenzando*—becoming a literary trenza—remains visible on the pages of this book.

First Strand: Ramona González

The trenza's first strand represents the selected Spanish-, as well as a few English-language writings, of González. Her organic and place-based writing style reflects the voice and actions of people from the barrios of south El Paso—*la voz de la frontera.* Borderlands scholars Debra Castillo and María Córdoba note that "the Chicana writer attempts to piece together an alternative, rooted, genealogical tale."

They also contend that "women authors tend to leave behind old literary and social conventions in order to conceive innovative writing forms, and to posit new subjectivities."[7] I selected writings from my grandmother's collection, unique in voice and form, that tell stories of the people and reveal the fullness of their characters. These writings, along with their translations, include "Los libros," which represents a genre I call a *cuadro*. I borrowed the term from *cuadros de costumbres*, a genre Spanish and Latin American writers and artists used to depict everyday manners and customs in a provincial setting in the late eighteenth and early nineteenth centuries.

González infused her own literary style and form into this more traditional genre. Her cuadros are shorter and focus on a singular cultural element of the barrio. Other work collected here includes "Adíos, barrio Chihuahuita" and "Barrio Chihuahuita, 1972," two personal reflections on the barrio; "Por vida de estas santas cruces yo viví en estos barrios" (By the Life of these Holy Crosses I Lived in These Barrios), a "long-short story" written in short character vignettes; "Mi tiendita" (The Little Store), another lengthier short story about the customers and events surrounding the barrio grocery store González opened in 1934; the cuadro, "El sol" (The Sun); a poem, "El vuelo" (The Flight); and a fable, "El pájaro zenzontle y el conde" (The Mocking Bird and the Count).

González's archival collection of writings includes textbook examples of historical documents—yellowed, delicate typewritten pages with penciled-in comments—and several literary styles of poetry, autobiography, and *costumbrismo,* depicting everyday life and the intimate cultural customs of a borderlands people. Intended to be read as autobiographical, her work addresses the traditions of people from the barrios who have been hidden and overlooked—characters such as *el camotero* (the sweet potato salesman); don Leandro, the milkman from Chihuahuita; doña Martina, the main character of "Por vida," a larger-than-life, outspoken midwife and barrio bootlegger; and José

Antonio, the beloved gay barrio boy who could paint and arrange a sales window better than anyone. As the narrator of her own lived experiences, González emerges as one of the many characters she depicts. She expressed herself most authentically in Spanish—*un rechazo*, a rejection, of an Anglocentric way of knowing. Yet her writings are not those of the radical Chicana protest that began to emerge in the early 1980s, such as from Cherrie Moraga or Gloria Anzaldúa.[8] Explicit social protest was not her style. Instead, she delivers a rich Chicana narrative voice, confident in a remembrance of place and her people.

Second Strand: Mi papá / My Father

The second strand of the trenza represents my father, Neil J. Devereaux, who completed the English translations of my grandmother's Spanish writings. He holds a doctorate in Spanish linguistics and Hispanic literatures from the University of Texas at Austin. I believe he was the best fit for this work, not only because of his expert fluency in Spanish. For more than thirty-five years, he was a professor of Spanish linguistics and literature at Angelo State University. For more than fifty years in the Texas cities of San Angelo and El Paso, he also worked as a translator of legal and literary texts. In the many interviews I have conducted with my father, he explains my grandmother's writings from his perspective as an expert in Latin American literature. He recognized the literary elements of *costumbrismo* in her writings and helped me coin the term cuadros to categorize some of them. He referred to my grandmother as an *ingenio lego*, or lay genius, a phrase occasionally used to describe Miguel de Cervantes, author of such works as *Don Quixote*. *Un ingenio lego* describes a self-educated author or artist who excelled at their craft yet lacked the pedigree of a university degree or other formal training. In reading González's works today, my father notes that my grandmother's writing "escapes the limitations of the barrio and her own education" and captures a universal appeal.

Education and fluency of language alone do not make a good translator. In 2021, a rare controversy erupted in the world of translation politics and spilled into the public arena.[9] Questions about identity and accessibility regarding translated writings crossed the globe, with translation becoming an unusual center of discussion. Serious inquiries—who can or should translate foreign language texts—challenged the status quo of translation work. For example, should a white male be able to translate a Black woman's work or a Chicana's writings? Can the translator do the writing justice? I believe so. Translation creates an ongoing dialogue between a diversity of people and cultures. As a democratic endeavor, translation does not depend on the translator's race or gender but on whether the translator can render a strong representation of the original. Translation of texts, literary or otherwise, stands as one of the oldest forms of communication and shared respect between two cultures. It should not be locked into rules of identity politics.

However, in translation, proximity to one's subject or culture does matter. My father knew doña Ramona personally and closely interacted with her as a son-in-law, reading her work as early as the 1970s. He recalls that during visits to El Paso, when I was three or four years old, she would pass her typed-up writings to him. With a stack of papers on the table, she asked him to edit her work, saying, "Me los puedes editar, por favor?" As a young doctorate in linguistics, my father hesitated to correct her work; he believed that his academic expertise would diminish her authentic voice. Decades later, having spent years in Mexico and more than fifty-five years participating in the life of the barrios of San Angelo and El Paso, he understood and appreciated the language she spoke and used in her writings, the language of *la gente del barrio*. As an Anglo with an adopted Mexican spirit and heart, my father's expertise has proven fundamental to the recovery effort of these writings.

Third Strand: La nieta / The Granddaughter

The trenza's final strand represents the personal, historical, and analytical perspective I bring to González's work. First and foremost, she was my maternal grandmother. I am a Texas-born and raised *mestiza*, a Tejana, the daughter of an Anglo father and Mexican American mother. I dwell at the border of two complementary cultures, languages, memories, and places. My mother taught my siblings and me *español primero*. Spanish was our home's first language. This borderlands culture, its ways of seeing the world dualistically, is imprinted on my skin and in my bloodlines with a centuries-long history of struggle. I am connected to *la frontera* that tethers the US–Mexico border communities of El Paso and Ciudad Juárez, a sprawling and dynamic metropolis. The Anglo side of my identity—that of university professor and researcher—pulls at me with a hard Western logic that at times takes me down an empty road of platitudes coupled with a sometimes unfulfilling culture that focuses too much on standards of learning or mere material comfort. My *mexicana* side—the side that believes in *curanderismo* (folk medicine), *hechizos* (spells), and *limpias* (spiritual cleansings), and frequently involves me speaking to my deceased grandmother—reaches for the deep well of knowledge from my *antepasados* (ancestors). At times this ancient knowledge comes within grasp; at other times it slips away. While I was writing this book, I felt this ancient knowledge mixing with the words of my dual existence to become something new. I plumb these two sides of myself to analyze González's writings and tell her story.

I also write and research González's history from a feminist perspective. Taking this approach to writing history, especially that of a borderlands Chicana writer, means I make a more personal connection with the writing. I invoke feminism in this work not as a radical stance but as a position from which to ask questions: Where are the women in any given historical event or era? How does the inclusion of women and their writings in the historical narrative shift the tone and perspective of that time? Along these lines, a recovery and contextualization of writings like González's should be viewed not as a rewriting of history but as the addition of a missing historical perspective. I consider the ways Texas history texts have systematically written women out of their pages. This book recovers a part of the missing history of Texas that is intertwined with writings from the past. This narrative takes twists and turns and stops and starts, reflecting the way González remembered and wrote about her barrio.

History also dwells in places. I lived in El Paso for twenty years, through my thirties. I walked the dusty, hot city streets. I visited Chihuahuita and Segundo Barrio, interacting with residents—elders, shoppers, children. I crossed the Rio Grande with family or friends to attend church services, teach, shop, eat, and visit the barrio communities of Ciudad Juárez, El Paso's *ciudad hermana*, or sister city. As they nurtured my grandmother and her daughters, these communities also became part of my daily routine. I acquired a personal intimacy and love for these communities, which offered me a unique, culturally rich perspective on what many today consider the "laboratory" of the United States in the twenty-first century—a multicultural tapestry where native sons and daughters, Mexican Americans and Spanish speakers, claim a legitimate birthright. Like my grandmother, I experienced the vicissitudes of El Paso's local cross-cultural spaces, its streets, schools and libraries, corner stores, and barrios. Because of these memories, I hold a deep affinity and reverence for the *mezcla* of this cross-border community.

Cerrando el círculo: Closing the Circle

I believe we carry a recollection of moments, events, and traumas experienced by our ancestors. We naturally bring a self-awareness of our past and understanding of how it connects with our present. It's what some people call "in one's DNA." I think of this connection as *ancestral remembering.* In writing this book, I found the stories I wrote about my grandmother—about collecting and preserving her writings, about her telling family stories to the younger generation, about her wanting to continue her education—to be autobiographical. Her stories have become my stories. I take the reader back to moments in the González family where we exchanged stories such as "La bruja de Missouri Street" and created our own family urban legend. Although my grandmother wrote extensively, the greater volume of her works went unpublished. We glimpse a moment where González accepts, late in her life, that her writings, beyond *El Grito's* 1973 special edition, will not be published. My mind flashes to instances when she wrote her first poems and cuadros.

Rarely were women of my grandmother's generation either inclined or encouraged to write. What, I wonder, was the impetus for González to start? I believe the desire to write lived in her spirit from an early age, and she was seeking to answer the calling of an ancestral remembering. Her family history leads off with a story of migration to *la frontera*, settling into El Paso's Chihuahuita, and struggling to gain access to an American education in El Paso during the Great Depression. Stories of Chihuahuita are all too often captured from an outsider's view, detached and limited to the circumstances of objective events. In contrast, González's unpublished writings reveal images and events—in the kitchen, bedrooms, front patios, neighborhood sidewalks, corner grocery stories—that routinely occurred in this historic barrio but were seldom seen from the outside. After she left the barrio, she discovered how a basic high school education and a lifetime of experience would enable her to positively shape her writings. During her lifetime, González's gift of literacy came full circle. At the end of her life—the beginning of my young adulthood—I read my own poetry to her. I believe she saw her gift of family literacy bloom in those spoken words.

Memorias ancestrales/
Ancestral Rememberings

Stories are saved in the voice.
Stars shine in long nights, those old rivers,
And the raspy telling begins. "En tiempos pasados…"
    —PAT MORA, "Feeding the Winds"

History echoes a community's collective memory of events, people, and places. It easily disappears if we do not add our own stories to this written collective, don't question longstanding narratives, or fail to recover lost and missing perspectives. Without these actions, history fades. Part of this fading of history is due to the exclusion of voices from the greater community—people who have experienced events, times, and places firsthand but do not have their ideas recorded. If the voices of the local people don't appear in the pages of history, then certainly, women's voices are absent.

Historical and literary texts of the US–Mexico borderlands and of Texas are particularly one-sided, too often narrated and romanticized from the perspectives of men—sometimes men not even from the city or region. In El Paso, for example, the writings and perspectives most widely known and celebrated are those of Leon Metz, a borderlands historian from West Virginia, and W. H. Timmons, a longtime academic historian at the University of Texas at El Paso who was born in Missouri. Neither men are native to El Paso, nor to Texas, yet they are regarded as local history experts. The popularity of their writing begs the question: Where is the local perspective? Whether local or otherwise, histories penned by men about the American Southwest are frequently based on a male-centered mythos of war, mission trails, railroads, bandits, saloons, expeditions, conquest, bootlegging, and politics. This mythical male narrative—especially that of the US–Mexico border featured in histories, novels, and movies—remains so powerful in the psyche of the American conscious that the myth effectively marginalizes and silences other voices.

Of course, there are native Texan poets, writers, and historians who have taken the charge to write about their people. These folk heroes include Américo Paredes, who is best known for *With a Pistol in His Hands: A Border Ballad and Its Hero* (1958) and *Folklore and Culture on the Texas–Mexican Border* (1993). Arnoldo De León takes a closer look at the people in his numerous books on Texas history and *la frontera,* including *The Tejano Community, 1836–1900* (1982) and *Tejano West Texas* (2015).[1] Paredes's and De León's histories counter the early Anglocentric views of Mexican Americans and their experiences in Texas, broadly expanding the repertoire of Texas storytelling. These historical perspectives have done much to advance the voices of Mexican Americans. I approach this project, however, wanting to make space for the perspectives of Mexican American women.

Until the 1990s, when a greater effort on the part of feminist historians commenced to recover women's history, if women appeared in male-oriented histories, their participation was often limited to a short paragraph, sometimes depicting them as housewives, cooks, or prostitutes. This trend toward including women's perspectives has shifted in the last two decades of published Texas history, led by such historians as Cynthia Orozco, Vicki Ruiz, Susan Roberson, and Angela Boswell.[2] Lois Marchino's *Grace and Gumption: The Women of El Paso* is a borderland historical corrective that portrays prominent women in El Paso as business owners, writers, healers, philanthropists, nuns, and artists. Writing specifically about women from El Paso, Marchino notes that "many women's stories have become part of oral history and folklore only, never written at all, or never published, or expressed in letters and diaries long ago discarded."[3] Renowned El Paso historians and autobiographers like Yolanda Leyva, Monica Perales, Selfa Chew, and Lucy Fischer-West have contributed important narratives about women in the El Paso border region. Yet women's stories are limited in comparison to the volumes centered on the border's male mythos. With women's voices almost absent from the El Paso borderlands history, this history remains, at the very least, incomplete. *A Story of Stories* offers a counternarrative and a link to this missing history.

El Paso's geographic isolation and cultural uniqueness has resulted in its historical exclusion. Organizations have led more recent efforts to bring the city into historical prominence. In 2016, for example, the National Trust for Historic Preservation, recognizing the trend of fading history in the El Paso borderlands, included two of the city's barrios, Chihuahuita and Segundo Barrio, in its annual list of America's Most Endangered Historic Places. Segundo Barrio was also listed on the National Register of Historic Places in 2021.[4] This designation asks the El Paso community to preserve the barrio's architectural and cultural heritage and seek new ways to recover and promote unheard stories and voices from its silent majority, to help El Pasoans deepen their civic appreciation and understanding.

Cuentos viejos / The Old Stories

Our ancestors, especially *nuestros abuelos* (our grandparents), carry the memories of the old stories. Those elders we have had the privilege of sharing meals, stories, and time with offer us a glimpse into their pasts. Their pasts simultaneously become our own. Our ancestral stories teach us about ourselves and explain things we may not know, such as why we are drawn to certain interests or places. Each one of us carries family stories, memories of small or grand events that play out as movies in our minds. These moments become etched into our DNA and penetrate our souls. Glimpses of these times emerge in our dreams and fade into our daily realities, shaping our present moments as much as our futures. If circumstances and family affairs align, we may be so fortunate as to hold physical possessions that are passed down from generation to generation: letters, quilts, oral stories, recipes, music, pictures, journals, and other objects that carry memories and the spirit of our ancestors into the present. By both luck and providence, my family has such a magical possession: a collection of roughly 750 pages of poems, stories, fables, and autobiographies written by my maternal grandmother, Ramona González. This veritable treasure trove remained hidden for more than thirty years. Her stories of relocation, life experiences, people of the barrio, and the magic of her barrio community were passed down orally to the younger generations at family gatherings and in daily *pláticas*.

When my grandmother was in her eighties, my family—my three siblings, parents, aunts, uncles, and many cousins—would join her for dinners in El Paso to reconnect and share stories from a time before the freeway ran through town. At my *tía*'s home on Robinson Road, we'd come together after the evening meal. As the Chihuahuan desert sunset cast its charm across the sky, the *sobremesa* (table talk) turned to the history of the González family neighborhood of the 1930s. Talk of the evening transported us to the intersection of Missouri and Ochoa Streets where my grandparents ran a grocery store. The stories opened with my uncles bringing the magic of the desert to the dining room. We laughed at the jokes our *tíos* told and the tales of youthful mischievousness on the streets around the El Paso High School neighborhood. Their personal accounts evoked images of dusty trails on the nearby Franklin Mountains, bustling school hallways filled with students, and the bright desert sun and star-filled skies. Their accounts also evoked the surreal—visiting spirits, shamans, and desert tricksters.

Our uncle, *tío* Manuel, invited us into a spoken panorama of images of don Manuel González, our deceased grandfather who was born in Zacatecas, Mexico. We relived the apparitions that periodically appeared to family members years after his death. We heard of his love for Mexico and its culture. These stories conjured vivid descriptions of cobblestone roads, Mexican adobe-tiled homes, post-colonial Zacatecas, and the González family's journey to the US border. Our family took all these stories to heart, and they defined our identity and belonging in the family—a Mexican trait even today. Wide-eyed and locked onto each word, we children listened to these tales of mischief. Once the laughter subsided, a moment of silence settled among us.

That silence was a cue for a retelling of our family's main story. My cousins and I would beg our grandmother, "Tell us the story, abuela! Tell us about la bruja!" Seeing her family gathered to listen to her stories, our grandmother's wrinkled face would become enlivened. In her later years, she tended to slouch slightly to one side in her chair. With her glasses slightly drooping and with wrinkles and gray hair, she wore a baseball cap to block the brightness of the dining room light. As the family matriarch, she sat at the head of the table. She would begin recounting the family legend of the community witch, "La bruja de Missouri Street." Her words, a *mezcla* of Spanish and English, added to the magic of the occasion and took us deeper into the history of El Paso, bringing to life another time and place haunted by shadows and ghosts. Through her words, we walked down dark empty streets and dusty unpaved roads, a bright moon often hanging in the desert sky. Our grandmother began: "En ese tiempo, todos conocían a sus vecinos. Eran así casi como familia. En una noche, tranquila y oscura, ya con todos dormidos, la vecina de enfrente salió a fumar.

Ni siquiera habían pasado unos minutos cuando vio alguien vestido de negro caminando en medio de la calle." (In that time, everyone knew their neighbors. They were almost like family. One night, tranquil and dark, when everyone was asleep, the neighbor lady from across the street came out to smoke. It wasn't even a few minutes before she saw someone dressed in black walking down the middle of the street.)

"La bruja de Missouri Street" tells the story of a mysterious woman believed to have attempted to curse our family. Times were difficult in 1934, and not everyone wanted my grandparents' grocery business to thrive. The people of Missouri Street neighborhood, steeped in the custom of *brujerías* (witchcraft), a common belief in Mexican culture, became frightened, forming a midnight watch to capture the witch. The story goes that on the next night the people waited for her. That night was illuminated by a full moon and, as if on cue, a cloaked figure appeared from the shadows at midnight. When the approaching figure realized that the people of the neighborhood were waiting for her, she ran down a dark alleyway. The people pursued and cornered her. Trapped, she picked up a piece of coal and quickly sketched an image of a horse on the wall. As the people approached her, she turned with a *whoosh* of her black dress, cackled aloud, and riding away on horseback, disappeared into the wall.

Told over and over again at family gatherings, "La bruja de Missouri Street" never ceased to grip our collective imagination. We identified with the story's magic and my grandmother's way of illuminating its mysteries. It connected us to a mixture of our Mexican and borderlands heritage, Catholicism, and magical realism. Through her storytelling, González passed these cultural beliefs on to us.

Years after these gatherings, I often wondered if my grandmother's stories were destined to remain merely an oral tradition of my family's. With a mixture of good fortune and foresight, she *had* recorded them. As it turned out, our grandmother's unpublished writings languished in an unmarked family archive. It was only after discovering her writings—stashed away in a cardboard vegetable box—that my family came to see our grandmother as our scribe and perhaps also a scribe for the El Paso community. How could we not have known about these writings? How could they have remained a secret for so long? I will never have the answers, nor do I need to know.

Our grandmother, a second-generation Chicana with a high school education and a passion to write, tirelessly recorded on an old typewriter the moments, events, and experiences of the people she shared a community with. Her stories, her people. And now there is the telling of how we discovered those stories to weave our family's *herencia* (heritage) of oral storytelling into the borderlands *legado* (legacy) of these writings.

El descubrimiento / The Discovery

One Saturday afternoon in fall 2015 in El Paso, my mother called with a tone of urgency in her voice. "Come over to the house right now! We have the missing writings of your *abuela*!" When I arrived, my family was sifting through an old vegetable box, reading some of the more than 750 pages of Spanish language poems, short stories, fables, and *dichos* (sayings). My *tía* Norma had brought the papers from her house in Austin, where they had been stored safely for several decades. Suddenly, we were reading our grandmother's thoughts penned forty to fifty years earlier. Her words flew off the page and came rushing into our family circle. Each page represented an original typewritten document, with some handwritten, all with some literary significance. Skimming the pages, we could see that some were unfinished—works in progress—with word and phrase strikethroughs and handwritten notes in the margins. Other pages were neatly typed—what could have been final drafts. "What shall we do with these writings?" my family asked, overwhelmed by this discovery.

Looking to my family, I said, "Please, entrust me with them. I know

Los Pajaritos

Los Pajaritos cantan en la mañana, cantan en la tarde.
Los puedes escuchar en el bosque y en el jardin. Los Pajaritos
del bosque se trepan muy alto, alto para cantar con toda su
fuerza. Poreso el canto de Los Pajaros es tan hermoso y sonoro.

¿Haz visto en alguna ocasion, como los Pajaros hacen su nido?

Los Pajaritos todos nacen de huevitos que ponen las Pajaricas.
Los Pajaritos tienen dos patitas y un piquito y dos alitas. Por
eso tienen que hacer un nido en donde nacer. Los Pajaros papas
ayudan a hacer y formar el nido. Con palitos, hilos que recojen
en los harboles y pelos y cerdas de animales. Todo esto forma un
buen nido para que nazcan los Pajaritos.

En el jardin de lucidas flores, pasean a picar las tiernas
ojas. Luego se van a buscar granos por los campos. Van llenos de
contento, volando pora aire, libres, cantando sus cantares.

Hay un pajaro muy especial, muy hermoso en sus trios. Este
pajaro es el Ruiseñor. ¡Canta al amanecer, canta al atardecer y te
canta al anochecer! ¡Que bonito!

El Ruiseñor endulsa con su trio el ambiente silencioso y
oscuro. Para el no hay noche, cuando el quiere cantar, canta. El
canta sobre la cumbre de los arboles, entre jardines de flores y
en los verdes campos. El Ruiseñor resplandece en su canto.

          Niño ....
               Escucha su canto ....
                    Y el de todos los Pajaritos.

Los niños, están compuestos de plantas flexibles,
y materiales como, hilos, cerdas, ramas secas pero
blandas; tejidos como se pudiera, con esfuerzo,
una con el otro hasta formar algo como Tela resistente. Nos pareciera que un pajaro o pajarito
sería casi imposible de que sin objeto, así, lo
terminara también un animalito o ave que sin
otra ayuda más que su pico y sus patitas.

El Pajaro es el constructor del nido, el acarrea
de todo lo que cree es útil para la Construccion de su
nido. Pedazos de planta suave, años, secas pero no huesos,
algodon y luego, se hace deuorcido, luego, la Pajarita se quita sus propios plumones

Sample page of Ramona González's original writing, from "Los pajaritos."

exactly how to preserve them." Since that day, and with the help of my father, I have scanned all of my grandmother's writings and digitally cataloged and organized them under a digital finding aid. González's writings capture a slice of borderlands heritage of far West Texas and the Mexican American immigrant experience, flavored with a uniquely Mexican sensibility and identity. Her writings address El Paso history, border barrio folklore, and Chicano literary history from an early to mid-twentieth century perspective. She took it upon herself to record her community's history at a time when Mexican American women rarely wrote and were much less published. Her vision and work are nothing short of revolutionary. The collection intersects with the history of El Paso's barrios and their people and sheds light on cross-border civic movements that spanned over a century, from prerevolutionary Mexico to the 1970s, capturing these social movements as well as my maternal family's connections to Mexico.

As it happens, most of my immediate family members, including my grandmother, are Mormon, and we hold a strong belief in the importance of genealogy. Because of this belief, we have gone in search of our ancestral roots. Some of my family, including González's younger sister Blaza and my mother, Sandra, traveled to northern and central Mexico in the 1980s to visit the Catholic churches, which at one time were the official registrars. They visited centuries-old Catholic churches in the cities of Zacatecas and Parral, Chihuahua, to locate our genealogical records, obtaining certificates of family births, baptisms, and deaths. After poring over countless dusty archives, my family successfully assembled more than two hundred years of family history. Their efforts paint a rich picture of where and how my ancestors lived in Mexico, which no doubt influenced González's childhood and, ultimately, her writings.

Central to the family genealogy project and analysis of González's writings are interviews I conducted with her four children: my aunt

Norma, *los cuates* (the twins), Manuel and Ismael (both now deceased), and my mother, Sandra. I sought specific answers about my family's lineage and influences: What language was spoken in the home? What was González's early childhood like? What value did she place on education? Who were some of her biggest influences? Did she write privately or share her work? Each answer from my family and clue I received helped me piece together this ancestral remembering.

To honor my grandmother's work, I have maintained the spirit of her writings. González wrote primarily in Spanish, which reflects her everyday interactions *con la gente de su barrio.* I present her writings as she wrote them in their original textual form. The manuscripts our family uncovered were not final drafts, and the Spanish text does not read in a standardized form. González read and spoke Spanish fluently but experienced limitations in her knowledge of the written language. She never attended formal Spanish classes but learned it from her daily interaction in the barrios, in Sunday school classes, and with her family. Importantly, this knowledge of everyday colloquial Spanish gave her a literary advantage. She wrote in the language of the barrio and not a polished form of Spanish. As a result, she occasionally misplaced or missed accents in words like *hábito, lágrimas, pláticas, más, ojalá,* and *así.* These errors could also be attributed to the limited technology of 1960s- and 1970s-era typewriters, which could not type accented words. We see in the original manuscripts where she added a number of diacritic marks.

González also misspelled several of what are called "eye spelling" words, which one must see in order to spell them correctly. If the writer has not read the word, it is easy to use an *s,* for example, instead of a *z,* as in *cerveza* (cervesa) or *cabeza* (cabesa). The same is true for the letters *b* and *v,* whose phonemic values are identical, as in *cerveza* (cerbeza or cerbesa or cervesa) or *cabeza* (cavesa or cabesa or caveza). These slight errors in the manuscripts offer a glimpse into González's

willingness to write. To create a reader's edition, these errors have
been corrected throughout the text. She also used words, phrases,
and common idioms of the barrio, such as *no nos haga jale, hacerle
pendejo, pilón, lonches, dar por violin,* which have been translated to best
reflect their colloquial meaning. Regardless of these occasional mis-
spellings and missed accents, González retains her rich storytelling
voice in the vernacular of her time and place, which reflects the true
beauty and significance of her writings.

Noticias de portada / Front Page News

Four years into this project, I received an envelope full of newspaper
clippings from my mother. On yellowed, delicate paper, one clipping
revealed a November 14, 1975, *El Paso Times* front-page interview
with González. It answered some of my questions and sparked new
ones. The columnist, Joe Quintana, began, "Even over the phone
Ramona González's voice calms, soothes. And when she laughs her
soft, tranquil chuckle, the world seems warmer, just a better place to
live." As I read his commentary, my grandmother's soothing laugh at
family meals resonated in my mind. The article also revealed some
of González's life influences. "[Ramona's] intense belief in the value
of education came from her mother [Ascención] 'who never went
to school and who learned to read and write by writing on walls with
charred sticks,' Mrs. González said. Her mother also influenced her
writing, but 'it was her daughters who encouraged [her],' she added."[5]

The article also cited González's then recent inclusion in *Worthy
Mothers of Texas, 1776–1976,* a special bicentennial collection sponsored by the Texas Mothers' Committee. Described as a dedicated
mother and grandmother, corner grocery store owner, published
writer, and community activist, González was one of only two Mexican
American women profiled in the anthology. Her youngest daughter,
my mother, wrote the commemorative biography for the work:

Why should Ramona González be a bicentennial mother? She

represents the best of two traditions. She is Mexican in that she re-
tained the best of her cultural heritage for her children and grandchildren—food, stories, a strong sense of family and pride in the
Spanish language, for we learned Spanish and English at home
without difficulty. She is American in that she taught us the virtues
of thrift and responsibility; instilled in us a spirit of independence;
through example showed good citizenship by always casting her bal-
lot; and counseled two generations to seek a continuous education
made possible only in this country.[6]

Like my grandmother, thousands of Mexican American women in
1960s and 1970s El Paso and throughout *la frontera* were negotiat-
ing their roles in two cultures and two languages while working and
raising children. Invisible to the public, they formed the backbone
of El Paso's everyday life as maids, seamstresses, laborers at El Paso
Laundry, waitresses, cooks, nannies, cashiers, salespersons, and store
accountants. The majority did not hold a high school diploma, which
possibly kept them from changing their immediate circumstances.
Despite growing up in a new era of possibility and change, they struggled with limited upward mobility and opportunity.

My grandmother's stories and those of the thousands of ordinary
Mexican and Mexican American women never made it into the history
books. Unfortunately, the stories of too many of these determined,
resilient women are lost. My grandmother's writings honor these El
Paso women, her contemporaries. Understanding the significance of
the powerful gift my grandmother left behind, I am determined not
to let her stories vanish.

Un cuento de cuentos/
A Story of Stories

Asked if she was wealthy, Mrs. González laughed, "Oh, no, I'm hard working, that's all," she replied. Then after a moment's reflection, she said, "I'm wealthy in lots of ways. My children. I have a lot of books. That's my wealth."

—*El Paso Times* INTERVIEW, 1975

By the time she was in her mid-eighties, Ramona González had tried for almost a decade to publish her writings with limited success. In 1973 five of her short stories appeared in the first of a book series published by *El Grito: A Journal of Contemporary Mexican American Thought, Chicanas en la literatura y el arte.*[1] This edition would go on to become a landmark collection of one of several emerging Chicano/a literary texts, including *Aztlán, El Grito del Norte,* and *Encuentro Femenil.*[2] Publication in *El Grito* gave González a taste of sharing her work, and it fueled a desire to write and publish more. Although beginning her work relatively late in life, she would write more than 750 pages of original prose and poetry, most of it in Spanish. She published a few other pieces, such as "Prueba de fe" (Test of Faith), in a local Mormon Relief Society circular in April 1969 but little else.[3] In spite of the limited publication exposure, González was determined to overcome her disappointment. She spent several decades writing her memories of the El Paso barrios where she grew up, believing that her words held relevance then and into the future.

In summer 1989, at the age of eighty-three, González spoke one afternoon over the phone with Rodolfo (Rudy) Hernández, her son-in-law. They discussed how the world was shifting toward faster technology and she felt she just couldn't keep up. She also commented on her failure to publish more of her writings. Rudy said, "Creo que tus papeles todavía valen y cuentan mucho para el futuro de nuestra familia y esta comunidad. Dámelos y yo te los cuido." (I believe your writings are worthy and count a great deal for the future of our family and community. Give them to me, and I will take care of them.)

González agreed. "Sí, tendré todos los manuscritos listos en la caja cuando llegues. *¡Pero prométeme que los vas a cuidar bien!*" (Yes, I will have all the manuscripts ready in the box when you arrive. But promise me that you will take good care of them!).

Days later, in her small El Paso apartment, González began gathering her cleanly typed manuscripts. She organized her writings according to style: a stack for her short stories, poems, riddles, and dictionary terms; and another stack consisting of some two hundred pages of *dichos*. Reading a few of them, she smiled and remembered the joyous afternoons she had spent with her *comadres* writing down each of their *dichos: Un bien, con un mal se paga.* (Return good for evil.) *Verla paja en el ojo del vecino y no ver la viga en el nuestro.* (Seeing the speck in the eye of your neighbor, yet not seeing the beam in your own.) *Andar entre la cruz y el agua bendita.* (Between a rock and a hard place.) *El que tiene tienda que la atienda, sino que la venda.* (Putting first things first.)[4] For González, the amusement and simple pleasure triggered by these *dichos* lingered on the pages and in her mind.

"Tal vez—maybe," she may have thought, "these writings are not

```
                              Los Libros

            Este Libro es tuyo, muy tuyo. Te lo regalo para que
        lo veas y si quieres lo leas y tendrás más felicidad.
            Unos versos hay esparcidos en tu Libro. Son como esca-
        leras de astros que llevarán tu pensamiento alto, muy alto.
        Te sentirás gozoso cuando los leas y los comprendas.
            Son cuentos y versos para ti, todos para ti. Por medio
        de palabras en el cuento y en el verso, oirás cantos armon-
        iosos,Verás otras tierras, sentirás los deseos de ver estre-
        llas lejanas y raras,relumbrar en una noche clara. Te darán
        ancias de recrearte en las aromas de raros jardines y flores.
        Y te divertirás viendo los matíces de diferentes aves.
            !Mas, que triste es cuando un Libro lleno de encantos, de
        olores de claveles y rosas, de relumbrantes estrellas, de le-
        janas tierras y de mil maravillas, que tu tienes en tus manos,
        y no lo ábres para leerlo y recrearte en los hermosos retablos!
            Admira, niño, los Libros como un tesoro. Cuida tus Libros
        y goza en ellos, en las figuras pintadas, ya sean de la natu--
        raleza o de cosas. Los paisajes desconocidos los verás en las
        fotos y en pinturas en las ojas de tus Libros. Con tus Libros
        pasarás los mejores tiempos de tu vida.

                Lee, Niño,....
                        Lee Libros buenos.....
                                    Y serás Riquisimo.....
```

Original text of the cuadro "Los libros."

ready to reach the world. My ideas are perhaps old-fashioned. Is it possible that one of my children or grandchildren will read them and be inspired to write, too?"

Returning to the task at hand, she arranged the fables and cuadros. She took the first cuadro from the stack, read it, and possibly wondered, "Will anyone ever read these writings?" "Los libros" rested at arm's length. She leaned in to pick up the document. Fingering the text, her mind raced to the day some thirty years earlier when she wrote it. One morning in 1958 or so, while she was taking care of her first granddaughter, Raquel, González worried aloud, "What will be

Raquel's *herencia*? What will be my *legado* to my family?" Her memory perhaps drifted to her mother, Ascención Rodríguez, remembering the sacrifices she had made in journeying to the United States at the turn of the century. Then almost 60 years before, her mother's bold move ensured that a young González received an education and an opportunity for a better life.

Thinking of her family—past, present, and future—González picked up a pen and notebook and penciled the first line of "Los libros." She spoke words of guidance to young Raquel as her thoughts poured onto the page. "Este libro es tuyo, muy tuyo. Te lo regalo para que lo veas." (This book is yours, very much yours. I give it to you so you can see it.) A phone call from Norma, González's oldest daughter and Raquel's mother, broke the quiet of the morning. While they chatted, Raquel sat quietly on the floor playing with her toys. She grabbed one of the many books scattered nearby and turned the pages as if she could already read. After the brief call, González picked up her pen and continued, "y si quieres lo leas y tendrás más felicidad" (and if you want to read it, you will have great happiness.) A few days later, after several edits and corrections, she typed out the full cuadro. It is translated here.[5]

BOOKS

This Book is yours, very much yours. I give it to you so you
can see it and if you want, you'll read it and you will have more
happiness.

A few verses are scattered in your Book. They are like stairways
of stars that will carry your thoughts high, very high. You will feel
joyful when you read and understand them.

They are stories and verses for you, all for you. Through words
in the story and in the verse, you will hear harmonious songs,
you will see other lands, you will feel the desire to see distant and
rare stars shining on a clear night. They will make you desire to

recreate in the aromas of rare gardens and flowers. And you'll
have fun watching the nuances of different birds.

But how sad it is when a Book full of fascinations, of fragrances
of carnations and roses, of sparkling stars, of distant lands,
and thousands of wonders, if you do not open it to read it and
recreate in the beautiful tableaux. Hold the Books in high
esteem, child, like a treasure.

Take care of your Books and enjoy the painted figures, whether
they are from nature or from things. You will see unknown
landscapes in the photos and paintings on the pages of your
Books. With your Books you will spend the best times of your life.

Read, child…

Read good Books…

And you will be extremely rich…

In "Los libros," González conveys her understanding of the importance of literacy, not only to Raquel but to the next generation of
readers. Not having attended college, our family's matriarch made
sure her four children did. By the time she wrote "Los libros," her
children were grown and had obtained a college degree or were in
the process of obtaining one. The classic immigrant success story un-
folded with González's children being among the first generational
wave of Mexican Americans of the 1960s to receive their college
degrees in greater numbers. Manuel became an engineer; Ismael,
a pharmacist; Norma, a university professor and college dean; and
Sandra, a public high school teacher and community activist. Her
children would collectively carry on the González legacy with twelve
grandchildren. Through her own struggle with limited opportunities,
yet newfound successes in a new country and era, González saw the
positive impact education and literacy creates in one's life. Wanting
to reach the younger generation, she portrayed the benefits of literacy in such a way that it appealed to children. In her mind's eye, she

imagined and wrote that books mirror a "stairway of stars" and that literacy would make the reader "extremely rich." In her lifetime, she would write forty-two poems and ten cuadros for children, including "Niño, cuida tu salud," "Ilusiones," "Joyas," "Lluvia de estrellas," and "Juegos."[6]

During that summer, González accepted with resignation that her remaining work would not be published. Her time had passed. She covered her typewriter for a final time and collected the papers spread across the table. Working through the heat of the day, she placed these memories and stories—her "gran plato de palabras"—into the vegetable box. As Rudy had promised, soon after the phone call he collected the box. Stored in a closet for three decades, it continued to hold the key to González's identity, memories, and dreams. In 2016, when my *tío* Rudy was dying from Parkinsons, he revealed the box full of González's writings to our family. Unfortunately, we do not know the chronology of her writing, or the order the pieces were placed in the box. Taken as a whole, however, the topics and choice of language in which she wrote say a great deal about her intended audience and message. This emphasis on Spanish-language writings suggests González was intentionally reaching for and claiming her personal heritage and ancestral roots.

Cruzando fronteras / Crossing Frontiers

While González's life began in a barrio in the desert sands of far West Texas, her family's history stretches back to Chihuahua, Mexico, at the turn of the twentieth century. Punctuated first by revolutionary fervor and then the Mexican Revolution (1910–17), the politics and policies of the first two decades of the twentieth century were a period of turbulence and upheaval in Mexican society. Tens of thousands of Mexicans, including my grandmother's family, fled the violence to relocate in Texas border cities like El Paso, which they knew as "El Paso del Norte." Material poverty may have been the reality of the

Severa Valles, Ramona
González's grandmother
(left), and Ascención
Rodríguez, González's
mother (middle), with an
unknown woman.

early days of González's life. But neither she nor her family suffered
from a poverty of spirit or mind. That inner fortitude and grit appear
throughout her writings. Her bicultural, bilingual upbringing was,
and still is, commonplace in El Paso and other border towns. The
linguistic and cultural influences, for her, came from living so close
to Ciudad Juárez.

Her family had immigrated from Hidalgo del Parral, Chihuahua,
the city through which the Mexican National Railroad crisscrossed
the state of Chihuahua and where revolutionary leader Pancho Villa
would be assassinated in 1923. González's mother, María Ascención
"Chona" Rodríguez (1869–1940) was born in Parral's Barrio Rayo.[7]

At the time Hidalgo del Parral stood as a small pueblo inhabited
by Tarahumara and Concho peoples. Parral was a bustling regional

commercial center famous for its silver mining, which dated back to the sixteenth century and Spanish colonialism. Wealth from these mines, however, remained with the ruling class. Pervasive economic inequality persisted, which was the norm for centuries across Mexico. The indigenous and poorer, uneducated segment of society was exploited for work as indentured labor in the mines. Under the dictatorship of Porfirio Díaz (1875–1910), parts of Mexico were modernized and accumulated great wealth. But those same economic policies, based heavily on labor exploitation, devastated the lives of the common people in Mexican rural villages like Hidalgo del Parral. The women of my family, my great-great-grandmother Severa Rodríguez and great-grandmother Ascención Rodríguez persevered through the economic devastation that spread to northern Mexico before the revolution, making already bad living conditions worse.

Our family does not know the details of Ascención's daily life in Mexico. We can, however, imagine her life through various historical facts. She married Jesús Chafino in 1886 at age seventeen in Carrizal, a small rural community ninety miles north of Parral. For those women not of the upper class in Mexico, daily life delivered a harsh existence, filled with menial labor and bitter acceptance of their fate. They married young, received little formal education, gave birth to large numbers of children, and often died in childbirth or from hardship. Mexican women had limited to nonexistent opportunity to earn their own money or independently provide for their families. Young girls from the lower classes could attend public schools. Most often, however, they acquired only a primary school education, equivalent to third grade, with limited attendance beyond that due to the high cost and obligations to help in the home. Girls had little choice in the matter. An education in Mexico was a privilege reserved mostly for the wealthy and upper classes. Many women from the lower class took up cleaning homes, washing laundry, sewing, selling what food they could make (such as tamales and tacos), begging on the streets, and occasionally resorting to prostitution. These traditional roles limited them even after they were allowed an education. Mexico's highly genderized social structure, which also prevailed in Mexican American communities in the United States, remained a space strictly for the social and economic advancement of men.

In 1896, a decade after Ascención and Jesús married, talk in the Chihuahuan barrios of Carrizal and the surrounding region of Villa Ahumada centered around opportunity and hope of employment brought on by the opening of the north-connecting Rio Grande, Sierra Madre & Pacific Railways. In Mexico, the mine and landowners paid abusively low wages. Speaking to one another, the workers protested the conditions, saying, "No nos pagan por nuestro trabajo. ¡Nos roban! Pero sí hay mucho trabajo—y bien pagado—en el norte." (They don't pay us for our work. They rob us! But there is a lot of work—and well paid—up north.) Those working in the mining system were only slightly better off than slaves. Thousands of Mexicans at the turn of the twentieth century were trapped in a prerevolutionary system of oligarchic rule and proletariat work—the very conditions Germany's Karl Marx assailed as conditions rife for social revolution. As it did for many, conditions of poverty for Ascención and her family became unbearable.

To escape, people looked north. Going south wasn't an option— the rest of Mexico merely held the likelihood of the same harsh conditions. But El Norte offered the promise of jobs, change, and opportunity. The railroad opened that path. Although train tickets were expensive, sometimes costing laborers more than several weeks' wages, the opening of the railroad that connected Chihuahua towns to El Paso inevitably set off a wave of immigration in the early twentieth century. With Ciudad Juárez and El Paso as a principal crossing point and connection to the rest of the United States, the West Texas town would experience a flood of Mexican immigrants in search of working opportunities and better lives.

La jornada / The Journey

We can only imagine their rail journey north from Chihuahua to Texas, which is not written down or documented, of more than a century ago. Desolate backcountry, hot desert days, and cold dark nights. Monsoon storms could have interrupted the trip, fueling trepidation and fear of the unknown. Chicana scholar Vicki Ruiz documents some of the forgotten experiences of women who journeyed north *al otro lado* searching for opportunities.[8] Much like the current migration stories, some followed their husbands, while others journeyed alone as single mothers or widows with children. The long journey through the Chihuahuan desert under a bleak, unforgiving sky, together with the uncertainty and risk of crossing into the United States, hinged in part on simple luck or sheer determination to succeed.

My great-grandparents Ascención and Jesús considered their options—stay in Chihuahua and hope for circumstances to change or leave. Along with hundreds of others, they decided to make the trip north to the US–Mexico border, to El Paso del Norte, the Pass of the North. For weeks before their journey, Ascención prepared the children, "Niños, prepárense. Viajamos al norte en unos días. Díganle adiós a sus amiguitos." (Children, prepare yourselves. We are journeying to the north in a few days. Say goodbye to your friends.) The family sold or gave away the few items they owned, packed clothes and food, gathered the pesos they had saved, and prepared their four children—Juana, Manuel, Antonia, and Carlos—for the several-days journey.[9]

On an August morning, in the dark and cool of daybreak, in what was probably 1899, Ascención, Jesús, and their children huddled in the back of a wagon filled with animal feed. They carried blankets and cloth sacks filled with provisions. The children slept while Ascención and Jesús kept watch. Wagon wheels crunched the gravel road as the clop of horses' hooves marked the time before sunrise. Though it

Mexican Central Railway train at station, ca.1880–97.

seemed an eternity, it was only several hours before they reached the train station, where they would wait indefinitely—possibly two or three days—for the train to Ciudad Juárez. When it arrived, they loaded into one of the cars, excited yet fearful for the opportunity to travel to a new and unfamiliar land.

Un sueño esperado / A Dream Awaited

In my mind's eye, I imagine Ascención and Jesús arriving at *la frontera.* A loud, high-pitched whistle and rising steam from the locomotive engine announced the train's appearance behind the rising dust. The train screeched to a slow stop in the booming northern Mexican pueblo of Ciudad Juárez across the river from El Paso. Out the window, Ascensión observed the endless blue skies and the Franklin Mountains off in the distance. Unfamiliar sights of buildings and people filled her eyes. A large crowd of people selling food—tacos or

Train station in Ciudad Juárez, Mexico, looking northeast with the eastern slope of the Franklin Mountains in the distance.

tortillas costing a single peso—from baskets and rolled-up blankets ran to greet the arriving train. Holding tightly to her children and the railing, Ascención stepped down from the car and scanned the scene.

She likely marveled, perhaps became frightened, by the large crowd that filled the stretch along the tracks and station and spilled into the streets. Makeshift markets with *puestos* (stands) of fresh farm produce and leather goods lined Avenida de 16 de septiembre and the unpaved connecting streets. The odor of human sweat mixed with food and smoke from the train as shouts to passengers turned her head in every direction. Loaded with provisions, Ascención and Jesús hustled past the crowds of vendors and travelers, nudging their four children through the dusty streets of Juárez. They blended in and disappeared among hundreds of other travelers from the far-flung corners of Mexico and other countries. That first evening, they likely remained in Juárez, possibly resting on the streets.

Early the next day, perhaps after a meal of *frijoles con tortillas* over an open fire, Ascención and Jesús, determined to cross the Rio Grande into the United States, again made their way past people walking, mingling, and selling their wares along the streets; aside adobe homes; and in front of the city's Catholic churches. The city bustled with action. By midday they arrived at the wooden Santa Fe Bridge.[10] Men with river paddles approached Jesús, asking if he wanted a ferry ride across. "¡Te llevamos al otro lado!" With only a few pesos in his pockets, Jesús waved off the offer. They would take their chances on the bridge. Ascensión and her family began the last leg of their walk and, as they crossed the river, El Paso del Norte slowly came into view. Scanning the Franklin Mountains, they saw hillside homes with what seemed like hundreds of steps that led to large brick buildings replete with balconies and patios. Ascensión may have marveled to Jesús, "Ahí deben de vivir los ricos." (That's where the rich must live.) Closer to the river and below the hillside homes sat hundreds of adobe homes that filled the horizon along the river's bank.

Weary from travel, Ascensión and Jesús stopped at the end of the Santa Fe Bridge to rest and take in the view. They looked over the immense, swiftly flowing Rio Grande, what Mexicans called the Río Bravo. They heard the dull roar of the river as it flowed downstream. Standing in awe, the couple no doubt gazed into the northern distance where the Franklin Mountains stood, tall and rocky, green from the monsoonal rains. With a backdrop of a deep blue sky, the mountains' splendor heightened the intensity of the scene. In mid-August, *la frontera* radiated a verdant, summer-desert green, with bosques of tall cottonwoods surrounded by lush green shrubs at river's edge. The Chihuahuan Desert's setting sun painted the sky a deep orange. A promise of a better life for the young family no doubt coalesced in this vision.

A buzz of activity whirled around them. The ding-ding of the Juárez street trolleys announced their departures. Crowds of people came and went across the bridge. Huddled together, the family of six stood in the immigration line. Whether fleeing poverty or political unrest, Mexicans coming to the United States filled a dire need for labor. For that reason, immigration enforcement did not resemble the level of interdiction and detention it does today. Immigration policy was much more relaxed along the international border in the 1890s, extending into the early decades of the twentieth century.[11] At the time my great-grandparents came, migrants crossing into Texas were not yet scrutinized, nor were they made to strip and endure the gasoline baths, full-body fumigations, and torment that would begin to be implemented in 1917.[12]

Now almost dark, the border post agent waved the family into the shade of the tree at the patrol booth. In heavily accented Spanish, he asked the requisite question, "¿De dónde vienen?" He scrutinized Ascención from head to toe.

Tired and nervous, his hat crumpled in his hands and held at his chest, Jesús replied, "Venimos de Carrizal, Chihuahua, señor. No tan lejos." His answer was, in part, a geographic one—being not far from the border, this was their home too.

"¿Y por qué vienen a El Paso?" the patrolman asked, no doubt already knowing what brought them here. He assessed their worn, dirty clothes, scant belongings, and the apprehensive children clinging to Ascención's *reboso* and long skirt.

"A buscar trabajo, señor." Ascención responded with a clear determination that they came to look for work.

Wanting to know what skills they had to offer, the patrolman continued, "¿Y qué trabajo hacen?"

Jesús spoke next. "Pues, yo pretendo buscar trabajo con el ferrocarril. Y mi esposa, p'os, ella puede hacer tamales muy ricos y limpiar casas, señor." (Well, I intend to look for work with the railroad. And my wife, well, she can make delicious tamales and clean houses, sir.)

The agent looked again at Ascención and Jesús, then at their

MEXICAN ADOBE HUTS   EL PASO, TEX.

Mexican adobe jacales, El Paso, ca. 1905.

children. The family eyed him cautiously. The agent knew that well-mannered Mexican women were always needed to cook and clean houses for the wealthy land and company owners living in El Paso's Sunset Heights, the affluent neighborhood a short distance from where they stood. Neither Jesús nor Ascención possessed contracts to work, which would have been preferable. Yet these youthful parents looked healthy and ready to work.

Turning to the patrolman who was about to replace him at his post, the agent said, "These Mexican women are a dime a dozen and men are always needed on the railroad or in the factories." Nearing the end of his shift and wanting to fill out as little paperwork as possible, he simply said, "Pasen." With this single utterance, Ascención and Jesús unhesitatingly crossed into this new land. The young parents hastened to pick up their bags and blankets, readied their weary children, and crossed into El Paso, Texas, los Estados Unidos; to what they were certain would be a better life.

El otro lado / The Other Side

The first stop for immigrants crossing into El Paso at the Santa Fe Bridge was Chihuahuita, or Little Chihuahua, named for its proximity to the Mexican state of Chihuahua. For those thousands of immigrants who came to El Paso, the familiar appeal of Chihuahuita, so close to Mexico, included its cultural familiarity. But as many Anglos living in El Paso perceived, the barrio's location was also its ultimate drawback. Being immediately across the river and at the edge of El Paso, it served to segregate the community culturally, economically, and geographically. Mexicans without means mostly lived in the south-side barrios, while Anglos and wealthy Spanish and Mexican residents lived in the affluent neighborhoods in the foothills of the Franklin Mountains.

El Paso's financial resources were strategically kept from south El Paso, which created grim living conditions. People in Chihuahuita struggled to survive. The Chihuahuan desert posed extreme weather conditions in summer and winter. With El Paso sitting at the southern end of the Rocky Mountains, winters proved to be brutally cold. Storms brought snow drifts as high as the rooftops of the adobe jacals. In the 1906 *El Paso Herald*, reporters wrote of the "great distress [that] exists among the Mexicans who live in adobe shacks in that part of the city known as Chihuahuita. Family after family have been found there on the verge of starvation and [in a] half-frozen condition."[13] Children there died daily of disease and malnutrition. Other reports detailed the barrio's summer flooding and stagnant, dirty water, which created unsanitary and unsafe conditions. Running water was not available in most barrio homes. Dirt floors and unsanitary conditions resulted in illnesses such as typhus and cholera. Living quarters were overcrowded and noisy. El Paso's city government ignored and even worsened people's plight by harassing them to change conditions they had little or no control over. Marginal living conditions persisted for many decades into the twentieth century.

In the middle of this struggle for survival, Ascención and Jesús discovered that living conditions, labor, and education opportunities depended on decisions made by the city government and the town's wealthy landowners. In some ways these circumstances were not much different than in their familiar Mexican pueblos of Hidalgo del Parral and Carrizal. One day Jesús left in search of a better job and never returned. What happened to him has forever remained a mystery. Months after his disappearance, Ascención gave birth to a fifth child, Ramona Rodríguez. (Ramona would later take González as her married name.) Born on a snowy winter's day on January 5, 1906, in a one-room jacal in Chihuahuita, Ramona would become one of seven children (Antonia, Juana, Carlos, Manuel, Hermenegildo, and Blaza) that Ascención, now a single mother, raised through determination and resourcefulness.

If living conditions remained dreadful in Chihuahuita, in the coming years opportunities for getting an education proved equally terrible. A young Ramona endured these harsh conditions of daily life in the barrio, and those memories emerge in her writing, particularly in one of her lengthier works, a memoir of her youth written in English and titled "Chamaca's Dilemma."

> Of course, not all six-year-old children are blessed or cursed
> with such extraordinary experiences as I was. The neighborhood
> circumstances were such that within a perimeter of half a block,
> fifty families were living in two-room apartments with at least three
> persons in each, and in several there were eight. In these two rooms
> crowded mostly with children, could there be an abiding peace?
> Especially if it was a two-story tenement? Probably there could be
> a whole day of tranquility, but then come evening, husbands beat
> wives, arguments and quarrels between children turned into fights

with mothers that later were continued by the fathers, and while the discussions and fistfights were being performed, the children would be playing with one another in the middle of the scuffle. [14]

In scattered references, González writes about not having shoes for school, sweeping and wetting down the dirt floors of her home, and supplementing her mother's income by cleaning houses and selling tamales. Although life in Chihuahuita posed difficulties and offered little stability to gain an American education, González escaped the barrio life, if only briefly. Ascención saw the importance of an education and sent her to Aoy Elementary School in Segundo Barrio and to visit family in nearby San Elizario.[15] González wrote in "Chamaca's Dilemma" that "the constant struggle of our mother was that we should improve ourselves by learning something. How could that be? My brothers went off to fight for their lives [in World War I], and I was the only one in school."

Educación y primeras influencias /
Education and Early Influences

Early recollections González shared with our family included events and people she remembered from Lincoln Park School, a now historic El Paso building constructed in 1868. Lincoln Park expanded its facilities in 1915, the year González enrolled at age eight.[16] At the time she spoke only Spanish, but she fondly remembered the Irish teachers making every effort to teach her and the other Mexican American children to speak and read English. Visiting the school sixty years later, she wrote of her memories of learning English in her unfinished piece "Lincoln Park School."[17]

> We were very excited and anticipated the opening of the new Lincoln Park School....After such a stirring recollection, I heard the wind passing through the empty windows, singing the songs of old.... With continuous effort, Mrs. Castle tried to teach us the song "The End of

a Perfect Day." The words were hard as we did not understand them, and we learned them by sound. We loved to sing "The Ole Oaken Bucket," but it mad[e] us sad, as did "The old Kentucky Home," "Old Black Joe," "The Swanee River" and many others....Although it was years later that I learned that these were songs of the south! Every time I hear "Home Sweet Home," it reminds me of my mother as she used to sing it in Spanish; it also reminds me of my old friends and companions...who have passed away or can't hear or see anymore. I dedicate this song to them.

Because of her public school education, González first heard English in song and at play. My *tía* Norma wrote that the teachers at Lincoln Park "were English and they were Irish, and they taught her and the others the Londonderry Air by singing it. That was their music program—no piano, no band, no orchestra, just these women's voices singing to these Mexican kids who were learning a foreign language. For the teachers, too, were immigrants whose roots lay much beyond the Rio Grande."[18]

Lincoln Park teachers were among the early educators in El Paso responsible for teaching English to native Spanish speakers. González describes the teachers' attempts to assimilate her and the other barrio children into the American culture. She doesn't write of harsh learning conditions or treatment, or of a colonizing mindset, but of the teachers' patience and willingness to teach. For González, learning English provided access to the broader American culture. The teachers at the school had such an impact on her that decades later she remembered their names:

Thanks to all those marvelous and extraordinary teachers, wherever they are: Mrs. Jones, Mrs. Castle, Miss Nancy Hammonds, Mrs. Standfill, Mrs. Hardgroves, Misses Leightons, and other dedicated teachers who remained after I left for high school. Who will say that someday, new memories and new songs will be heard again,

with more shouts, more stamping of feet, more whisperings, and
that someone else will hear them and enjoy those wonderful, awe-
inspiring…memories…of days gone by.[19]

These teachers—themselves newcomers to the United States and
sometimes themselves ostracized from this desert community—certainly impacted González. With their collective love of literacy, songs,
and play, the Irish and English teachers laid the early literary founda-
tions for González and many other immigrant children. Yet it would
be through her own perseverance and intellectual curiosity, including during summer vacations, that she mastered reading English.

Seeing her daughter's desire to learn, Ascención took advantage
of having family in the nearby village of San Elizario and the opening of El Paso's transportation system to the small pueblo east of the
city. In 1913 transportation in the city was expanding, and the Ysleta
Interurban streetcar opened, connecting El Paso to Ysleta del Sur
Pueblo, a Tigua Indian settlement that traces its origin back to 1682.[20]
Alone, at the age of nine or ten, González would climb aboard the
streetcar that traveled east from downtown El Paso to Ysleta. From
there she traveled farther down the valley to San Elizario, where she
stayed with family for several weeks. The former El Paso County seat
and a military presidio, San Elizario was a bustling village that attracted El Pasoans as a place to relive the lore of Spanish merchant
travelers and frontier life. When Ramona visited, many of its residents still had connections to the wealth of El Camino Real de Tierra
Adentro, the trail for transporting silver from Mexico to Texas and
up to Sante Fe. This trail directly connected the Spanish colonial
missions and the wealth of New Spain.

During her stay, the Grijalvas, a wealthy neighboring family,
opened their doors to Ramona and gave her unlimited access to their
vast library.[21] Their library, likely located in the adobe home's sitting
room, showcased tall wooden bookshelves filled with books in both

Ramona Rodríguez (González)
in the 1925 El Paso High
School yearbook, *The Spur*.

English and Spanish. Sitting in a chair while listening to the distant
commotion of women cooking and cleaning in the kitchen, Ramona
reveled in this magical place as a limitless opportunity to indulge in
learning. Those hot, far West Texas summer afternoons spent browsing and reading books sparked a love of literacy and education in
González. For several summers, she visited San Elizario and that
blessed library. During that time of absorbing stories and learning
new vocabulary, she also discovered her own imagination and gift
for words—in English and Spanish. She became an avid reader of
all literature. My *tía* Norma, recalls, "Having read much English and
American literature in school, doña Ramona was able to discuss with
me the works of such authors as the Brontë sisters, R. L. Stevenson,
Arthur Conan Doyle, Edgar Allan Poe, Oscar Wilde, Victor Hugo,
Shakespeare, and Dickens, among others, when these were assigned
to me in high school."[22]

Through Ascención's tireless work and self-sacrifice cooking and cleaning for families, Ramona had the time to study and earned a high school education, graduating from El Paso High School in 1925. At the turn of the twentieth century, a high school education equated to today's college education, especially for kids from the barrio. The yearbook shows that Ramona joined the Spanish Club, was on the volleyball and basketball teams, and enrolled in a four-year commercial course. According to family interviews, she dreamed of becoming a journalist, possibly inspired by the work of early women journalists, such as Peggy Hull's many articles in the *El Paso Morning Times*.[23] Cultural reasons and economic circumstances deferred that dream, but finally—after a life of raising a family, owning and running a grocery store, and assuming the traditional roles of a young Mexican American woman—the call to write resurfaced. Starting relatively late in life, most likely in her thirties or forties, she began to sketch out stories and recording the memories of early El Paso's Mexican American communities.

Our family cannot precisely identify when González started to write. We've wondered: Did she begin with pen and paper? Did she sketch out her ideas? We have no writing pads or journals, only her collected works. I long for an opportunity to rummage through her old desk in the small dining room, which held her typewriter surrounded by papers and books. Her quiet personality kept her from talking about her writing. No doubt this trait came from the conservative upbringing that shaped her traditional values. Mexican American women of that era just did not assert themselves or express their opinions. Writing remained a craft practiced mostly by men and was not something middle-class women typically did, in either Mexican or American culture.

My *tío* Ismael, one of her twin sons, remembered a gray typewriter in the living room of their house on Missouri Street. My grandmother specifically forbade him and his siblings to touch it, but he recalls that he never saw or heard her typing. As tradition likely dictated, she may have kept her writing a secret. In her cloistered writings, González combined the influences of her barrio upbringing with Mexican upper-class influences from her husband's family. Their pastimes included intellectual conversations in Spanish about Mexican literature from the late 1800s. No doubt her husband, don Manuel González Sr. (1900–1973), introduced these literary influences to her.

To understand my grandmother's culture and literary influences, it's essential to know more about my grandfather. Born in Zacatecas, Mexico, Manuel immigrated to the United States at the age of seventeen with his five older sisters. They came after the untimely deaths of his parents, Cesáreo and Lorenza González, related to difficulties of the war. During their travel to *la frontera,* those five sisters—Josefa (Pepa), Guadalupe (Lupe), Carmelita, Adelaida (Lala), and Antonia (Toña)—carried Mexico with them to their new home, a phenomenon termed *México de afuera* (Mexico from outside).[24] Pepa, the oldest of the five, worked as a schoolteacher in Zacatecas before and during the Mexican Revolution. Immediately after the brutal Battle of Zacatecas in 1914, Gen. Pancho Villa ordered the schools reopened. Everybody returned to school as ordered, but the teachers did not receive compensation for their work. Adding to this struggle, the other González siblings were too young to find work. With no recourse, the family of six children left their home and traveled north, initially to Ciudad Juárez. Two years later the family relocated to El Paso—again, a much easier task than doing so today because the El Paso–Juárez community was essentially one society and the demand for Mexican labor was constant. As did tens of thousands of other Mexican families who made the journey, they carried the memories and influences of life in such culturally rich and historic cities as Zacatecas.

Beginning in the late eighteenth century, Zacatecas had a reputation—within and outside Mexico—as a major center of wealth from mining and industry. Located in the silver-producing namesake state in central Mexico, it prospered and boasted all the amenities of an influential city. Manuel did not grow up materially wealthy, but he did acquire the cultural and educational influences that Porfirio Díaz, the Mexican president and dictator, encouraged as a show of wealth and political power by the land-owning class. Wealth gained during "the Porfiriato" influenced the daily life of every citizen, from schooling to dress to entertainment, making existence in Zacatecas an almost baroque experience. Music, opera, and zarzuelas—a Spanish influenced musical genre—along with painting and literature were broadly accessible to citizens and even practiced by the lower classes. French cultural influences were also strong, so a curriculum of music and French language filled the González home in those prerevolutionary years. Manuel's siblings learned to play piano and mandolin, forming a musical group that sang popular Mexican songs. Just under the surface of this period of relative social calm, however, simmered the early signs of violent revolution.

Díaz's regime came under attack as the conflict of the Mexican Revolution expanded, with Zacatecas as the central city to be captured because of its cultural and historical significance and wealth. In 1914 war broke out in the city. La Batalla de Zacatecas, one of the revolution's bloodiest battles, abruptly ended the idyllic, relatively comfortable lives of the González family and thousands of others. Violent and far-reaching, the revolution brought an awareness of the importance of education for the advancement of social equality and not just entertainment and leisurely pursuits. In the battle's aftermath, parents Cesáreo and Lorenza González died. The González children carried their hopes and aspirations, and their values—education, music training, self-reliance, strict gender roles, love of literature—to the United States, emigrating in 1917. These influences and love for the arts and culture remained with my grandfather Manuel, who no doubt passed on these intimate experiences to his young wife. Yet

Manuel also broke with tradition and leaned into the ideals of the Mexican Revolution, encouraging Ramona to write.

Manuel's sister Pepa lived with the couple, taking care of their children while Ramona ran the family's neighborhood store, González Grocery. Pepa held the family together and helped to instill the rich Zacatecan heritage and pride in the González children. *Las tías* held fast to many of the prerevolutionary Enlightenment norms that represented the elitist old guard of educated, wealthy Mexican families. They also maintained a duality, however, cultivating revolutionary ideas about women's progressive roles in society with respect to educational attainment, economic independence, and personal expression. For the aunts, coming to the United States offered the chance to realize a dream of acquiring more education for the girls of their families and pursuing economic opportunities. Provided they could obtain some high school education like the boys, El Paso in the early decades of the twentieth century offered a means to advance women like my grandmother.

By marrying into the González family, Ramona learned more about these deep Mexican traditions and cultivated the progressive philosophies of education based on these revolutionary ideals. She already possessed the personal drive to pursue an education and break free of social barriers that held Mexican women back. The thriving grocery store she owned was opened in the middle of the Great Depression in 1934 and closed in 1964 when the state seized the area under eminent domain to expand the local highway system. (The story "Mi tiendita" covers this portion of her life.) She also gained respect and prominence in the community as a dedicated member of the Church of Jesus Christ of Latter-day Saints. In the early 1920s, she attended the state's first Spanish-speaking Mormon congregation. She attended services at the Douglas Street chapel, now a registered Texas historic site.[25] As an active member for more than fifty years, González gained a deeper fluency in the Spanish language by teaching Sunday school lessons and engaging in weekly Relief Society efforts.[26] Her work with the Mormon Church gave her visibility in the community and independence that the Catholic Church did not offer to women. For her, these cultural and religious ties—the ideals of the Mexican Revolution, American idealism, the women's suffrage movement, and the Mormon community's focus on civic participation—created a unique cross-cultural mix of philosophies that would influence her writing.

A *Mezcla* of Beliefs

Descendants of Ramona González have always acknowledged our ethnic and cultural *mezcla*, which at times to outsiders can seem strange and even mismatched. My cousin Manny González III observed of our grandmother's eclectic beliefs: "Ramona was the product of a strange mixture of religious and philosophical thought. Included in this amalgamation of beliefs were Catholicism, folk herbalism, biblical evangelism, astrology, tarot and palm divination, and later in her life—in order to completely undermine any hope of normalcy—there were Mormon beliefs augmented by Rosicrucian[27] and other ancient beliefs embodied in the Popol Vu."[28] My grandmother was indeed a product of the border region and shifting cultural norms resulting from three wars: the Mexican Revolution and two world wars. The decades following World War II marked changing times that would openly challenge many traditions, leading to the civil rights movement. This personal mix of beliefs and influences appears in such works as "La mulata," a story about a *bruja* (witch) who is stalked and chased, then tried by a rural community, and "El funeral de don Pancho," a short story that recounts the death of a corrupt Chihuahuita police officer under mysterious circumstances. As matriarch, Ramona González's *mezcla* of ideas was not challenged; instead, many of them—belief in

God, Mexican folk remedies, American values of independence—
have been incorporated into those of our extended family.

El Grito: The Chicano Literary Movement

In the 1960s and 1970s, El Paso's history of Texas ranching and mining pioneers, stagecoaches, western gunslingers, and border saloons
captured the imaginations of millions of Americans in TV shows and
paperback novels. These narratives flowed from the typewriters of
Tom Lea, Leon Metz, and Dale L. Walker, and other local history
writers. Seeing the literary trends, González may have wondered:
What value would a Mexican American woman's stories about her El
Paso barrio community have? Who would want to read her stories?
Based on the fact she was unable to publish the rest of her work, the
sentiment may have been true then. The winds of literary change,
however, were blowing.

Women's perspectives, through various genres in creative writing
(poetry and short story) and a growing body of Chicano literature,
found an expanding audience. Seeking greater representation in all
civic areas, the Chicano experience of the 1960s and 1970s promoted
the social inclusion of inherited Mexican, indigenous, and Spanish
languages, cultures, and ways of life. González lived in and felt the
heartbeat of this experience, which was centered in the southwest-
ern states of California, Texas, Colorado, Arizona, and New Mexico.
The Chicano movement erupted in the early 1960s, and González
followed its literature and news. The Mexican American and Spanish
American voice became more widely read with publications like
Rudolfo Anaya's *Bless Me, Ultima*, Tomás Rivera's ... *y no se lo tragó
la tierra*, and Estela Portillo Trambley's *Rain of Scorpions and Other
Writings*.

The Chicano movement signified a social affirmation of Mexican
Americans who were actively protesting their stagnant educational,

economic, and civic opportunities. The movement's demands resonated throughout the nation and, more intimately, in the communities of El Paso. Cesar Chavez's United Farm Workers march from
Delano, California, to the state capitol of Sacramento in spring 1966
galvanized Chicanos and other Americans. In El Paso, the Chicano
movement resonated with labor strikes at the Farah Manufacturing
Company, which manufactured jeans and other apparel. Farah employed hundreds of Mexican Americans, but low wages, few benefits,
and growing pressure on employees to meet high production targets
pushed workers toward union representation. A strike ensued. As reported in *El Mestizo*, the official bilingual newsletter of Movimiento
Estudiantil Chicano de Aztlán at the University of Texas at El Paso,
protests erupted in the streets with Chicano high school students supporting the 150 Farah strikers.[29] As a voracious reader of the newspaper, González no doubt followed the United Farm Workers and Farah
workers' strike developments. Furthermore, she may have come to
identify with chicanismo as these civic movements came to life in her
community.

In his 1975 *El Paso Times* interview with González, the reporter
wrote, "Mrs. González is very empathetic about dual loyalties to
Mexico and the US. 'When I hear the national anthem from either
side, I get emotional,' she said, then added matter-of-factly, 'I am
Chicana.'"[30] Her claim to chicanismo reflected a bold move at the
time. The term "Chicana" carried militant connections to a growing
radical social movement. Irene Blea notes that "for striving toward a
different society, Chicanas were frequently thought of as deviant."[31]
The terms "Chicano" and "Chicana" had the effect of dividing members of the movement from Mexican nationals. Yet González found
her voice during this tumultuous time as a Chicana.

Connected with her identification, González's writing intersects
with the growing Chicano literary movement of the 1960s and 1970s.

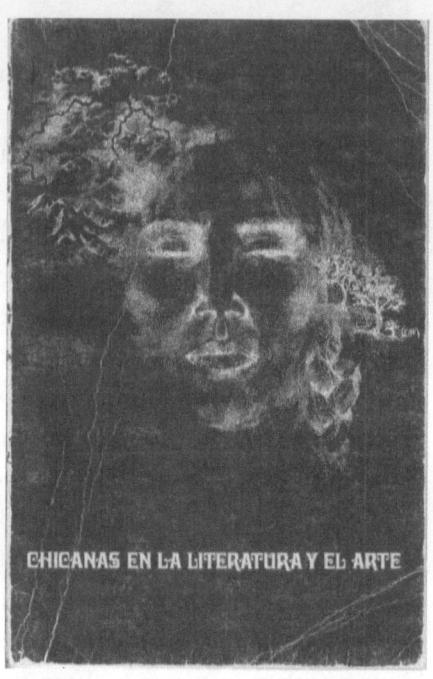

CHICANAS EN LA LITERATURA Y EL ARTE

Front cover of the September
1973 issue of *El Grito: Chicanas
en la literatura y el arte.*

At a time when it was difficult for women to gain literary exposure, she
published five Spanish short stories in 1973 at the age of sixty-six in a
special edition of *El Grito: A Journal of Contemporary Mexican-American
Thought,* titled *Chicanas en la literatura y el arte.*[32] *El Grito* exemplified
the literary Chicano movement. Chicano historian Dennis Lopez
notes, "Texts distributed by Quinto Sol from 1967 to 1974 stand as the
earliest and perhaps most influential scholarly and literary works of
Chicano movement participants struggling to forge an autonomous
and self-sustaining intellectual and creative space for the development and self-definition of the Chicano community."[33] The work collected in the special edition may have been a direct response to the
1972 Chicana Caucus meeting, where the National Chicano Political
Conference in San José, California, pledged support for Chicana issues of jobs, childcare, education, and abortion.[34]

Established by Octavio Romano and Nick Vaca, *El Grito*'s primary goal was to push against the prevailing negative, sometimes derogatory social science perspective on Mexican American culture. The journal later turned its focus to literary writing and published "the first modern anthology of Chicana/o literature."[35] It published works by prominent Chicano authors like Tomás Rivera, Rudolfo Anaya, Rolando Hinojosa, and Estela Portillo Trambley and solidified its impact by establishing the Quinto Sol Award, which each of these authors won. González was in the running for the literary prize in 1975, which Portillo Trambley won for *Rain of Scorpions and Other Writings*.[36] She is the only Chicana to have received the prize.

The Chicano literary community acknowledges González's writing on the first pages of *El Grito*'s 1973 special edition. The contributing editor, Portillo Trambley, wrote the introduction on Chicana writers, opening with the rhetorical question, "The voice of woman?" This question implies that a woman's voice in print is somehow antithetical and foreign in contrast to the widely published male voice. Portillo Trambley recognizes González's confidence as a fellow Chicana writer and speaks from a personal connection. "The substance of self-assertion as a woman and as a writer varies in the inlaid patterns of each individual reality. From the barrio experience made organic in hope and faith by Ramona González to the inward struggle of Lorenza Calvillo Schmidt in 'Birth.'"[37] We know that González succeeded at getting a few of her early works published. But did she continue to attempt to seek publication? I wish I could ask her myself. Instead, a letter that inexplicably came into my possession answered this question.[38]

La respuesta editorial: The Editorial Response

In early August 1974, González opened her mailbox to find a letter addressed to her from Herminio Ríos-C., editor of *El Grito*. It read:

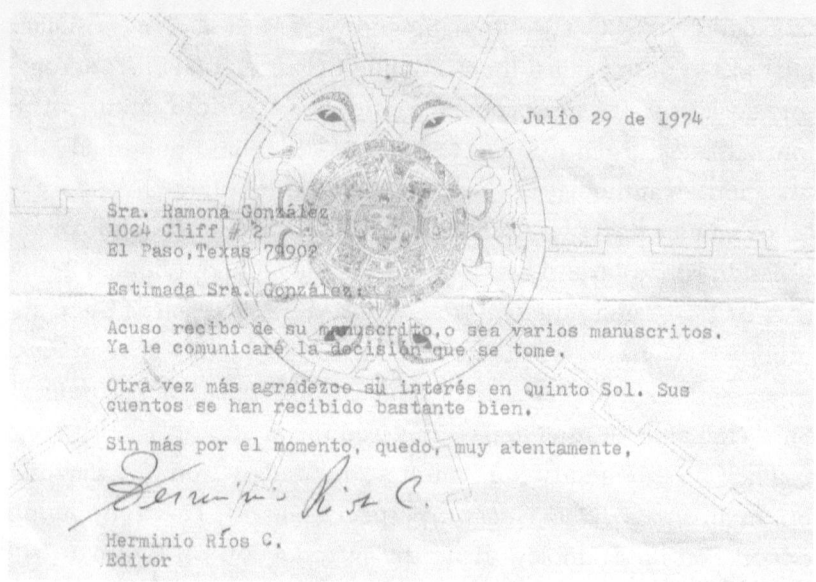

Julio 29 de 1974

Sra. Ramona González
1024 Cliff # 2
El Paso, Texas 79902

Estimada Sra. González:

Acuso recibo de su manuscrito, o sea varios manuscritos.
Ya le comunicaré la decisión que se tome.

Otra vez más agradezco su interés en Quinto Sol. Sus
cuentos se han recibido bastante bien.

Sin más por el momento, quedo, muy atentamente,

Herminio Ríos C.
Editor

Letter to Ramona González from Herminio Ríos-C., editor of *El Grito*, 1974.

Esteemed Mrs. González: July 29, 1974

I acknowledge receipt of your manuscript, that is, several
manuscripts. I will inform you of the decision that is made.

Once again, I appreciate your interest in Quinto Sol. Your stories
have been received quite well. Without more for the moment,
I remain, very sincerely,

Herminio Ríos C.
Editor

This letter remains the only correspondence we have regarding
her attempts at further publication. No editorial explanation exists
for why the rest of her works were not published. The journal closed
its doors in 1974, shortly after this letter was sent. For several years

after receiving this letter, González meticulously edited and cleanly typed her work, still trying to publish. In her 1975 interview with the *El Paso Times*, she revealed that "Quinto Sol, publishers of the anthology, have about twenty more stories [of mine] that they have promised to publish."[39] A contemporary reading of Quinto Sol reveals that the editors focused on scholarly aspects of the work it published and the academic credentials of its authors.[40] The publisher attempted to build cultural capital around the university setting, ignoring writers who did not fit this mold, such as my grandmother. Her other work was never published. But what happened to those manuscripts González sent them? Our family does not have copies, and that question may never be answered, as *El Grito's* archives remain lost to the public.

In 2021 my mother discovered additional evidence that my grandmother continued her efforts to publish her work. When she was cleaning out a closet, my mother found a faded manila envelope with a half-torn address sticker, still legible. The letter and envelope were addressed to "Ramona González, 1024 Cliff Drive, El Paso, Texas" and dated February 17, 1977. Inside the envelope she found no letter, only the forty-three-page copy of "Mi tiendita." The envelope originated from Tonatiuh International, which published Chicano literature in California. With no comments, the publisher had returned her story. We can only believe that González wanted much more than publishers at that time could offer. Her efforts to publish would pass to the next generation, one that would be ready to listen to her voice.

Chihuahuita,
el barrio de mi corazón

Lo más importante en el barrio era la gente, lo que hacían, y lo que
les acontecía. (The most important matter in the barrio was the
people, what they did, and what happened to them.)
    —RAMONA GONZÁLEZ, "El tesoro enterrado"

On a cool Chihuahuan desert morning in 1972, Ramona González,
sixty-six years old, got dressed in colorful pants, blouse, and a Mexican
rebozo, climbed into her 1965 Chevy Vega, and drove the few miles
south from her home on Cliff Drive to *el barrio de su corazón*. After
many years of absence, González had both a purpose and desire to
pay Chihuahuita a visit. She wanted to bear witness to its transformation since she had lived there fifty years earlier. Turning down
Stanton Street, the downhill road to Chihuahuita that leads through
downtown El Paso to the Rio Grande's edge, she saw Ciudad Juárez
on the horizon. Around the time of this visit, González was at the
peak of her literary production, having written several autobiographical accounts of the barrio, where she spent the first decade and a
half of her life before moving to Segundo Barrio nearby. She longed
to walk the streets of Chihuahuita, relive past events, and remember

the people and places of a time gone by. Her memory held the key to stories waiting to be told—of events not found in El Paso history books.

That morning González parked her car at one of the many border parking lots for tourists on Santa Fe Street. The daytime tourists rushed past Chihuahuita to cross into Mexico for the *mercados*, mariachis, and restaurants. But González lingered in the barrio. The desert sun beat down overhead. The cottonwood trees from her youth along the banks of the Rio Grande were no longer there to provide shade. On sidewalks that were once dirt walkways, she would have walked past El Paso Laundry, recalling her sister Juana working there in the 1910s. She visited the infamous two-story apartments where she once lived, known for the harsh living conditions and violent outbreaks of gang fights. Some of the old adobe homes still stood; a number of them more than a hundred years old. She possibly spent some time talking to Chihuahuita's longtime residents. To quench her thirst, she may have stopped in at Villalva's Grocery for an ice-cold soda. After spending the day walking the barrio, González arrived back at her apartment, realizing that the barrio that remained—absent of the cottonwood trees, the roaring waters of the Rio Grande, and unpaved streets—was only a fraction of what she remembered.

References to Chihuahuita appear in local newspapers dating back to 1896 along with interspersed citations and debates about the barrio through the next sixty years.[1] But in the late 1960s and early 1970s El Paso had all but forgotten—given up, even—on Chihuahuita. Except for a 1965 account of the great Rio Grande flood of 1897, hardly a word about this barrio appeared in city newspapers for over a decade. Known today along the border as the Ellis Island of the Southwest, Chihuahuita was established as the First Ward in south El Paso in 1887. Decades before, in 1818, Ricardo Brusuelas received a Spanish land grant and became the barrio's first known settler. Its fame traces back to its long history of settlements and passersby, but it's better known for proving its mettle as a tough, indomitable barrio. Few Texas neighborhoods can claim a centuries-long line of international politics that encompassed a revolution, geographic upheaval from mass immigration, and overhyped fear and propaganda against its residents. It overcame the odds by becoming a recognized, and now peaceful, historic Texas neighborhood.[2]

In 1972, El Paso appeared as a drastically changed city from when González was a child in the early 1910s. Over the course of sixty years, she witnessed its transformation from a small border city of about fifty thousand residents to a buzzing metroplex approaching half a million.[3] El Paso experienced geographic and civic upheaval leading to formalized immigration policies and construction of modern international crossings, along with the building of schools, stores, and an interstate highway; containment of the Rio Grande waters that flooded the city; and the clearing of trees along the riverbanks.[4] González relied on her memory of the barrio instead of the changes she witnessed that afternoon, and when she got home she typed what could be a letter to her proud, vibrant neighborhood.

ADIÓS, BARRIO CHIHUAHUITA

Era de mañana cuando fui a visitar el barrio Chihuahuita. Llevé mi automóvil guiado por todo el pavimento hasta llegar a un cerco junto al río Bravo y adjunto a una finca de negocios.

¿Hasta aquí llega el nuevo barrio Chihuahuita? ¿Cómo?

Ya no existía como antes. Mi madre nos había llevado a vivir al Chihuahuita hace setenta y dos años. Vivíamos en una de las viviendas de dos pisos, y mi mamá abrió una tiendita de abarrotes en la vivienda de la esquina.

La calle Chihuahua corría del norte al sur, realmente un poco corta. En esos tiempos cuando había inundaciones por las lluvias y el desborde del río crecido, la calle existía como un lodazal inmenso. Se estancaban los charcos alrededor de las viviendas. En una de muchas ocasiones, se desbordó el río y tuvimos que salir del apartamento y subir a un lugar más alto. Corríamos el riesgo de ser arrastrados hasta llegar al mismo río por la corriente rápida, de gran velocidad y fuerza. Todo lo que esa corriente veloz del río Bravo encontraba, se llevaba, fueran tinas, macetas, madera y otras cosas que se dejaban afuera. El agua entraba por una puerta y salía por otra, dejando charcos de agua adentro. Cuando ya pasaba la lluvia y el río se sosegaba, todos los chamacos salíamos y empezábamos a meternos a los charcos y en el lodo. ¡Qué gusto nos daba!

En esos años en el verano nos íbamos por la orilla del río una corta distancia, hacia el poniente, y podíamos jugar y correr a darnos gusto. Las orillas del río eran un campo húmedo con arbolitos pequeños y hierbas verdes y frondosas.

Ahora ya no soy libre para vagar por esa margen, ni por el campo verde y húmedo, ni de tomarme una de esas limonadas, o comer de esas sandías y melones, jugar al baseball y meter los pies en el agua fresca o gozar de la única frescura que había en tiempos de sol ardiente de verano, como lo hacíamos mi madre, mis hermanas y hermanos, las comadres y compadres, que yo conocí tan bien.

Cayendo la tarde volvíamos a nuestras casas o viviendas a descansar. La luna salía brillante, en veces sobre los que dormían afuera, pues nos acostábamos al piso duro y nos aguantábamos las incomodidades del ambiente en aquellos años pasados.

No se espanten, ustedes de las nuevas generaciones, de lo que les cuento de aquellos tiempos pasados—de no ser civilizados, o de ser incultos. Pues las circunstancias no permitían muchas cosas que en el presente se pueden—ser atentos, pulidos e instruidos.

Sí, había cultura y refinamiento. Recuerdo ir al "grito" a Ciudad Juárez el 16 de septiembre con mi listón tricolor, y mis hermanos y hermanas con sus banderas. Luego teníamos las procesiones por las

calles, y cuando se acercaba el que fuera el santísimo, nos hincába-
mos en el suelo hasta que pasara.

Era un barrio de festines. En mi casa nunca faltaban la comadre, el
compadre y los vecinos. Éramos seis hijos y cada uno tenía su padrino
y su madrina de bautismo y luego los padrinos de confirmación. Ojalá
que hubiera tiempo y lugar para contarles de todos estos padrinos y
madrinas que eran algunos y cada uno muy divertido.

El barrio tiene su historia, tal vez no esté escrita, pero por mi parte,
es oral. De tantos que llegaban al barrio unos se retiraban al norte a
trabajar, otros con ocupaciones de músicos, o reparación de zapatos,
otros carpinteros, y todos hundieron raíces en ese barrio.

Por mi tierna edad, tal vez, no tenía resentimiento contra pleitos,
borrachera o injusticias entre los mismos residentes, pero sí siento
nostalgia por ese terrón en donde jugué, corrí y formé muchos tras-
tecitos de lodo que dejaba el río.

Al mirar el barrio apenas puedo creer que en este lugar vivimos
algunos años entre ratos felices y ratos sin ninguna alegría. Mis hermanos y yo vimos la luna brillar, pensando que era nomás para nosotros. ¿Cuántas veces nos brilló? ¿Cuántas veces oímos los repiques
de las campanas de la iglesia? Los contábamos, uno, dos, tres…Mil
recuerdos me traen y a veces me viene ese silencio que me llena el
alma de tristeza.

Pues si ya es el fin de ese barrio deberíamos tener una despedida
con toda aquella gente, como yo, que vivió allí por necesidad o por
voluntad. Con frecuencia voy a darle vueltas al barrio, y es el mismo,
charcos de agua cuando llueve, falta de árboles y cercos, pero no falta
el calor humano entre los habitantes.

Adiós, Chihuahuita, entre poco te enterrarán como a nosotros los
viejos en los camposantos, después del servicio a nuestros semejantes
y familia. Me dejaste, mi barrio, una huella, una huella de ánimo para
seguir soportando las vicisitudes de la vida. Te vengo a ver por última
vez. Te agradezco.

GOODBYE, BARRIO CHIHUAHUITA

It was in the morning when I went to visit the barrio Chihuahuita. I took my car and drove all along the pavement until arriving at a fence next to the Río Bravo and near a group of small businesses.

The new barrio Chihuahuita goes all the way to here? How is that possible?

It no longer existed as before. My mother had taken us to live in Chihuahuita seventy-two years ago. We lived in one of the two-story tenements, and my mother opened a small grocery store in the house on the corner.

Chihuahua Street ran from north to south—really pretty short. In those times when there were floods because of rains and the overflowing of the swollen river, the street was like an immense swamp. The puddles around the houses stagnated.

In one of quite a few occasions, the river overflowed, and we had to get out of the apartment and climb to a higher place. We ran the risk of being dragged along all the way to the river itself because of the fast, swift current and its force. Everything that the Río Bravo's swift current encountered, it carried away—tubs, flowerpots, wood, and other things that were left outside. The water entered through one door and went out through another one, leaving water puddles inside. When the rain had passed and the river calmed down, all the kids came outside, and we began to jump into the puddles and the mud. What happiness it gave us!

In those years in the summer, we would walk along the riverbank a short distance, toward the west, and we could play and run to our heart's content. The banks of the river were a wet field with little trees and green, leafy weeds.

Now I am no longer free to wander along that riverbank, nor through the green, wet fields, nor to drink one of those lemonades, nor eat those watermelons and cantaloupes, nor to play baseball and stick my feet in the cool water to enjoy the only coolness that there was under the burning summer sun, as my mother, my sisters and brothers, godmothers and godfathers, who I knew so well, also did.

When night fell, we would go back to our houses or tenements to rest. The moon would come out radiant, sometimes shining on the ones who were sleeping outside. We made our beds on the hard floor and endured the discomforts of the surroundings in those years gone by.

Don't be frightened, you of the new generations, of what I tell you about those times gone by—of not being civilized or of being uneducated. Because circumstances didn't allow us to do a lot of things that nowadays we can—being courteous, polished, and educated.

Yes, there was culture and refinement. I remember going to the *grito* in Ciudad Juárez on the 16th of September with my three-colored ribbon and my brothers and sisters with their flags. We enjoyed the processions through the streets, and when the one that was representing the Holy One drew near, we would kneel on the ground until he went by.

It was a barrio of celebrations. In my house the *comadre*, the *compadre*, and neighbors were never absent. We were six children and each one had their own godfather and godmother of baptism and later, the godparents of confirmation. I wish that there were time and available space to tell you about all these godfathers and godmothers since there were quite a few of them and each one was full of fun.

The barrio has its history, perhaps it is not written, but as for me, it is oral. From the many that came to the barrio some left to go north to work, others had jobs as musicians or shoemakers, others were carpenters, and they all sank roots in that barrio.

Because of my tender age perhaps, I did not feel resentment against fights, drinking sprees, or injustices between the residents themselves, but I yearn for that small piece of earth where I played, ran, and molded a lot of dishes from the mud the river left behind.

When I look at the barrio, I can barely believe that in this place we lived some years amid happy times and times without any joy. My siblings and I saw the moon shining, thinking that it was only for us. How many times did it shine for us? How many times did we hear the ringing of the church bells? We counted them, one, two, three. They bring a thousand memories to me and sometimes that silence that fills my soul with sadness comes to me.

Well, if it is now the end of that barrio, we should have a farewell party with all those people who, like me, lived there out of necessity or by choice. Frequently I take a ride through the barrio, and it is the same, water puddles when it rains, a scarcity of trees and fences, but the human kindness among the residents is not missing.

Goodbye, Chihuahuita; in a short time they will bury you like us old folks in the cemeteries, after service to our fellowmen and family [is finished]. You left on me, my barrio, an imprint, an imprint of courage to keep on enduring the vicissitudes of life. I come to see you for the last time. I give thanks to you.

The Barrio has Its History . . . But as For Me, It's Oral

"Adiós, barrio Chihuahuita" reads as a personal yet historical piece, and it is one of the few writings González translated herself. The bilingual nature of her writing reflects how she perceived the borderlands. González wrote in two languages and in the first-person voice, sometimes even adopting the voice of a young girl living in the barrio. This approach mirrors that used by Mexican writer Nellie Campobello in *Cartucho and My Mother's Hands*.[5] Campobello wrote vignettes about the Mexican Revolution from a child's perspective. González also writes of the barrio in the way she experienced it—as a child. González reveals the vivid details of the geography, the floods of a wild Rio Grande that often crested its banks, threatening to overtake Chihuahuita's homes each year. In this short piece she articulates the community elders' steadfast determination, the hardships people endured, and the neighborhood *pleitos* (fights). González paints a picture in words of the countless people that lived in and passed through the barrio, workers of all kinds "sinking roots" there. In her other short works, such as "Cuentos: el patio, el compadre, el borracho y la maceta" (Stories: The Patio, the Godfather, the Drunk, and the Flower Pot), she profiles real people of the neighborhood: the guitar man who "would strum his guitar, and one could hear the harmonious notes" throughout the barrio; don Chinto, the barrio drunk who "entertained us with his stories and poems," the old woman who called the police when she thought someone had stolen her flower pots.[6]

González was not a university-educated historian, writer, or translator. Yet she wrote history in her own voice and style. She wrote comfortably in the vernacular of the English and Spanish of her time. What she lacked in formal education, she compensated for in self-education, being schooled on the steps of her adobe childhood home in the oral tradition of storytelling and being well read in American and Latin American literature. While her family lived in the barrio, her mother instilled in González a love of storytelling. Ascención enthralled her children on summer evenings when the heat broke, transporting them to another time, amusing and entertaining them with her stories. González also heard many lively stories from barrio residents while sitting outside the jacals and adobe homes after a day's work. These stories were generally told in a barrio dialect of Spanish.

Women's autobiographical writings, including the few that exist of El Paso community life, have rarely been given equal consideration as historical texts because they do not follow the male-centric narrative of travel, conquest, and life triumphs. Women writers, especially Mexican American women writers, focus on oral language, feelings, personal life, home activities, and interpersonal relationships.[7] Their narratives tend to conform to a greater experience of the social world.

Sisters Ramona Rodríguez
(González, left) and Blaza Chafino
in Chihuahuita, ca. 1913.

González then offers important literary and historical contributions from the perspective of a woman who grew up in a border barrio during the early twentieth century.[8]

González's five published writings in the 1973 special edition of *El Grito: Chicanas en la literatura y el arte*, reveal how her stories revolve around the spirit and the people of the barrio. "El tesoro enterrado" (The Buried Treasure) recounts how a young González believed she knew of a hidden treasure buried in the barrio. "El conjuramento" (The Incantation) tells of a barrio priest who magically prayed away the rain clouds that hovered over the barrio and flooded its homes. "Cuando tienes comezón" (When You Have an Itch) relates the story of a young González telling jokes with her friend Olga and learning the inappropriate language of the barrio. La Talaca narrates the story about an old skinny cow her family bought in hopes that it would produce nutritious milk. "El camotero (El vendedor ambulante)" (The Sweet Potato Salesman [The Street Vendor]) conjures the image of the vendor slowly walking through the barrio, calling out to people to buy his baked treats at day's end.[9]

Collectively these pieces paint a firsthand impression of the barrio streets, a mosaic of the hardworking yet happy community that was Chihuahuita in simpler times.[10] Indeed, these are historically significant pieces. Because González relied on her memory and firsthand knowledge to bring the reader close to the barrio, these stories convey a magical, timeless, even haunting quality. Each begins with a barrio philosophy—how the people thought, or how they chose to live their lives—followed by a snapshot of life in Chihuahuita in the very early twentieth century. One example of this technique is found in the opening of "El camotero (El vendedor ambulante) / "The Sweet Potato Salesman (The Street Vendor)":

En este mundo de terribles extremos, hacíamos comentarios y observaciones de las cosas que ya no son como eran anteriormente. Hemos notado ese cambio marcado y brusco en los empleos, en los grandes negocios e industrias cuyas operaciones nos llevan arrebatadamente sin poder hacer nada para detenerlo.

Con nostalgia y respeto recuerdo al vendedor de camote, que iba de puerta en puerta pregonando su vendimia con una voz de calidad de abrir el apetito. Con sonsonete típico mejicano decía, "Camoteeeee enmieladooooo, camoteeee enmieladoooo, dulce y calientito".

Corríamos afuera con deseos de saber y en veces de averiguar si en realidad el camote era lo que el camotero pregonaba al decir, "Dulce y calientito". Realmente no había que discutir; al ver la vianda se nos hacía agua la boca. Por mi parte, que yo recuerde, no he vuelto a saborear camote como el que nos vendía el camotero.[. . .]

Recuerdo al hombre: chaparro, de brazos fornidos y de tez morena. Sus ojos grandes de pestañas sin rizar miraban el alimento como si también afirmaran que estaba delicioso. Con mucho cuidado levantaba cada uno de los camotes con una cuchara de palo y con otro palillo como espátula, y minuciosamente los ponía en los trastes. Luego con la cuchara ponía, esmeradamente, la míel a cada uno de los camotes.

In this world of terrible extremes, we would make comments and observations about things that are no longer as they were before. We have noticed marked and sudden changes in jobs, in big business and industries whose operations carry us along hurriedly without our being able to do anything to hold them back.

Nostalgically and with respect, I remember the sweet potato salesman who went from door to door, shouting out his harvest with a high-pitched voice to whet our appetite. With a typical Mexican singsong voice he would cry out, "Camoteeeee enmieladooooo, camoteeee enmieladoooo, sweet and hot."

We would dash outside with eagerness to know and, sometimes to really find out if, in fact, the sweet potato was what the *camotero* was announcing when loudly calling out "sweet and hot." Really there was nothing to debate; when we saw the food, our mouths began to water. As for me, to the best of my recollection, I have never again tasted sweet potatoes like the ones that the *camotero* used to sell us.

I remember the man: he was short, with strong arms and a dark complexion. His big eyes with straight eyelashes gazed at the food as if to declare that it was delicious. With a great deal of care, he lifted each one of the sweet potatoes with a wooden spoon and another spatula-like little stick and then carefully put them on the dishes. Then, with great care, with a spoon, he put honey on each one of the sweet potatoes.

A Place (Not) Fit to Live

While González fondly reminisced of *la gente del barrio,* the El Paso community often misunderstood, ignored, disparaged, and occasionally exploited Chihuahuita's residents and their way of life. El Paso newspaper archives reveal these sentiments. In the early twentieth century a young González observed this willful neglect of Chihuahuita and its diminished relevance in the community. Later in life she questioned why the barrio had so often been impugned. In the first two sentences of "El barrio Chihuahuita, 1972," a supplement to her letter "Adiós, barrio Chihuahuita," she wrote, "Why are we just now becoming conscious of the barrio Chihuahuita? Precisamente porque ya lo estamos viendo agonizar, por la indiferencia y desprecio" (Precisely because we just now are seeing it lie dying, due to indifference and disdain).[11] Contrary to this statement, Chihuahuita had appeared as an occasional embarrassment for El Pasoans for more than seventy-five years and was often portrayed negatively.

A survey of El Paso newspaper archives shows a well-documented, one-sided history and debate about life in Chihuahuita at the turn of the twenieth century and the following two decades. Newspapers often labeled the barrio as a place to be feared by the Anglo community. In May 1914, for example, because of outbreaks of waterborne diseases like cholera and typhoid fever, the *El Paso Herald* published the editorial "The Chance El Paso Has Longed For" in response to a suggestion from Gen. John J. Pershing of nearby Fort Bliss that a sanitation system should be installed in Chihuahuita:

> There is no use in trying to blind ourselves to the shameful facts. El
> Paso has always neglected its plain duty down there [Chihuahuita].
> The city has not only neglected the elemental welfare of half its own
> population, but it has tolerated conditions in that section that have
> constituted a terrible menace to all the rest of the city. These things
> are not news, nor have they been concealed. The public is and has

been fully informed as to the truth about Chihuahuita, and the frightful death rate down there.[12]

Debates on how to improve Chihuahuita took place in public forums without consulting the people of the barrio, who predominately spoke Spanish. At these forums, the proposal to demolish the barrio became a serious option. In August 1914 the *El Paso Herald* resumed this disparaging theme of Chihuahuita in the editorial "Destruction That Means Progress":

"One block a week"—that is the program of the city health officer for the progressive destruction of the old and unsanitary tenements in Chihuahuita, the part of El Paso in which the Spanish-speaking laboring population chiefly dwells.

The editorial uses the term "progressive destruction" advisedly. It sounds contradictory. But no—with every block of those buildings destroyed, El Paso's self-respect will grow, the status of her workers will improve, the death rate will tend to decline, and greater happiness will dawn for our people."[13]

Some editorial coverage conveyed sympathy and even condemned the city council for its treatment of Chihuahuita residents. In 1915, a year before the city began clearing away a large expanse of the original adobe houses, the *El Paso Herald* ran the editorial "Just the Truth—That's All." It reads, "Our continual, heartless, senseless neglect of our people in that section [Chihuahuita] in the matter of school facilities constitutes a black chapter in our record.... More than 3,000 children of school age in this city are not attending any school.... Most of the 3,000 are children of Spanish-speaking parents."[14] These early twentieth-century editorials coincide with the "white man's burden" thinking that British writer Rudyard Kipling promoted, an attitude that was rampant in many of the opinion pieces on Chihuahuita, the "stepchild" of the Anglo community's ambitious civic and commercial aspirations. This kind of reporting on Chihuahuita persisted for decades.

In the 1910s these opinions circulated weekly in the *El Paso Times*, *El Paso Herald*, and other local papers. The rhetoric sparked fear of a "contamination of disease" from the Mexican people that were crossing, as well as those already in the area. In 1917, the *El Paso Herald* reported on the "forced baths" Chihuahuita residents were required to take, as communicable diseases and influenza struck fear in the hearts of El Paso residents. "Herding the Mexicans of Chihuahuita to the government bathhouse for their 'annual dip' is the daily duty during two months in the year of the inspector of tenements and boarding houses in the southside." The article continues, "Bedding and clothes, as well as the owners, undergo a thorough cleansing. They are all bundled into the auto, and off they go to the government bathhouse at the international bridge."[15] Along with forced baths, the people of Chihuahuita were often subjected to hostile, even racist, actions by inspectors. The 1917 article quoted an inspector saying that "if he [an elderly Chihuahuita resident] didn't come, he [the inspector] would kill him, and he did not care how Grandpa came to his sad end."[16]

David Romo, a historian of events that occurred at the El Paso border and in Chihuahuita, found that the baths consisted of using toxic mixtures of gasoline, kerosene, sodium cyanide, cyanogen, sulfuric acid, DDT, and Zyklon B, a form of hydrocyanic acid.[17] These petroleum-based baths were given not only to residents of Chihuahuita but also to Mexican citizens crossing into the United States well into the 1950s and 1960s during the bracero program.[18] The people of neighboring Juárez and those in the El Paso barrios were not completely silent on this matter. In January 1917, Carmelita Torres, a domestic worker crossing into El Paso, protested the baths in an incident that became known as the Border Bath Riots.[19]

A routine reference to Chihuahuita as a place to be feared or forgotten, or unfit for habitation, became embedded in the collective fabric of Chihuahuita residents and the people of El Paso. Yet like many residents of Chihuahuita and Segundo Barrio, González did not address these dehumanizing "delousing" baths in her work. Omission of these events was likely deliberate. Having lived in Chihuahuita until 1917, she may or may not have experienced them herself. González's writing focuses on positive aspects of the barrio, however, such as resiliency in the face of such public misperceptions.

Chihuahuita: A Slice of Aztlán

Early historical references to Chihuahuita paint an unwelcoming and unflattering image of the barrio. In sum, the newspaper coverage proclaimed to residents, "You don't belong." Yet in González's autobiographical accounts, we learn that she and her family, along with countless others, found beauty in its form and ways in order to survive and thrive in the barrio. I contend that Chihuahuita represented the slice of Mexican homeland that residents, short- or longer-term, called their own. With such difficult conditions and public opinions to endure, why did so many from Mexico decide to come north and choose to remain there? What significance does the El Paso border region hold to these people, even those just passing through? Most Mexican families along the border did not speak of the humiliation they experienced with the gasoline baths. They endured this treatment, or worse, to remain with family, stay employed, and forge ahead in life.

For centuries this region had been called El Paso del Norte. Those who traveled through or stayed followed an innate understanding of ancient indigenous migration and movement. Their journey was not random. For centuries, the indigenous and mestizo people of Mexico, even Spanish Franciscans and conquistadors, believed that there existed a mystical, rich place somewhere in the north. The knowledge keepers and storytellers never gave an exact location, but when travelers arrived, they recognized it as such. The hundreds of Spaniards who set out to find gold in El Dorado referred to this place in the north as the Seven Cities of Cíbola or Grand Quivira. They failed in their quest.

While explorers may not have found gold, according to Pérez de Villagrá, a chronicler and legal officer of the don Juan de Oñate expedition of 1610, they found a paradise along the Rio Grande a few miles upstream from today's Chihuahuita. Villagrá wrote in his travel log, "Joyfully we tarried 'neath the pleasant shade of the wide spreading trees which grew along the riverbanks. It seemed to us that these were, indeed, the Elysian fields of happiness, where, forgetting all our past misfortunes, we could lie beneath the shady bowers and rest our tired aching bodies."[20] The riparian area Villagrá mentions housed a grove of flourishing trees and lush green surroundings. For good reason, early settlers in the border region called it El Bosque, the place where trees are plentiful. The late seventeenth century marks the time before the massive industrialization and division of the region's land, and it lives in the memory of those who inhabited the border. Today, El Bosque, without the trees but lined with cement roads and sidewalks, contains the Chihuahuita and Segundo barrios.

With the full range of possibilities before them, thousands of immigrants followed the compass and trailed migratory routes to the north. As they passed through harsh jungle and desert lands, travelers likely dreamed of a slowly unfolding reality. Spaniards discovered what the indigenous and mestizo people already knew—the land north of the Rio Grande was Aztlán, the mythical ancestral homeland of the Aztecs. A Nahua word, Aztlán means "the land of herons" and represents a verdant and fruitful land in Aztecan culture where people once freely inhabited the lands and thrived. For travelers going north, Chihuahuita represented Aztlán. Weary from their travels, many made homes in Chihuahuita and Segundo Barrio. These communities offered a familiar Mexican culture while holding promise of a new life and renewed opportunities. With Mexico and the United States in such proximity, these communities served as an ideal setting for a meeting of two nations.

As a Chicana participating in the emerging culture of the 1960s and 1970s that embraced the idea of Aztlán, González would have agreed with the claim that Chihuahuita was part of this chosen land. Michael Pina says that "Chicanos interpreted their nationalist cause as more than a political movement; they were involved in the regeneration of sacred time and space, as the ultimate concern of Chicano nationalism sought to transcend the existent temporal and spatial barriers and establish a homeland."[21] Considering Pina's view of Aztlán, I contend that Chihuahuita held (and still holds) an ideal image of homeland for its residents, a place between two places.

A Meeting of Two Nations

From the banks of the Rio Grande, one's eyes take in the stark escarpment of the Franklin Mountains, covered with green prickly pear, creosote bushes, and long-armed ocotillo. From either side of the river, the Chihuahuan desert's beauty greets the eye, even more so after rain or snow. Since the establishment of El Paso in 1680 and Ciudad Juárez a year later, these sister cities have exchanged commerce and shared a common culture, language, and heritage. Mexico and its influences spilled into El Paso, hence the name Chihuahuita. Today a historical signpost on El Paso Street announces a welcome to the barrio. Across the street stands a two-story brick building constructed in the 1890s. El Paso Laundry & Cleaners, one of the few remaining structures in Chihuahuita built over a hundred years ago, sits at 901 South Santa Fe Street, only a few yards from the Rio Grande. A black and silver historic plaque displayed on one of the sand-colored brick columns notes that El Paso Laundry served as a steady source of employment for men and women living in Chihuahuita for almost eighty years. Those included my *tía abuela*,

Juana López, who was Ramona's older sister. The building, however, holds a greater history.

On October 16, 1909, the steps outside of El Paso Laundry hosted a cordial meeting between President William Howard Taft and Mexico's president, Porfirio Díaz. Military from both sides marked the meeting with a twenty-one-gun salute to commemorate two nations' presidents coming together in a show of peaceful talks. The *El Paso Morning Times* reported:

> The boom of cannon, the ringing of bells, blowing of whistles and yells from a hundred thousand throats welcomed William Howard Taft, president of the United States of America, when he arrived yesterday morning to write El Paso's name large in the history of America, and with Porfirio Díaz, president de la Republica de los Estados Unidos de México, to mark an epoch in the history of the two great nations of the Western Hemisphere.[22]

At the turn of the century this meeting established Chihuahuita as the symbolic crossroads and common space between the United States and Mexico.

The following year the Mexican Revolution would break out and spill into the borderland region. While many El Pasoans took to viewing the unfolding revolution as a spectator sport from the roof of the El Paso Laundry, the war horrified Chihuahuita residents. Stray bullets and artillery flew daily across the border and into the barrio, lodging into buildings and occasionally killing or wounding people.[23] Ramona was four years old when the revolution began and likely did not remember these early events. But she grew up in the shadow of the conflict, which raged for seven years, and certainly experienced some of the war's social, economic, and political effects. As with most young children living in difficult situations, Ramona assimilated the massive shifts happening around her—poverty, war, racism, immigration policies, public health sanitation, and growing income inequity from unbridled capitalism. Children are often more aware of life's realities than adults realize, as attitudes are still forming, and young people's lives are more intertwined with a rich sense of perception. Later in her life, Ramona captured how she understood the politics and opinions surrounding Chihuahuita, in a short reflection.[24]

EL BARRIO CHIHUAHUITA, 1972

Tiene su historia el barrio Chihuahuita, así como los barrios al norte de la calle Texas tienen la suya.[25] La historia del barrio Chihuahuita y la historia del Segundo Barrio nunca han compartido una historia común. Además, las distintas historias de los dos barrios no tuvieron lugar en la historia de los paseños, los anglos. Esta fue una de las causas porque el barrio se desarrolló y creció a su manera hasta el presente, aparte de unas adiciones de la electricidad, drenaje y pavimento que se hicieron de compromiso de los que establecieron comercios y grandes negocios en el barrio. No se hicieron estas mejoras para el bien de los vecinos del barrio sino para las empresas—esta es la indiferencia.

Por esas razones el barrio creció, así como anotaré en los siguientes cuentos.

Yo pasé mis primeros años en el barrio Chihuahuita. Cuatro de mis hermanos nacieron en el barrio. Nos criamos en esa cultura llena de diversas maneras expresivas, palabras y frases de sentimiento. Allí nos conocíamos todos, compartíamos buenos y malos días, aunque escasamente lo sabíamos. Las responsabilidades de los habitantes eran de poca importancia a menos que fuera algo único de la persona o familia. Sin embargo, esas responsabilidades, como dije, tan livianas como el aire, son tan fuertes como el acero a la hora de la hora.

EL BARRIO CHIHUAHUITA, 1972

The barrio Chihuahuita has its history, as well as the barrios north of Texas Street have theirs.[26] The history of the barrio Chihuahuita and the history of the Segundo Barrio have never shared a common history. Furthermore, the different histories of the two barrios did not have a place in the history of the *Paseños*, the Anglos. This was one of the reasons why the barrio developed and grew up in its own way down to the present, aside from some additions of electricity, drainage, and paving that were carried out due to the commitment of businesses and large enterprises in the barrio. These improvements were not made for the good of the residents of the barrio but in the interest of the companies—this is indifference.

For those reasons the barrio grew up in the way that I will make note of in the following stories.

I spent my first years in the barrio Chihuahuita. Four of my siblings were born in the barrio. We were raised in that culture filled with diverse ways of expression, words and phrases full of feeling. There we all knew each other, shared good and bad days, although we hardly realized it. The responsibilities of the residents were of little account unless it was something unique about the person or family. However, those responsibilities, as I said, as light as air, are as strong as steel at the moment of truth. (Translation by Ramona González.)

Livianas como el aire, tan fuertes como el acero
Light as Air and Strong as Steel

González's recollection of the border barrio doesn't focus on the harsh poverty, the difficulties of the Mexican Revolution, or the unbearable sanitary conditions. With the lens of a cultural anthropologist, she wrote of how the people of the barrio transcended their troubles. One of these moments of truth occurred during the Mexican Revolution. In one of her few English-language pieces, González recorded an event that demonstrated how the people of Chihuahuita came together in the rescue efforts of Mexican wounded soldiers. This piece reads counter to the newspaper reports of cross-border shootings that took place during the battles. It opposes the near-voyeuristic experience of watching battles being waged on the Mexican side of the river from the rooftops of Chihuahuita and downtown El Paso. Unlike those detached war spectators, Chihuahuita and Barrio Segundo residents witnessed the suffering of their Mexican countrymen and women, and they acted. González wrote the following account on the revolution's tragedies at the border and how residents reacted.

A 1910 EPISODE[27]

In 1910 an episode took place here in south El Paso, of which there has been no record in any of the history writings. Also, there were no screaming headlines in the newspapers, or mention of a compassionate emergency, and yet this event happened in a fortuitous way, bringing Mexican and Anglo-American residents in El Paso together to share their feelings.

This incident, which was one of so many never heard widely, was different from all the rest because of its quality and effort executed.

Thinking about this incident, you would say that the women's lib was taking precedence in this orphan barrio. We want to share this episode with the rest of the Chicanos.

In those years, years of war-torn Mexico, hospitality among *paisanos* was a necessity for survival. No matter how poor or how meager the provisions of the refugees, those standing in need could depend upon help to share their scanty supplies.

Early one morning in 1910 a little girl, Luz, played unconcerned with other children outside of her home. Suddenly, rifle shots rang all around the Segundo Barrio. One shot zipped close to Luz's head. Promptly her mother sent the other children home and took her daughter inside, as she had all along known that Madero's forces were attacking Ciudad Juárez, Chihuahua, Mexico.

From side to side in the Second Ward, excitement ran wild. Some said that the Mexicans were attacking El Paso and others, that the war was being fought here. The men of the barrio called a meeting at the

Alamo Park, a large, vacant piece of land, with a few trees around it. There the reason for the wild shots hitting some of the taller buildings was cleared. The people were told that Madero had attacked Ciudad Juárez and none of the residents of the United States would be hurt, unless accidentally.

Among the hundreds of people who attended this meeting was a young *señorita*, Jenny Napoles, and her four sisters. Jenny was a vivacious young girl with initiative, and immediately she rounded some of her young friends and formed a *comitiva* (retinue). Her father knew some of the military men in Juárez and with his help, Jenny brought the wounded to this side [of the border] and gave them medical attention.

In less than two days, she had twenty-two recruits. She divided the girls in groups and gave them commissions. Some to tend to the wounded, to go into the neighborhood and ask for bedding, others to beg for food and utensils for the provisional hospital.

Two blocks from their home, there was a recently vacated two-story tenement house. The construction was solid but had been neglected.

At night a crew of young boys and men cleaned and whitewashed the rooms to be ready for the wounded Mexican soldiers.

The men had to work at night as they had jobs during the day, from sunup to sundown, but they did not ignore the needs of their paisanos and countrymen, especially knowing that Madero was fighting a good cause.

These girls who became mothers, many have passed away and few are alive, but being so young at the time, I remember with nostalgia that they contributed with their grain of sand.

Gente de mi barrio
People of My Barrio

González had always wanted to be a journalist. She read the daily newspaper religiously and noticed the often-biased reporting of

events. Her own account of the 1910 episode highlights the conspic-
uous absence of Mexican people in the local newspaper accounts.
Fortuitously, she filed this account for the benefit of future generations. The event she wrote about involved hundreds of people—
Anglos, Mexicans, and Mexican Americans—who brought relief to
the wounded Mexican soldiers. Impactful, humanitarian moments
like this showed a degree of community unity in a crisis and solidified
González's connection to the barrio. Coverage in the El Paso newspapers too often overlooked the hearts and minds of the people of
its south-side barrios, relying more on the opinions of its Anglo community and outsiders. At the very least, residents of El Paso's barrios
were misunderstood, seen as a group to be controlled or feared. In
the 1970s this top-down approach to reporting gradually began to
change.

Beginning in 1976, with the formation of the Chihuahuita
Improvement Association by Fred Morales, Chihuahuita's community situation steadily improved. In a 1977 article, "Chihuahuita:
Forgotten But Not Gone,"[28] Morales spoke about how Chihuahuita
was barraged with routine nightly gunfire and had to deal with flood-
waters, the occasional corpse in the Franklin Canal, and railroad
accidents. He identified a range of nightmarish events that seemed
hard to imagine for an obscure community like Chihuahuita. These
collective events became a geopolitical wound that has never completely healed. But Morales conveyed a continuous upbeat perspective: "Maybe we look at things a little differently here," he wrote. "We
want to fight for some of the same things other barrios want. But we
think we can work things out if we're just given a little of the same
help that other areas of El Paso are given. We've done a lot to help
ourselves."

A shift in perspective emerged in the news coverage of the barrio in 1979. A weeklong series, "Chihuahuita USA," appeared in
the Kaleidoscope section of the *El Paso Times*. One of the features,

"Señora's memories mirror Chihuahuita passages," included a historical perspective from one of Chihuahuita's lifelong residents, Elisa Villalovos Mora Garcia, who was born in 1911.[29] In the featured article, a drawing of Garcia appears alongside a flood of images of the events that materialized outside her Chihuahuita home: border travelers, funeral processions, soldiers, bandits, river floods, and old adobe buildings. Covering two pages, the article recounted her memories of the barrio, beginning with the early moments, struggling to feed her siblings, surviving harsh poverty, and uncovering ghosts of the community's past.

In the interview's first portion, Garcia discusses the name of her section of the barrio, Barrio de la Mancha Roja, or Red Stained Barrio, saying it was so termed "because hoodlums or gangsters used to live there."[30] She recounts her memories of the Mexican Revolution and the women soldiers who followed Pancho Villa, the 1919 death of her father, booze and drug smugglers, and more. "Everything came across the border from Mexico and passed Garcia's family front porch—black-market coffee, sugar and liquor, and all kinds of drugs from marijuana to cocaine," the article reports. "Arms crossed the river in the opposite direction."[31] Garcia was given the space to tell her story about life in Chihuahuita, which she believed held no importance to those outside the barrio. To those still living in the barrio, however, it remains their home, and those who have moved on seem to never forget it. The reporter gives Garcia the last word. "'I believe,' she says looking at her work-worn hands, 'when you come into this world, you're marked with your destiny.'"[32]

González, born four years before Garcia, may have lived next to her. Ascención may have spoken to Garcia's mother. Like the Garcia family, the Rodríguezes relied on their neighbors. Considering how hundreds of people lived in a single block of the barrio, the likelihood of knowing or interacting with one another was not a distant reality. Garcia's oral history reflects a rich, intimate past of the people of

Chihuahuita that was rarely recorded in newsprint, essays, or books. Chihuahuita shares equally in the foundation of El Paso's civic history; yet few, if any, written historical accounts exist. Like González, Garcia and her stories are hidden in the archives, both private and institutional, waiting to reemerge and tell a story of their people. Recovery and retelling of these stories bring *la gente* to life, making them relevant in our time.

Chihuahuita remains an important barrio geographically and historically. As the city's oldest border barrio, it has suffered the pains of straddling two major regional cities. It retains the history of some of the state's most important events, spanning the 1880s establishment of the Southern Pacific Railroad, a 1909 meeting between the presidents of the United States and Mexico, an occasional front-seat view of Mexican revolutionary battles, and the immigration wave that has continued mostly uninterrupted since the late nineteenth century. Since its establishment in 1887, Chihuahuita has transformed from a cottonwood-lined riverbank with periodic floods full of sometimes vulnerable adobe homes to a community of cultural identity, pride, and openness. Some of the original adobe houses still exist, with many families living in the neighborhood for generations, spanning a hundred years. The remnants of an old Mexican barrio endure, and the barrio remains strong by embracing its heritage. González's pieces on Chihuahuita provide a more intimate perspective on this special community seldom seen by others.

Cuentos del barrio/
Stories from the Barrio, Part I

Por vida de estas santas cruces,
yo viví en estos barrios

By the Life of these Holy Crosses,
I Lived in These Barrios

"Por vida," one of González's lengthier pieces, is full of dialogue and rich descriptions of Chihuahuita. The story's opening pages foretell a theatrical drama with a list of characters (*la gente*) she knew while living in Chihuahuita the first nine years of her life. (Her family moved to nearby Segundo Barrio in 1917.) Eleven vignettes focus on nine distinct characters and two specific barrio events. Multidimensional characters include doña Martina, the barrio midwife and widely reputed bootlegger, and her children; the milkman, don Leandro; the "gay boy," José Antonio; and a dwarf, Licha. Each vignette begins with González's philosophical commentary on the barrio, as if she were looking for potential answers to life in the stories of her youth. She also highlights the politics of identity reflected in the 1920s. Throughout, she uses the terms *prieta,* or dark one, and *güera* to discuss what in the barrios was known as *el complejo de color* or "the complex of color."

Elsewhere she highlights the characters' physical traits. The reader should understand that in the 1960s, when González wrote this piece, she held racial and ethnic values from the 1920s; the following decades were not sensitive to nuances of identity.

The final section of "Por vida" celebrates a wedding between two young barrio residents, Jony, a veteran returning from World War I, and Gaby, who worked as a maid. With this literary piece ending in a marriage and the birth of a child, González may have relied on literary master William Shakespeare, whose comedic plays often end with such celebrations. The story's upbeat conclusion also showed that she held an optimistic view of the barrio and its residents.

"Por vida" can be classified as creative historical fiction written through the lens of realism. Realism, as Jerome Stern notes, is a creative approach to historical fiction and presents the idea that "art [is] not only about extraordinary events, amazing places, and spectacular characters, but [can] be fashioned from everyday life. Realism justifies fiction that stresses observation of characters, scenes, events, and problems that are familiar to regular folks."[1] Stern offers an important detail about realism that connects to González's writing style: "Realists felt they were doing more serious work than the writers of wild adventure stories and improbable love stories, whom they called Romanticists, because realists tried to show how people actually lived and suffered and dealt with their problems."[2] Given the love my grandmother had for the people of Chihuahuita, she sought to portray the barrio's reality and not to rely on the narrative portrayed by outside influences.

"Por vida," then, reveals a writing style I call *barrio realism.* The short story follows everyday occurrences in Chihuahuita, such as immigrants moving into the barrio, the ways large numbers of people lived in proximity, and the work they did to make a living. It deals with class, ethnic discrimination and identification, cross-border perceptions of war, and managing dual loyalties to Anglo and Mexican cultures and identities. Incidents include the floods of the Rio Grande, bootleggers and late-night drinking parties, dairy farms that populated the barrio, the role of traditional midwives, the outbreak of the Mexican Revolution, and the murder of one of the barrio's food vendors, don Teodoso, which actually occurred.[3] In short, the work reflects a simple yet radical witness-bearing of Chihuahuita's residents in the early decades of the twentieth century brought to life.

POR VIDA DE ESTAS SANTAS CRUCES, YO VIVÍ EN ESTOS BARRIOS[4]

Personajes del cuento

La familia de doña Martina, la partera
   Sus hijo Jony, el héroe. Pronunciado en el barrio "Yoni"
   Jenny
   José Antonio
   Licha
   Toncha
   Dos hijos más no mencionados
Lecheros
Chano (Nepomuceno)
Familia de don Leandro
   Sus hijos
      Cuatro jóvenes no nombres dados
      Otra sin nombre
      María la mayor y otra sin nombre
      María Cristina
Facundo, el padre de una de mis amigas quien murió en la epidemia
El esposo de Tita
   Sus hijos
      Su hija Chelo
      Cuatro hijos más sin nombres

Familia de Crucita

  Sus hijos

    Tonya

    Pepín

    Chale

    La Chata

Familia de doña Patrocinio

  Sus hijos

    Gabina

    Lola

    Juan de Dios

Otros

    Don Domingo y su esposa, Panchita

    El Melcochero, don Teodoso

    Palmira, novia de Pepín

Mis amigas

    Tomasita

    Chelo

    Ema

    Juana, fallecida

doña Martina, la partera

Recorriendo los años, cuadros de mi niñez se arrojan en mi mente, urgiendo que los ponga yo en ánimo de nuevo. Yo no me daba cuenta que las experiencias de la vida pudieran llegar a ser unas memorias de un pasado y que ya no se repetirían jamás. Ahora sé que ciertos incidentes y vidas, de hace muchos años pasados, se destacan, enfocándose contra el borrón de años, y están en mi memoria vivamente imprimidos para llevar a ustedes hacia atrás a ver aquellas personas de barrios con quienes vivimos muchos años, y de quienes su lucha parecía implacable.

Cuantos años han ya pasado, cuarenta, cincuenta o más, y todavía me maravillo de doña Martina. Fuimos vecinas, nos frecuentamos casi de diario, nos ayudamos unos a otros. Nuestras familias nos tratamos por nombre, sobrellevamos nuestros malentendidos y todavía me maravillo de doña Martina.

No recuerdo el tiempo exacto cuando conocí a doña Martina. A mi parecer ella ya estaba en el barrio cuando nosotros fuimos a vivir allí.

Durante mi vida, cuántas personas ideales, cuántas caras bellas han pasado rápidamente de un lado a otro en mi mente y se han desvanecido ante mí como una sombra. Parece algo de hechicería, mas una hechicería rara por la cual esta cara vieja, cara sin ningún color, marchita y arrugada, ha ganado lugar y un establecimiento en mi memoria.

¡El cuerpo de doña Martina, la partera, era pequeño, dando la impresión y una idea inicial, si en cualquier tiempo las mejillas de ella habían sido de tez morena y limpia, pues ni rastro quedaba, dejando huellas únicamente de arrugas profundas!

Sus ojos de mirada maliciosa y de viveza resaltaban en su cara ajada cuando sonreía, siendo su sonrisa medio burlona y con visaje que mostraba los dientes fuertes, aunque manchados por el cigarro. Su risa iluminaba su cara y también su risa nos contaminaba.

Doña Martina tenía siete hijos, cuatro mujeres y tres hombres. Empezaré a contarles que la disciplina no existía en ese hogar. ¿Cómo se gobernaba esta familia? Se dice que los métodos de usar la fuerza para gobernar la familia son muy eficaces, pero en esa casa no había tal cosa, ni fuerza palpable ni cariño demostrado. Tal vez estaba oculto y en esto doña Martina no usaba ni fuerza ni amor. Y a mi parecer había más bien indiferencia.

Digo así, porque si alguno de la familia, chico o grande, quería fumar, "¡Pos que fumen!" Si querían tomar intoxicantes, aunque en ese tiempo estaba en vigor la ley de la Prohibición, no había venta de ningún intoxicante, no obstante, doña Martina con la mayor indiferencia les decía, "¡Cabrones, que beban!"

Una de las hijas mayores ya casada había ido a vivir al estado de Arizona y de allá vino con la novedad de hacer "home brew", una especie de cerveza hecha en casa. Tiene otros nombres, como "moonshine" y "booze." Toncha, otra hija, comentaba a mi madre, diciendo, "Crucita, para todo hay maña." La familia tomaba de este producto, el cual aprendió doña Martina a elaborar con perfección, pero les advertía con palabras de mordacidad, "Beban con medida porque es para sacar unos cuantos centavos."

Los únicos a quienes no les agradaba la bebida eran Licha, la enana, quien decía, "¡Yo ni oler esa porquería tan apestosa!" y José Antonio, el joto, declaraba con visajes y haciendo cola a las palabras, "Yoooo no tomo esas cosaaasas tan horriblessss."*

Por primera vez, doña Martina entró actuando en nuestra vida, fue en la necesidad que había de una partera para mi hermana, Tonya, a quien ya se le aproximaba su parto. Mi madre la solicitó para ya cuando fuera la hora necesaria.

Ella no tenía título de obstetricia, y decía, "Crucita, yo sé sacar muchachos". Cobraba una bagatela por su trabajo. Cuidaba de los entuertos, de los cólicos de las parturientas o de los niños, con sus hierbas cultivadas por ella misma.

Su casa, podía decirse, contaba su historia. Era de remiendos, tal vez empezó con un cuarto y se le fue añadiendo según la necesidad. La puerta daba a la calle y cuando entraba uno a la sala, desde allí se veían las otras piezas y la cocina. Al lado de la casa en donde le pegaba más el sol, había el jardín de doña Martina, mejor atendido

---

* Originating in the late nineteenth century, the term *joto* in Mexican and Mexican American communities was often used in a derogatory way to signal that a man was gay or had effeminate characteristics. Writing within the historical context of 1915, González's use of *joto* aligns with its open use in Mexican barrios. However, she also uses it to show a positive aspect of this character's community contributions.

que la casa y el cual producía las hierbas curativas, utilizadas para las parturientas. Ella cultivaba las hierbas y plantas con todo esmero.

En la cocina había una estufa de leña, grande, una mesa de madera larga y ancha alrededor unas sillas desquebrajadas. Las paredes de las habitaciones enseñaban el asolamiento, la negligencia, no por abandono porque allí vivían, sino por faltar el "con qué" hacer las reparaciones.

José Antonio se afanaba por arreglar las cortinas viejas color rojo, pero ya por el sol o por el uso, habían quedado casi un rosa medio sucio y algo rotas y deshiladas. Su uso envejecido no era áspero ni tampoco la indigencia del hogar daba en cara, pues en el barrio éramos todos parejos en muebles de casa.

Había semanas en que doña Martina no tenía trabajo y ella en desesperación e impaciencia decía, "Maldita garza, cabrona, ¡ahora está en huelga!" Y en seguida se ponía a proyectar para sacar centavos. Dos de sus hijos casados, una mujer y un hombre, no le ayudaban en nada, únicamente iban a tomarse su jarro de "homebrew" e ir a los bailes que ella misma organizaba, "paserle la roncha a la vida".

Toncha, quien tenía el hermoso nombre de María Antonieta, vivía sola. Ella trabajaba en el barrio de los gringos. Este barrio lo separaba al de los mejicanos, la única calle que era la primera pavimentada. Para allá las de los gringos todas estaban bien cuidadas y las de nosotros, chuecas, lodosas y con bordos y peñascos y de pilón la eterna arena. Cuando llovía y caían aguaceros, el arroyo se repletaba del agua abundante.

Si por alguna razón algún trabajador o persona quería atravesar para llegar a su casa, pues tenía que rodear y andar, atravesando los cenagales y en partes se formaba lodo y barro, para llegar al mentado puente para poder cruzar. Este arroyo llegó a crecer tan inmenso, con el tiempo se formó una laguna y permanecía de año a año.

Como decía, Toncha compró su terrenito que a resumidas cuentas, y con los años, era un terreno abarcando casi la cuadra. Mi madre la visitaba y de vez en cuando yo maliciaba que mi madre le "tiraba las cartas" para decirle la suerte a Toncha. Toncha platicaba que no le agradaba la vida en casa de su madre y menos como la trataban los hijos, principalmente los casados y la Jenny. Quizás Toncha también disimulaba el oprobio que le causaban los defectos de José Antonio y Licha, la enana.

En los sábados y domingos por la tardecita, aparecía una linterna encendida colgada en un lado de la puerta de la casa de doña Martina, lo cual anunciaba el baile (unos vecinos decían el fandango y otros decían "chorchas") o fiesta en la noche.

Mi madre no me permitía ir a las fiestas de adultos, aunque mi hermano Pepín le rogara. Pues en una ocasión al estilo de muchachas curiosas, dos de mis amigas y yo fuimos únicamente a asomarnos al baile, viendo únicamente por las ventanas. Eran tres músicos rascuaches, un harpa antigua, una guitarra y un violín rechinón. ¡Aparentemente los músicos e instrumentos no se tomaban en cuenta, lo importante era el baile, iban a bailar y bailaban! Los jóvenes, impacientes por empezar a bailar, platicaban y hacían ruido como niños pequeños. La salita estaba repleta con vecinos conocidos, amistades de doña Martina y de sus hijos y también de nuestra familia, mi hermano Carlos, "el Chale", y mi hermano Pepín, a quien le encantaba el baile y aprendió bien a bailar.

La Jenny, quien se presentó por milagro, aseada y con los labios húmedos y algo pintados, pero disparejamente, bailaba en los brazos de Julio, su novio.

La impresión que dejó grabada en mi memoria este baile, nunca olvidaré. Precisamente, los músicos tocaban un vals. Muy empeñosos se mostraban las parejas. ¡No importaba nada en este mundo en ese momento, nomás el de bailar!

Repentinamente se oye la voz de doña Martina, ronca e imponente, "Abran sala, hijos de la chingada". Los danzantes se apartaron y quedaron inmóviles a la mitad de la salita y los músicos también quedaron quietos.

"Qué, ¿no oyen o están sordos, cabrones"?

Realmente no sabían qué hacer en el lugar tan reducido.

"¡Les digo que abran sala!" mandaba doña Martina.

Las parejas acataron, haciéndose a un lado y abriendo camino en medio. Al parecer ninguno se afrentó por las palabras de doña Martina, pues la conocían lo mal hablada que ella era. Las palabrotas de doña Martina no pasaron desapercibidas para mí, en esos momentos vino a mi mente un incidente acontecido muchos años atrás y me recordó, efectivamente, el terror causado por las mismas palabras mal dichas de doña Martina.

¡Ya amanece y no hay ni un muerto!

Al empezar la revolución del 1910 en México, toda la gente que pudo se pasó a los Estados Unidos Americanos a refugiarse de las amenazas de bandidos, de rebeldes y otros peligros por los cuales estaba pasando el país. Entre gente buena se pasaban muchos maleantes, pues los puertos de inmigración no eran vigilados.

"¡Ya amanece y no hay ni un muerto, hijos de la chingada!" ¡Qué horror entraba en la vecindad oír estas palabrotas en las noches oscuras! Eran malhechores quienes con toda la boca gritaban y nos llenaban de temor y espanto.

Nadie se atrevía a contestar, menos arriesgarse a asomarse a la ventana para saber quienes eran. Después de pasar un rato de silencio, se repetían de nuevo las abominables palabrerías tan ofensivas. Volvíamos a estremecernos de nuevo. Al largo tiempo cuando nadie les sacaba pleito, se cansaban y se retiraban. Los sustos eran frecuentes y escandalizaban al barrio.

¡Acontecía esto en el barrio Chihuahuita en el que, según se decía, "rasuraban con hacha!" Amanecían muertos y asesinados ya por esos maldicientes en sus parrandas o en pleitos, y también algunos inocentes. Temíamos a los desalmados.

Al oír el espantoso ruido de pasos y estruendos como de bestias y, según uno de los niños, se acercaban a devorarnos, corríamos a la cama grande de mamá. "El corazón de Jesús nos libre". Eran las palabras de nuestra madre tratando de esconder o disimular el miedo. A medio amanecer, mi madre nos llevaba a nuestros lechos, los cuales eran el suelo, pero yo me quedaba con ella. Contaba yo en ese tiempo con únicamente seis años de edad, no obstante hacía ya muchos años que había fallecido mi hermano Pepín. Lo tengo muy presente, con su pelo ondulado con la partidura a un lado y en el otro le quedaba un rizo rebelde no queriendo domesticarse. Sus ojos eran negros con miradas penetrantes, sus cejas anchas y tupidas. Inquietas y agudas miradas eran de cariño para todos sus hermanos y su madre, mas yo era su consentida.

Mis dos hermanos eran menores que mi hermana Tonya, y demasiado jóvenes, y naturalmente temblaban con aquellas injurias e impropiedades de esos hombres. Mas, ¿qué podíamos hacer? Quiero mencionar a mi hermano porque era un muchacho consciente, pese a que todavía usaba el pantalón debajo de la rodilla con medias negras, pues así ocultaban más lo sucio y lo remendado en las rodillas y en los talones.

En las mañanas oscuras, temprano iban a vender periódicos. Cuando volvían, comían algo y salían los dos juntos a buscar "chambas". Siempre traían algunos centavos ayudando a descargar mercancías o en algún otro trabajo liviano. Éramos huérfanos de padre. Mi madre con la eterna preocupación de que nosotros pudiéramos mejorarnos en alguna manera.

Ella misma se inquiría, "Pero ¿cómo puede ser así, que nos mejoremos? Ya ven lo que pasa en el barrio".

Días después llegó el colmo de los males. Había un hombre melcochero, don Teodoso, gordo y chaparro, moreno y con el pelo muy corto, casi pelón. Tenía manos gordas con dedos que parecían no haber la mano de tan abultados, pero muy ágiles. Cuando mi hermano Pepín me daba un centavo, corría a comprar una melcocha.

El melcochero era rápido para hacer melcochas. En un instante, en una charola grande, golpeaba y estiraba la masa y prontamente tomaba un pedazo y lo arrollaba en las palmas de las manos, formando, como con magia, la melcocha. ¡Luego la movía y con velocidad aprensaba las orillas de la melcocha con el pulgar y el índice, les daba una torcidita y les marcaba unas orejas! Me fascinaba esta demostración de elaborar melcochas.

Una mañana se oía una algazara o un bullicio en el barrio. Casi dormida salí, pues no podía esperarme ni un momento más a saber lo acontecido. ¡Válganos! ¿Qué pasa? ¡Era don Teodoso a quien se lo llevaban en la ambulancia! Había amanecido asesinado en su casa. Tal vez por robarle los miserables centavos que se ganaba en la venta de sus sabrosas melcochas.

"¡Este sí ya es el colmo!" se quejaba mi madre con fuerte sentimiento. Don Teodoso era buena gente y buen vecino. No había ninguna razón para causarle la muerte.

Buscamos casa fuera de ese barrio. A los cuantos días nos movimos a otra vivienda. ¿Mejoramos en algo? No como quería nuestra madre, pero no murmuramos....

Nos establecimos en el barrio. Mi hermana Tonya, quien apenas cumplía los escasos quince años, había ido a trabajar a una lavandería, de las ocho de la mañana hasta las cinco o seis de la tarde, en el mango. Los días de invierno no eran tan dificultosos como los del verano. En aquel entonces no se gozaba de abanicos ni de aire acondicionado, únicamente el calor que salía del vapor del mango. ¿Fue mejoramiento?

Aquí también en este lugar había refugiados de México. Pero después de buscar trabajo y no encontrar, se fueron a vivir en donde "se barría el dinero con la escoba". Tal vez buscaban las Siete Cuidades de Cíbola en California. ¡Qué ilusiones tan hermosas, porque yo también las creía!

El barrio se prestaba para ser sociable. Las pláticas se trataban de la política, pero mejicana, nada de los gringos. Únicamente cuando se llegaba el día de la elección y los candidatos ofrecían sacos de harina y botes de manteca en cambio de votos para el que tenía más que ofrecer, eso es de comestibles.

Aprendí de partidos políticos de México, y el porqué de la revolución. ¡Hasta el presente no me agrada saber nada de lo bueno del presidente Porfirio Díaz! Mi favorito e ideal político fue y es Francisco I. Madero, mártir, la víctima de la democracia mexicana. Don Porfirio, el tirano de México. Todo esto fue inculcado cuando yo era niña.

A menudo se formaban grupos partidarios de los dos presidentes. Las conversaciones, los acaloramientos y altercaciones y grandes disputas, aprendidas escuchando y fisgando todo el día. Para mí duraron toda mi vida.

Los periódicos mejicanos eran leídos con ahínco y a veces con lágrimas, de la manera ocasionada por el asesinato del presidente Madero. Los vecinos mandaron decir misas por su alma y por largo tiempo guardaron luto con un listón negro ancho puesto a la manga del saco o camisa. Los llantos fueron por un héroe mejicano… También yo acompañaba a llorar a gritos, guardaba el luto y aborrecía a los culpables.

A pesar de todo esto, la pugna constante de nuestra madre era que mejoráramos en aprender algo. ¿Cómo podía ser así? Mis hermanos se lanzaron a luchar por la vida y yo era la única en la escuela. Por medio de periódicos, los cuales eran el único elemento de tener literatura para aprender a deletrear y a leer.

Pasaron los años. En nuestra familia llegó un cambio el cual fue de mucha trascendencia en nuestras vidas, especialmente la mía. Por lo pronto se olvidó la política y nos ocupamos en los asuntos familiares. Mi hermana se casaría, su novio había regresado de California y traía lo necesario para el matrimonio.

Mi hermano Chale trabajaba en una botica llevando y entregando a domicilio. Recuerdo con nostalgia sus afanes con su bicicleta de "segunda", mas yo pienso que ya era de quinta mano, se "ponchaba" tan seguido. Me supongo que mi hermano componía y reparaba esas llantitas más que los mandados que hacía.

Pepín trabajaba en unos establos, enganchaba los tiros de caballos a los coches y preparaba a los caballos para alistarlos cuando los solicitaran. Era buen trabajo, pero deseaba otro. Con el tiempo fue a trabajar al "City Water Works" ayudando a cuidar unas maquinarias, y era trabajo, según nosotros, de categoría.

Al fin se casó mi hermana Tonya. Yo le eché de menos más que todos. Por lo pronto la visitábamos casi a diario. Les diré que todavía veo las viviendas en donde vivía mi hermana, buenos recuerdos me dan.

Después mi madre y hermanos compraron un terreno retirado del centro en donde radicábamos. La casita de dos cuartos se había construido en las orillas de la ciudad. Explicaré que en ese tiempo todavía era condado y no ciudad. El agua estaba afuera. El escusado de "hoyo", mis hermanos le nombraron vulgarmente "mi tormento", estaba lejos de la casita. A ellos no les agradaba este lugar, pero nuestra madre pensaba, era mejor vivir en donde hubiera espacio. Realmente el espacio estaba a nuestras "anchas", pues era la última casa del barrio. Las lomas de arena, mezquites y chamizales eran nuestro vasto espacio.

Este barrio todavía llegó a ser otro barrio. ¿Mejor? El tiempo dirá, decía mi madre. Ella se empeñó en criar gallinas y un puerco que nos tomó un año para medio engordarlo. Mis hermanos ya ganaban lo suficiente para pagar la casa y el lote y también los comestibles no abundantes, pero si taxativos.

Basta de lo que aconteció hace algunos años, volvamos al baile.

Las palabras de doña Martina de "ábran sala" no me dieron pavor como las anteriores en el barrio Chihuahuita. No comprendía yo el porqué, pero sí me provocaban pena y al mismo tiempo risa a mí y mis amigas. Poco a poco conocí y aprendí algo de esa mujer, doña Martina.

No olvido cómo se paraba en medio de la salita, un cuerpo femenino, tal vez viejo y escaso, pero con voz rasposa y seca, decía, "Ábran
sala, hijos de la chingada…" La figura andrajosa de esa mujer me
daba la impresión de una actitud de alteza con sonrisa de satisfacción
y risa entre los dientes, gozando quizás por la turbación causada a los
danzantes. Recorría de un lado a otro; tan pequeña se mostraba en
medio de muchachas y muchachos muy altos.

Se acercaba junto a Pepín y le decía, "¡Oye, Pepín, como estás largo,
ya no crezcas!" Con sonrisa burlona y con miradas de arriba a abajo.

Mi hermano únicamente contestaba, sonriente, "Sí, doña Martina".

"¿Bueno, 'ora qué esperan, cabrones? ¡Bailen!" Y con el mismo
gusto y ánimo al empezar a bailar con ese mismo espíritu de energía
joven, seguían bailando como si nada hubiera pasado.

Alguien comentó que a doña Martina tal vez se le había pasado
la mano en el "home brew", y otro que tal vez tenía otra cerveza o
bebida mejor que la que vendía. Era cosa de diversión.

La Jenny

Hacía tiempo que Juana ya no quería el nombre de Juana; quería, y
por fin logró, quedársele el nombre de Jenny. Ella pensaba, y parte
de la familia le hacía segunda, que ella era bonita y bella por su piel
blanca. Efectivamente Jenny era superior por la simple razón de "en
la tierra de los ciegos, el tuerto es rey", y según la regla fija, hasta la
fecha, principalmente en nuestros barrios mejicanos, la blanca, la
rubia es la bonita y la hermosa. La Jenny no era güera sino más bien
blanca, con ojos zarcos no grandes, pero de mirada atractiva. Su pelo
amelcochado.

Rara vez se encontraba la Jenny bien acadia; era morosa y descui-
dada. Tenía el hábito de ponerse una madeja de su pelo en la boca y
estarla pasando por la boca hasta dejarla empapada de saliva. Tenía
dieciséis años de edad y tenía novio, de nombre Julio, quien era
amigo de mis hermanos.

Para estas fechas, el barrio sufría espantosamente de los rigores de la Primera Guerra Mundial. Y en una ocasión fui a llevarle a doña Martina unas calabacitas. Al entrar a la sala, me sorprendí algo, pues allí estaba Jenny con Julio. Saludé y pregunté por doña Martina. Contestó Jenny que al momento venía y que me sentara. Pues no sé si sería al momento o no; yo estaba atentamente embobada en la plática de Jenny y Julio.

"¿Ya sabes que hay guerra, Julio?" inquirió Jenny.

"Cómo no, Jenny. ¿Por qué me preguntas?"

"¿Por qué no te das de alta en el ejército o en la marina?"

"¿Yo, Jenny? ¡Te he dicho que por esa misma razón vine a este país, por la revolución en mi tierra! ¡Ahora quieres que vaya a una guerra que no sé quién o por qué se pelea! Que según sé, es una guerra que se empezó en Europa, hace años. ¿Qué no?"

"No, no, Julio, no me reburuje. Yo tampoco sé de qué se trata esa guerra, pero dice Jony, mi hermano, que él se va antes que le hablen". Los labios húmedos de la boca de Jenny se mostraban desdeñosos y aún más, porque la madeja de pelo no cesaba de ser bañada de saliva en su boca.

Había algo en la cara de Jenny que no le estaba, según a mi parecer, así como cuando uno oye una cuerda de algún instrumento sonar discordante. Después me di cuenta, era la boca de labios delgados, ancha, y cuando hablaba no pronunciaba bien las palabras y se podía decir que su plática era un lenguaje de ella misma. Yo le entendía bien, así hablaban muchos del barrio.

No pudieran entender lo que ella hablaba si yo lo escribiera, y tal vez ni escribirlo pueda.

La conversación parecía ponerse algo acalorada, más a mí no tomaban en cuenta y platicaban como si yo no existiera.

"'Ora, 'ora, diga que tiene miedo Julio, por eso no quiere ir a la guerra. ¿Qué no?" Atrevida la Jenny, pero estaba algo nerviosa y más pelo mojaba.

"Mira, Jenny, desde ahorita te diré que no peleo ni en mi tierra ni en ninguna otra. En México pronto se establecerá la paz y espero volver a trabajar las tierras de mi padre junto con mi hermano Salomón. ¡Pero pelear, nomás no!" Julio se manifestaba firme en su decisión. Una sonrisa de desdén y de inquietud se notaba en los labios húmedos de la Jenny.

Posteriormente supe que había cierto entendimiento entre Jenny y Julio: cuando ella cumpliera los diecisiete años, contraerían matrimonio. Posible fuera que la Jenny quisiera ir a vivir a México y no sabiendo cómo explicarse, provocara al novio en esta manera.

Mucha duda había en los ojos de Jenny. Implicaciones y acusaciones con ciertos ademanes de impaciencia en su conversación con su novio, Julio. El noviazgo no caminaba de acuerdo.

Licha, la enana

Algunas personas nos esforzamos para conseguir algo. Luchamos contra enfermedades, tratamos de librarnos alguna cosa como la injusticia y la amargura del destino, así en este barrio la gente era una de luchar continuamente…desapercibidamente.

Licha fue la última hija de doña Martina. Ya tenía más de quince años de edad y aún no había llegado a crecer a su debida estatura. La cara la tenía bien fea. ¡Qué contraste tan vivo! Era todo lo contrario a su hermana, Jenny. Su semblante parecía uno de anciana, no con arrugas, sino por su cutis grueso y de color amarillento, asemejándose a un pellejo seco. Tenía ojos grandes y se esforzaba para levantar los párpados. Debajo de los ojos le caían bolsitas o rollitos de piel, dando la apariencia de una persona que tiene mucha edad.

Los labios descoloridos, para moverlos al hablar, las extremidades de la boca no se movían, únicamente la parte de los labios de en medio. Su pronunciación era dificultosa, su voz algo ronca y rasposa. ¡La infeliz muchacha no podía reír!

Su cuerpecito extraordinario, pequeño, parecía barril, redondo con piernas muy bajitas y los brazos como de niña, mas las manos grandes y gruesas.

Realmente Licha era un fenómeno. Les diré que para el trabajo no era fenómeno inútil, era una esclava. Planchaba subida en un cajón para alcanzar la tabla. Lavaba trastes y remendaba la ropa. Licha regaba el jardín de doña Martina y cuidaba las flores rebeldes y las hierbas para los enfermos de su madre.

Licha no era falta de entendimiento pese a su gran defecto físico. En ocasiones se rebelaba. Su hermana Jenny tenía maneras intolerables con Licha. Le ordenaba con voz grosera, "Licha, traime esto, y haz el otro". Naturalmente Licha se rebelaba.

Ya enfadada, se quejaba con la madre, diciendo, "Mamá, ¿cómo quieres que yo haga todo para estos huevones, empezando con la Jenny? Nomás está echada en la cama durmiendo y pensando en el novio. ¡Yo me canso, saben!" Licha no podía llorar.

"¡Vete de aquí, fenómena odiosa! ¿Pos, pá qué quieres servir?" Con mal talante le hablaba Jenny a su hermana. Licha se retiraba con una retreta de palabras, raspando la voz; no se le entendía lo que decía, pero no hacía lo que Jenny mandaba.

Doña Martina parecía estar sorda a las riñas de sus hijas. Y cuando no estaba en la elaboración del mentado "home brew", estaba entretenida con sus menjurjes y sus hierbas, las cuales anudaba en pedazos de tela o las ponía en frascos y otras en paquetes de papel y los guardaba. A ella le daba lo mismo que se pelearan y se dijeran sus defectos. Cuando la cansaban, les gritaba, "¿Qué quieren que yo haga? No me frieguen, cabronas". Asunto terminado.

Licha se retiraba a su única protección, el trabajo.

José Antonio, el joto

Por lo general, casi todos los escritores tienen un código, como se dijera, un código secreto o uno de guardar y señalar los acontecimientos, no como eran ni son, sino como quisieran que fueran. En donde en parte, aunque pobres, sus hábitos son buenos, sus aspiraciones ideales, sus modales de puritanos y así por lo consiguiente. Lo que yo escribo realmente fue gente de barrio, sus costumbres y sus pobrezas, así como las escribo. Los defectos de esta familia de doña Martina son sin iguales porque nunca he sabido de dos personas de una misma familia que tengan defectos de los más notables y perceptibles como los de Licha y José Antonio.

José Antonio, quien por tradición se llamaba Antonio, como su bisabuelo, el cual había dicho a sus hijos con orgullo, "El nombre de Antonio aparecerá en todas mis generaciones futuras". Toncha y su hermana mayor, cuando oían a su madre platicar de su abuelo, decían con algo de mofa, "Para bien o para mal, amén".

En realidad, José Antonio era hermafrodita, teniendo los caracteres distintivos de ambos sexos. Doña Martina, su madre, y el resto de la familia no ocultaban el defecto de J. Antonio.

A menudo comentaba la madre a la mía, diciendo, "Crucita, parece, o más bien dicho, ¡Dios me ha castigado! Así dice la vieja doña Patrocinio que tal vez yo, por ser tan pecadora y mala, me ha dado fenómenos en mi familia". Se desesperaba y retrocedía a palabrerías.

Mi madre trataba de consolarla, "No se puede hacer nada con esa cuestión, doña Martina. Hay que soportar lo bueno y lo malo de la vida, ¿no le parece?"

"Está bien, Crucita, pero esa gente que no deja a uno hacer lo que pueda. Como te dije, de la vieja, ¡ella se asusta de mí! Yo también me puedo asustar y hasta espantar de lo que dicen de ella. ¿Crucita, que no sabes que la güera, Gaby, se la robó doña Patrocinio?" Excitada por lo que desembuchaba, bajaba la vista y sacudía la ceniza de la vieja de cigarro.

"Será eso un cuento; usted sabe cómo los 'sueltan' de vez en cuando, doña Martina". Mi madre se apenaba.

"Mira, Crucita, seré chismosa y cuentista como quieran decirme, pero yo de mí no cuento mentira, no soy fabulosa. Les puedo decir quien lo asegura, si se presentara el caso. Pero a mí qué me importa. Pero vale más que esa vieja no le busque al gato tres pies, porque le haya cuatro. Así dice el dicho". Temblaba doña Martina y le chupaba a la bachicha de cigarro hasta que no tenía que fumarle, luego la tiraba y al rato encendía otro.

Resumía el cuento. "Qué no te has fijado como es prieta ella y prieta como ella sola; hasta las encías de los dientes las tiene negras! Así tendrá el corazón, porque yo ni me meto con ella para nada. Los otros dos, la chapa Lola y Juan Dios, ¡son prietos! ¿Y Gaby? Güera, bonita frondosa. Es rubia, Crucita, ¿qué no? Fíjate y lo verás, ¡es más güera que mi Jenny!"

A toda la plática mí madre movía la cabeza, aprobando lo que doña Martina exponía. "Tal vez Gaby es hija de gringo".

Una risa maliciosa y graciosa apareció en los labios de doña Martina, y con la mayor naturalidad del mundo, contaba sus relatos y sospechas. "Mira, yo digo de mí parte, la Jenny sí es hija de gringo; ni me asusto ni lo niego y aunque quisiera, ¡ya ves a mis demás hijos! ¿Pero que diga doña Patrocinio eso? Pura 'chet' [caca]". Terminaba la conversación con enfado y disgusto. Hacía pausa y con aire de perversidad, decía:

"¿Oye, Crucita, que no sabes que a mi Jony le cuadra la Gaby?" Se encaminaba así a la puerta para retirarse y con una risa escondida en la boca dijo, "Ya me voy, Crucita, a ver que dicen esas paridas empedernidas".

Vuelvo con J. Antonio. Él no era alto, pero sí delgado, aunque nunca se notaría por la razón que su ropa siempre fue segunda o tercera mano. Los pantalones le quedaban guangos y la camisa con mangas demasiado largas y él con ligas en las mangas se arremangaba poco. Luego se fajaba el cinto y le resultaban pliegues alrededor. Pobre muchacho.

Para J. Antonio no había el cariñoso nombre de Toño, como a

su hermana Toncha. Tampoco no se cambió su nombre al "agringado" Tony, como su hermano Jony, y Juana a Jenny. Su nombre era J. Antonio y así le llamaban todos.

El corte de pelo no lo conocía él, y si bien le iba, cada año. Lo usaba largo y poco aceitado para que se mantuviera en su lugar, y se le formaba una colita de pato atrás en el cogote. El pobre intentaba ser medio presumido, mas no era posible. También diré que era muy decente y fácilmente se atemorizaba. Yo le tenía lastima. J. Antonio daba la impresión de no tener esperanza ninguna... Se mostraba sumiso, sin ánimo, y a más de esto, todo era vergüenza y se mortificaba con las palabras maldichas de su madre. Él no gritaba, no se exaltaba y no se quejaba. En las fiestas o bailes en su casa, él ni Licha aparecían por ningún lado. Amigos, paseos o cines no los conocía J. Antonio. Tal vez estaba preparado para el agravio y prevenido para toda ofensa e insulto en callar.

Él había llegado a todo su crecimiento pero los de la familia se avergonzaban de su estado y él lo comprendía. Su misma madre, doña Martina, no era persona quien, por el maldito "qué dirán", tratara de ocultar o disimular el defecto de su hijo, cuando menos no echarle en cara a cualesquiera ocasión su imperfección.

Cuando la cigüeña se ponía en huelga, doña Martina andaba de malas. Llegaba a mi casa con su palabrerío, echándole la viga a J. Antonio. "Ya me canso ése cabrón verijón de J. Antonio; no lo saco de la casa ni a palos. Que en ninguna parte le quieren dar trabajo, que no lo pueden ocupar, y que sé yo que más. No sé qué hacer".

En otras ocasiones llegaba animada. "Crucita, ay, te encargo a San Antonio. Su niño tiene los deditos quebrados y J. Antonio lo va componer. Dice Lola que le paga bien. Ojalá que sí, fíjate que estamos limpios hasta del estómago".

¡Yo no podía imaginarme ver a J. Antonio sentado pacientemente arreglando unos deditos de un santito tan pequeño como el niñito de dos pulgadas de largo de pies a cabeza! Pero hubieran visto cuando lo terminó. Los deditos formados de yeso y pintado el santo su hábito en sus colores naturales y vivos; los dejó casi nuevos. Doña Martina, con poco aire de orgullo ocultado, decía, "¡Pero que cabrón muchacho; te digo, Crucita, que parece mujer!"

J. Antonio era callado, no por mal humor o genio sino por falta de quien lo animara y lo alegrara. Quizás él pensaba que no podía agradar a nadie. Y traté más con J. Antonio cuando su madre, por la impaciencia y necesidad, y también para aprovechar la oportunidad de las onzas de oro pagadas por Leandro, le facilitó una tiendita de abarrotes. Los dos hermanos de J. Antonio, a reniegos y maltratados, le ayudaron a construir un cuarto pegado a la casa.

No les miento, era una miniatura el cuarto de tienda, ¡de doce por diez pies! Apenas se abría la puerta y ya estaba el mostrador. La ventanita la cubrió con una cortina graciosa. Los floreros con flores hechas por él mismo, de papel de china. Ahí era su casa, su castillo, se pudiera decir. Vendía azúcar, frijol, arroz y alpiste en paquetes para dar a cinco centavos. Dulces y galletas a centavo. Realmente era una juguetería lo que hacía J. Antonio.

A mí me gustaba ir a la tienda más bien a fisgar que a comprar. Lo encontraba ocupado haciendo flores, limpiando el mostrador y pesando sus comestibles. Componía y adornaba cuadros de fotografías con holanes de papel o de tela de encaje, acomodándolos alrededor de cuadro, y se veían muy bien, aparte de esto le pagaban unos cuantos centavos, ¡pero le pagaban!

Con una sonrisa rara y forzada, ojos medio mansos, contestaba a mi pregunta de admiración, "J. Antonio, ¿tu tocas el violín?"

"Muchacha, yo no tocooo el violinnn...loo estoooy componiendo. Le falta el puente y una cuerda y cuando lo arregle, entonces lo afinareeeee". Aparte de ronca su voz, era gangosa

y les hacía cola a las palabras.

Quizás él notó la admiración grande mía, porque cuando me entregó el mandado, me dio un caramelo de pilón.

Y más grande todavía fue mi sorpresa que ya, al retirarme de su tiendita, J. Antonio, la sonrisa permanecía en sus labios. En esto y en otras cosas semejantes, se ocupaba J. Antonio, el joto, y exponía sus mercancías a la raquítica clientela y ganaba el mezquino sustento de vida.

Don Leandro

¿Acaso tenemos derecho a la felicidad? ¿Cómo pudiéramos demandarla y a quién? Tal vez se ignora ese sentimiento tan furtivo en esta vecindad. Como pudiéramos robarnos un poco en ésta vida tan llena de miseria y tan desgraciada como, decía doña Martina… Pues lo ignoramos…

Sucedió que un día de pleno invierno, doña Martina llegó a mi casa. Noté la inclemencia del frío y más aún cuando ella se cubría la cara con las manos en la boca por la cual arrojaba el aliento así calentándose poco las manos heladas. Doña Martina cubría sus espaldas con un tapado negro gastado hasta verse los hilos ralos.

Ahora haciendo recuerdos de ella, pienso que tal vez ella ya se había olvidado, si acaso, todo lo que era un tapado nuevo. Los zapatos viejos y en ese tiempo tan frío, con las suelas gruesas de lodo y gastados de cruzar los terregosos y enlodados lugares para ir a ver a sus parturientas.

Apresuradamente me preguntó, "¿Chata, ón ´tá tu mamá?"

"Anda dándole comida a las gallinas, ya viene, doña Martina".

"Buenos días, doña Martina, ¿qué hace tan temprano y con tanto frío?" Ya sabíamos a que llegaba.

"Crucita, anda… dame una taza de café, que me muero de frío; aquellos cabrones, huevones, no quieren levantarse. Licha es la única, pero hace un café del diablo. El tuyo es el sabroso, Crucita". Se tomaba su café caliente y lo saboreaba con gusto. Se sospechaba que algo traía, como un secreto. Su proceder era uno de confusión y ahitamiento en sus movimientos ligeros y poco temblorosos.

Al rato y después de su primera taza de café, doña Martina nos daba a conocer algo que tenía en mente. Nosotros esperábamos.

"Qué les cuento, ¡me mandó hablar con don Leandro!" Su voz ronca pero con poca emoción en la sorpresa. "Tomasita me dijo su papá quería verme". Sus ojos brillaban y esperaban ánimo.

"¿No le dijo para que la necesitaba, doña Martina?"

"Anda, Crucita, ¿pos pa' qué sirvo yo?" Se tomó su café con una tortilla de harina, exclamando con gusto, "Qué bueno está tu café y muy calientito". Se cubrió su cabeza con el tapado negro y en voz baja, como si dijera un secreto, dijo, "De allá pa' 'ea te digo".

Doña Martina salió al frío troteando.

Don Leandro fue uno de tantos quienes vinieron de México y se refugiaron en este país. Y fue también él que compró más terreno que los demás refugiados. ¡Estableció la lechería más grande en ése tiempo, comprando más de doscientas vacas lecheras!

La primera vez que vi a don Leandro fue en tiempo de invierno. Me dejó la impresión de un hombre ruso, con el gorro de lana gruesa embutido hasta de las orejas y un poncho tan largo que le daba hasta los tobillos. También era rareza ver, especialmente a un hombre con una bufanda enredada al cuello, no obstante, larga y muy útil para el invierno.

A las cuarto de la mañana su vozarrón se oía por todo el barrio: "Cambo, cambo". Así les llamaba a las vacas y obedecían porque una por una salía del corral y atravesaba el camino para ir al establo para ser ordeñadas. Si por ansia de comer, alguna de las reses, con amplias ubres y echando chorros de leche por el camino, se metía en el establo equivocado, a cornadas la quitaba la dueña.

Don Leandro era hombre corpulento y de grande fuerza pese a sus sesenta años de edad. También era enérgico con sus hijos y con sus tres hijas. Tomasita la menor era mi amiga íntima. Los hijos habían heredado los hombros anchos y poderosos de su padre. Con la primera luz de la madrugada, padre e hijos se empeñaban en ordeñar y en preparar la leche y la entregaban en las tiendas. Al regresar y haber comido sus alimentos, limpiaban los establos y daban pastura a las vacas. También ellos ponían y quitaban los arreos de los caballos y bajaban las cajas de botellas vacías y los galones; luego aseaban los carros y los dejaban listos para el siguiente día.

Don Leandro disponía en todo. Ordenaba a sus hijos con arrogancia y palabras insolentes. Sus ojos se encendían debajo de cejas gruesas y rojizas si los trabajos y tareas las desempeñaban despacio. Realmente los obligaba a trabajar duramente. Si por alguna razón se revelaban o repelaban, les golpeaba con piales y con palos o con lo que encontrara cerca.

Muy lindas muchachas las dos hijas mayores de don Leandro. En el trabajo de la casa eran hacendosas. También al igual de los hermanos trabajaban en la casa y en lavar frascos y utensilios de metal pesados. También eran muy ordenadas y obedientes.

Se dice que para el amor no hay linderos. No obstante don Leandro, con su limitación tan ceñida para sus hijos e hijas en su libertad personal, en los asuntos del amor la astucia vence obstáculos.

Enseguida de la lechería de don Leandro, un joven con el nombre Facundo estableció otra lechería; por supuesto, era mucho más pequeña que la de don Leandro. Facundo, listo y con la ambición de hacer la vida en un país extraño, siendo él también refugiado, trabajaba con afán en su negocio. Pasando el tiempo se enamoró de María, la hija mayor de don Leandro. María correspondía el amor de Facundo. Le cubrían todos los que le rodeaban menos su padre, quien no sabía nada de las saliditas de su hija por las noches o cuando tenía tiempo desocupado y lo aprovechaba. Tomasita me contaba del noviazgo; con temor decía: "¡*La divina comedia* cuando mi papá se dé cuenta! Pero todos queremos a Facundo, también mí madrastra".

Se va llegando el día en que don Leandro supo del tatole. Los dos novios en esa ocasión únicamente platicaban en el corral que separaba las casas de ambos. Nadie anticipó para evitar la catástrofe. Don

Leandro casi se volvió loco; gritaba insolencias y bufaba como toro cuando lo tienen atado y vacas están cerca.

Todo el barrio aplaudió cuando Facundo como todo un "macho" se enfrentó a don Leandro y le gritó para darse a entender sobre la algazara formada por toda la familia y los alaridos y amenazas de don Leandro, diciendo en voz alta: "Yo quiero la mano de su hija para casarme, don Leandro".

Intentó don Leandro golpear a Facundo como hacía con sus hijos, pero Facundo le habló terminantemente: "Mire usted, don Leandro, no me toque para nada porque verá lo que le pasa si lo hace; será el último día que usted permanece en este país, se lo advierto".

Con estas palabras se aplacó el furioso padre de María, quien con lágrimas en sus ojos y con grande angustia se retiró oyendo las palabras de su padre: "Jamás volverás a salir de esta casa para nada. ¿Entienden todos?"

Poco tiempo después, clandestinamente, Facundo traspasó el negocio de la lechería. Con ayuda de los hermanos y hermanas de María y cuando menos se esperaba, María y Facundo se huyeron. En el camino se casaron y se fueron rumbo a California. Tomasita contó que recibieron una carta por conducto de una vecina con las nuevas.

Un jubileo grande había entre los vecinos del barrio cuando supimos lo que sucedió, eso era el matrimonio de los novios. El padre fue injusto con su hija tan buena, pero nadie le reclamaba.

Tomasita me contó lo que sucedía en su casa. Ellos habían quedado huérfanos de madre en Chihuahua. Después su padre se casó de nuevo con María, la presente esposa, quien era sumisa y dócil. Ahora el problema pendiente (seis meses después que se casó la hija) era que su madrastra ya había perdido dos criaturitas, nacían muertas o tenía abortos. Él, don Leandro, aferrado a que le viviera un hijo o una hija de él y María.

En estos trámites andaba doña Martina con don Leandro y dijo o había dicho que le contaría a mi madre lo ocurrido. Llegó Martina apresuradamente a mi casa; gustosa le decía a mi madre, "¡Mira, Crucita, mira lo que dio don Leandro!"

En la mano apoyaba una onza de oro de cinco pesos mejicanos. En ese tiempo el oro mejicano valía lo mismo o estaba a la par del dinero americano. Cinco pesos en oro eran cinco dólares.

Gran gusto tenía la mujer y se mostraba el ánimo vivo en su cara arrugada, diciendo, "¡Hasta le besaría los pies al viejo por esta onza, Crucita!"

"¿Qué pasó, diga, doña Martina? ¿Quién está enfermo?" mi madre quería saber.

"Fíjate, quiere don Leandro que María tenga familia y dice que ya van algunas creaturas que nacen muertas. ¡Y fíjate que dice que me paga lo que yo quiera si le hago vivir de él!" Yo nunca había visto lo feliz que se mostraba doña Martina.

"¿Puede hacer algo usted, doña Martina?" mi madre preguntaba medio asombrada.

Doña Martina hizo a un lado el tapado como si le estorbara para hablar y gesticular, y se paró así como se paraba cuando decía, "Abran sala" y le dijo a mi madre con cierta afirmación: "Crucita, yo sé mi negocio y además ¡esta es mi chanza de una vida entera! He esperado este momento media vida. ¡Aquí, Crucita, se darán cuenta quien soy yo! ¿A quién le debo esto qué sé? A naiden, nomás a mí misma. Ahora dirá ese viejo cabrón desgraciado de don Domingo que estoy sedienta de dinero; ¡pa' maldita la cosa me sirve a mí el dinero, Crucita!"

Descansaba un rato y volvía a resumir su plática. "Me quitaré de 'pendejas' y te diré que dijo don Leandro, Crucita. Muy manso el viejo estaba. Primero yo le dije que si él quería tener hijos y que le vivieran, tenía que hacer lo que yo le mandara. Él dijo que sí estaba dispuesto a lo que yo le digiera".

Se sentía satisfecha doña Martina. Se fumaba un cigarro.

"Pos yo le dije, terminantemente, 'Mire, don Leandro, usté no tocará a su mujer por dos meses y le prometo que su mujer tendrá un hijo. Lo cumplo si no, no, ni me hable otra vez'".

Tiró su cigarro medio fumado y encendió otro. Ya era la hora de comer y mi madre sin preguntarle le sirvió un plato de caldo de gallina y su sopa.

"Crucita, Crucita, 'ora estoy de plácemes. ¡Miren que platillo tan rico, como para el rey!" Mientras saboreaba el alimento con aquel gusto, nos contaba lo demás.

"El viejo es muy macho. Fue anuente a lo que le pedí. Examiné a María y está perfectamente bien. Volví a decirle a don Leandro que su mujer era joven y no había razón porque no tuviera familia bien, pero tenía que hacer lo que le dije. Ya me voy, Crucita, y gracias por tu comida tan buena. Ya me voy a ver a esos cabrones. Esta onza levanta hasta los muertos, Crucita".

Carlotita

Pocas personas piensan en ser compasivas con los menos afortunados, lo cual sería una noble acción. Evidentemente, así sucedía con Carlotita, mi vecina cercana.

Carlotita era buena persona con nosotros. Su esposo era lechero, pero no refugiado, original de Nuevo México. Él y sus hermanos eran muy unidos y se ayudaban uno al otro. Tenían tiendas de abarrotes, vendían leña, hacían adobes y fincaron casas para alquilar.

Tita, como le decíamos por cariño, era alegre y le encantaban las fiestas y bailes. No pasaba una semana o dos sin hacer fiestas; el día de santo, el bautismo o la confirmación de alguno de sus hijos, los cuales eran cuatro hijos y una hija, Chelo, mi amiga.

La primera vez en que conocí a esta familia fue cuando me invitó Chelo a su celebración de cumpleaños. Mi hermana Tonya tenía un vestido de hermoso color rosa con encajes, y ella sugirió a mi madre hacerme un vestido. ¡Fue un vestido precioso! Pero había otro impedimento. No tenía regalo que ofrecerle a mi amiga. ¡Malaya, si yo sabía de llevar presentes a fiestas!

Realmente no teníamos con que comprar algo. Para mí, Chelo tenía todo. Por segunda vez, mi hermana vino al rescate. En su casa tenía un rosal frondoso y me trajo una cubeta de las flores más lindas que pudo haber. Fue el regalo más apreciado por mi amiga. En la fiesta, nos sirvieron nieve, producida de la crema pura de la leche, la cual Chelo y yo descremamos para ese propósito. Como ese manjar no he vuelto a probar. Y esto era que fue hecha la nieve en garrafa movida a fuerza de brazos poderosos. Ellos le decían a la nieve "leche nevada".

Mi madre no me permitía ir a otras fiestas de compadres y comadres. Además, yo no tenía mucho interés en los bailes y menos en donde se servía el famoso "home brew". Lo que encantaba y deleitaba eran las carnes frías preparadas por doña Patrocinio. Pero la única que la ocupaba para este trabajo era Tita. Pues ella tenía con que pagarle. Cuando ella iba a la casa de Chelo a preparar las salchichas, más bien dicho salchichones por lo ancho, a nadie permitía entrar a la cocina en ese día. Era una cosa de mucha habilidad lo que hacía doña Patrocinio. El secreto de esa elaboración se fue con ella hasta el sepulcro. Ni aún a sus hijas dejó la receta para preparar tan exquisito manjar. En la primera oportunidad que tenía mi amiga Chelo, me daba lonches de ese salchichón.

Tita no sentía ningún agrado o gusto a doña Martina. Casi con tono de desprecio le decía a mi madre, "¡Crucita, por ninguna razón puedo yo ver ni a J. Antonio, ese joto, ni a esa enana! Nomás no. ¿Para qué hago amistad con doña Martina? Y si tengo amistad con ella naturalmente tengo con su familia". No la criticaba ni tampoco la frecuentaba. Le evadía.

En ese tiempo la situación económica empeoraba con la Primera Guerra Mundial. Este incidente es uno de tantos que ocurrió por aquel entonces. Para poder comprar un saco de harina de trigo, por ley teníamos que comprar lo doble de harina de maíz. Siendo que Tita no le gustaba cocinar, le regalaba la harina de maíz a mi madre, quien en cambio le obsequiaba tamales, o cosa así por el estilo, que a Tita no le gustaba preparar. Tita sabía bien la necesidad de doña Martina, pero lo ignoraba adrede.

Cuando Tita le llevaba la harina a mi madre, a escondidas de Tita mi mamá se la mandaba a doña Martina con la advertencia, "Chitón, chitón, doña Martina". Ella entendía el dicho común "Con el rey y la Inquisición, chitón".

Al siguiente sábado por la noche, la linterna aparecía al lado de la puerta de la casa de doña Martina. Esa noche sería de baile y fiesta, pues los entusiastas de baile ya sabían que indicaba la linterna. También se servirían antojitos, como champurrado y gorditas de maíz, "los sopes". Se sentía feliz doña Martina porque ya sería otra manera de luchar por la vida.

Las vidas se gastan inútilmente, nomás existiendo y vidas se echan a un lado como ropa gastada con el uso. Y aquí en el barrio, la vida proseguía y proseguía, hasta que llegó la escoria de la epidemia de gripa, o como se llamó "influenza española", azotando por todos lados y no haciendo excepción. Caminaron ricos y pobres, bonitas y feas, perfectos e imperfectos.

Lo más impresionante para mí de esta epidemia fue cuando se enfermó mi madre y no sabíamos que tenía. Los primeros auxilios se los dio doña Martina con hierbas sudoríficas, que según se decía en ese tiempo era bueno para moderar la enfermedad. Mi madre estuvo más de dos meses convaleciente y se alivió. Mi hermana Tonya la lidió.

Apenas se estaba recobrando de la enfermedad cuando tuvimos la funesta noticia que mi hermano Pepín había muerto de la gripa en el fuerte Travis en Texas. Esto retardó más la convalecencia de mi madre.

A mi amiga Chelo ni a mi nos pegó la gripa, tampoco a doña Martina. Temprano en las mañanas aparecía en mi casa con sus menjurjes para curar, ¡y apenas lo creo! Tengo el cuadro estampado en mi mente de aquellos enfermos, tirados en el suelo, en las camas o donde caían.

Primero fuimos a la casa de Chelo. Doña Martina nos mandó hacer una olla grande de café negro. Ella espolvoreó hierbas secas y nos mandó a dárselo a Tita, la madre de Chelo, luego al padre y a cuatro hermanos de Chelo, quienes al parecer ya no tenían vida. ¡Doña Martina no se atrevía a dejarse ver de Tita!

De ahí fuimos con otra amiga mía y de Chelo, no obstante, no conocíamos a su familia, le dimos también café fuerte y negro con los polvos hierbas. Su madre ya estaba moribunda y también mi amiga Catalina; a ellas no nos dejó doña Martina verlas. Después cuando otras amigas mías se dieron cuenta que andábamos de ayudantes de doña Martina, nos llamaron a ver a sus familiares, quienes eran también dueños de lecherías. Pues doctores no podían ir a las casas tan retiradas del centro. Uno que otro aparecía en el barrio, pero tenían, según decían, más trabajo en el centro; realmente no se preocupaban por los de barrios tan distantes.

Tengo memoria viva de doña Martina cuando veía a aquellos cuerpos inertes. Ella mostraba tristeza en su cara; no obstante, nos animaba y ella por delante, sus faldas sacudidas por el viento, la seguían detrás de ella a paso ligero.

Don Leandro mandó por doña Martina. Aunque él no estaba enfermo, nomás mi amiga Tomasita, quien casi estaba inconsciente; le aplicamos el café y los polvos. Le ayudamos a doña Martina arrastrar un galón de leche, de los grandes pesados; fue presente de don Leandro, al rehusar dinero doña Martina.

También visitamos a Lola, la del santo San Antonio, el cual no quiso sanarla, según ella, y a los cuantos días murió de la gripa. Pero doña Martina no se daba por vencida. Aparte de estos enfermos de la gripa, ella no olvidaba a sus parturientas. Esta vez dejaba a los maridos encargados de ellas cuando se aliviaban.

También la muerte cargó con doña Patrocinio, dejando a tres huérfanos. Juan al poco tiempo se dio voluntario al ejército, y Lola, la chapa, se quedaba en casa y Gaby, la güera, trabajando. Hubo algunos otros muertos en el barrio pero les cuento de los conocidos.

Recuerdo, platicado por mi amiga Chelo, de cómo su padre supo lo que había hecho doña Martina y sin consultar a su mujer, Tita, les mandó a sus trabajadores, sin preguntas ni murmuraciones, dejaran a doña Martina dos frascos grandes de leche todos los días. Esta fue muestra de gratitud inspirada por la fina demonstración desinteresada de doña Martina.

Jony, el héroe

Es curioso y he aprendido, ahora recordando de aquellos tiempos, que para muchas personas bajo presión, tienen algo de humor en situaciones algo tremendas. Esto se puede aplicar a doña Martina.

A fin de ese año, se había terminado la guerra, pero las angustias y pesares continuaban. Empezaron a llegar los soldados veteranos y traían recuerdos de los que no volvieron. Mi hermano Pepín fue el único quien no volvió con vida; todos los del barrio volvieron, a Dios gracias.

Mi madre por fin recobró su salud, pero no había ánimo en la casa, únicamente recuerdos de aquel hermano quien nos quiso tanto y luchó por el sustento de todos y aún después de su muerte siguió con una pensión para mi madre para el resto de su vida; pese a que después de pasar tanta amargura y necesidad, no llegó el socorro hasta dos años después de la muerte de nuestro hermano. No sabíamos de tal ayuda y menos de inquirir de lo que se ignoraba.

En los primeros meses del año, no obstante, el luto en el barrio era notable; doña Martina y su familia estaban de parabienes. El Jony había regresado con felicidad y de ribete, el Jony volvía aclamado ¡héroe! Únicamente en el barrio, y esto en lo íntimo del barrio, nos dimos cuenta de que el Jony era héroe.

"¡No entiendo cómo es héroe, este cabrón!" Palabras favoritas de doña Martina, medio burlonas, pero con algo de orgullo disimulado. Fue Jony con su madre un día a darnos el pésame por la muerte de mi hermano. Él sabía lo que queríamos a Pepín.

Les diré cómo era Jony. ¡Juan era el Jony y nomás! ¿Nomás? "Ay, veremos, dijo un ciego", corre el dicho. Él tenía mucho parentesco indio, escaso de cuerpo pero con fuerza física pero invisible. Jony era muy amigo de mi hermano Chale y eran jugadores de "baseball".

También eran buenos "pitchers" y buenos corredores. Doña Martina quería que sus hijos tuvieran trabajos de hombre; eso era "¡pico y pala!" pero los infelices con esos cuerpitos ni siguiera les daban chanza para ver si eran útiles. Sí, trabajaban en chambitas pequeñas. En una ocasión mi hermano Chale y él fueron a buscar trabajo, y al fin encontraron en el Western Union Telegram, de mensajeros. Duraron allí un año y luego Jony se fue al ejército y mi hermano a la marina.

En las pláticas de familia no podemos comprender cómo llegó a ser héroe. ¡Se pudiera decir que fue un milagro! Digo así porque el Jony era un pedacito de hombre igual de la madre. Los otros hermanos, aunque delgados, pero no de tan baja estatura como Jony.

Figúrense, él solo destruyó cuatro nidos de ametralladoras, ¡una por una a punta de granadas! Nos platicaba de sus experiencias en el campo de batalla y decía no quería ni acordarse, pero le rogábamos y al fin concedió nuestro deseo.

"Pos no sé pa' qué me dicen que soy héroe", contaba él con su sonrisa de muchacho travieso.

"¡Yo estaba haciendo lo que me habían mandado, nomás! Pos me enseñaron otras mañas y me decían cosas pa' transformarme en no sé qué, Crucita. Me querían hacer cruel y animal, pos así eran todos. Pero yo no quería matar y era lo que oía, 'Mata, mata'. La guerra es mala, Crucita". Gotas de sudor aparecían en la frente de Jony.

Doña Martina lo escuchaba y comentaba por la quinta o más vez,

"Apenas lo creo que este cabrón muchacho pudo salvarse, ¡y luego que sea héroe!"

Continuaba el Jony, "Les digo que yo no soy matón, nomás por que sí. Pos llegamos a un bosque en Alemania, y ya estaba medio quemado de bombardeos. Llegábamos allí porque veníamos de 'corrida'. Éramos como cuarenta compañeros y apenas empezamos a sentarnos para tomar agua o fumar, cuando inesperadamente llovió sobre nosotros el ataque de fuego, primero por viento y luego por tierra. El jefe nos gritó corriéramos a donde fuera. No nos dijo dos veces. Yo arranqué a un árbol y vide las raíces secas y desenterradas; me metí debajo de las raíces con un miedo que me ensucié los pantalones. Vi lo que pasó a mis compañeros, ¡tendidos en todo el campo y yo con vida! Ahí en la mampara del árbol me estuve no sé cuanto tiempo. Paso a paso salía en la noche y luego me metía otra vez debajo del árbol; pos las luces de los 'searchlights' no me dejaban. En la madrugada salí arrastrándome a gatas y créanmelo con lágrimas; quité una cantina de uno de los cuerpos y otro me surtió de pantalón, aunque guango, pero me lo planté. Me eché andar pa' contra del combate. Me perdí. Me cansé y andaba muerto de se', pero seguía andando no sé pa' donde.

"Pos que de repente me topaba con un soldado alemán, tal vez venía como yo, derrotado y sufriendo el cansancio y la se'. Los dos cargábamos armas y granadas, pero no quisimos matarnos, ¿pos y pa' qué, Crucita? Nos enfrentamos y nos saludamos al estilo militar y él se fue por su lado y yo por el mío".

"¡Jony, diles como mataste a los de los nidos!" doña Martina animaba a su hijo Jony.

"Pos ní yo mismo sé, mamá. ¿Pero acuérdese, Crucita, como jugábamos Chale y yo al baseball? Pos yo era bueno pa' pitchar. Cuando los de los nidos disparaban sus ametralladoras, yo contaba y sabía que había un ratito de descanso en su arma, y luego era cuando yo aprovechaba, aventando la granada y muy acertada, así los destruía un por uno. Fueron cuatro y a mí ni me tocaron. ¡Ahora dicen que soy héroe! ¡Hágame favor, Crucita!"

Después Jony soltaba una risita, luego se extendía a una sonrisa grande. Podía verse ese relámpago infinitésimo de triunfo en sus ojos. ¡Pero desapareció tan rápidamente como apareció!

"Y les digo a todos yo no soy matón". Así terminó su cuento.

"¿Qué piensas hacer ahora, Jony?" le preguntaba mi madre.

"Qué lástima Chale no esté aquí, Crucita. Él y yo teníamos pensado hacer un negocio, pero él se enlistó cuatro años, pos t'avía le faltan más de dos. Mientras voy a componer la casa de mamá".

El semblante de Jony era enjuto y moreno, ojos inteligentes, pero lo bueno fue que le había acostumbrado a tener sus espaldas derechas y enseñaba más confianza en sí mismo. Pienso yo ahora que por pequeño que fuera el triunfo alcanzado, sobre un ser tan desconocido y vituperado en su propio barrio, no dejó de saborearlo un instante, aunque disimuladamente.

Don Domingo

En nuestras meditaciones de ensueños, de diario nos empeñamos en justificarnos a nosotros mismos porque no nos agrada sufrir la pena de estar erróneos; no obstante, tenemos constantemente ilustraciones de nuestras propias debilidades y errores.

Una ilustración se puede observar en los siguientes eventos. Una noche de invierno, estando yo ya dormida y naturalmente en el suelo, oí una voz muy amable y empujándome a la misma vez a darle lugar para ella, diciendo, "Chatita, Chatita, muévete más allá, pero más".

Entre dormida y despierta comprendí que era Panchita, la mujer de don Domingo, vecino de la siguiente cuadra. Pronto me volví a dormir. A la mañana siguiente, me despertó un toquido en la puerta y mi madre fue a ver quién era.

"Perdone, Crucita, buenos días. ¿Está aquí Panchita?" La voz labiosa y amable era la de don Domingo.

"Sí, don Domingo, aquí pasó la noche Panchita, pero ella dijo que usted quería golpearla".

Para ser tan temprano en la mañana, el hombre ya andaba bien rasurado y peinado. De pronto allí en el marco de la puerta, y extendiendo los brazos a los lados y formando cruces con los dedos pulgares e índices, decía con voz persuasiva y afectuosa, "Por vida de estas santas cruces que no toqué a Panchita para nada, Crucita, ¡pregúntele delante de mí!"

Yo me quedé azorada con lo que decía don Domingo y además cuando vi la cara de Panchita, detrás de su cara trigueña con el lunar negro al lado de sus labios llenos y rubíes.

Mi madre fue con Panchita y le inquirió, "Panchita, aquí está don Domingo. Viene por ti, ¿te quieres ir?"

Su semblante al momento cambió a uno de desafío y respondió fuerte para que oyera su marido, "Sí, vuelvo a mi casa, pero me tratarás mejor, ¿es así, Domingo?"

Don Domingo contestó, fingidamente o no, no lo sé, así, "Mi amor, te juro que no probaré ese maldito trago que le dicen 'home brew'. Sí, vamos, mi vida". Salieron los dos.

Don Domingo fue quien vendió a mi madre y hermanos la Talaca, la yegua flaca. Lo conocíamos bien, era risueño y poco cachetón. Esto me trae a memoria de cuando yo compraba la leche a don Domingo. En la mañana, Panchita ya tenía afuera, debajo de un árbol frondoso, una mesa con un mantel blanquísimo y una jarra de leche, tortillas calientes y otros alimentos, a mi parecer, muy sabroso. Don Domingo muy aseado, me invitaba a acompañarlo al desayuno.

El hombre era presuntuoso. Tenía un carro con dos tiros de caballos, los cuales alquilaba para carga o lo que se ofreciera. Por donde él tenía que pasar todos los días a sus negocios era por cerca de la casa de doña Martina. No había otro camino, a menos ir a rodear por el puente que estaba algo retirado. Por este camino atravesábamos para llegar más pronto, y a la escuela o a tomar el tranvía, y así por lo consiguiente.

Don Domingo indagaría, tal vez, el propósito de la linterna en la puerta de esa casa. Cuando se dio cuenta de lo que significaba, yo me imagino que esto le dio a él una idea, por la siguiente razón.

Días después de este acontecimiento, don Domingo fue con mi hermano Pepín y le dijo, más bien lo aduló así: "Pepinito, yo sé que usted sabe bailar flamantemente y quiero hacerle una invitación a un baile el sábado a las siete, ¿qué dice?"

"Mire, don Domingo, con mucho gusto aceptaría, y gracias, pero tengo cita con una amiga y no la veo hasta el sábado en la tarde. No sé qué hacer".

"Pepín, eso es fácil, invítela. Mi casa la gobierno en buena conducta, y además yo no cobro nada. ¿Lo espero, eh? Los espero". Solícitamente se mostraba don Domingo.

Pepín le platicó a mi madre. ¡Las costumbres en esa época todavía eran convencionales y no le pareció bien o propio a ella que una muchacha señorita aceptara una invitación acompañada de únicamente su amigo o novio! Era propio que una persona de confianza o un familiar acompañara a la señorita a fiesta o baile.

"Mira, mamá, tú también vas al baile, ¿quieres?, para que conozcas a Palmira. ¡Es alta y elegante!" Con movimientos exagerados en los ojos y boca, mi hermano se mostraba contentísimo. Le gustaba bromear con mi madre, pero ella aceptó ir al baile y yo con ella.

Don Domingo decoró la sala amplia y el piso encerado para bailar. Invitó a los hijos de don Leandro, quienes no bailaron por la simple razón que no sabían ni dar un paso. Ellos se estacionaron en la puerta y en la ventana. Don Domingo se enfadó con ellos de rogarles que pasaran a la sala. El más joven de los hermanos parecía pretender a mi amiga Chelo, y ella también le hacía ojitos, pero no aprendió a bailar jamás. Al fin se casó él con mi amiga Chelo como tres años después. Pero ese es otro cuento.

Palmira fue la sensación del baile. Ella y mi hermano hacían una pareja ideal. La concurrencia, como había comentado don Domingo, era gente de "roce". Pregunté a mi madre qué era esa palabra y dijo que era "roce social", personas no corrientes.

Completamente diferente era Palmira a las muchachas del barrio. Entre la concurrencia estaba Gaby, la güera, su hermana Lola, la chapa, vestida de un traje muy ajustado, y después, mis amigas y yo la recortábamos y nos moríamos de risa porque pensábamos el vestido se le reventaría de tan apretado y escotado. Que parte de ser ajustado y escotado, se le notaba la línea que divide los senos, más nos reíamos. Había otras vecinas no conocidas por ustedes.

Gaby, muy simpática, no era maliciosa como Palmira. Su cuerpo esbelto, pero no era alta. Iba ataviada con cuello alto y manga larga, y don Patrocinio sentado al lado de sus hijas.

Las muchachas estaban recelosas de Palmira, pues don Domingo era toda atención con ella. En medio de la sala, salió él muy "panter", como decían en el barrio, y dijo, "Yo soy el bastonero". Manifestaba su ánimo cuando en voz alta decía, "Abran sala". Medio me estremecí porque yo creía que él diría lo que doña Martina le añadía.

Confiado en sí mismo, repitió, "Abran sala, muchachos". Cuando se hicieron a un lado, continuó don Domingo, "Caballeros y señoritas, los molesto en escuchar lo siguiente: tenemos entre nosotros a un joven y una señorita quienes nos presentarán un baile no bien conocido por estos lugares. ¡Es el tango! Un aplauso para Pepín y la señorita Palmira quien lo acompaña".

Efectivamente, mi madre y yo nos sentíamos orgullosas de mi hermano. "¡Mamá, yo no sabía que Pepín bailaba tan bonito!"

"No hables, hija, deja ver el baile".

Los músicos eran mejores que los de doña Martina; no obstante, eran nomás cuatro. Mi hermano y Palmira se lucieron en bailar tango. Este es un recuerdo de mi niñez que jamás olvidaré, entre tantos que nos dejó ese querido hermano.

Mi hermano Chale tuvo compasión de la chapa Lola y de otras que bailaban y no dirían que se quedaron "sentadas" o "calabaceadas". El bailó con todas.

Les aseguro que, si hubiera estado Jony, él se hubiera dado vuelo con todas las muchachas. Lo que le faltaba de cuerpo, le sobraba para bailar; como decía su madre, "Baila como trompo". Mas él no fue invitado y no tenía "roce" y además Jony era fiel a su madre, quien también tenía esa noche baile en su casa.

Al día siguiente, doña Martina llegó a mi casa más tarde de lo acostumbrado. Se mostraba muina y de mal talante.

"Ese viejo desgraciado cabrón, me quiere hacer mal, Crucita, y lo sé. No me puede ver ni pintada, viejo tal". Así expresaba la indignación que tenía a don Domingo.

"Por qué, doña Martina, ¿qué pasa?" preguntó mi madre.

"¿Que no sabes que le mete cizaña a don Leandro? Que no me ocupe a mí, que consulte a un doctor y no sé qué más pendejadas, viejo metiche, condenado. Ya me dijo María, la de don Leandro. Yo a ese viejo cabrón no le hago nada, ni siquiera le hablo al sanababiche".

Doña Martina se tomaba su café con esperanzas de satisfacer su estómago y pacificar sus nervios.

"No entiendo todavía qué pasa ni por qué es así don Domingo con usted, doña Martina".

"Pos ni yo sé por qué me ha cogido de blanco. Pero ha de haber sido Panchita. Hace varios días, fui a comprar carne a la tienda de don Venustiano. Llegó también Panchita, y me vio pagar con una onza de oro".

" 'Doña Martina, ¿de dónde con onza de oro?' preguntó el carnicero con admiración, y Panchita estaba de fisgona. Y le contesté, 'Pregúntele a don Leandro, Venustiano, si quiere saber'."

"'¿Ah, don Leandro, eh? No sabía que usted trabajaba con él'".

"'Hay muchas cosas que usted no sabe, Venustiano'. Yo me salí, pero se quedó Panchita". Muy indignada estaba la infeliz mujer.

"¡Realmente, yo no me imaginaba que don Domingo tuviera esa alma para querer perjudicarla, doña Martina!" Mi madre se mostraba preocupada y confusa. "¿Qué le ha dicho don Leandro a usted?"

"Nada, Crucita, para allá voy al rato. Mira, Crucita, ¿ahora no te fijaste que me hace la competencia porque él supo de la onza de oro que Panchita dijo? Él cree que me va a derrotar; pues está equivocado, el viejo cabrón infeliz. Él no saca muchachos como yo, Crucita, como yo. No estoy esperanzada a que bailen ni a vender el nickle para poder vivir, Crucita. ¡Yo vivo hasta sin comer!

"Crucita, de tan endiablada que vengo, no te dije las nuevas. Fíjate que María, la de don Leandro, está gorda. Me mandó hablar el viejo. Voy a ver qué pasa. Ojalá que salga todo bien. Gracias por tu sabroso café. Como siempre, tú me quitas tantas penas, Crucita".

Gaby

Gabina, la de la cara risueña, la muchacha rubia, hablaba poco y lentamente, pero cuando miraba, era una mirada que parecía querer leer en el fondo del corazón. Los muchachos del barrio se fijaban en ella, pero únicamente como amiga conocida y vecina estimada. Tal vez no se podía llevar más amistad por la razón de que don Patrocinio no quería que sus hijas trataran con "piltrafa", y naturalmente este nombre precisamente implicaba al Jony. Quizás doña Patrocinio sospechaba algo de su hija Gaby.

Como mencionaba anteriormente, en aquella época las ideas y costumbres que después de la Primera Guerra Mundial dominaron no estaban en moda, de que una muchacha saliera a paseo con un muchacho pretendiente, con el permiso de la madre. De todas maneras, ellas y ellos se daban sus salidas cuando podían. En ocasiones, según contaban, Gaby y su hermana Lola rogaban a doña

Patrocinio que las llevara al parque a pasear. Les cumplía su deseo la madre.

Los muchachos del "team" de baseball incluían a Chale, mi hermano, y a Jony. Tal vez de corazón a Gaby le agradaba el "muchachito", como ella llegó a decirle con cariño. No era tanto interés en el paseo como era la única manera de ver al Jony, aunque de lejos.

Gaby trabajaba, pero nadie sabía en qué ni en dónde. Un día en una reunión de amigos allí en mi casa, preguntaba Jony a quien supiera qué era lo que hacía Gaby.

"¡Pues se viste tan bonito, tal vez es secretaria!" comentó Julio, el novio de la Jenny.

"No me digas, fregado. ¿Y tú como sabes?" Jony estaba disgustado y también sospechoso.

"¿Qué no se han fijado cómo viste? ¡Con un sombrero de cinco pesos!" dijo Julio.

"Hay nomás, hay nomás, fregado". Jony movía la mano contra Julio que se detuviera.

Jony no quería confesar, pero los muchachos amigos lo obligaron a exponer su sentimiento con relación a Gaby. "Yo les voy a decir una cosa. Yo no valgo nada. Realmente no tengo que ofrecerle a tan linda muchacha, pero que carambas, si ella correspondiera a mi amor, ¡yo me volvería loco!"

Los amigos se rieron afablemente de la declaración de su amigo Jony, que nunca esperaban que él dijera tal cosa. Continuó Jony: "Y si es asina, como dice mi amigo Julio, pos ni modo. Yo no soy nada. No sé nada. Soy un cabrón, como dice mamá".

"Jony, Jony, hay que tener paciencia y valor para vivir bien la vida. Miren, yo con Palmira, pues no encontraba como hablarle, pero me di valor, y ella contesto a ser mi novia. No te des, Jony".

"Oigan, ¡pero esa vieja nana no la deja ni respirar! Cuando la veo en el parque, pos nomas la veo y le echo ojos, pos no puede ni reír, con el 'polizonte [policía] a un lado'".

En nuestro barrio carecíamos de lo moderno, de lo necesario para adornar o embellecer ya en muebles o en las personas. No obstante, Gaby tenía ingenuidad de transformar aquello sencillo y de poco costo a algo de moda y de gracia.

Y esta era la razón porque decían que Gaby se vestía "elegante". No era la calidad de prenda de tela, sino ella se proporcionaba el vestido adecuado a su medida, no corto ni largo, más denotado algo de su propio gusto, haciéndose pertenecer más a lo femenino. Se podía decir que Gaby era algo "old-fashioned".

El hermano de Julio, Salomón, había estado escuchando a la conversación y el interpuso, "Mira, Jony, yo trabajo de aquel lado del puente, ayudándole a don Camerino en los abarrotes. Y he visto a Gaby pasar en las mañanas, pero no me he fijado a dónde realmente va a trabajar. Pero si quieres saber, mañana te lo diré".

Así quedaron. Y al siguiente día, fue una de risotadas y de guasa que no podían ninguno de los muchachos contenerse.

Salomón, el hermano de Julio, contó lo siguiente: "Eran las siete de la mañana cuando yo esperaba que la Gaby saliera de su casa. Fíjense que no trabaja muy lejos de su casa. Pasando el puente, entró en la casa de unos gringos que son clientes de Camerino, mi patrón, y a quienes yo les he llevado mercancía".

Todos estábamos (¿dónde me iba yo a escapar de oír tal cuento?), atentamente. Esperábamos a Salomón que continuara aquello tan importante.

"¡Ándale, fregado, dinos qué paso!" urgía impacientemente Jony.

"No me lo van a creer. Jony, no te enojes. Me mandaron a espiar y yo fui. Fíjate, Jony, ¡la Gaby es gata!"

"¿Qué? ¿Qué? ¿Qué?" inquirieron todos a la vez.

Siguió con su relato Salomón: "Me esperé, realmente no sé, pero como decía mi hermano Julio que Gaby se viste con sombrero de 'cinco pisos´ y que parece secretaria, pues yo no podía entender o pensar cómo, en esa casa, ¡Gaby fuera secretaria!"

Esperaba Salomón que Jony le reclamara algo, pero todos estaban atentos a saber el fin. "Gaby entró a la casa y yo vigilaba. ¡Luego al rato salió con vestido de casa y unas chanclas y un trapo enredado en la cabeza a barrer el patio y tirar basura al callejón!"

"¡Gaby es gata! ¡Gaby es gata!" Qué risa tenía el Jony. Luego se extendió a una carcajada y todos soltamos una risa de gusto y también de desilusión.

"¡Ora, Jony, es tu chanza! ¡Ora, que sí le llegas!" Chale animaba con mucha alegría a su amigo.

"Ojalá y no esté soñando, muchachos. Apenas lo creo. Les diré algo de sorpresa para ustedes: a mi madre siempre le ha gustado la Gaby. Pero hasta tiemblan mis rodillas al pensar hablarle, pero lo voy a hacer muchachos, se los cumplo".

El pedacito de hombre lo cumplió. Le habló a la Gaby y Gaby le correspondió. Ella le aclaró que su madre no estaría de acuerdo y sería mejor que ella no supiera hasta después.

A los cuantos días Jony se fue al ejército. La fue a esperar a su trabajo y los dos se pasearon en el barrio gringo. No necesitaron muchas palabras; sus semblantes decían todo. No obstante, el Jony tenía el sentimiento de incertidumbre. Cubrió de repente de impulso grande y se sintió optimista.

Gaby sentía que el día tendría que llegar el cual ella esperaba con ahínco. Jony le propuso matrimonio y se casarían tan pronto como llegara de la guerra. Ella aceptó.

Jony sabía que la madre de Gaby no lo quería. "¡Esa vieja de los ojos de rana!" no lo podía ni ver. "Pero quiero tanto a Gaby que no me importa. ¡La quiero como a naiden y mi madre la quiere mucho y con eso basta!" Así decía el enamorado Jony.

Cuando regresó Jony, visitó a Gaby. Le habían escrito de la muerte de doña Patrocinio y que su hermano Juan de Dios se había enlistado en los "marines".

Todos en el barrio nos platicábamos del noviazgo de Gaby y de Jony. Cómo admiraba a su novia y qué linda se veía su Gaby con traje negro. Se esperaron para la boda casi un año, pues era ley de la gente guardar luto por un año.

Toncha le regaló bastante de su terreno para que Jony fincara una casa para él y para Gaby. Lo curioso del caso era que Jony no encontraba trabajo, ¿y si "te casas con que la mantienes?" le preguntaba Jenny y también doña Martina. Sus amigos ya no estaban en el barrio y él no sabía en qué ocuparse para ganar el sustento de su futura esposa y tal vez de hijos. Se desesperaba. Todos los días visitaba su terrenito. Lo limpiaba de hierbas y escombros y lo admiraba. Se sentía contento con su propiedad.

Un día notó el barro que dejaban las aguas del arroyo cuando se retiraban de la orilla de toda la propiedad. Esto le dio la gran idea, la cual cambió el curso de su vida. No esperó nada. Al día siguiente se puso en obra. Compró paja, y con arena y el barro, se puso a hacer adobes. Doña Martina le aconsejaba de lo que ella sabía y produjo suficientes adobes para la construcción de su casa y la futura de Gaby. La enjarró y la blanqueó. Y Gaby quería un jardín como el de su futura suegra, y también el Jony se lo concedió.

"Adobero" fue el título del "pedacito de hombre" y del "muchachito", como le decía con cariño la Gaby. De vez en cuando le decían el "héroe". A él le daba lo mismo. Él era feliz con Gaby, y ya.

Era en el mes de abril. El sol brillaba, y el aire estaba fresco, pero no frío. Toda la familia de doña Martina, desde la madrugada, andaban en pie preparándose para el matrimonio y la boda de Jony y Gaby.

Por primera vez, vi a doña Martina vestida en ropa nueva y también con zapatos estrenados y una capita. Al parecer, doña Martina estaba muy orgullosa de usarla, pues era un regalo de su futura nuera.

Chelo y Jenny, madrinas, se lucían con vestidos de azul pálido. La Jenny parecía una princesa con el gorrito azul pálido y pegado a la cabeza encima del pelo largo amelcochado y brilloso. El joven acompañante no quitaba la vista de tal belleza. Allí se oyó el murmullo del compromiso de matrimonio de la Jenny con el compañero, el padrino. Fue un amigo de Jony y también compañero de la guerra en Europa. Por medio de Jony, su hermana conoció a este joven y se enamoraron tanto uno como el otro. Pronto, después del matrimonio de Jony, ella también se casó y se fueron a vivir a California, y según después supe, vivieron muy felices.

En esos días, a doña Martina no le interesaba nada de nada. Nomás era Gaby y su hijo, y realmente andaban en las nubes. También eran días de gala para el barrio en cuanto a los eventos de los últimos meses.

Jony apenas había llegado de la guerra y traía poco dinero. Y con el pago de Leandro a doña Martina, la tiendita de J. Antonio fue transformada en una tienda grande y llego a tener buena clientela. El barrio crecía y nuevas familias fincaban casas nuevas.

También la casa de doña Martina se vistió de nuevo. La Jenny se tornó en señorita hacendosa, cosa rara. Ella y J. Antonio colgaron cortinas nuevas y sacaron los tilicheros y acomodaron algunos muebles nuevos. Las paredes se encalaron y los marcos de las ventanas y puertas se renovaron. También era notable que el nombre de "joto" no era mencionado. Licha se entregaba como siempre al trabajo de la casa y cultivaba las hierbas en el jardín de su madre. Ya más bien, se plantaban flores, pues las parejas casadas consultaban doctores, y la generación moderna aspiraban a lo nuevo y lo modernizado. Ya no consultaban a la "partera". Consultaban a doctores, siendo que ya se disfrutaba de más dinero.

Un día, Tita fue a visitar a mi madre. Ella y la familia hacían preparativos para moverse de su terreno ocupado por tantos años. Tita se sentía triste por dejar a sus amistades de este barrio, pero la realidad era que el plazo de tiempo para cambiar la lechería se cumpliría pronto. Tita se sentía apesadumbrada por el cambio. En la plática de buen rato, ella contaba lo siguiente:

"¿Crucita, recuerdas a don Chen [Epomuseno], al que le rentamos los tres cuartos de las viviendas de la esquina? ¿Te acuerdas también de que llegaron de refugiados y mi marido y yo les ayudamos con leche y huevos a toda la familia? Nos dijeron que estaban necesitados. Cuál fue nuestra grande sorpresa que ahora que compramos el terreno para cambiar la lechería, Cheno fue quien compró un inmenso espacio. Pero mucho, Crucita, y estableció la lechería más grande de todas".

"Apenas lo creo, Tita. Si tú no lo contaras, yo no lo creía". Se asombró de esta información, mi madre, porque realmente no se esperaba esto. Pues, los conocimos bien y las muchachas fueron conmigo a la escuela. No decían que eran pobres, pero se mostraban de tal manera.

"Siento mucho dejarlas a ustedes, nuestras amigas de años, pero tenemos que hacer lo que la ley manda. Queremos que nos visiten y si por alguna razón no tienen en qué ir, me telefonean y yo mando por ustedes. El número de teléfono es el mismo", anunció Tita. Ellos fueron los primeros en tener ese lujo, y yo creo que los únicos.

El barrio perdió a todos los lecheros. La ley los mandó lejos. Perdimos buenos amigos y vecinos. Las madrugadas sin el grito de don Leandro eran lóbregas y silenciosas. El grito de "Cambo, cambo" se fue a otro barrio. Las amigas mías íntimas también se fueron. Para mí no encontraré otras amistades como ellas. Las quise mucho.

Aún hasta la fecha nos telefoneamos y platicamos. Sabemos cuántos hijos tuvieron y qué vida llevan. ¡Amistades y amigas para siempre!

Cuando doña Martina asistió el parto de María, la de don Leandro, no tuvo ninguna dificultad. Lo difícil del caso fue la niña tan delicada. Nos contaba doña Martina de la niñita, quien parecía una muñequita de China o de porcelana, era tan primorosa niña. Su pelo medio color de rosa subido y sus ojitos verdes con pestañas oscuras y largas y enrizadas.

Tres o cuatro veces por semana y los primeros días, iba en la mañana y tarde a ver a la niña. Nada se hacía en la pieza de María y de la niña, María Cristina, sin consultar a la partera.

Un cambio notable vino sobre don Leandro en su casa y con otros de la familia. Al lado de su mujer e hija se mantenía haciendo cariños a su hijita y proclamando por todos lados que no había tal niña como la de él, hermosa y más hermosa como nadie. El padre efectivamente hablaba la verdad.

En una ocasión, don Domingo conversaba con don Leandro, pero me dijo mi amiga Tomasita que su padre nunca mencionó lo que platicó con don Domingo. Y fueron algunas pláticas que los dos tuvieron. El caso fue que un día resultó don Leandro dueño de la propiedad de don Domingo, quien de la noche a la mañana desapareció él y su mujer. Unos vecinos dijeron que fue rumbo a California, y muy buen dinero pagó don Leandro por la propiedad.

Doña Martina nos contó que, a ella, le mostró tres cajones llenos de onzas de oro, de cinco, diez y de veinte. Y con asombro ella decía, "Fíjate, Crucita, tiene varias petacas de monedas de oro y cada vez que yo voy a ver a María y a la niña, me ofrece que escoja lo que quiera del oro. Pero Crucita, como siempre, nomás una tomo, y eso de a cinco pesos".

"¿Por qué no coje más si él le ofrece, doña Martina?" inquiría mi madre, con ojos llenos de admiración.

"Crucita, más que nadie, tú sabes cómo me aborrecen algunas vecinas, y yo sin deberla ni temerla, porque jamás sabré y ni quiero saber. Como te dije antes, yo únicamente quería saber qué podía yo hacer en estos partos y en estos enfermos como la niña de don Leandro. Es todo, ya sé. ¡Dinero, oro, me salen sobrando, Crucita! Pa´ maldita la cosa lo quiero". Satisfecha se mostraba doña Martina.

El sietemesino

Ahora, cuando tengo tiempo desahogado, recuerdo placenteramente los cuentos de doña Martina. Eran cuentos de sus parturientas y de algunos otros enfermos a los cuales ella daba hierbas para curarlos. El siguiente es el más fresco que tengo en mi memoria.

Había un padre de varios hijos. Su nombre era Cirilo, quien era muy estricto con su hija la mayor, así como don Leandro con toda su familia. La hija fue compañera de escuela mía y de mis otras amigas, quienes ustedes ya conocen en estas hojas. Se llamaba Ema. Era coqueta y le gustaban los muchachos. Nosotras sabíamos cuando Ema se iba a hacer "la zorra" pero no decíamos nada a nadie.

Por fin tuvo un novio formal y el papá de ella pensó que era prudente que "la alborotada" mejor se casara. Pues se casó Ema.

Resulta que la hija, quien tenía únicamente los diecisiete años, y sucedió lo que tenía que suceder, a los siete meses tuvo su primer hijo. Doña Martina la asistió como partera.

Don Cirilo, cuando vio a su nieto, robusto, vigoroso y perfecto, sospechó algo y se enfureció. El marido joven notó al suegro tan indignado. Le entró miedo y corrió a la casa de doña Martina.

"Doña Martina, por vida de su madre o por lo que más quiera, le pago lo que usté quiera o hago lo que me diga, ¡pero dígale a mi suegro que mi hijo es sietemesino!" Arrodillado en el suelo le suplicaba a doña Martina el pobre muchacho.

Esa misma noche, don Cirilo fue a la casa de doña Martina. Él todavía iba encolerizado contra la hija y el yerno. Le preguntó, "Usté me dice, doña Martina, si esos condenados me quieren hacer cabrón. Usté me dice la verdad. ¿Es mi nieto sietemesino?"

¡Se reía la mujer con unas ganas! "¡Hasta alcahueta me hacen esos cabrones! Crucita, yo pensé, pues ya se casaron. Ya hicieron la suya, ¿y ahora qué? El niño está perfectamente bien de salud. No sé qué quiere el viejo Cirilo". Con su risa maliciosa, pausaba.

"No tenía otra cosa que hacer nomás de mentirle a don Cirilo!

Yo le dije, 'Don Cirilo, su nieto es sietemesino'. Fue todo lo que yo le dije".

"Mire, doña Martina, la trago porque usté lo dice, pero agarraba a esos condenados cabrones y los fregaba".

En su ancianidad, doña Martina nos contaba las gracias de sus nietos, los hijos de Jony y Gaby. "Fíjate, Crucita, a que no me crees que mi nietecita la Biny [Gabinita] me ha quitado un poco lo maldiciente, eso es en frente de ella. Déjenme contarles. ¡Un día yo estaba jugando con ella, pues la canalla muchacha apenas tendría unos tres años, si mucho!

"El caso fue que yo estaba platicándole a Gaby de algo y luego me empecé a quejarme de algún cabrón y le decía a Gaby, 'Yo tengo la culpa, naiden más, porque soy una buena cabrona'".

Pensando yo, ahora, en ese cuadro tan feliz, tan lleno de nostalgia, mi garganta se atiranta y mis ojos se ponen borrosos. La veo tal y como la vi parada y diciendo, "¡Abran sala, hijos de la chin…!" Nunca cambiará, doña Martina.

"De veras que no pensaba que la niña se fijara en lo que yo contaba a Gaby. ¡Qué equivocada estaba! La Biny se acercó a mí y como defendiéndome con toda su alma y moviendo su cabecita de un lado a otro, decía en su vocecita de niñita, pero sutil y penetrante para que fuera oída, dijo, '¡Mamá, Tina no cabona, no cabona!'

"El Jony la iba a nalgear pero yo no lo dejé. Le dije que me pegara a mí. Él dijo que cuando yo dijera malas palabras delante de Biny, él le pegaría a la niña y así me dolería más a mí y aprendería a refrenarme. Hay tienes tú, Crucita, que he aprendido a no maldecir. Es el chiste más cabrón de mi vida, te juro, Crucita"

Nos reímos con ganas de las pláticas de doña Martina. Nos las contaba con calma, ya no de pasadita como lo hacía en años pasados cuando llegaba a mi casa y se tomaba el café y se salía al frío o al sol y muchas veces a las polvaredas de arena.

El fin se ha llegado de despedirnos de aquella vida en ese barrio tan querido. Mi vida fue repleta como pocas niñas y jovencitas han tenido. Aquella palabra de la cual mi madre tal vez ya la olvidó, "¿Mejoramos?", ya no se menciona. Ya se palpa en la amistad y convivencia entre todos los vecinos que conocimos.

Aunque nuestras vidas no fueron de cosas abundantes materiales, pero sí de cuentos, eventos, chistes y actividades, fueron de sobra.

¡Algunos tal vez se han olvidado de los acontecimientos de la gente del barrio, y otros jamás pudiéramos!

Siento que el aprecio de la gente una por la otra se ha perdido en la opulencia, en el tropel y la prisa. La falta de esta estimación hace perder aquella comunicación tan necesaria para una vida completa y significativa.

Sí, aquellos tiempos ya no volverán, y como dice el dicho, "Los tiempos pasados son los mejores". ¡La memoria es hermosísima!

Recuerdo a doña Martina parándose en medio de la cocina de mi casa, y yo pensaba, "¿Ahora que pasará con ella?" De curiosa yo le pregunté, "¿Doña Martina, que va a hacer ahora que ya nomás le queda J. Antonio y Licha?"

Con su risa extraordinaria burlona en su boca con dientes manchados, decía, "Pues, Chata, ya parece que se fueron mis enemigos, y me importa un chingado. Puedo hacer lo que se le ponga a esta cabeza cabrona, ¿qué no?"

Cómo se llena el aire en ola tras ola de recuerdos. La risa escondida entre los dientes, luego se desparramaba en toda su cara, y nos contagiaba; también nos reíamos y luego soltábamos las risotadas las tres. Qué feliz se mostraba doña Martina, con su taza de café en una mano y un cigarro en la otra.

Por un momento violento quisiera volver a esos tiempos y gozar de la calma de la risa encantadora de esa vieja inolvidable.

Una cosa que a través de los años me ha impresionado de esta gente, que, aun tan pobres, tan ignorantes y faltos de instrucción, malhablados y maldicientes, como doña Martina, no recuerdo un robo o raterías, ni viciosos, ni borrachos en las calles, tampoco asesinatos o muertos en pleitos, ni asaltos con arma de ninguna especie. Lo he pensado y no puedo comprender el porqué.

Y todavía una figura sobresale entre esa mezcolanza, entre toda la gente del barrio: doña Martina. Sí, y todavía me maravillo de doña Martina.

By the Life of These Holy Crosses I Lived in These Barrios

Characters of the Story

The Family of doña Martina, the Midwife

Her children

Jony—the hero. Pronounced in the barrio "Yoni"

Jenny

José Antonio

Licha

Toncha and two children but not mentioned

Milkmen

Chano (Nepomuceno)

Family of Don Leandro

His Children

4 young people, no names given

María, the Oldest

Another unnamed

María Cristina.

Facundo. The father of one of my friends who died in the epidemic

The husband of Tita

His daughter

Chelo

4 more children unnamed

Family of Crucita

   Her children

      Tonya

      Pepín

      Chale

      La Chata

Family of doña Patrocinio

   Her children

      Gabina

      Lola

      Juan de Dios

Others:

   don Domingo and his wife Panchita

   The "Melcochero," don Teodoso

   Palmira, girlfriend of Pepín

My friends: Tomasita, Chelo, Ema, and Juana, deceased

Doña Martina, the Midwife

Going back through the years, pictures of my childhood are thrown into my mind, urging me to bring them back to life. I didn't realize that the experiences of life could become memories of a past, and that they would never ever be repeated. Now I know that certain incidents and lives from many years ago stand out, focusing against the blur of years, and they are vividly imprinted in my memory, so I can take you all back to see those people from the barrios who we lived with for many years, and whose struggles seemed unrelenting.

How many years have passed, forty, fifty, or more, and I still marvel at doña Martina. We were neighbors, we got together almost daily, we helped each other. Our families called each other by first names, we overcame our misunderstandings, and I still marvel at doña Martina. I don't remember the exact time when I met doña

Martina. In my opinion she was already in the barrio when we went to live there.

During my lifetime, how many ideal people, how many beautiful faces have swiftly passed from one side to the other in my mind and have vanished before me like a shadow. It seems to be like something out of sorcery, but a strange sorcery by which this old face, a face without any color, withered and wrinkled, has gained ground and a place in my memory.

The body of doña Martina, the midwife, was small, giving the impression that if at any time her cheeks had been of a dark and clean complexion, there was no trace left, leaving behind only deep wrinkles!

Her eyes had a malicious and lively look and stood out in her withered face when she smiled her half-mocking smile, and her face showed her strong teeth, although stained by cigarettes. Her laughter lit up her face and made us want to join in, too.

Doña Martina had seven children, four girls and three boys. I will begin by saying that discipline did not exist in that home. How was this family governed? It is said that using methods of force to govern the family are very effective, but in that house there was no such thing, no palpable force or demonstrated affection. Maybe it was hidden and in all this doña Martina used neither force nor love. And in my opinion, there was indifference instead.

I say so because if someone from a small or large family wanted to smoke, "well, let them smoke!" If they wanted to drink intoxicants, even though the law of Prohibition was in force at that time; there were no sales of intoxicants. Nevertheless, doña Martina with the greatest indifference said to them, "bastards, let them drink!"

One of her oldest daughters, already married, had gone to live in the state of Arizona, and she came back with the novelty of making homebrew, a kind of homemade beer. It has other names like "moonshine" and "booze." Toncha, another daughter, would say to my mother, "*Crucita*, there is a way out for everything." The family profited from this product, which doña Martina learned to brew to perfection, but she warned them with words of mordacity, "Drink it sparingly because its purpose is to bring us in a few extra cents."

The only ones who didn't like the drink were Licha, la Enana (Shorty), who said, "I wouldn't even smell that stinking filth!" And José Antonio, *el Joto* (gay boy), making ugly faces and stringing out his words, declared, "I do not drink those hoooooorrible thiiiiiings."

The first time doña Martina came to be an active part of our life was because my sister Tonya, who was already approaching her delivery time, needed a midwife. My mother asked for her when her time arrived.

Doña Martina had no obstetrical degree, and she said, "Crucita, I know how to take out babies." She charged a trifle for her work. She also assisted with postpartum pains, with the colic of the women in labor, and with the children, using herbs she grew herself.

Her house, it could be said, told its own story. It was a patchwork. Maybe it started as one room and was added to as needed. The door opened to the street, and when you entered the living room you could see the other rooms and the kitchen. Beside the house, where the sun beat down the most, was doña Martina's garden, which was better cared for than the house, and which produced the healing herbs used for the women in labor. She grew the herbs and plants with great skill.

In the kitchen were a large wood stove, a long, wide wooden table, and a few broken-down chairs. The walls of the rooms showed their devastation and neglect, not because of abandonment, because they lived there, but because of a lack of funds to do repairs.

José Antonio was struggling to fix the old red curtains, but because of either the sun or use, they had become an almost half-dirty rose color and were somewhat torn and frayed. This was not because of rough treatment but from long-time use. The house's poverty was not readily apparent, because in the barrio we were all about on the same level with respect to household furniture.

There were weeks when doña Martina didn't have work, and, in despair and impatience, she said, "That damn stork, the bitch, now she's on strike!" And then she started to plan for how to get some money. Two of her married children, a woman and a man, did not help her at all. They only came over to drink a pitcher of her home-brew and go to the dances she organized, "to thumb her nose at life."

Toncha, who had the beautiful name of María Antonieta, lived alone. She worked in the gringos' neighborhood. This neighborhood was separated from the barrio of the Mexicans only by a street, which was the first one to ever be paved. Beyond that, the gringos' streets were all well cared for; ours were in disrepair, muddy, and with piles of dirt and big rocks, and to add to all that, the ever-present sand. When it rained and downpours fell, the streams filled up with large amounts of water.

If for some reason a worker or person wanted to get to their house on the other side, they had to go around and walk, crossing through quagmires and in some places through mud and slush, to get to the so-called bridge in order to cross over. This stream grew so immense that over time a small lake formed and remained there from one year to the next.

As I was saying, Toncha bought parcels of land that together, finally, over the years, almost covered the whole block. My mother would visit her, and every once in a while I suspected that my mother "would read the cards" to tell Toncha her fortune. Toncha was saying she didn't like her life in her mother's home and liked the way the children treated her even less, especially the married ones and Jenny. Perhaps Toncha also concealed the shame that the physical defects of José Antonio and Licha, la Enana, caused her.

On Saturdays and Sundays in the early afternoon there appeared a lighted lantern hanging on one side of the door of doña Martina's house, which announced the dance. Neighbors called it the fandango and others called it a *chorcha*, or noisy party, a party at night.

My mother wouldn't allow me to go to the adult parties, even though my brother Pepín begged her. Because once, just like young curious girls, two of my friends and I went just to peek, only looking through the windows. Three lousy musicians played an old harp, a guitar, and a squeaky violin. Apparently, the musicians and instruments were not very important; what was important was the dance. They were going to dance and they danced! The young people who were eager to start dancing, talked and made noise like little children. The living room was filled with well-known neighbors, friends of doña Martina and her children, and also of our family, including my brother Carlos, "Chale," and my brother Pepín, who loved dancing and learned how to dance well.

Jenny, who showed up, miraculously, all spruced up and with moist and painted lips (but unevenly), danced in the arms of Julio, her boyfriend. I will never forget the impression that this dance left in my memory. Just then the musicians played a waltz. The couples were unrelenting. Nothing in this world mattered at all at that moment, just dancing!

Suddenly you could hear the hoarse and imposing voice of doña Martina, "Get out of the way, you bastards." The dancers moved away and stood motionless in the middle of the room, and the musicians also remained quiet.

"Can't you hear or are you deaf, you bastards."

They really didn't know what to do in such a small place.

"I'm telling you to get out of the way," ordered doña Martina.

The couples complied, stood aside, and made a space in the middle of the room. Apparently, no one was insulted by doña Martina's words, because they knew how foul-mouthed she was. Doña Martina's curses did not go unnoticed by me. At that moment an incident occurred to me that happened many years ago, and that actually reminded me of the terror caused by the same ill-spoken words of doña Martina.

Dawn is already here and there's not even one dead person!

At the onset of the 1910 Revolution in Mexico, all the people who could, crossed over to the United States to take refuge from the threat of bandits, rebels, and other dangers the country was undergoing. Among the good people, many thugs crossed over, because the immigration check points were not monitored.

"Dawn is already here and there's not even one dead person, mother fuckers." What horror came into the neighborhood hearing these curses in the dark nights! They were hoodlums who shouted at the top of their lungs and filled us with fear and terror.

No one dared answer, much less risk looking out the window to find out who they were. After a moment of silence, the offensive, loathsome words were repeated again. We all trembled again. After a long time, when no one came out to fight with them, they got tired and left. These scares were frequent and scandalized the barrio.

This happened in the barrio of Chihuahuita where, it was said "There they shaved with axes!" People were found dead in the morning, murdered by those evil-tongued persons during their wild parties or their fights; some were innocents. We feared those soulless men.

When we heard the frightful sounds of footsteps and noises like the howling of beasts, we ran to Mamá's big bed. According to one of the children, they had come to devour us! "May the heart of Jesús deliver us." These were the words of our mother trying to suppress or conceal her fear. At the breaking of dawn, my mother would take us to our beds on the floor, but I would stay with her. At that time, I was only six years old; nevertheless my brother Pepín had died many years before. I can still see him, with his wavy hair parted on one side and on the other side he had a rebellious curl that didn't want to stay put. His eyes were black with piercing looks, his eyebrows were broad and bushy. He had a restless and penetrating gaze, which was one of affection for all his brothers and sisters and for his mother, but I was his favorite.

My two brothers were younger than my sister Tonya, very young, and naturally trembled at the insults and improprieties of those men. But what could we do? I want to mention my brother [Pepín] because he was a conscientious boy, although he still wore his pants just below his knees with black stockings, because they hid more of the dirty places and the patches on his knees and heels.

In the dark mornings, they went out to sell newspapers early. When they returned, they ate something and the two of them went out together to look for "odd jobs." They always brought in a few cents by helping to unload merchandise or in some other light work. We were fatherless orphans. My mother had the eternal concern that we could improve in some way.

She asked herself: "But how can it be, that we can improve? You now can see what happens in the barrio."

Days later, the most evil thing possible happened. There was a man who sold toffee, don Teodoso, who was fat and short, dark complected, and with very short hair, almost no hair. He had fat hands with fingers that didn't seem to fit on his hands because they were so bulky, but they were very agile. When my brother Pepín gave me a penny, I would run to buy a piece of toffee.

The toffee maker was quick to make the candies. In an instant, on a large tray, he beat and stretched the raw candy and promptly took a piece and rolled it up in the palms of his hands, forming, as if by magic, the toffee. Then he moved it and quickly squeezed the edges with his thumb and index finger, gave it a twist and crimped the ends! I was fascinated by this demonstration.

One morning a commotion and an uproar was heard in the barrio. I went outside nearly asleep, because I couldn't wait a moment more to find out what had happened. Oh my goodness! What's happening?

It was don Teodoso, who was being taken away in the ambulance! He was found murdered in his house at dawn. Maybe to steal the miserable pennies he earned from selling his tasty toffee candies.

"Now this is the last straw!" my mother lamented with great emotion. Don Teodoso was a good man and a good neighbor. There was no reason to kill him.

We looked for a house outside that barrio. A few days later we moved to another home. Did we improve somewhat? Not like our mother wanted, but we didn't complain.

We settled into the new barrio. My sister Tonya, who was barely fifteen years old, had gone to work in a laundry, from eight in the morning until five or six in the afternoon, at the mangle. The winter days were not as difficult as those of summer. In those days there were no fans or air-conditioning, only the heat coming from the steam of the mangle. Did my mother consider that to be improvement?

Here, too, in this place, there were refugees from Mexico. But after looking for work and not finding it, they went to live where the "money was swept up with a broom." Maybe they were looking for the seven cities of Cíbola in California. Such beautiful illusions—I believed them too.

The neighborhood lent itself to being sociable. Talk was about politics, but Mexican politics, nothing about the gringos. Except when Election Day arrived and the candidates offered sacks of flour and cans of lard in exchange for votes for the one who had more groceries to give.

I learned about Mexican political parties and the reason for the revolution. To this day, I don't like to know anything about the good side of President Porfirio Díaz! My favorite and ideal politician was and is Francisco I. Madero, the martyr for Mexican democracy. Don Porfirio is the tyrant of Mexico. All this was brainwashed into me when I was a child.

Groups of supporters of the two presidents were often formed.

The conversations, the heated discussions and altercations, and big disputes were lessons learned by listening and observing all day long. For me they lasted my whole life.

The Mexican newspapers were read earnestly and sometimes with tears, because of the way the assassination of President Madero happened. The neighbors ordered masses to be said for his soul and for a long time they showed their mourning with a wide black ribbon placed on the sleeve of their coats or shirts. Their tears were for a Mexican hero.... I also cried out loud, was in mourning, and hated the guilty ones.

In spite of all this, the constant struggle of our mother was that we should improve ourselves by learning something. How could that be? My brothers went off to fight for their lives and I was the only one in school. The only sources of literature that I had to help me learn how to spell and read were newspapers.

Years passed. In our family there came a change that was very important in our lives, especially in mine. For the time being we forgot about politics, and we dealt with family matters. My sister would get married; her boyfriend had returned from California and brought everything necessary for the wedding.

My brother Chale worked at a pharmacy, picking up orders and delivering to homes. I remember nostalgically the problems with his second-hand bike, but I think it was already fifth-hand. It so often had flat tires. I guess my brother fixed and repaired those little tires more times than the number of deliveries he made.

Pepín worked in stables; he hooked up the horse teams to the buggies and prepared the horses to get them ready for when they were called for. It was a good job, but he wanted a different type of job. In time he went to work for City Water Works where he helped take care of some machinery, and it was high class work, according to us.

At last, my sister Tonya got married. I missed her more than anyone. For a while we visited her almost daily. I will tell you all that I still remember the house where she used to live that brings back good memories to me.

Later my mother and brothers bought a plot of land far from the center of town where we used to live. The two-room cottage had been built on the outskirts of the city. I will explain that at that time it was still a county and not a city. The water was outside. The outhouse, which was jokingly referred to as "my torment" by my brothers, was far from the house. They did not like that place, but our mother thought it was better to live where there was some space. Really, we had a lot of space because it was the last house in the barrio. The sand hills, mesquite trees, and chamiso patches were our vast space.

This barrio turned into still another barrio. Better? Time will tell, my mother would say. She set out to raise chickens and a pig that took us a year to halfway fatten up. My brothers were already earning enough to pay for the house and the lot and the groceries, which were not abundant, but a necessity.

Enough of what happened a few years ago, let's go back to the dance.

The words of doña Martina about "get out of my way..." did not frighten me like the previous ones in the barrio Chihuahuita. I didn't understand why, but they did cause me to feel pity and at the same time gave me and my friends a laugh. Little by little I got to know and learned something about that woman, doña Martina.

I can't forget how she stood in the middle of the room, a woman's body, perhaps old and boney, but in a dry, raspy voice, she said, "get out of the way, you bastards." The ragged figure of that woman gave me the impression of arrogance with a smile of satisfaction and laughter between her teeth, perhaps enjoying the disturbance caused to the dancers. She paced back and forth; she appeared so small among the very tall girls and boys.

She approached Pepín and said, "Hey Pepín, you are really tall,

don't grow anymore!" With a mocking smile she looked at him up
and down.

My brother just answered, smiling, 'Yes, doña Martina.'

"Well, what are you waiting for, you bastards? Dance!" And with
the same gusto and zest they began to dance with that same spirit
of youthful energy, they kept dancing as if nothing had happened.
Someone commented that perhaps doña Martina had gone a little
too far with the "homebrew," and another said that maybe she had a
better beer or drink than the one she was selling. It was fun.

La Jenny

Juana had not wanted the name Juana for a long time; she wanted,
and finally succeeded in keeping, the name Jenny. She thought,
and part of the family agreed with her, that she was attractive and
beautiful because of her white skin. Indeed, Jenny was superior
for the simple reason that "in the land of the blind, the one-eyed
man is king," and according to the fixed rule, to date, mainly in
our Mexican barrios, the white girl, the blond girl is attractive and
beautiful. Jenny was not blond but rather white, with not very large
blue eyes, but she was attractive to look at. Her hair was toffee
colored.

Jenny was rarely neat and well dressed; she was sloppy and un-
kempt. She had the habit of putting a hank of her hair in her mouth
until it was soaked with saliva. She was sixteen years old and had a
boyfriend named Julio, who was a friend of my brother's.

By this time, the barrio suffered horribly from the rigors of the
First World War. On one occasion, I went to bring some squash to
doña Martina. As I entered the room, I was somewhat surprised,
for there was Jenny with Julio. I greeted them and asked for doña
Martina. Jenny answered that she was coming right back and I
should sit down. Well, I don't know if it was just at that moment

or not, but I was absorbed in the conversation between Jenny and Julio.

"Do you know there's war on, Julio?" Jenny asked.

"Of course, Jenny. Why are you asking me?"

"Why don't you join the army or the navy?"

"Me, Jenny? I told you that for that very reason I came to this country, because of the revolution in my country! Now you want me to go to a war where I don't know who is fighting or why! And according to what I know, it's a war that started in Europe years ago. Isn't it?"

"No, no Julio, don't mix me up. I don't know what the war is all about either, but Jony, my brother says that he's going before they call him up." The moist lips of Jenny's mouth were scornful and even more because the hank of hair did not stop being bathed in saliva in her mouth.

There was something in her face that was not right, in my opinion, just as when one hears a string from an instrument that sounds discordant. Later I realized it was the mouth with thin lips, wide, and when it spoke it did not pronounce the words well and it could be said that when it spoke it was in a language all of its own. I understood her well; many people spoke that way in the barrio. Some people wouldn't understand what she was talking about even if I wrote it down for them, and maybe I wouldn't even be able to write it.

The conversation seemed to get a bit heated, but they didn't pay attention to me and talked as if I didn't exist.

"Okay, now you say Julio's afraid and doesn't want to go to war. Right?" Jenny is bold, but she was a little nervous and there was more wet hair.

"Look, Jenny, right now I'm telling you that I won't fight in my country or in any other. Soon peace will be established in Mexico and I hope to return to work the lands of my father, along with my brother Salomón. But fight, I just won't!" Julio showed himself to be firm in his decision. A smile of disdain and uneasiness could be seen on the wet lips of Jenny.

I later learned that there was some understanding between Jenny and Julio; when she turned seventeen, they would get married. It might have been possible that she wanted to live in Mexico, and didn't know how to explain it. She would provoke her boyfriend in that way.

There was a lot of doubt in Jenny's eyes. There were innuendo and accusations with some gestures of impatience in her conversation with her boyfriend, Julio. The future man and wife were not in agreement.

Licha, la Enana

Some of us strive to get something, we fight against disease, we try to free ourselves from something like injustice and the bitterness of destiny, so in this barrio people were in continuous struggle . . . unnoticed.

Licha was the last daughter of doña Martina. She was now more than fifteen years old and had not yet grown to her proper height. Her face was very ugly. What a vivid contrast! She was quite the opposite of her sister Jenny. Her countenance looked like that of an old woman, not with wrinkles, but because of her thick yellowish complexion, which resembled dry skin. She had big eyes and struggled to lift her eyelids. Underneath her eyes were small bags or rolls of skin that gave the appearance of a person who is very old.

Her lips were discolored, and in order to move them to speak, the extremities of her mouth didn't move, only the part in the middle of the lips. Her pronunciation was difficult, her voice somewhat hoarse and raspy. The unfortunate girl couldn't laugh!

Her extraordinarily small body looked like a barrel, round with short legs and arms like a child, plus large and thick hands.

Really, Licha was a freak of nature. I will tell you all that for work, she was not a useless freak of nature, she was a slave. She ironed standing on a box to reach the ironing board. She washed dishes and mended clothes. She watered doña Martina's garden and took care of the rebellious flowers and herbs for her mother's sick patients.

Licha was not lacking in understanding despite her great physical defect. Sometimes she rebelled. Her sister Jenny had intolerable manners with her. "Licha, bring me this, and do that." Naturally, Licha rebelled.

She was already angry when she complained to her mother, saying, "Mom, how do you expect me to do everything for these lazy bums, starting with Jenny? She's always lying in bed sleeping and thinking about her boyfriend. I get tired, you know?" Licha could not cry.

"Get away from here, you hateful freak. Well, just what do you think you are good for?" Jenny spoke to her sister in a bad way. Licha would retreat with something like a military call but with words, using her raspy voice. No one could understand what she was saying, but she wouldn't do what Jenny ordered.

Doña Martina seemed to be deaf to her daughters' quarrels. And when she was not busy making the so-called homebrew, she would amuse herself with her potions and herbs, which she knotted into pieces of cloth or put in jars or paper packages and put them away. She couldn't care less if they fought and called each other names. When they got her fed up, she would shout at them, "What do you want me to do? Don't bother me, you bastards."

Licha retreated to her only protection, work.

José Antonio, el Joto (the gay boy)

Generally, almost all writers have a code, as they say, a secret code or one of holding back or pointing out events, not as they were or are but as one would want them to be. Where in part, although poor, their habits are good, their aspirations are ideal, their manners are puritanical, and so on. What I write about, really, is barrio people, their customs and their poverty, as I see them. The defects of doña

Martina's family are unequaled because I have never heard of two people from the same family who have physical defects of the most striking and perceptible kind, such as those of Licha and José Antonio.

José Antonio was traditionally called Antonio, as was his great-grand-father, who had proudly said to his children, "The name Antonio will appear in all my future generations." Toncha and an older sister, when they heard their mother talk about their grandfather, they would say with some mockery, "for better or for worse, amen."

In fact, José Antonio was a hermaphrodite, having the distinctive characteristics of both sexes. Doña Martina, his/her mother, and the rest of the family didn't hide his defect.

Often José Antonio's mother commented to mine saying, "Crucita, it seems, that actually, God has punished me! So says old Mrs. Patrocinio, that maybe because I am so sinful and bad, He has given me freaks of nature in my family." She was sinking into despair and regressed into empty speech.

My mother tried to comfort her, "You can't do anything about that matter, doña Martina. You have to endure the good and the bad things of life, don't you think?"

"It's okay, Crucita, but those people don't let one do what they're capable of. As I told you, the old woman is scared of me! I can also frighten myself and even be intimidated by what they say about her. Crucita, don't you know that the *güera* (blondie), Gaby, was kidnapped by doña Patrocinio?" Excited by what she was spilling the beans about, she looked down and shook the ash off her old cigarette.

"It's probably a tall tale. You know how people let go with those rumors from time to time, doña Martina." My mother was feeling regretful.

"Look, Crucita, I may be a gossip and a storyteller, or whatever you want to call me, but I do not tell lies. I don't invent fables. I can tell you who will back that up, if it comes down to that. But what do I care? But that old woman better not look for three legs on a cat, because she'll find four. That's what the saying says." Doña Martina trembled and sucked on her cigarette butt until she had nothing left to smoke, and then she lit another.

She resumed the story. "Haven't you noticed how she is brown and brown as she can be, even the gums of her teeth are black! Her heart is most probably like that too, so I don't mess with her at all. Her other two childrren, Lola and Juan de Dios, are dark! And Gaby? Güera, pretty, light color. She's blond, Crucita, isn't she? Look and you'll see, she's lighter complected than my Jenny!"

Through all that talk my mother was shaking her head, approving what doña Martina was revealing. "Maybe Gaby's a gringo's daughter."

A malicious and comical laugh appeared on doña Martina's lips, and with the greatest naturalness in the world she told her stories and suspicions. "Look, I say that for me, Jenny is a gringo's daughter. I'm not scared nor do I deny it, even if I wanted to. You can look at my other children! But just let doña Patrocinio say that. Pure *chet* (caca)." The conversation ended with anger and disgust. She paused and with an air of perversity, said, "Listen, Crucita, don't you know that my Jony likes Gaby?" She was going toward the door to leave and with a laugh hidden inside her mouth, said, "I'm leaving, Crucita. Let me go see what those expectant mothers say."

I go back to J. Antonio. He was not tall, but he was thin, though one would never notice for the reason that his clothes were always second- or third-hand. His trousers fit him loosely, and the sleeves of his shirt were too long. He had rubber bands on his sleeves, which he rolled up a little. Then he tightened his belt, which made folds around his waist. Poor guy.

For J. Antonio, there was no affectionate name like Toño, like his sister Toncha had. Neither was his name changed to the "gringoized" Tony, like his brother Jony, and Juana to Jenny. His name was J. Antonio, and that's what everyone called him.

He hardly knew what a haircut was, and if he was lucky, he got one every year. He wore it long and lightly oiled to keep it in place, and a ducktail was formed in the back of his neck. The poor guy tried to be halfway cocky, but it wasn't possible. I will also say that he was very decent and easily frightened. I felt sorry for him. J. Antonio seemed to give the impression that he had no hope at all. . . . He was submissive, with no spirit, and besides that, everything about him was shameful, and he was mortified by his mother's curse words. He didn't shout; he didn't get excited, and he didn't complain. At parties or dances in his house, neither he nor Licha showed up anywhere. Friends, outings, or movies were unknown to J. Antonio. Maybe he was prepared for any affront and forewarned against any offense and insult, to be silent.

He had reached his full growth, but the members of his family were ashamed of his condition, and he understood it. His own mother, doña Martina, was not a person who, because of the accursed gossip, tried to hide or disguise her son's defect, at least not to throw his imperfection in his face on any occasion.

When the stork went on strike, doña Martina was always in a bad mood. She would come over to my house with her idle chatter and say all kinds of bad things about J. Antonio. "I am sick and tired of that queer bastard, J. Antonio. I can't get him out of the house with a club. He says that they don't want to give him a job anywhere, and that they can't hire him, and who knows what else. I don't know what to do."

On other occasions she came around very animated, "Crucita, please say a prayer to San Antonio for me. Lola's little saint figurine has broken fingers and J. Antonio is going to fix them. She says she will pay him well. I hope so because we are all cleaned out even from our stomach."

I could not imagine seeing J. Antonio sitting patiently tending to the tiny fingers of a little figurine who was two inches long from head to foot! But you should have seen when he finished it. The little fingers were made of plaster, and he painted the saint's habit in its natural and living colors, and he left them almost like new. Doña Martina, with an air of concealed pride, said, "But what a bastard that boy is. I tell you, Crucita, he acts like a woman!"

J. Antonio was silent, not because of bad humor or bad temper but because of the lack of someone to encourage him and make him happy. Maybe he thought he couldn't please anyone. And I dealt more with J. Antonio when his mother, because of impatience and need, tried to make good use of the golden ounces paid by Leandro and provided him with a grocery store. J. Antonio's two brothers, with all their moaning and abuse, helped him build a room added onto the house.

I'm not lying to you all; it was a miniature room for a store, at twelve by ten feet! Right next to the open door was the counter. He covered the little window with a charming curtain. The vases with flowers were made by him, from crepe paper. It could be said that this was his house, his castle. He sold sugar, beans, rice, and birdseed in packages for five cents. Sweets and cookies for a penny. It was really a toy store that J. Antonio made.

I liked going to the store for looking rather than for buying. I found him busy making flowers, cleaning the counter, and weighing his groceries. He repaired and decorated picture frames with photos in them by placing paper ruffles or lace cloths around the pictures, and they looked very good, and besides, he was paid a few cents. But they did pay him!

With a rare and forced smile and almost gentle eyes, he answered the question I asked out of respect, "J. Antonio, do you play the violin?"

"Girl, I don't plaaaaay the violiiiiin … I'm juuuuust fiiiiiixing it. It is missing the bridge and a string and when I fix it, then I'll tuuuuuune it." Besides his voice being hoarse, it was twangy and he strung out his words.

Perhaps he noticed my great admiration, because when he gave me my groceries, he gave me a candy for free.

My surprise was even greater that as I was leaving his little store, the smile remained on J. Antonio's lips. In this and other things like it, J. Antonio, el Joto, busied himself and showed his goods to the sparse clientele and earned a paltry living.

Don Leandro

Do we perhaps have a right to happiness? How could we demand it and from whom? Perhaps that fleeting sentiment is unknown in this barrio. How could we steal a little of it in this life so full of misery and so wretched? As doña Martina said, "We just don't know...."

It happened that one day in the middle of winter, doña Martina arrived at my house. I noticed the inclemency of the cold and even more so when she covered her face with her hands in her mouth, through which she expelled her breath and warmed her hands a little that way. Doña Martina covered her back with a worn-out black top-coat through which one could see the thin threads.

Now as I am remembering her, I think that maybe she had already forgotten everything about what a new topcoat was like. The old shoes, and in that cold weather, with soles thick with mud and worn down from crossing the dirt and mud to go to her expectant mothers.

Hastily she asked me, "Chata, where's your mom?"

"She's feeding the chickens; she's coming, doña Martina."

"Good morning, doña Martina, what are you doing so early and in such cold?" We already knew the reason she had come.

"Crucita, come on, give me a cup of coffee, I'm dying of cold, those bastards, lazy butts, don't want to get up. Licha is the only one up, but she makes coffee like a devil's brew. Yours is real tasty, Crucita." She drank her hot coffee and savored it with gusto. We suspected that she had something up her sleeve, like a secret. Her behavior was confusing and haphazard with her slight, trembling movements.

After a while and after her first cup of coffee, doña Martina let us know what she had on her mind. We were waiting for that.

"What can I tell you, Don Leandro summoned me." Her voice was hoarse but with little emotion about the surprise. "Tomasita told me her dad wanted to see me." Her eyes sparkled and hoped for encouragement.

"Didn't she tell you why he needed you, doña Martina?"

"Hey, Crucita, well, what am I good for?" She drank her coffee with a flour tortilla, exclaiming with gusto, "Your coffee is really good and very warm!" She covered her head with the black topcoat, and in a low voice, as if she were telling a secret, she said, "From there and for her, I'll tell you later what happens."

Doña Martina trotted out in the cold.

Don Leandro was one of many who came from Mexico and took refuge in this country. And he was also the one who bought more land than the other refugees. He established the largest dairy of that time, buying more than two hundred dairy cows!

The first time I saw don Leandro was in wintertime. He gave me the impression of a Russian man with a thick woolen cap pulled up to his ears and a poncho so long that it extended to his ankles. It was also a rarity, especially, to see a man with a scarf around his neck; however, it was long and very useful for winter.

At four o'clock in the morning his loud voice was heard all over the neighborhood. "Cambo, Cambo." That's the way he called the cows and they obeyed because one by one they left the corral and crossed the road to go to the stable to be milked. Maybe for an eagerness to eat, one of the cattle, with large udders pouring streams of milk along the road, went into the wrong stable, it was gored and removed by the true owner.

Don Leandro was a husky man with great strength, despite his sixty years of age. He was also aggressive with his sons and his three daughters. Tomasita, the youngest, was my close friend. The children had inherited the wide and powerful shoulders of their father. With the first light of dawn, father and sons got to work milking and preparing the milk, and they delivered it to the stores. When they returned, having eaten their food, they cleaned the stables and fed the cows. They also took off the horses' harnesses and took down the boxes of empty bottles and gallon cans; then cleaned the wagons and left them ready for the next day.

Don Leandro made the decisions in everything. He ordered his children with arrogance and insolent words. His eyes lit up beneath thick, reddish eyebrows if the work and chores were done slowly. He really forced them to work hard. If for some reason they rebelled or complained, he beat them with pails and sticks or whatever he found nearby.

The two daughters of don Leandro were nice girls. They were hard-working around the house. Also, like their brothers, they worked for the farm, washing bottles and the heavy metal utensils. They were orderly and obedient.

It is said that for love there are no boundaries. Nevertheless, even with don Leandro's restrictive limitations for his sons and daughters in their personal freedom, in the matters of love, cunning overcomes obstacles.

Right next to don Leandro's dairy, a young man named Facundo established another dairy. Of course, it was much smaller than don Leandro's. Facundo was bright and had ambitions to make a life in a foreign country. Since he was also a refugee, he worked eagerly in his business. As time passed, he fell in love with María, don Leandro's eldest daughter. María reciprocated the love of Facundo. All those around her covered for her except for her father, who knew nothing of his daughter's nightly outings or when she had spare time and took advantage of it. Tomasita told me about the courtship and fearfully said, "It will be the Divine Comedy when my dad finds out. But we all love Facundo, including my stepmother."

The day was approaching when don Leandro would learn of the affair. On that occasion the two lovers would only talk in the corral that separated their houses. No one could help the catastrophe from happening. Don Leandro almost went crazy [when he found out], shouting insults and snorting like a tied-up bull when the cows are nearby.

The whole barrio applauded when Facundo, as a real *macho*, confronted don Leandro shouting to make himself understood above the uproar created by the family and the shouts and threats of don Leandro. He said, "I want the hand of your daughter in marriage, don Leandro."

Don Leandro tried to hit Facundo as he did with his children, but Facundo spoke to him in no uncertain terms: "Look, don Leandro, don't touch me at all. You'll see what happens if you do. It will be the last day you remain in this country. I'm warning you."

With these words, María's furious father calmed down, and she, with tears in her eyes and with great anguish, left as she heard her father's words: "You will never leave this house again for anything, do you all understand?"

A short time later, clandestinely, Facundo transferred the business of his dairy. With the help of María's brothers and sisters, and when everyone least expected it, María and Facundo ran away. On the way they got married and headed to California. Tomasita said that they received a letter through a neighbor with the news.

There was great rejoicing among the neighbors of the barrio when we learned about the marriage of María and Facundo. The father was unfair with his good-hearted daughter, but no one complained to him.

Tomasita told me what was happening in her house. They had been orphaned from their mother in Chihuahua. Later their father got married again to his present wife, María, who was submissive and docile. Now the unresolved problem (six months after the daughter was married) was that her stepmother had already lost two babies who were either stillborn or miscarriages. Don Leandro was determined to have a living son or daughter with María.

Doña Martina and don Leandro were having talks about this, and she had said that she would tell my mother what happened. Martina arrived at my house, gladly telling my mother, "Look, Crucita, look what don Leandro gave me!"

In her hand she held an ounce of gold in five Mexican pesos. At that time Mexican gold was worth the same or on par with American money; five pesos in gold was five dollars.

The woman was very pleased, and she showed a lively disposition in her wrinkled face, saying, "I would even kiss the old man's feet for this ounce, Crucita!"

"What happened? Tell me, doña Martina, who is sick?" my mother wanted to know.

"Listen to this, don Leandro wants María to have children and he says that there already have been some babies who were born dead. And listen to this, he says he'll pay me whatever I want if I make a child of his live!" I had never seen doña Martina so happy.

"Can you do anything, doña Martina?" my mother asked in half-amazement.

Doña Martina set aside the topcoat as if it were obstructing her from speaking and gesturing, and she stood up just as she did when she was saying "get out of the way." She said to my mother with a certain amount of affirmation: "Crucita, I know my business, and this is a chance of a lifetime! I have waited for this moment for half my life. Here, Crucita, they will realize who I am! Who do I owe for what I know? Nobody, just myself. Now, that old disgraceful bastard don Domingo might say I'm thirsty for money. What damn good is money to me, Crucita!"

She rested for a while and started talking again. "I'll stop with the stupidities and tell you what don Leandro said, Crucita. The old man acted very unaggressively. First, I told him that if he wanted to have children and he wanted them to live, he had to do whatever I told him. He said he was willing and prepared for whatever I told him to do."

Doña Martina felt satisfied. She was smoking a cigarette.

"Well, I told him, categorically, 'look, don Leandro, you will not touch your wife for two months and I promise that your wife will have a child. I'll make it happen, and if I don't, don't speak to me ever again.'" She threw down her half-smoked cigarette and lit another. It was time to eat, and my mother, without asking, served her a bowl of chicken soup.

"Crucita, Crucita, and now I'm here to congratulate you. Look what a dish, fit for a king!" While doña Martina savored the food with gusto, she told us the rest.

"The old man is very macho. He was agreeable to what I asked. I examined María and she is perfectly fine. I went back to tell don Leandro that his wife was young and there was no reason why she couldn't have children easily, but he had to do as I told him. I'm leaving now, Crucita; thanks for your good food. I'm going to see those bastards; this gold ounce even raises the dead, Crucita."

Carlotita

Few people think of being compassionate to the less fortunate, which would be a noble act. This was evidently the case with my close neighbor Carlotita.

Carlotita was a good person to us. Her husband, a milkman but not a refugee, was a native of New Mexico. He and his brothers were very close, and they helped each other. They had grocery stores, sold firewood, made adobe bricks, and set up houses to rent.

Tita, as we lovingly called her, was cheerful and loved parties and dances. Not a week or two passed without them having a party because of a birthday, baptism, or confirmation of one of their children—four sons and a daughter, including Chelo, my friend.

The first time I met this family was when Chelo invited me to her birthday celebration. My sister Tonya had a beautiful pink dress with lace, and she suggested that my mother make me a dress. It was a beautiful dress! But there was another snag. I had no gift to offer my friend. Darn it! But I knew about taking presents to parties!

We really didn't have any money to buy something. For me, Chelo had everything. For the second time my sister came to the rescue. In her house she had a leafy rose bush, and she brought me a bucket of the most beautiful flowers I ever had been. It was the gift most appreciated by my friend. At the party we were served ice cream, made from whole cream, which Chelo and I skimmed for that purpose. I have not tasted anything like that delicacy again. And this was because the ice cream was made in a large jug moved by the force of powerful arms. They called the ice cream "snowy milk."

My mother wouldn't allow me to go to other parties of compadres and comadres. Besides, I didn't have much interest in the dances and even less in those where the famous "homebrew" was served. What I really enjoyed were the cold meats prepared by doña Patrocinio. But the only one who hired her for this job was Tita, because she could afford it. When she went to Chelo's house to prepare the large sausages, no one was allowed to enter the kitchen on that day. Doña Patrocinio made something that required a lot of skill. The secret of making that sausage went with her to her grave. She didn't even leave the recipe for such an exquisite delicacy to her daughters. At the first opportunity, my friend Chelo gave me sandwiches made of that sausage.

Tita didn't like doña Martina at all. Almost in a contemptuous tone she would say to my mother, "Crucita, there is no reason for me to like J. Antonio, that queer, or that dwarf! There just isn't. Why should I make friends with doña Martina? And if I have a friendship with her, then naturally I have one with her family." She didn't criticize her; she avoided her.

The economic situation was worsening because of the First World War. The following incident is one of many that occurred at that time. In order to buy a sack of wheat flour, by law we had to buy twice as much corn flour. Being that Tita did not like to cook, she would give the corn flour to my mother who in exchange gave her tamales or something else that Tita didn't like to prepare. Tita knew doña Martina's need well, but she ignored it.

When Tita took the flour to my mother, without Tita's knowledge my mother sent it to doña Martina with the warning, "Not a word, not a word, doña Martina." She understood the common saying "With the king and the Inquisition, not a word."

The following Saturday night, the lantern appeared next to the door of doña Martina's house. That night there would be a dance and a party—the dance enthusiasts already knew what the lantern meant. Snacks, such as *champurrado, gorditas de maíz,* and *sopes* would also be served. Doña Martina felt happy because this would be another way to fight for their life.

Lives are spent uselessly, just existing, and lives are put aside like worn-out clothes with use, and here in the barrio, life went on and on, until the scourge came from the flu epidemic or Spanish flu as it was called, striking everywhere and not sparing anyone. The rich and poor, beautiful and ugly, perfect and imperfect walked together.

What struck me most about this epidemic was when my mother became ill and we didn't know what she had. Doña Martina gave first aid with sudorific herbs, which were said to be good at moderating the illness. My mother convalesced for more than two months.

She was just recovering from the illness when we received the tragic news that my brother Pepín had died of the flu at Fort Travis in Texas. This set back my mother's convalescence.

My friend Chelo and I didn't get the flu, and neither did doña Martina. Early in the morning she would show up at my house with her healing mixtures. I could hardly believe it! I have the image stamped in my mind of all those sick people we visited, lying on the floor, in the beds, or wherever they fell.

First we went to Chelo's house. Doña Martina had us make a large pot of black coffee and she sprinkled in dried herbs and sent us to give it to Tita, Chelo's mother, and then to the father and Chelo's four siblings, who apparently were no longer alive. Doña Martina didn't dare allow Tita to see her!

From there we went to another friend of Chelo's and mine; however we didn't know her family. We gave her strong black coffee with herbal powders too. My friend Catalina and her mother were already dying. Doña Martina didn't let us see them. Later when other friends of mine realized that we were doña Martina's helpers, they called on us to go to their relatives, who also owned dairies. The doctors couldn't get to the houses, which were so far removed from downtown. One or two showed up in the barrio, but according to what they said, they had more work downtown. They really didn't care about people from such remote neighborhoods.

I have a vivid memory of doña Martina when she saw those lifeless bodies. She showed sadness in her face; however, she encouraged us, and she went in front, her skirts ruffling in the wind, and we followed behind her at a brisk pace.

Don Leandro sent for doña Martina. He was not sick, but my friend Tomasita was almost unconscious. We rubbed on the coffee and the powders. We helped doña Martina drag a gallon of milk, the heavy kind. It was don Leandro's gift, since doña Martina refused money.

We also visited Lola, the one devoted to the saint San Antonio, who, according to her, refused to heal her. And in the next few days she died of the flu. But doña Martina did not give up. Apart from those people who were sick with the flu, she didn't forget her expectant mothers. This time she left the husbands in charge of them when they were giving birth.

Death also took doña Patrocinio, leaving three orphans. Juan soon after volunteered for the army and Lola, the shorty, stayed at home;

Gaby, the blondie, was working. There were some other dead people in the barrio, but these are the ones I knew.

I remember—this was told to me by my friend Chelo—how her father found out about what doña Martina had done. Without consulting his wife, Tita, he ordered his workers, without questions or complaints, to leave two large jars of milk for doña Martina every day. This was a token of gratitude inspired by doña Martina's fine and generous act.

Jony, the Hero

It is curious, and I have learned, now remembering those times, that many people under pressure find some humor in formidable situations. This can be applied to doña Martina.

By the end of that year the war had ended, but the anguish and sorrows continued. The veteran soldiers began to arrive, and they brought back memories of those who did not return. Only my brother Pepín did not return alive; everyone else in the barrio returned, thank God.

My mother finally recovered her health, but there was no spirit in the house, only memories of that brother who loved us so much and fought for the livelihood of everyone. Even after his death, he continued with a pension for my mother for the rest of her life. Although after going through so much bitterness and need, the assistance didn't arrive until two years after the death of our brother. We didn't know of any such help and less about inquiring about what we didn't know.

In the first months of the year, however, the mourning in the barrio was striking. Doña Martina and her family were in great shape. Happily, Jony had returned to top it all off. He was returning as an acclaimed hero! Only in the barrio, and just among the intimate friends and family of the barrio, did we learn that Jony was a hero.

"I don't understand how he is a hero, that bastard!" Those were doña Martina's favorite, half mocking words but they were said with some concealed pride. Jony came over with his mother one day to give us their condolences for the death of my brother. He knew how much we loved Pepín.

I'll tell you what Jony was like. Juan was Jony, and that's all! No more? "We'll see, said a blind man," as the saying goes. He had a lot of Indian relatives, so he was small in body but he had invisible physical strength. Jony was a close friend of my brother Chale; they were both baseball players.

They were good pitchers and good runners. Doña Martina wanted her sons to have men's jobs; that meant "pick and shovel" jobs, but unhappily with those small bodies they weren't even given a chance to see if they could be useful! Yes, they worked odd jobs. On one occasion, my brother Chale and Jony went to look for work, and at last they found some at Western Union Telegram as messengers. They lasted there a year, and then Jony went into the army and my brother into the navy.

Our family wonders how he became a hero. You might say it was a miracle! I say it was because Jony was a snippet of a man like his mother. The other brothers, though they were thin, weren't as short as Jony.

Just imagine, he alone destroyed four machine gun nests, one by one, by using grenades! He told us about his experiences on the battlefield and said he didn't want to remember, but we begged him and finally he granted our wish.

"I don't know why they tell me I'm a hero," he said, with his mischievous boy's smile.

"I was just doing what they had ordered me to, that's all! They taught me other special skills and told me things to transform me into I don't know what, Crucita. They wanted to make me cruel and animal-like, because that's what they were all like. But I didn't want to kill, and that was what I heard, 'kill, kill.' War is bad, Crucita." Drops of sweat appeared on Jony's forehead.

Doña Martina listened and commented for the fifth or more time, "I can hardly believe that this bastard boy could save himself, and then for him to be a hero!"

Jony continued, "I tell you I'm not a killer. We reached a forest in Germany, and it was already half burned because of the bombings. We got there because we were in a hurry. There were about forty of us buddies, and we barely started to sit down to drink water or smoke when, unexpectedly, a fire attack rained down on us, first through the air and then by land. The squad leader shouted at us to run wherever we could. He didn't tell us twice. I headed for a tree and saw the dry and dug-up roots. I got under the roots with such a fear that I messed my pants. I saw what happened to my buddies, stretched out across the field and with me alive! There I was screened by the tree for I don't know how long. Step by step I went out into the night and then I got under the tree again because the searchlights wouldn't let me get out. At dawn I went out crawling on my hands and knees and believe me, it was with tears in my eyes. I took a canteen from one of the bodies and another provided me with pants. Even though they were too big, I put them on. I started to walk away from the combat. I got lost. I got tired and I was dying of thirst, but I kept walking, I don't know where."

"Then I suddenly ran into a German soldier. Perhaps he was in the same shape I was in, defeated and suffering from fatigue and thirst. We both carried rifles and grenades, but we didn't want to kill each other. What for, Crucita? We stood up and saluted each other military style and he went on his way, and I went mine."

"Jony, tell them how you killed the ones in the nests!" doña Martina encouraged her son.

"Well, I don't even know myself, Mom. But remember, Crucita, how Chale and I played baseball? Well, I was good at pitching. When the ones in the nests fired their machine guns, I counted and knew there was a little pause in firing their weapons, and that was when

I took advantage. I threw the grenade and with very good aim, and that's how I destroyed them one by one. There were four of them and they didn't even touch me. Now they say I'm a hero! Give me a break, Crucita!"

Afterward Jony chuckled, then that spread into a big smile. One could see that infinite lightning of triumph in his eyes. But it disappeared as quickly as it appeared!

"And I tell all of you, I'm not a killer." That's how his story ended.

"What are you going to do now, Jony?" my mother asked him.

"What a shame Chale is not here, Crucita. He and I had planned to start a business, but he enlisted four years ago and he still has more than two to finish. Meanwhile I'm going to repair Mamá's house."

Jony's face was thin and dark, with smart eyes, but the good thing was that he had grown accustomed to keeping his back straight and he showed more self-confidence. I think now, however, that no matter how small the triumph he achieved, for having been so unknown and vituperated in his own barrio, he didn't stop savoring his new status for a moment, albeit slyly.

Don Domingo

In our meditations about daydreams, we daily strive to justify ourselves because we don't like to suffer the pain of being wrong. However, we constantly experience examples of our own weaknesses and mistakes.

An example can be seen in the following events. One winter night, when I was already asleep, naturally on the floor, I heard a very kind voice and felt pushing at the same time. Someone was saying, "Chatita, Chatita, move over farther, just a little more."

Between being asleep and awake, I understood that it was Panchita, the wife of don Domingo, our neighbor from the next block down. I soon went back to sleep. The next morning, I was awakened by a knock on the door and my mother went to see who it was.

"Excuse me, Crucita, good morning. Is Panchita here?" The smooth-talking, kindly voice was that of don Domingo.

"Yes, don Domingo, Panchita spent the night here, but she said you wanted to beat her."

For being so early in the morning, the man was already well shaved and combed. Suddenly there in the doorway, extending his arms to both sides and forming crosses with his thumb and index fingers, he said in a persuasive and affectionate voice, "By the life of these holy crosses, I did not touch Panchita at all, Crucita, ask her in front of me!"

I was terrified by what don Domingo said, and even more so when I saw Panchita's face, dark with the black mole beside her full, ruby-red lips.

My mother went over to Panchita and asked, "Panchita, don Domingo is here. He's coming for you; do you want to leave?"

Her face instantly changed to one of defiance, and she answered loudly so that her husband could hear. "Yes, I'll go back to my house, but you will treat me better, won't you, Domingo?"

Don Domingo answered like this, in a false way or not I don't know. "My love, I swear I'll never again take a sip of that damn drink called 'homebrew.' Yes, let's go, my darling." They left.

Don Domingo was the one who sold Talaca, the skinny mare, to my mother and brothers. We knew him well; he was always smiling and a little bit plump in the cheeks. This reminds me of when I bought milk from don Domingo. In the morning Panchita already had a table outside under a leafy tree, with a very white tablecloth and a jug of milk, hot tortillas, and other food, all very tasty, indeed. Don Domingo invited me to join them for breakfast.

That man was presumptuous. He had a wagon with two teams of horses, which he rented for hauling loads or whatever was needed. He had to pass near doña Martina's house every day to get to his businesss. There was no other way, except to go around to the more distant bridge. We would cross over by this route to get there sooner, and to get to school or to take the trolley, and like that.

Don Domingo would perhaps inquire about the purpose of the lantern by the door of that house. When he realized what it meant, I imagine that gave him an idea.

Days after what happened, don Domingo went over to see my brother Pepín and said, rather he flattered him like this: "Pepinito, I know you can dance real well, and I want to give you an invitation to a dance on Saturday at seven. What do you say?"

"Look, don Domingo, I would gladly accept, and I thank you, but I have a date with a friend and I won't see her until Saturday afternoon. I don't know what to do."

"Pepín, that's easy. Invite her along. I manage my house with good behavior, and besides I don't charge anything. I'll expect you, okay? I'll expect both of you." Don Domingo was acting very courteously.

Pepín talked to my mother. The customs at that time were still conventional, and it did not seem right or proper to her that a young lady should accept an invitation accompanied by only her friend or boyfriend! It was proper for a person of confidence or a relative to accompany the lady to the party or dance.

"Look, Mom, you go to the dance too, will you? You can meet Palmira; she is tall and elegant, with exaggerated expressions in her eyes and mouth." My brother was very happy. He liked to joke with my mother, but she agreed to go to the dance and I agreed [to go] with her.

Don Domingo decorated the large living room and waxed the floor to dance on. He invited don Leandro's children, who didn't know even one dance step. They situated themselves at the door and in the window. Don Domingo was angry with them and begged them to come into the living room. The youngest of the brothers seemed to go after my friend Chelo, and she also made eyes at him, but she had never learned to dance either. About three years later, he married her. But that's another story."

Palmira was the sensation of the dance. She and my brother made an ideal couple. The crowd, as don Domingo had said, were all "highbrow" people. I asked my mother what that word was, and she said it meant "of high social class," not just ordinary people.

Palmira was completely different from the girls from the barrio. Among the crowd was Gaby the "blondie," her sister Lola the "shorty," who dressed in a very tight dress. My friends and I cut her down, and we were dying of laughter because we thought the dress would burst; it was so tight and cut so low. Aside from being tight and low, you could see the line that divides the breasts. We laughed even more.

There were other neighbors who are not known to you all. Gaby was very nice, not malicious like Palmira. Her body was slender, but she was not tall. She was dressed in a high collar and long sleeves, and Don Patrocinio sat next to his daughters.

The girls were distrustful of Palmira because don Domingo gave all his attention to her. In the middle of the room, he came off as very "badass," as they would say in the barrio; he said "I am the real *cabrón*." He expressed his feelings when he said in a loud voice, "Get out of my way." I almost shuddered because I thought he would say what doña Martina had added to that.

Confident of himself, he repeated, "Get out of my way, boys." When they stepped aside, don Domingo continued, "Ladies and gentlemen, I interrupt you now to tell you the following: We have among us a young man and a young lady who will show us a dance which is not well known in these parts. It's the tango! Let's hear an applause for Pepín and Miss Palmira, his partner."

Indeed, my mother and I were proud of my brother. "Mom, I didn't know Pepín danced so well!"

"Don't talk, daughter, let's watch the dance."

The musicians were better than doña Martina's; however, there were only four of them. My brother and Palmira really put on a show dancing the tango. This is a memory of my childhood that I will never forget, among so many that our dear brother left us.

My brother Chale took pity on Lola the shorty and others he danced with so they wouldn't say that they remained seated or were wallflowers. He danced with all of them.

I assure you that if Jony had been there, he would have been the star of the show with all the girls. While he lacked body size, he had more than enough to dance. Like his mother said, "he dances like a spinning top." But he was not invited and he had no social graces, and besides, Jony was faithful to his mother, who also had a dance in their house that night.

The next day, doña Martina came over to my house, later than usual. She looked like a woman who was out of sorts and in a bad mood.

"That old bastard, he wants to hurt me, Crucita, and I know it. He really hates me, the old so and so." This was how she expressed her sense of outrage for don Domingo.

"Why, doña Martina, what's wrong?" my mother asked.

"You mean you don't know that he is stirring up the pot against don Leandro? I don't care if he doesn't hire me and consults with a doctor and I don't know what other crap, the damned old buttinski. María, don Leandro's wife, already told me all that. I don't do anything to that old bastard, I don't even talk to the *sanababiche* [son of a bitch]." Doña Martina drank her coffee in hopes of filling her stomach and calming her nerves.

"I don't yet understand what is happening or why don Domingo is acting this way with you, Doña Martina."

"I don't know why he chose me for a target. But it must have been because of Panchita. Several days ago, I went to buy meat from don Venustiano's shop. Panchita also arrived and saw me pay with an ounce of gold. 'Doña Martina, where did you get an ounce of gold?'

the butcher asked with admiration, and Panchita was looking on. And I answered, 'Ask don Leandro, Venustiano, if you want to know.' "

"Ah, don Leandro, eh? I didn't know that you worked with him."

"There are things you don't know, Venustiano. I went out, but Panchita remained behind." The miserable woman was indignant.

"I really didn't imagine that don Domingo had that kind of soul to want to hurt you, doña Martina!" My mother was worried and confused. "What has don Leandro said to you?"

"Nothing, Crucita, I'll get to that in a little while. Look, Crucita, now didn't you notice that he's giving me competition because he found out about the ounce of gold from Panchita? He thinks he's going to defeat me, well, he's wrong, the wretched old bastard. He doesn't deliver babies like I do, Crucita, like I do. I'm not pinning my hopes on the fact that people will dance nor on selling the nickel to live on, Crucita. I can live even without eating!"

"Crucita, because I came in so filled with the devil, I didn't tell you the news. Notice that don Leandro's María is pregnant. The old man called me over to speak to me. I'll see what happens. I hope everything turns out well. Thanks for your tasty coffee. As always, you take away so much grief, Crucita."

Gaby

Gabina, the one with the smiling face, the blond girl, spoke little and very slowly, but when she looked at you, it was a look that seemed to want to read in the depths of your heart. The boys in the barrio looked at her, but only as a well-known friend and esteemed neighbor. Maybe she could not have anything more than friendship because don Patrocinio did not want his daughters to deal with "trash," and of course this implied Jony. Perhaps doña Patrocinio suspected something about his daughter, Gaby.

As I mentioned earlier, at that time the ideas and customs that dominated after the First World War were not in fashion, for a girl to go out for a walk with a boy suitor [even] with the permission of the mother. They all went out when they could. Sometimes, according to what they said, Gaby and her sister Lola begged doña Patrocinio to take them to the park for a walk. The mother would comply with their wish.

The boys on the baseball team included my brother Chale and Jony. Perhaps in her heart Gaby liked the "little boy," as she came to call him fondly. It was not so much interest in the walk, as it was the only way to see Jony, although from a distance.

Gaby worked, but no one knew at what or where. One day at a meeting of friends in my house, Jony asked anyone who might know what it was that Gaby did.

"Well, she dresses so nice, maybe she's a secretary," commented Julio, Jenny's boyfriend.

"You don't say, jerk. And how do you know?" Jony was disgusted and suspicious too.

"Well, haven't you noticed how she dresses up? With a five-peso hat!" Julio said.

"That's enough, that's enough, you jerk." Jony waved his hand for Julio to stop.

Jony didn't want to confess, but his buddies forced him to tell them his feelings about Gaby. "I'm going to tell you one thing. I'm not really worth anything. I don't have anything to offer such a pretty girl, but what the hell, if she reciprocated my love, I would go crazy!"

His friends laughed good-naturedly. They never expected him to say such a thing. Jony continued, "And things are like my friend Julio says...well, what the heck, I'm not anything. I don't know anything. I'm a bastard, like Mom says."

"Jony, Jony, you have to have patience and courage to live life well," said Pepín. "Look, like with me and Palmira, I couldn't find any way to talk to her, but I got up the courage and she answered yes to being my girlfriend. Don't give up, Jony."

"Hey, but her old grandmother won't even let her breathe! When

I see her [Gaby] in the park, I just look at her and give her eyes. She can't even laugh, with the cop on the beat."

In our barrio, we lacked modern things, and had only the necessary things to decorate or beautify either in furniture or in people. Not surprisingly, Gaby was good at transforming simple, inexpensive items into something fashionable and in good taste.

And this was the reason they would say that Gaby dressed elegantly. It was not the quality or type of cloth, but rather that she proportioned the dress according to her size, not short or long, but rather implying something of her own taste, making herself seem more on the feminine side. You could say that Gaby was somewhat old-fashioned.

Julio's brother Salomón had been listening to the conversation and interjected, "Look, Jony, I work on the other side of the bridge helping don Camerino with the groceries. And I've seen Gaby pass by in the mornings, but I haven't noticed where she really goes to work. If you want to know, I'll tell you tomorrow."

They agreed on that. And the next day, they were laughing and joking so much that none of the boys could contain themselves.

Salomón, Julio's brother, recounted the following:

"It was seven o'clock in the morning when I was waiting for Gaby to leave her house. She didn't work very far from her house. On the other side of the bridge, she entered the house of some gringos who are clients of Camerino, my boss, and who I've delivered merchandise to."

We were all ears (how was I not going to listen to such a story?). We were waiting for Salomón to continue that very important piece of news.

"Go ahead, halfwit, tell us what happened." Jony was impatiently urging him on.

"You all aren't going to believe me. Jony, don't get mad. You all sent me to spy on her, and I went. Look, Jony, Gaby is a maid!"

"What? What? What?" they all asked at once.

Salomón went on with his story. "I waited. I really don't know her but since my brother Julio said that Gaby dresses in a five-peso hat and looks like a secretary, well I just couldn't understand or believe how in that house Gaby was going to be a secretary!"

Salomón hoped Jony would ask something, but they were all listening to hear the end. "Gaby went into the house, and I watched. She came out wearing a house dress and flip-flops and a rag on her head in order to sweep the yard and throw out trash in the alley!"

"Gaby is a maid! Gaby is a maid!" Jony really was laughing. Then he burst into a belly laugh and everyone, including me, let loose laughing with gusto and also from disappointment.

"All right, Jony, this is your chance. I'm sure you'll get through to her!" Chale happily encouraged his friend.

"I just hope I'm not dreaming, guys. I can hardly believe it. I'll tell you something that will surprise you. My mother has always liked Gaby. My knees are shaking at the thought of talking to her, but I'm going to do it boys, I'll do it!"

The little bit of man did it. He spoke to Gaby, and Gaby responded. She made it clear that her mother wouldn't agree and it would be better if she wasn't told until later.

In a few days Jony was going into the army. He went to wait for her at her work and the two walked in the gringo neighborhood. They didn't need many words; their faces said it all. However, Jony had a feeling of uncertainty, but he suddenly covered himself with a great impulse and felt optimistic.

Gaby felt that the day she longed for would have to come. Jony proposed to her, and they would get married as soon as he got back from the war. She accepted.

Jony knew that Gaby's mother, "that old Frog eyes," did not like him, not even a little bit. "But I love Gaby so much that I don't care. I love her like no one else and my mother loves her very much and that's enough!" So said Jony in love.

When Jony returned, he visited Gaby. They had written to him about the death of doña Patrocinio and that her brother, Juan de Dios, had enlisted in the Marines.

All of us in the neighborhood talked to each other about Gaby and Jony's courtship. How he admired his girlfriend and how pretty his Gaby looked in her black suit! They waited for the wedding for almost a year, since it was the law of the people to mourn for a year.

Toncha gave him enough of her land so Jony could build a house for himself and Gaby. The odd thing about it was that Jony couldn't find work. "And if you get married, how do you support her?" Jenny and doña Martina asked. His friends were no longer in the barrio, and he didn't know what to do to earn enough to support his future wife and perhaps children! He was desperate. Every day he went to his land, cleared it of weeds and debris, and admired it. He felt happy about his property.

One day he noticed the stream waters as they receded from the edges of the property. This gave him a great idea that changed the course of his life. He didn't wait for anything. The next day he went to work. He bought straw, and with sand and mud he started to make adobe bricks! Doña Martina advised him on what she knew about it, and he made enough bricks for the construction of a house for his future wife, Gaby. He plastered and whitewashed it. Gaby wanted a garden like her future mother-in-law's, and Jony made that for her too.

"The adobe man" was the title of the "little snippet of a man" and the "little boy" as Gaby affectionately called him. From time to time, they called him the "hero." It was all the same to him; he was happy with Gaby, and that was it!

It was April. The sun was shining, and the air was cool but not cold. Doña Martina's whole family was up and about early in the morning, preparing for the wedding and marriage of Jony and Gaby.

For the first time, I saw doña Martina dressed in new clothes and also for the first, she was wearing shoes and a small cape. Apparently she was very proud to wear it, since it was a gift from her future daughter-in-law.

Chelo and Jenny, the bridesmaids, wore pale blue dresses. Jenny looked like a princess in her pale blue bonnet worn close to her head, on top of her long, shiny, dark blond hair. Her young escort did not take his eyes off such beauty. There were rumors of Jenny's engagement to her escort, the godfather. He was a friend of Jony's and a fellow soldier from the war in Europe. His sister met this young man through Jony, and they fell in love. Soon after Jony's marriage, she also got married and moved to California. And as I later found out, they lived very happily.

In those days doña Martina was not interested in anything other than Gaby and her son. They really were on cloud nine. Those were also days of celebration for the barrio with respect to the events of the last months.

When Jony returned from the war, he had a little money, and with the payment of don Leandro to doña Martina, J. Antonio's little store was transformed into a large one and with a large clientele. The neighborhood grew and new families were building houses.

Doña Martina's house was also dressed in new furnishings. Jenny became a hard-working young lady, a rare thing. She and J. Antonio hung new curtains and removed all the worthless stuff to make room for some new furniture. The walls were whitewashed, and the windows and doors were renovated. It was also remarkable that the term *joto* was not mentioned again.

Licha dedicated herself to the housework as usual, and to growing herbs in her mother's garden. Rather, flowers were planted instead, since married couples consulted doctors and the modern generation wanted new and modernized things. They no longer consulted the midwife; they consulted doctors, and they had more money available.

One day Tita went to visit my mother. She and the family had made preparations to move from the land they lived on for so many years. Tita was sad to leave her friends in this barrio, but the reality was that the time frame to move the dairy would be up soon. Tita felt sorry about the move. In our talk, which lasted quite a while, she related the following:

"Crucita, do you remember don Chen (Epomuceno)? We rented the three rooms in the house on the corner to him. Do you remember also that they came as refugees, and my husband and I helped them with milk and eggs for the whole family? They told us they were in need. What a great surprise that now that we have bought the land to move the dairy, Cheno was the one who bought an immense area, but really large, Crucita, and established the largest dairy of all!"

"I can hardly believe it, Tita. If you weren't telling me, I wouldn't believe it." My mother was astonished by this information. We really didn't expect this, because we knew them well and the girls went to school with me. They didn't say they were poor, but they showed themselves to be.

"I'm sorry to leave you all, our friends for years, but we have to do what the law orders. We want you to visit us, and if for some reason you don't have any way to get there, you phone me and I'll send someone for you. The telephone number is the same," Tita announced. They were the first to have that luxury, and I think the only ones.

The barrio lost all the dairy farmers. The law sent them away. We lost good friends and neighbors. The dawns without the shouts of don Leandro were gloomy and silent. The shout of "Cambo, Cambo," went to another barrio. My close friends left too. I will not find other friends like them. I loved them very much.

Even to this day, we telephone and talk to each other. We know how many children they had and what kind of life they are living. Friendships and friends forever.

When doña Martina attended at the delivery of María, don Leandro's wife, she had no problems. The difficult thing about the case was the delicate child. Doña Martina told us about the little girl who looked like a doll made from china or porcelain; she was such a beautiful girl. She had intense almost rose-colored hair and green eyes with dark, long curled lashes.

Three or four times a week and for the first few days, I would go in the morning and afternoon to see the girl. Nothing was done in María's and the little girl, María Cristina's room without consulting the midwife.

A noticeable change came over don Leandro at home and with others in the family. He remained at his wife and daughter's sides, caressing his little daughter and proclaiming everywhere that there was no such child as his, more beautiful than anyone. The father did indeed speak the truth.

Don Domingo conversed with don Leandro on occasion, but my friend Tomasita told me that her father never mentioned what they talked about. And the two had quite some talks. The reality was that one day don Leandro became the owner of don Domingo's property when he disappeared overnight. He and his wife just disappeared. Some neighbors said they headed for California, and that don Leandro paid very good money for the property.

Doña Martina told us she showed her three drawers filled with ounces of gold in five, ten, and twenty peso coins. With astonishment, she said, "Look, Crucita, he has several pieces of luggage filled with gold coins, and every time I go to see María and the child, don Leandro offers for me to get what I want from the gold, but, Crucita, like always, I just take one coin and that is one of five pesos.

"Why don't you take more, if he offers it to you, doña Martina?" my mother asked, with eyes full of amazement.

"Crucita, most of all, you know how some neighbors hate me, although I don't owe them or fear them. I'll never know why, and I don't want to know. As I said before, I only wanted to know what

I could do in those deliveries and with those sick people like don Leandro's little girl, that's all I know. Money, gold, are not necessary for me, Crucita. Why in the hell should I want it?" Doña Martina was satisfied.

The Preemie

Now when I have free time, I remember pleasantly the stories of doña Martina. These were stories about her expectant mothers and about sick people to whom she gave curative herbs. Following is the one I have freshest in my memory.

There was a father of several children. His name was Cirilo, and he was very strict with his eldest daughter, just like don Leandro was with all his family. The daughter was a schoolmate of mine and my other friends who you already have gotten to know in these pages. Her name was Ema; she was flirty and liked the boys. We knew when Ema was going to play hooky from school, but we didn't say anything to anyone.

She finally got a formal boyfriend, and her dad thought the "wild one" would be better off married. So Ema got married when she was only seventeen years old. What had to happen did happen, and seven months later she had her first child. Doña Martina attended as a midwife.

Don Cirilo, when he saw his grandson, sturdy, vigorous, and perfect, suspected something and became enraged. The young husband noticed that his father-in-law was so indignant that he was afraid and ran to doña Martina's house.

"Doña Martina, by the life of your mother or whatever you love most, I'll pay you whatever you want or do whatever you tell me but tell my father-in-law that my son is a preemie!" Kneeling on the floor, the poor boy, he begged doña Martina.

That same night don Cirilo went to doña Martina's house. He was still angry at his daughter and son-in-law. He asked her: "You tell me the truth, doña Martina, if those damned kids want to make me out to be a fool. You tell me the truth. Is my grandson a preemie?"

The woman laughed enthusiastically! "Those bastards even want to make me out as a procurer! Crucita, I thought, since they were married, they would have already done what they did, and now, so what? The child is perfectly well, I don't know what old Cirilo wants!" With her malicious laughter, she paused. "I couldn't do anything else but lie to don Cirilo. I said to him, 'Don Cirilo, your grandson is a preemie.' That was all I said to him."

"Look, doña Martina," he said, "I'll swallow that because you say so. If not, I would grab those damn bastards and beat the shit out of them."

In her old age, doña Martina told us cute stories about her grandchildren, the children of Jony and Gaby.

"Look, Crucita, you aren't going to believe me, but my little granddaughter, Biny (Gabinita), has taken away a little of my cussing, that is, in front of her. Let me tell you. One day I was playing with her, and the little devil was barely three years old, if that. The thing was, I was talking to Gaby about something and then I started to complain about some bastard and I said to Gaby, 'It's my fault, nobody else's, because I'm a good bitch [*cabrona*].'"

Thinking now of that happy picture, so full of nostalgia, my throat tightens up and my eyes get blurry. I see her now as I saw her then standing there and saying, "Get out of my way you *hijos de la chin* [you dirty bastards]." Doña Martina will never change.

"I really didn't think that the little girl would notice what I was telling Gaby, but how wrong I was. Biny approached me and, as if defending me, with all her soul and moving her head from one side to another, she said, in her little girl's voice, clear and penetrating so she could be heard, she said, "Mamá. Tina not *cabona*, not *cabona*!"

"Jony was going to spank her, but I didn't let him. I told him to hit me. He said that when I said bad words in front of Biny, if he hit the little girl that would hurt me more and I would learn to restrain myself. There you have it, Crucita, I have learned not to curse. It's the fucking joke of my life, I swear, Crucita."

We laughed heartily about the things doña Martina said. She told us about them now, calmly, not just in passing, as she had in years past when she came over to my house and drank coffee and then went back out into the cold or the heat and often, into the blowing dust storms.

The time has come to say goodbye to that life in that barrio, so dear. My life was rich like that of very few young girls. Those words, which my mother may have already forgotten, "Are we better?" are no longer mentioned. The answer is felt in the friendships and togetherness among all the neighbors we knew. Although our lives were not abundant with material things, but rather of stories, events, jokes, and activities, they were more than full.

I feel that the esteem the people have one for the other has been lost in opulence, in crowds and haste. The lack of this esteem makes us lose that communication so necessary for a complete and meaningful life.

Yes, those times will not return, and as the saying goes, "The old times are the best." The memory is beautiful!

I remember doña Martina standing in the middle of my kitchen, and I was wondering what will happen to her now. Out of curiosity, I asked her, "Doña Martina, what are you going to do now that you just have J. Antonio and Licha left?"

With her extraordinary, mocking laughter coming from that mouth filled with stained teeth, she said, "Well, Chata, it seems that my enemies have all gone, and I don't care a *chingao*. I can do whatever is put into this bitchy head, can't I?"

How the air fills with wave after wave of memories! The laughter was hidden between our teeth, then it spread all over our face, and it was contagious. We also broke into belly laughs and then all three of us would laugh! How happy doña Martina was, with her cup of coffee in one hand and a cigarette in the other!

For one fierce moment, I would like to return to those times and enjoy the calm of the charming laughter of that unforgettable old woman.

One thing that over the years has impressed me about those people, who, even being so poor, so ignorant and lacking in education, so ill-mannered and swearers like doña Martina—I don't remember robberies or burglaries, drug addicts or drunks in the streets, murders or deaths in street fights, or assaults with weapons of any kind! I've thought about it, and I can't understand why.

And still one figure stands out among all that hodgepodge, among all the people of the barrio—doña Martina. Yes, and I still marvel at doña Martina!

González Grocery,
el alma del barrio

"There is no question that the sight of a boarded-up corner grocery
strikes a chord of sadness in the soul."
—BENJAMIN FORGEY

My family's history in El Paso resembles similar American immigrant
stories not often spoken of, which occurred in the early decades of the
twentieth century in cities across the country: the foundation of corner grocery stores. My grandparents, doña Ramona and don Manuel,
opened González Grocery in the middle of the Great Depression in
1934. Their business venture mirrored the opening of corner grocery
stores across America. Also known as mom-and-pops and bodegas in
Hispanic neighborhoods, corner grocery stores like theirs marked
the beginning of a long and colorful history of grocery store retail
in lower- and middle-class communities. These stores exclusively
catered to their communities: urban, ethnic, and striving for their
place in a new country. Immigrant families began moving to New
York, Chicago, and Los Angeles, and other large cities, and Puerto
Rican, Jewish, Italian, and Mexican neighborhoods flourished, most
of them anchored by the corner grocery. Keenly aware of their own

food culture, entrepreneurial families recognized a need to provide unique foods and services to the community. The corner grocery store was born. Architect and urban development critic Benjamin Forgey notes that "corner stores—especially corner grocery stores—became ubiquitous in American cities because they were needed and convenient, and they fit the typical urban geometry."[1] Community members treated these mom-and-pop stores as the backbone to the communities they served.

By operating a corner grocery in an American city, immigrant families were telling their communities, "We belong here and are here to serve you." Business thrived. The stores came in all shapes and sizes and served their communities reliably. The storefronts often functioned as businesses out front and housed families in the back quarters. Even through the corporate grocery store explosion of the 1960s and 1970s, many mom-and-pop stores flourished, and some remain open today. Arwa Haidero observed that they "reflect the fabric of our nation through their abundant diversity, and the vital role that immigrant shopkeepers have played."[2]

Many American cities remember and still support their beloved corner grocery stores. El Paso is no exception. Its bodegas and corner stores thrived in Chihuahuita and Segundo Barrio and in the neighborhoods south of Schuster Avenue. Several stores operated for generations, among them Silva's Supermarket, which began as Abarrotes Faro in 1919 and closed in 2019, one hundred years later. El Paso corner stores that were established in the early twentieth century and remain open today include Sunset Grocery in historic Sunset Heights, La Tiendita de Irma in Segundo Barrio, Moon Grocery on Brown Street, and Villalva's Grocery in Chihuahuita.

As early as the 1880s, Mexican and Chinese immigrants opened grocery stores in El Paso to invest their hard-earned capital in the neighborhoods where they lived and raised their families. Occasionally, only a few urban blocks from each other, these family markets served

Grocery store owner standing in the doorway of an El Paso mom-and-pop shop, ca. 1915.

as safe places where people of the community gathered to exchange stories of struggle or success, news of births or marriages, divorces or deaths. They provided a connection to local and even national news, such as offering a newspaper to share, as many residents could not afford a newspaper subscription. AM radio often played in the background as customers mingled at the butcher counter or simply looked out the window at passersby.

The central role of corner grocery stores increased during local and national crises, such as when men went off to war or labor groups organized for strikes. The stock market crash of 1929 brought fear and uncertainty to every household across the country. The Great Depression hit El Paso hard. Texas historian Robert McKay notes that "the effects of the Depression on Mexican businesses was perhaps greatest at El Paso, where hundreds of commercial enterprises closed."³ Despite these obstacles, Ramona and Manuel González took a risk in 1934 and opened their store on the corner of Missouri and Ochoa Streets. Neighbors with the best of intentions warned the young couple of the possible financial pitfalls of such a move during difficult economic times. The Gonzálezes could potentially lose their entire investment.

My grandparents fully understood life's hardships in those gritty times. While they came from different economic backgrounds—my grandmother from the barrio and poverty, my grandfather from a middle-class family who immigrated from well-heeled Zacatecas, Mexico—they shared in their experiences of adversity. In her 1975 *El Paso Times* interview, González explained that the Great Depression struck during her first pregnancy and Manuel lost his job, a reality that befell many men at the time. Fortunately, Ramona and Manuel had converted their cash savings into gold. Like many people at the time, Manuel didn't trust banks. González recalled in the interview, "We persisted with [our] plans and opened the store. After selling the gold, we started a grocery store with $158 including $50 credit. After a while, it became a big store in the barrio." As she recalls in "La tiendita," establishing the business came over time and with it came eventual financial success. Because González Grocery served as my family's root and lifeline—taking on a life of its own at times—stories of its community reputation and role were frequently shared at family gatherings.

The details I remember most from these stories emphasized the key role González played in managing the business. She ran the front counter, kept the accounts, learned to butcher, and worked as the cook for the small storefront restaurant they opened during lunch hours. She had learned accounting skills from her classes at El Paso High School and cooking from living in the barrio. Her words from the 1975 *El Paso Times* interview reflect her perseverance. "'For twenty-six years, I worked hard in that store,' she said, adding, 'I wanted my children to go to college.'"

There are moments in the young lives of curious grandchildren—those blessed to have their grandparents, even great-grandparents alive—when they muster the curiosity to ask about their past hopes and aspirations. It's difficult to imagine our elders when they were young. Yet knowing our elders' dreams and aspirations as youth helps us imagine them in the prime of their lives and connect their aspirations to ours. One such moment presented itself to me while I was living with doña Ramona. At age twenty, I had entered my second year at the University of Texas at El Paso. With little warning, I asked my grandmother, "Did you ever want to attend college?" The question, I could tell, took her by surprise. She took a sip of her coffee and wiped her mouth. Casting her eyes back to me after a brief stare into the distance, she said, "Women, especially *mexicanas,* just didn't go to college at that time. *Pero sí, quise asistir.* We also didn't have the money." A moment of silence came between us as if to let the reality of what she had said penetrate my mind. The conversation abruptly ended as the sound of a car engine and accompanying honks announced that my ride to school had arrived. Jumping up, I kissed my grandmother on the cheek, grabbed my backpack, and joined my friend out front.

For many years, the weight of that moment has remained with me. As this memory flashed before me decades later, I realized I was living her dream, benefiting from her personal sacrifices and years of hard work. Had we continued that conversation, she likely would have recounted the path that she took instead of continuing her education—working downtown, meeting my grandfather Manuel, getting married, opening the corner grocery store, struggling through the Depression, and experiencing the shared sacrifices of food and gas rationing during World War II. She likely would have explained the

public anxiety that society felt during the social upheaval of the civil
rights and Mexican American movements of the 1960s and 1970s.
Her life choices and experiences enriched her perspective and values, and they would serve her well when she wrote the short story "Mi
tiendita." Looking back on what I know of her life, I imagine some of
the more poignant moments.

No es posible / It's Not Possible

"*¡Mamaaaa, ya llegué!*" shouted a youthful Ramona as she arrived
home from school one afternoon in spring 1925, a few months before
her high school graduation. As she entered the house on Durazno
Street, the screen door slammed behind her. The bright El Paso
sun guided her steps to the kitchen where her mother had a pot of
frijoles boiling on the stove. The earthy, warm smell of cooking hit
Ramona's senses. Full of hope for the future, she announced that she
had an opportunity to attend Texas College of Mines and Metallurgy.
"¡Me están hablando en la high school de las muchas oportunidades
que hay de ir al colegio! Ya han abierto el colegio para las mujeres
desde 1916." (They are talking to me at high school about the many
opportunities to attend college! The local college has been open to
women since 1916.)

Ascención responded, "¡Ay, mija! Ya sabes que no tenemos el dinero para que vayas al colegio. Aún más, las mujercitas no deben de
entrar en un lugar solo para hombres. ¿Tienes amigas que preten-
den ir? Esperaba que encontraras un trabajo para ayudar aquí." (Oh,
dear! You know we don't have the money for you to attend college!
And young women should not enter a place only for men. Do you
have friends who plan to go? I was hoping you would find a job to
help out here.) Ramona's mother's response merely affirmed the
realities that women, especially Mexican American women, of the
1920s had to endure for another half-century: limitations on societal
advancement related to gender, social status, and money.

Ramona said, "Pues, sé que mis amigas como Ruth Zelman, Betty Johnson y Francina Harde tal vez vayan. Y pues, ya sé que no tenemos el dinero para mi educación." (Well, I know my friends Ruth Zelman, Betty Johnson and Francina Harde might go. And well, I know that we don't have the resources for my education.) A long pause followed. Her voice trailed and even broke. She added faintly, "Sí, ya encontraré un trabajo." (Yes, I will find a job.) The conversation ended with no further discussion.

Ramona served herself a bowl of fresh frijoles and tortillas and ate her lunch in silence, thinking over the prospects of education after graduation. The smiles and laughter of her friends who were headed to college no doubt punctuated her thoughts. These impulsive "flashes of the day" disappeared as quickly as the bowl of frijoles before her. Rooted in her Mexican upbringing, she knew her first responsibility was to her family. After finishing her chores, she flew out of the house, taking a bus to meet her friends in downtown El Paso.

During the Roaring Twenties, El Paso's downtown benefited from an economic boom, with the opening of clothing shops, banks, bakeries, cafés, and other businesses in and around the city's historic San Jacinto Plaza. That thriving economy didn't necessarily benefit everyone, however. As a single mother, Ascención needed help supporting the family. In her advancing years, she could only clean homes or sell beans and tamales for so long. With or without much formal education, Mexican American families were often left out of the prosperity. Mexican women, in particular—who had less formal education than the men did—often worked as domestic employees or did food preparation or laundry work. None of these options helped them get ahead economically.[4]

Ascención had done what she could for Ramona to get a high school education. She graduated from El Paso High School in 1925, at a time when a diploma in the hands of a Mexican American woman was indeed a rare possession. With this educational attainment alone, she raised her family's social advancement position by a large margin; she now had the skills to become an accountant. Those skills allowed her to seek work at places beyond El Paso Laundry where her sister, Juana, worked or to toil as a maid in Sunset Heights, making less than a dollar a day. In the weeks after graduation she found a job as an accountant at Given Brothers Shoes downtown.[5]

Amid the bustle of downtown life in the 1920s Ramona met and fell in love with Manuel González, a salesman at Tres B Department Store and a Mexican immigrant from Zacatecas. His immediate family of five orphaned siblings fled to the United States during the Mexican Revolution. Immigrating at the age of seventeen, he adapted but never fully assimilated to the American way of life. Ramona's *mexicana* side mixed with her American roots attracted him; she carried sensibilities from both cultures, speaking Spanish, being hardworking, independent, honest, and dedicated to family. Living along the Mexican border, Manuel sought a companion that could both appreciate his *mexicanidad* and help him navigate American society and culture.

Equally smitten, Ramona introduced Manuel to her mother. He won over his future Mexican mother-in-law with his *mexicanidad*— his easy politeness and earnestness to work, coupled with smooth and flowery conversation in Spanish. His tall, slender build, black slicked-back hair, a wide and welcoming smile, framed with a long, slim face and dark brown skin, captured both mother and daughter's attention. He carried the best of both sides of the border—a barrio-rooted, blue-collar sensibility mixed with a Mexican educated flair. The courtship began slowly, but it wasn't long before Manuel proposed marriage.

In September 1930, a year after the Great Depression hit, Manuel and Ramona started their life together in their house on Campbell and Montana Streets in central El Paso. Following Mexican custom, the couple lived with Manuel's family, which included his four

Ramona and Manuel González
as newlyweds on the banks of
the Rio Grande, ca. 1930.

sisters—Pepa, Lala, Lupe, Toña—and Lupe's son, Armando. Life seemed to settle into an easy routine. Three of the sisters worked, while Toña took care of Armando and did the housework. Manuel and Ramona commuted to their downtown jobs. The Depression's effects, however, lurked behind everyday and major decisions.

Miedo y riesgo / Fear and risk

In 1931, with the excitement of her marriage diminishing, Ramona could not find sleep for several nights. News on the streets and in the papers reported the looming economic fallout from the Depression. People she knew began losing jobs they once thought stable. Friends lost their house cleaning jobs, and some even continued to work for no pay. Now desperate, people in the barrios looked for whatever work they could find: cleaning houses, selling used goods, shining shoes, delivering newspapers, washing cars, picking up trash, even occasional begging in the streets. Ramona writes in "Mi tiendita" that "there was also plenty of time to spare, but there was nothing to do. Jobs were scarce. The employment offices were packed with people, and they were even lining up outside, and the lines were endless. Groups of men could be seen on the street corners, waiting to be hired, but there was nothing to hire them for."

My grandparents experienced the Great Depression differently. As a Mexican citizen, Manuel quickly lost his job and became one of many unfortunate men who could not find new work. He regularly crossed into Ciudad Juárez to work, including baling hay or cleaning restaurants. After six months of looking, he landed a job as a shoe salesman at the Popular, the main department store downtown. As an educated American citizen, Ramona was more secure in her employment. She managed to keep her job and save a little every month. The Depression, however, quickly became the least of her worries.

By 1931, social uncertainty and distrust in American society had spread beyond the economy, almost like a cancer. Ethnocentric, scapegoating Americans began claiming that the Mexicans were taking jobs from white men. The same hysteria spread through California and Texas where Mexican American populations had always resided. This rhetoric brought tense moments of fear to the streets and into the homes of Mexicans and Mexican Americans across the Southwest. Francisco Balderrama notes that "with the deterioration of the United States economy after 1929, between 400,000 and 500,000 Mexicans and their American-born children voluntarily returned to Mexico. More than half of these departed from Texas."[6] Regardless, authorities quietly coordinated repatriation plans to deport Mexicans in an attempt to mitigate the effects of joblessness among white Americans.

In El Paso, Anglo-American households and businesses relied heavily on the cheap domestic and industrial labor of documented and undocumented Mexicans. They held jobs in the laundries, on the railroad, in the emerging Farah clothing factory, and at the

Asarco smelter. Even with the huge reliance on Mexican labor along the US-Mexico border, immigration authorities deported large numbers of Mexicans. Unskilled and semiskilled Mexican and Mexican American workers would be denied the better-paying jobs as xenophobia surged across the United States during the Great Depression. Balderrama says that "the massive deportation dragnet struck terror in Mexican communities across the nation."[7] This news was often underreported in local papers but spread quickly through the Mexican American communities.

A conversation with Luzita, a friend who had recently returned from Los Angeles, struck fear into my grandmother's heart. At a chance meeting, Luzita shared the following story: "No puedo creer la suerte que me tocó. No fui ese día a la placita por tener que cuidar a mijo. ¡Y qué bueno! La migra bloqueo las salidas de las calles y juntaron casi 400 personas, todos mexicanos, y los mandaron pa´tras a México." (I can't believe how lucky I was. I did not go to La Placita that day because I had to take care of my son. And what luck! The border agents blocked the exits of the streets and gathered almost four hundred people, all of them Mexican, and sent them back to Mexico.)

As Luzita spoke, Ramona saw the look of fear flood her eyes. "Ay, Ramoncita, por favor, cuídate y también a don Manuel y sus hermanas. He oído que lo mismo está pasando aquí en El Paso." (Oh, Ramona, please take care of yourself, don Manuel, and his sisters. I have heard the same thing is happening here in El Paso.)

Ramona's hand slowly covered her mouth in disbelief, and she responded between breaths, "*¡Ay, Luzita, que terror!* Espero que tu familia esté bien. Sí, nos cuidaremos mucho. Muchas gracias." (Oh, Luzita, what terror! I hope your family is well. Yes, we will take great care of ourselves. Thank you so much.)

This was how Ramona learned of the Mexican repatriation and deportation raids being waged against Mexican Americans in California and beginning to occur in Texas.[8] These raids were not well reported, if they were reported at all, but she kept this information in the back of her mind. Despite the news, she proceeded with her plans. The González household would be spared the fate of deportation, but news of these efforts to deport Mexicans no doubt unsettled them.

Ramona continued to work at Given Brothers while Manuel worked as a shoe salesman and his sisters did odd jobs to make ends meet. Like so many other Mexican Americans in the El Paso barrios, the oldest sibling, Pepa, crossed daily into Juárez to teach at a school. Occasionally, the government there did not pay teachers as Mexico was also suffering from severe fiscal austerity. Lack of reliable pay only heightened the family's financial anxiety. With dire circumstances gathering like a Texas summer storm, the González household struggled to make ends meet. Ramona knew she needed more.

Decades later, Ramona recalled the Great Depression in family stories. She learned countless lessons from witnessing her family persevering. To make ends meet, her mother opened a portion of their adobe home as a store to sell tacos and household items. Ramona noticed small grocery stores opening around the barrio and downtown. As a second-generation Mexican American, blessed with an education, she knew she needed to take a different path. She believed the family could increase their income if they applied themselves. In her midtwenties, married with a child, and in the trough of the Great Depression, Ramona would take some risk and become an entrepreneur.

One afternoon in 1934, she told her husband over lunch, "Don Manuel, tengo una idea."

"¿Dime, Ramoncita, qué piensas? Qué rico tu caldo, ¿eh?" (Tell me, Ramoncita, what are you thinking? Your soup is wonderful.) As he enjoyed her *caldo*, he asked Ramona to go on.

"Quiero abrir una tiendita de abarrotes. Y antes que me digas no, escúchame." (I want to open a small grocery store. Before you tell me no, hear me out.) She commented on the trend of stores opening and being successful. "Hay varias tiendas que han abierto en Segundo Barrio. Por ejemplo, he visto Abarrotes Faro ya ha crecido mucho. ¡Creo que abrieron en 1919 y andan muy bien!" (There are several stores that have opened in Segundo Barrio. For example, I have seen that Abarrotes Faro has already grown a lot. I think [the store] opened in 1919 and is doing very well!)

Doña Ramona's suggestion to open a grocery shifted to a personal plea: "Me acuerdo bien de que mi mamá abrió una tiendita chiquita en Chihuahuita cuando era niña. También nos hizo mucho bien. Realmente, nos salvó." (I remember well that my mom opened a little store in Chihuahuita when I was a child. It did us a lot of good. Really, it saved us.)

Not wanting to risk losing the gold and little money they had saved, Manuel responded, "Ramoncita, me gusta tu idea, pero si no te has fijado estamos en medio de una gran depresión económica, y no podemos ver el final de esto." (Ramoncita, I like your idea, but if you haven't noticed, we are in the middle of a great economic Depression, and we can't see the end of it.) He kept eating as they spoke.

Their debate deepened. Ramona reminded him that they could rent a house and convert it to a store with their savings. "Mira, Manuel, tenemos $158 en dinero americano. Con este dinero, podemos rentar una casa que vi de renta en la calle de Missouri y Ochoa." (Look, Manuel, we have $158 in American money. With this money, we can rent a house that I saw on Missouri and Ochoa Streets.)

Ramona painted an idealistic image of how the young couple could blend business with living at home. "Lo de al frente tiene espacio amplio para un lugar donde vender abarrotes y comida preparada. Lo de atrás, se puede usar como nuestra habitación." (The front has ample space for a place to sell groceries and prepared food. We can use the back as our home.)

Rubbing her growing belly, she winked and said, "¡Pepa y Lala

pueden vivir con nosotros y cuidar los niños que seguramente vienen!" (Pepa and Lala can live with us and take care of the children
who are surely coming!)

Reluctantly, Manual wondered aloud, "Suena como buena idea,
Ramoncita, pero ¿cómo vamos a manejar todo?" (Sounds like a good
idea, Ramoncita, but how are we going to manage everything?)

Ramona did not concern herself with the impracticality of the suggestion. She saw the possibility. She said, "¿Y qué es 'todo'? ¡Tenemos
una buena oportunidad para empezar un negocio! Y ya sabes, todos
tienen que comer. ¿Qué no?" (And what is "everything"? We have a
good opportunity to start a business! And you know, everone has to
eat! Why not?) She persisted, adding, "¿Qué dices, Manuel?" (What
do you say, Manuel?)

Manuel didn't answer immediately. He took a few weeks to think
through the proposal and talked to his sisters, friends, and neighbors.
Coworkers at the Popular reminded him that the Depression's effect
on incomes everywhere would mean store customers might not be
able to pay for their goods. He was still skeptical, unconvinced of the
potential of his wife's proposal. The couple had more conversations
about finances, living arrangements, and the what-ifs of the venture.
Resisting any pessimistic urges from Manuel or his sisters, Ramona
finally persuaded her husband to invest their savings and open what
would be called González Grocery. From then on, Manuel placed
complete trust in Ramona's judgment and determination.

González Grocery opened on July 4, 1934. Although business
started slowly, with many customers indeed buying on credit, González
Grocery became the heart of the El Paso community. It served about a
two-mile-square block: the community north of the Southern Pacific
railroad tracks and Missouri Street, south of Arizona Street, and east
of Campbell Street including Ochoa, Virgina, and Saint Vrain Streets.
Close to their homes, people in the area grew to rely on the store's
varied services. All four of Ramona's children—my mother, Sandra;

González Grocery at the corner of Missouri and Ochoa Streets, ca. 1942.

Norma; and the twins, Manuel Jr. and Ismael—worked in the store, learning the value of hard work and thrift. Norma, who worked there on Saturdays, remembered her father telling her, "We don't cheat our customers. Yes, we make a profit, but not by cheating them." With Ramona managing the receipts and money, González Grocery would become a trusted community store known for reasonable prices and being a place to congregate.

Ramona gained a reputation as a cook, meat butcher, accountant, teacher, and even community counselor. She never shirked from helping families, extending store credit when other businesses refused, serving as interpreter of city ordinances, and even blessing the children of barrio families before World War II. In an interview, my *tía* Norma said, "Ramona did not use rationing stamps during the war. That was too white and too rigid a system. She went by who needed what." González Grocery served the small El Paso community for almost thirty-five years. After the family closed the business, the building became the Mormon's Bishop Storehouse, where the church collected and distributed food for those in need, and served as classrooms for Mormon Bible study, which Ramona taught for five years.

My grandmother's civic leadership and community role highlights the González family's civic contribution to El Paso from the 1930s to the 1960s. According to friends and family, she was a steady presence in the store. She could be seen waiting behind the counter for customers, walking the aisles, answering customers' questions, recommending items in both English and Spanish, and listening to customers' news reports. When the state purchased the property in 1964 under eminent domain, as part of the federal highway interstate program, my grandmother did not consider the destruction of her store as progress. In "Mi tiendita" she shares how the loss of the grocery store destroyed part of the barrio she and her community knew and loved. While grieving those necessary losses as El Paso grew into a regional city, her descriptive writings of that place and time remind us of who we are, where we come from, and where we are going—our collective ancestral remembering.

Cuentos del barrio/
Stories from the Barrio, Part II

"Mi tiendita"
"My Little Store"

As with the first story of this book, "Por vida de estas santas cruces," "Mi tiendita" is a first-person account of the people of the community where González lived. Shifting among El Paso neighborhoods, the story takes the reader to the doorsteps of González Grocery on the corner of Missouri and Ochoa Streets, just north of the railroad tracks. "Mi tiendita" opens in El Paso in 1965 with González standing in the checkout line at one of the new grocery stores. Amid flashy signs, newfangled products, and people filling their shopping carts, she experiences a pang of disconnection from the store's slick modernity and buzz. Disappointed, she gets into her car and drives off, not knowing her destination. She wrote, "Dejé atrás todo lo enorme y grande; me perdía en esa inmensidad." (I left behind all that was huge and big; I was lost in that immensity.) This feeling of being lost and disinterested in the presence of social change takes her to the literal edge of self-destruction. She can no longer return home to González Grocery. It no longer exists. Instead, she drives to a construction site along the newly built Interstate 10, where she contemplates the destruction and transformation of her community: the sidewalks, the gated homes, the front patios, and gardens. González sees the place where she had once lived and thrived as now only a pile of dirt.

Early in the story, González once again invites her muse, *su memoria*, to reconstruct the now demolished community. She flashes back to 1934, the year she and Manuel opened the grocery. Readers relive some of the many interactions with the many lively customers—Chana, Pancho, Correo, Rubén, Chorty, don José, and more—that brought her peaceful and festive days, the struggles to make ends meet during the Depression, and rationing during World War II, and, ultimately, the closing of the grocery. We are invited into the intimate, and sometimes painful, details of the lives of people from the grocery store's neighborhood. As a point of comparison to American literature, "Mi tiendita" parallels the play of *Our Town* by Thornton Wilder that brings the audience up close to the everyday people of Grover's Corner.

Doña Ramona González—wife, grandmother, and community pillar—earned the love and trust of an El Paso community both self-aware and proud of its heritage. "Mi tiendita" captures *el corazón*—the heart—of a time and place that no longer exists but whose heartbeat lives on today.

Mi tiendita

¡El supermercado era inmenso! Los anuncios multicolores sobresalían. Las líneas de casilleros repletos de botes de diferentes alimentos. Cómo admiraba yo la grandeza de esta tienda. Sus carteles modernos, adornados con brillantes colores, presentaban ciertos productos y parecían verdaderos platillos de comidas muy apetitosas, que tenía uno que comprarlas para saborearlas. ¡Cómo cambió todo!

Al tiempo de entrar, llevaba yo ánimo y confianza, mas cuando saludé a los empleados, ellos respondieron forzadamente. Me sentí desairada y olvidé parte de lo que quería comprar. Empujaba yo mi canasta lentamente, mas las personas, quienes estaban apresuradas, tomaban latas o cajas y sin más, las aventaban en sus canastas y seguían en su afán. Parecían robots (autómatas de formas humanas) desinteresados y fríos. Canasta daba contra canasta, empujando para salir pronto. Contemplaba todo esto con asombro.

Aquí nadie me conocía, ni había con quién hablar. Reinaba el sonido de latas o frascos al caer en las canastas, al igual que el sonido de registros marcando las compras. Después me acerqué a la cajera para pagar, y fue lo mismo, ni una sonrisa ni adiós, y mucho menos gracias. ¡Me dio escalofrío! ¡Qué extraño este ambiente!

La apuración de la gente me llevaba como corriente de agua en la arena. Los empleados sacaban las bolsas de mandado arrebatadamente y los clientes apresurados detrás de ellos. No quedaba tiempo de platicar ni de darles gracias. ¡Tal vez se imaginarían que esto quitaba el tiempo! ¡Yo no comprendía! ¡Qué complicaciones! Los trabajadores, aseados y peinados, al parecer muy competentes, mas se mostraban indiferentes.

Dejé atrás todo lo enorme y grande; me perdía en esa inmensidad. Me subí en mi auto. Arranqué sin rumbo. Me sentía desanimada. La tristeza me ahogaba. De repente me di cuenta adónde me dirigía. ¡A la tiendita! Qué alegría sentía. Quería darle la última visita. La alegría fue pasajera, pues el lugar en donde había existido la tiendita estaba cubierta de montañas de tierra y había quedado enterrada debajo de la monstruosa carretera. Hubiera querido introducirme debajo de aquella montaña para volver a sentir aquel gozo de nostalgia que sentí cuando vivía en la tiendita.

Las maquinarias gigantes movían la tierra y la dejaban caer en aquel lugar de tantos recuerdos. Las temerosas grúas, con sus cadenotas, daban ruidos ensordecedores. Luego al otro lado de la carretera, el tren daba aullidos largos y tristes, y más aumentaba mi pena, porque aquel lugar ya estaba despoblado y lóbrego. Se acabaron las casas de los que fueron amigos, clientes y vecinos. Se acabaron también los jardines, junto con las cercas desquebrajadas.

Cesó el movimiento brusco. Reflexioné. El tren pasó y descansaban las maquinarias y grúas. Luego fue un silencio. ¡Que alegría sentí! Por mi mente se pasaban acontecimientos ensoñadores.

¡Empecé a desenterrar la tiendita!

Recorriendo el desfile de los años, me intriga aquella vida en la tiendita. Vidas familiares, amistades íntimas y más que todo la de los vecinos, clientes y no clientes, a los cuales apreciamos con todo corazón. Había algo en común, en aquellos tiempos, que nos unía a toda esta gente, y esto era la escasez de trabajo, la pobreza y la inquietud por falta de dinero. Nos procurábamos los unos a los otros para compartir de alegrías y pesares. Sobre penas, angustias y dificultades, aprendimos a congeniar. Para mi esposo, mi familia y para mí, fue una escuela que nos enseñó y nos dio madurez para cruzar las márgenes con más facilidad cuando hubiera nuevas márgenes que cruzar.

La tiendita nació en esos años de intranquilidad e inseguridad. Cuando primeramente abrió los ojos, fue en un barrio pobre, desconfiado y desconocido, mas esperábamos mucho de ese caserón tan grande, destartalado y enfermizo.

Nuestra esperanza en vencer la escasez era la tiendita, y teníamos la confianza que no nos quedaría mal. ¿Qué si hablara la tiendita? Nos dijera, tal vez, con mucha razón, "¡Qué traje tan grande me ordenaron; quizá muera antes de estrenarlo!" Mas yo contestaría, y le contesto, con orgullo y satisfacción, "Lo estrenaste, ¡se te ordenó otro más grande y creciste a llenarlo por todos lados y luego para arriba!" Pues la tiendita llegó a ser "La Tienda" grande del barrio. Para surtir ese caserón, recorrimos por toda la ciudad en busca de enseres. Algunos amigos de mi esposo habían clausurado sus tiendas de abarrotes y pudimos conseguir vitrinas, mostradores, una hielera y una báscula, y de pilón nos dieron los casilleros de madera; pues decían los tenderos, "¿Ya pa´ qué los queremos? Ya no sirven."

Pagamos por los enseres $50 y era necesario tazar el poco capital que nos quedaba; todavía había que comprar los comestibles y artículos de primera necesidad. Invertimos otros $50 en abarrotes y solicitamos crédito por otro tanto.

Cuando cayeron en cuenta nuestros amigos de que abriríamos una tienda de abarrotes, vinieron a la novedad. "¿Oigan, qué de veras piensan abrir una tienda de abarrotes?"

"Ya empezamos, miren", tranquilamente contestábamos.

Tercos y dudosos continuaban, "¿No saben que están cerrando diez tiendas de abarrotes por mes aquí en la ciudad?"

"No, no sabemos."

Impacientes con nosotros, continuaban, "Ustedes no saben nada de abarrotes, están locos, ¡de veras!" Y nos advirtieron, "¿Qué no se dan cuenta que hay una depresión?"

Ciertamente no sabíamos nada del negocio de abarrotes, ni tampoco de depresión. Únicamente nos dimos cuenta de que el trabajo estaba sumamente limitado y era difícil encontrarlo. Mi esposo fue uno de los primeros en perder su empleo, mas aprendió el trabajo de dependiente trabajando en una tienda propiedad de una familia judía. Esto nos hacía pensar que deberíamos de hacer algo, y pensamos en una tiendita.

La apertura de la tiendita fue el día 4 de julio de 1934, el cual dijo mi madre que era de buen agüero. Malaya ni se acordó la gente de la tiendita. No se pararon ni moscas ese día. Al día siguiente nos dice una vecina, "¿Por qué no fueron al Parque Washington? Estuvieron tan buenos los lonches, sodas, ¡ay, nos dimos vuelo! ¡Todo nos dieron de violín, nieve, dulces y galletas!"

¿Quién se iba a acordar de la pobre tiendita?

Más tarde, nos dicen, "¡Oye, Raymon, si vieras, ¡qué suave estuvo ayer que fuimos al parque! Nos dimos un 'treat', pero padre. Nos hartamos de todo lo que nos dieron, fíjate, sandía, melones y sodas; comimos hasta que nos llegó al gaznate." Ofelia estaba toda quemada del sol de julio, pero satisfecha de haber ido a la celebración del cuatro.

"Oye, y tronamos cuetes hasta que nomás", continuó, dichosa.

¿Mas de compras? ¡¡Nada!!

Pensábamos en lo que nos habían dicho las amistades, y aún más, nos esforzábamos a que la tiendita fuera un éxito, pese al acosamiento. Era preciso que insistiéramos para que la tiendita tuviera vida, pues la vida de la tiendita era la vida de todos nosotros.

También pensábamos cómo podríamos atraer clientela. A los pocos que iban, les ofrecíamos lo que teníamos con sonrisas y ánimo, y les mostrábamos buena voluntad para chicos y grandes.

Mi esposo ideó en una manera para tener más negocio. Llamó a los muchachos de la vecindad y les dijo, "Muchachos, les juego a los 'checkers', ¿qué dicen?"

Animados, contestaban, "Seguro, don Manuel, nomás no nos haga jale." Al rato se amontonaron los chamacos.

"Muchachos, les voy a jugar a lo parejo." Mi esposo los dejaba ganar, por supuesto, sin darse cuenta los chamacos. Lo que ganaban era un dulce, y cuando mucho, una soda.

Al siguiente día venían los padres o madres con don Manuel. "Don Manuel, me fía, ¿qué dice si le pago el día que raye?" Les fiábamos, casi todos pagaban, y a uno que otro les teníamos que cobrar, pero pagaban.

La tiendita guardaba los secretos, tribulaciones, gozos y quejas de las personas que la frecuentaban. Uno de los primeros clientes de la tiendita fue "el Chorty"; le decían así porque era muy bajito, muy chaparrito, sin embargo, muy trabajador y ahorrativo. Chorty trabajaba con el ferrocarril, el cual quedaba a una cuadra al sur de la tiendita, en la "casa redonda", casa para servir a las locomotoras. Él hacía el aseo de las vías y yardas. Para las cinco de la mañana, ya él estaba trabajando. Usaba pantalones de mezclilla, los cuales le quedaban muy "guangochudos", y una cachucha que le daba hasta el cogote. Andaba siempre con la carrucha colmada de piedras y palos que recogía en la limpieza de las yardas y vías.

Entraba a la tienda a refrescarse y siempre le hacía cariños a mi hijita de un año de edad. "¿Quieres que te baile la botella?" la preguntaba con una sonrisa alegre. La niña le movía la cabecita que sí. Chorty se quitaba la cachucha, se alisaba el pelo y se ponía una botella de leche vacía en la cabeza y con una mano en la cintura y otra moviéndola como ala, bailaba la botella. No pasaba tiempo en que se oyera, "¡Muchachos, muchachos, Chorty está bailando la botella!"

Los muchachos corrían y con agitación esperaban que de un momento a otro la botella se estrellara en el piso. Realmente era una sensación ver al hombre ponerse la botella y bailarla sin que se cayera.

Los compañeros de trabajo de Chorty lo apreciaban. Era muy cumplido y nunca dejó de trabajar. Lo más curioso de este hombre fue que al cabo de los años, él ya pensionado, todavía iba muy temprano a hacer la limpieza de las vías del tren. Los compañeros, los cuales eran todos anglos, decían, "Chorty, vete a tu casa; ya no trabajo." El nomás se reía y al siguiente día allí estaba muy de mañana en el trabajo.

Un día llegó a la tiendita medio triste y me dijo, "Señora, si me hace el favor de llenarme estos papeles, están en inglés y no sé qué quieren que yo haga". Me relató lo que había sucedido.

Chorty y su esposa fueron a darse un paseo a México y optaron por llevarse una colección de monedas de oro, americanas y mejicanas. Cuando regresaron, la inmigración se las decomisó. Nadie sabía de esta colección; tenía ya años juntándolas. Las monedas de oro y cualquiera otra cosa de oro fueron prohibidas, y aun poseerlas era contrabando. El gobierno federal quitó la circulación del oro, mas Chorty no se dio cuenta porque no sabía leer ni escribir, ni en inglés ni en español. Le escribí cartas y llené blancos para que le devolvieran sus monedas, pero nunca las volvió a ver. Chorty no murmuraba nada.

Cuando recién abierta la tiendita, una mañana temprano, mi esposo estaba con la espalda a los mostradores de dulces, galletas y otras golosinas cuando vio de reojo salir corriendo a un muchacho. Mi esposo lo siguió. El muchacho llevaba puños de dulces. Fue mi esposo con la madre, la cual le dijo, "No tengo tiempo de chismes. Vaya con la abuela, lo tiene muy chiple, a ver qué hace."

"Pepino se llevó unos dulces del aparador, Chalía, dice su mamá que le diga a usted." Mi esposo lo dijo como que fuera broma, y así lo tomó Chalía, diciendo, "Carajos muchachos. Mire, don Manuel, otra vez que hagan esto, dígame, don Manuel, yo le pago. Diantre de diablos."

No era gran cosa lo que se llevó el chamaco, pero podía llegar a más si no le parábamos el alto. Pero nunca se repitió esto, pues era buena familia y hasta la presente llevamos buena amistad con todos.

Chalía, la abuela, fue también una de nuestras primeras clientes. Tenía el defecto de ser coja, mas era de buena salud. Dios la guarde en su seno, era muy franca. Decía, "Ustedes no tienen el sagú que a mí me gusta. Ordénenlo y se los compro. Me gusta mucho esta tiendita". Ella fue también la que nos dio la primera orden grande; siempre fue un gozo atenderla y platicar con ella.

Chalía fue nuestra primera cliente/amiga y fue la última. Recuerdo cuando habíamos ya clausurado la tiendita, pues la compró el "Highway Commission" y por allí pasaría el "Expressway", que fue una de las carreteras más grandes que se ha visto en El Paso. Chalía nos hablaba por teléfono (pues ya teníamos ese lujo), y nos decía, "Ramoncita, quiero un botecito de esos ejotes que ustedes tenían y un botecito de caldo de gallina, pero que estén buenos. Ustedes ya saben, nadie más que ustedes saben lo que a mí me gusta". Lo comprábamos en otra tienda, no obstante. Chalía ya tenía más de cinco nietos y otros tantos bisnietos. Ya estaban ancianitos Chalía y su esposo, y sus nietos la comprendían. "Cómo es necia esa vieja, parece que todo mundo está a su disposición", decía Felisa, con gesto de grande disgusto, cuando se encontraba a Chalía en la tiendita.

"¿Que no los cansa?" insistía Felisa. Nos sonreíamos. Insistía otra vez y teníamos que decir algo. "Mire, Felisa, hay un dicho que dice, 'El que tiene tienda que la atienda; si no, que la venda'". Y tomábamos la conversación como broma. Luego ya platicábamos de otra cosa y se retiraba aplacada y de buen humor.

Felisa era una mujer muy alta y muy delgada, por lo tanto, se notaba huesuda. Tenía cinco hijos y un marido rezongón. Todo le parecía mal y nunca entablamos conversación ninguna. A pesar de que era viejo, ni su propia familia le daba gusto y nunca se paró en la tiendita. Su mujer, Felisa, iba a disipar de los malos ratos que él le daba. Ella compraba lo que al marido se le olvidaba, y siempre él compraba los comestibles. Con los años Felisa adquirió crédito en la tiendita y compraba suficiente, pues ya la familia era mucha.

Los hijos de Felisa iban a la tiendita para que les ayudáramos con sus tareas de escuela, la matemática y gramática. Los padres no entendían ni jota de inglés y se impacientaban con ellos, y Felisa los mandaba conmigo. Yo estaba capacitada para ayudarles con sus estudios, había graduado de El Paso High School. Después ya no venían llorando por los regaños de los padres; venían contentos cuando necesitaban la ayuda. Cuando los vecinos se daban cuenta, ellos también mandaban a sus hijos a que les ayudara.

Pasado un día de Navidad, llegó Felisa a la tiendita, muy triste, y dijo, "Mire lo que me regaló mi hijo y mi nuera". Era un par de zapatos de un estilo antiquísimo. "¿Qué, no hubiera podido regalarme otra cosa mejor?" Los aventó en el mostrador con desprecio.

"Felisa, tal vez no tienen lo suficiente para un regalo mejor".

"Sí, tienen, y saben lo que quiero, pero es la mujer la que compró estos zapatos, yo estoy segurísima. Pero ni crean que me los voy a poner, no tienen chiste". Felisa se sentía lastimada y en realidad quería mucho a su hijo, pero no a la nuera.

Si acaso la tiendita estaba menesterosa de negocio, no faltaba quien la colmara de conversaciones alegres, cuentos y picoteos. En esos años gozábamos de tiempo como para despilfarrar y por lo consiguiente, había tiempo para dar oído a las lamentaciones y apuraciones, y no se diga a chismes.

Una noche de invierno, oímos golpes fuertes en la puerta de la tiendita y se oían gritos alarmantes. "Por favor, ábreme la puerta, don Manuel, ¡por vida suya!" Corrimos, abrimos la puerta. Era una de las vecinas. La conocíamos bien. Entró como relámpago, despavorida, con el pelo alborotado, y trataba de esconderse. Detrás de ella, entró otra vecina y le gritaba con ira, "Diablo, te voy a alcanzar. No le abra don Manuel, no la deje entrar, a esa hija de un tal por cual". Se echaba encima para seguir jaloneándola, pero mi esposo la detuvo. Estaban cansadas; habían correteado algunas cuadras.

Quedaron contemplándose la una a la otra, parecían perros y gatos, gruñendo y listas para agarrarse y desgreñarse. Mi esposo les dijo, "Apacígüense, muchachas, tienen niños, vale más que ya no se peleen. Dejen de estar en esa condición. Miren como vienen. No permitan que sus hijos las vean así; después será penoso decirles qué pasó".

Se aplacaron, y después de oír otros consejos, se fueron de una por una. No se atrevieron a salir juntas. Las conocíamos por muchos años, y a sus maridos también. Siguieron casadas con los mismos maridos y tuvieron más hijos, y al parecer se mostraban muy dichosos. Así aprendíamos de la naturaleza humana.

Como en todos los barrios y vecindades, siempre hay muchachos y muchachas. En este barrio abundaban y si hiciera lista de todos los vecinos conocidos, tendría que escribir un libro. Mencionaré los más inolvidables y destacados acontecimientos de algunos de estos.

Rubén, el de sobrenombre "Jotinche", contaba únicamente con diez años de edad y era un muchacho muy precoz. Tenía ojos enormes y pelo abundante y ondulado. Su cara era redonda y con labios gruesos y desdeñosos. Era hábil y listo para observar, averiguar y, no se diga, para poner sobrenombres a todo mundo. Me ayudaba a entretener a mi hija, paseándola en su cochecito, mientras yo me ocupaba en otros quehaceres, y cuando mi esposo estaba fuera de la tiendita. Este muchacho tenía mucho amor propio, por lo consiguiente era muy honrado. No era capaz de tomar nada de la tiendita; yo tenía toda confianza en él.

Siendo que fue en verano cuando abrimos la tiendita, Rubén se pasaba horas platicando o dando detalles de todos los vecinos que vivían en el barrio. Vivía una familia numerosa, los cuales eran todos muy bajitos de estatura, y él les dio el nombre de "tepocates", y además eran muy prietitos y salían en cantidad a jugar afuera. También había otros muchachos. Vivían en la casa enseguida de Chalía. Eran de hombros inclinados y les puso los "sapos". Por más que insistíamos que no diera sobrenombres, o apodos, más adrede lo hacía. Después nos acostumbramos a estos apodos y fueron aceptados, aun el de él mismo, Jotinche.

Una tarde llevó a sus hermanas para que las conociera, las cuales eran muy bonitas de cara, ¡pero las piernas! ¡Qué piernas! Zambas, hasta decir basta; parecía que habían sido criadas estribadas en caballo. También Rubén me contó que su padre trabajaba en el Banco de Juárez; esto lo oyó una de las vecinas, con el apodo de "Correo del Bravo". Juárez es una ciudad hermana de El Paso, Texas. Todos los días el padre de Jotinche se iba en el tranvía a su trabajo, mas no sabíamos cuál era su oficio. Era buen hombre; únicamente tenía el defecto de gustarle el vino.

El Correo del Bravo era el nombre de uno de los periódicos mejicanos y por eso se le dio el nombre a la vecina de Correo. Llevaba y traía las noticias, por no decir chismes. Rubén y Correo se tenían mala idea, sospechaban uno del otro, y nosotros, de malos, decíamos que estaban en competencia, a cuál más, cuál menos.

Correo era achaparrada y rechoncha, ojos grandes y claros y daban miradas maliciosas. Tenía dos hijos y un marido holgazán y ella le decía "huevón" cuando se disgustaba con él, y "tiene callos en las nalgas". Nomás estaba leyendo los periódicos y revistas, y con sarcasmo decía que "vivía de sus rentas". Ciertamente a este hombre nunca se le conoció trabajo ninguno, nada más el de la parranda.

Yo adivinaba y acertaba cuando Correo tenía algún cuento de chisme. Se mordía las uñas hasta llegar a la carne y siempre andaba con los dedos sangrientos y más cuando no podía desembuchar lo que traía dentro. Rentaba tres o más apartamentos para poder vivir y mantener a su familia. Ella hacía todo el aseo y pintaba, destapaba los resumideros y sembraba su jardín. Tenía dos o más jaulas de pájaros, y todavía tenía tiempo de saber de las vidas de otros. Me daba asombro.

La mayoría de los vecinos rentaban uno o dos cuartos para poder ayudarse. Las casas eran viejas y tenían varios cuartos, y los moradores de estas casas se reducían a lo menos que podían para sacar con qué pagar la renta, el agua, luz y gas, o el petróleo, que era lo que la mayoría de la gente usaba, estufas de petróleo.

Les daré un por menor de cómo vivían los vecinos en ese tiempo. Los vecinos de la acera de enfrente rentaban a tres diferentes personas, los que seguían más allá de los de Correo, la cual familia se componía de ocho hijos los cuales eran huérfanos de padre y la madre trabajaba para mantenerlos; a ella también le fiábamos y era buena paga. Pese a ese familión, todavía rentaba dos cuartos. Los padres de Jotinche, aparte de sus tres hijos que les quedaban, tenían para rentar un cuarto más, a una muchacha que se las daba de artista y que tocaba el piano, quien enseñó a Jotinche a tocar algunas piezas de música, por supuesto, muy sencillas. Jotinche también aprendió de ella dos o tres bailes; el que aprendió mejor fue "La carioca". Lo bailaba muy lucido.

Chalía, ella no rentaba, sino que allí vivían su hijo y toda su familia. En la casa enseguida de Chalía vivían los "sapos". Esta familia era numerosa, sin embargo, allí vivía un compadre, su esposa y un hijo. Pasando esta, estaba una familia, y tenían un padre que no se le conoció ningún vicio, excepto el de no trabajar. La esposa se oía seguido, "Quería rentar un cuarto", pero él no la dejó, porque como él decía, "No tenemos necesidad de rentar, yo trabajo y a mi familia no le falta nada". Y nunca rentó cuartos.

En esos años, casi no había familia que no rentara uno o dos cuartos, porque si al jefe de la casa le faltaba el trabajo, era una desgracia, y ahora si le faltara un esposo a una madre con familia, huérfanos de padre, se morirían de hambre. Nadie de las que conocimos, quienes no tenían trabajo, llegó a tal grado. Trataban de hacer lo mejor que podían, como lo hizo la madre de los que vivían enseguida de Correo. Tenía una hija de quince años, muy bonita y graciosa, según decía Correo.

"¿Qué no saben que mi vecina de enseguida casó a su hija con el gringo, dueño del 'filling station'?" Realmente todos estábamos azorados.

"Pero ese viejo le sirve de abuelo", dijo la nuera de Chalía.

"Tal vez a la otra la case con el árabe de la tienda de ropa".

"Nadie sabe lo que hay en el costal, solo el que lo carga".

Comentarios que, si los hubiéramos visto de otro punto, hubiéramos comprendido lo que sufría esta familia. Una niña de ocho años no iba a la escuela por cuidar de los otros chiquillos, que siempre se veían flacos, mugrosos y de pilón eran peleoneros. Después que se casó la hija mayor, se aliviaron algo las penas. El yerno era buena gente con la familia de la esposa. Todos los cuñaditos ayudaban en el trabajo de la gasolinera y el hombre no ha de haber sido tan viejo, puesto que la esposa tuvo hijos de él, y para el pesar de algunos vecinos, los chiquitillos eran güeros y bien parecidos.

No era fácil para la gente rentar cuartos de sus casas, pues trataban de hacer su vida, aunque batallaran para congeniar con los inquilinos, que seguido abusaban de la bondad de los que rentaban.

Esto me recuerda de una señora, Elena, persona tan fina, y como suele decir, "buena alma". Ella parecía no conocer el enojo. Un día fue a la tiendita, muy acongojada y desanimada, y me confesó, "Raymon, figúrese que la inquilina que tengo, usted ya la conoce, es sola, y por compadecerme de ella, le renté el cuarto más grande. Ella no tenía hielera y mi hijo me regaló una, nuevecita, para la Navidad. Otra vez me compadecí de ella y la dejé que pusiera su leche fresca que le traían de un rancho, porque la de la tienda no servía, y se la traían cada tres días. Mire, usted Raymon, ¿cree que yo soy injusta? Luego para acabarla de moler, trajo a otra hermana a vivir con ella, porque la hija ya no la aguantaba en su casa, y sin decirme a mí, también trae su comida a mi hielera y fueron y sacaron mi comida y pusieron lo de ellas. ¿Cree usted que esto es justo?" Elena me contó esto pausadamente.

No sabía yo qué contestarle a esta mujer tan bondadosa y tan servicial. A la inquilina junto con las hermanas, tenía otra más, las conocía de mustias y santiguadas. Realmente eran malas por la simple razón de que no tenían necesidad de rentar de esta pobre mujer Elena un cuarto cuando una de ellas tenía una casa grande y la rentó para ir a vivir en el cuarto que no tenía ni hielera ni calentador. El hijo de Elena se dio cuenta de lo que hacían estas viejas, y las echó para fuera, pero no se fueron hasta que le dieron una buena maltratada a Elena. Y de ribete, le robaron a Elena cosas que ella les había prestado mientras que vivían en el cuarto. Mucho sufrió Elena con esa gente.

Un día Correo entró a la tiendita, muy horonda y con una sonrisa maliciosa, y me dijo, "Oiga". Siempre empezaba su conversación así.

"Oiga, Raymon, ¿qué es que dice Jotinche que su papá trabaja en el Banco de Juárez? De veras, cómo le gusta a ése recargárselas. ¡Se parece a la madre! ¡Es puro barrendero de pisos en el banco!" Y soltó la carcajada, haciendo cimbrar a la tiendita. Pareció que la risotada había llamado a Rubén, o este ya la traía entre ojos, y la estaba espiando. Finalmente, los dos se enfrentaron cara a cara. Jotinche ni siquiera parpadeó. Se le notaba a Rubén la cólera por encima, y en esos momentos, no temía ni a los toros de lidia. Me supongo que este sospechó a Correo de circular el chisme de su padre, de que trabajaba en el banco. Y sin chistar y de mal talante, se estacionó en la tiendita hasta que Correo salió con su sonrisa y mirada de coyote.

Al siguiente sábado en la tarde, Jotinche entró encarrerado, tratando de esconderse. Detrás de él, uno de los hijos de Felisa, quien era muy chiple y buscaruidos, se detuvo en la puerta y le gritó para provocarlo.

"Jotinche, anda ayúdale a tu papá. Ya viene haciendo culebrillas y se le van cayendo todas las tortillas en la banqueta. Ándale".

Esta explosión le prendió un cuete a Rubén. Los ojos le saltaban y echaban chispas, y contestó, "Qué te asustas, Cabezón, ¿no te veo que tú le ayudes al tuyo cuando viene borracho y lo tienen que sostener para que entre a tu casa? ¿Eh? Y a él se le caen las botellas de cerveza, ¿eh? ¿Eh?"

El Cabezón le dio un cerrón a la puerta de la tiendita, como si le debiera algo la pobre puerta destartalada, mas no contestó. El piquete le dio en donde más le pudiera doler. Rubén era un diablo bien hecho cuando se trataba de pelear con palabras, porque con los catos era correlón. Cabezón era muy llorón, y con lágrimas y el moco colgando se fue lleno de cólera. Rubén se sentía avergonzado por la burla de su padre, y se escondió detrás del tanque de petróleo hasta que notó ver pasar a su padre. Callado y de mal humor, salió lentamente de la tiendita.

Los padres de la vecindad eran, a cuál más, cuál menos, gustadores de beber. Por los sábados en las tardes, unos porque tenían con qué embriagarse y otros porque les gustaba andar de coleros, hacían desfile. Pasaban por en medio de la calle, por las banquetas, hablando tontería y media. Lo curioso del asunto que causaba tanto entretenimiento a toda la vecindad era que al levantar la mano para maldecir o hacer oraciones elocuentes imaginarias, no podían sostenerse y se daban contra el suelo. Nadie los ayudaba a levantarse y se iban a gatas y como podían, hasta que se enderezaban solos.

Entre estos ebrios que hacían sus peregrinaciones cada sábado, había un sastre con cinco hijos, un encalador muy alegre y otro encalador que se vanagloriaba de ser pintor, un borracho de diario, y, de ribete, holgazán; su mujer le decía el "huevón". Otro era un curro a quien se le veían lápices detrás de las orejas, en los bolsillos de la camisa, otros en la bolsa de pecho del saco, mas no sabía ni siquiera poner su nombre, y cuando, según él, se le subían las copas, ¡¡jamás era la cerveza!! ¡Era el vino! De todos modos, se bambaleaba y por más que se esforzaba, no dejaba de estrellarse contra las paredes y cercas de las casas. Verdaderamente era un convite el que presenciábamos en los sábados por las tardes.

Debemos de darle mención honorífica al marido de Correo del Bravo. Éste no hacía desfile, sino que hacía parranda por días, y todo el barrio se daba cuenta cuando regresaba...Las chanclas, los pantalones y otras pertenencias de él estaban regados en frente de su casa, mas Correo no chistaba nada de esto. Y decía Jotinche, "Huh, de eso no se hace reportaje", mofándose y con gozo impúdico.

Rubén siempre andaba esperando su chancita para la venganza. Él sufría de estimación inmoderada de sí mismo. Se sentía ofendido y buscaba satisfacción de su agravio. Llegó la hora de la represalia.

"Oye, Raymon, a que no sabías que el marido de Correo era contrabandista". Fue tanto la sorpresa que me causó mareo. "No", contesté, y con risa satírica, sutilmente continuó. "Yo sé que no sabías nada de esto y más si quieres, también estuvo en la cárcel y lo iban a deportar". Realmente yo no sabía ni jota de este asunto; naturalmente no había qué comentar. Rubén sentía cierto gozo en la chismografía.

Pasaron unos días y volvió a la tiendita. Noté que estaba de buen humor y pensé darle consejos. No mencionando nombres ni casos, le dije, primeramente, que debería tratar bien y respetar a su padre, y sin más ni menos, me contestó, más bien dicho, repostó, "Yo, ¡¡¿yo ayudar a mi papá cuando viene todo borracho por la calle?!!" Se mostraba altivo y con desprecio continuo, "Huh, nunca. Prefiero no comer tortillas. Que se lo lleve Judas. No se le quiere quitar esa maña de beber, pues que se caiga, a mí no me importa." Se fue enfurecido.

La tiendita hacía pininos y daba sus pasitos. Se animaba más el negocio. No obstante, las ventas eran de centavos, mas mi madre me decía, "De grano en grano, llena la gallina el buche". Así era ese tiempo, las cosas no costaban mucho pero no había con qué comprarlas.

También había mucho tiempo de sobra, mas no había qué hacer. Eran raros los trabajos. Las oficinas de empleos se repletaban de gente y todavía hacían colas afuera, las cuales eran interminables. Grupos de hombres se veían en las esquinas, esperando que los ocuparan en lo que fuera, mas no había en qué ocuparlos.

Pasaron años con la escasez de trabajo hasta que el gobierno federal halló la manera en qué emplear a los hombres y mujeres necesitados. La gente aceptaba el trabajo que fuera, pues no era según sus capacidades. Esto me trae a memoria una americana. Ella había sido gerente de una compañía de préstamos, y yo trabajé con ella en la oficina como su secretaria. Llegando la Depresión, clausuraron la oficina, no obstante, era una de las más prestigiadas del estado.

A cuatro cuadras de la tiendita, hacia el oeste, el gobierno abrió una oficina para solicitar trabajadores. Esta americana tenía que pasar por la tiendita para llegar a esta oficina. En una de estas pasadas, llegó a tomar un refresco y nos reconocimos, platicamos. Llorando me contó a qué grado había llegado en empleo. "Yo ya vivo sola, porque mi madre, a quien tú conoces, fue a vivir con mi otra hermana y yo, ni casa ni trabajo tengo. Figúrate, ¿a dónde crees que me mandaron a trabajar, estos infelices, desgraciados? En una fábrica en donde separo hilachos, garras y otras cosas que realmente ni quiero mencionarlas. Siendo que yo puedo desempeñar trabajo de contadora o puedo tener otro trabajo de categoría. Ahora trabajo con negras, filipinas, mejicanos, borrachos, viciosos, ¡¡y no sé quién más!!" Lloraba a mares. "Pues, necesito el sueldo, aunque es realmente una miseria, pero ¿qué puedo hacer? Tengo que vivir".

Me compadecía de mi patrona de hacía ocho años. Así era el tiempo.

Había padres de familias quienes ya conseguían únicamente dos o tres días de trabajo, y tenían gusto tener esos días de ocupación, aunque el sueldo era poco, mas era un sueldo seguro. Las mujeres de casa lo hacían rendir, economizando todo lo que podían, comprando de diario sus provisiones, y en verdad, no había con qué comprar para una semana.

Volviendo a las ventas de centavos. En esa época se compraba algo con un centavo, es decir dulces, pero señores dulces, como los de orozuz, que eran unos chirriones de a yarda, y duraban tanto como una chupaleta de dulce que dura un día chupándose. Un centavo compraba una galleta de maíz o un marranito, tan sabrosos, por cierto, que ya no los hacen lo mismo. Con tres centavos se compraba una lata de leche y en especial dos por cinco centavos. Piezas de pan francés calientito. Por tres centavos se compraban en la tiendita, a las cinco de la mañana, leche fresca con la crema encima a la pinta. Es por esta razón que digo que las ventas de la tiendita eran de centavos.

Hablando de centavos, recuerdo de una negrita muy viejecita y muy, pero muy gordita, la pobrecita. Hacía grandes esfuerzos para andar; no obstante, vivía una media cuadra de la tiendita, se tardaba en llegar. Día tras día llegaba a la tiendita a comprar una pieza de pan francés o dos panes de huevo y una lata de leche chica. Cuando le entregaba el cambio, siempre le regalaba a mi hijita, a quien yo cargaba en los brazos, un centavo y le hacía cariños en su pelo negro y brilloso.

Todo ser humano tenemos algo de fetichismo, eso es superstición. Y yo no era la excepción. Se decía que un regalo de una gente negra era buena suerte, y naturalmente todos creemos en la buena suerte. Y los centavos que la negrita le daba a mi niña se los guardaba en un bote. Tal vez fue la suerte, pero al cumplir mi hija un año, tenía ya lo suficiente para poderle comprar una póliza que a los veinte años recibiría un pago de $500, lo cual recibió.

La infeliz negrita vivía sola y tal vez sufría de alguna enfermedad, porque realmente era dificultoso para ella andar. Los muchachos del barrio corrían cuando se acercaba. Sin embargo, ella nunca maltrató a ninguno. Siempre saludaba y sonreía, mas nadie le contestaba. Era una cosa notable cuando acariciaba a mi niña, su voz sutil y dulce, y con sus manos y dedos ya viejos, arrugados y cenizos, le alisaba su pelo sedoso. Y en torno, la niña le daba una sonrisa de inocencia y dulzura. La negrita murió sola en su cuarto que le rentaban. Y la encontraron dos o tres días después que había muerto.

Había días en que las comadreras tenían una afinación mutua, parecía aconsejarse. Relatos de pleitos, necesidades, tristezas y gozos y no se diga de sacar la garra. Era el colmo en la tiendita. Si hubiéramos podido pasar en una grabadora todos los cuentos que se oían en esta tiendita, hoy causarían chiste y serían una gracia, verdaderamente.

En este día traían unas tijeras muy filosas y la que pagó el pato fue una vecina, quien ni se metía con alma creada, muy trabajadora y muy caritativa. La cuñada de ella fue la que empezó el recorte. Animadísima les dice a las que estaban en la tiendita, en la hora que iban a comprar para hacer la comida, "Muchachas" (eran un montón de viejas), "qué les cuento, ¡la Nena fue a rejuvenecerse!"

Estalló una bomba en los oídos de las lengonas que estaban con hambre de oír un chisme. "¿Qué dices?" preguntaron al mismo tiempo, y se juntaron a hacer bola, como los futboleros cuando se juntan a aconsejarse para su siguiente jugada. Así estas mujeres tenían un "huddle", y más cuando se trató de la Nena, la cuñada de la que relataba el cuento.

"Figúrense, tiene moretones en la frente y detrás de las orejas. Les digo esto y casi no lo creo, pero no tiene ni una arruga en la cara. Espérense, espérense. La pobre no ha salido para nada, ya va en seis meses, porque los moretones no quieren desaparecerse".

Las risotadas y los comentarios hacían temblar las ventanas de la tiendita, y se oían a una cuadra de lejos.

"¡Oye, platícales cómo se viste la Nena!" preguntaban a la cuñada.

"¡Nomás la vieran!" Y se ponía las manos en la cabeza y no podía contarles porque no podía contener la risa, y las demás junto con ella. Se calmaba y seguía. "Miren, se pone una bata, pero fina, no crean, color morado, larga, luego se anuda un listón amarillo, amarillo canario, eh, en su pelo, oigan, oigan, estilo Cleopatra". Esto causaba risas a San Antonito, decía una vecina. Les corrían las lágrimas de risa, y seguía la confusión, pues todas querían dar su opinión o preguntar algo.

"Esperen, eso no es todo. ¡También se pone unas pantuflas amarillas y negras enlazadas con cintas amarillas!" Imagínense a la cuñada con la mano en el aire y otra en la cintura, ojos restirados mirando al suelo, pasearse por toda la tiendita, la cual gozaba de bastante espacio. Más risas y aplausos. Era un espectáculo que jamás he visto en mi vida.

"Oye, oye, ¿qué no dicen que tiene al pobre marido embrujado?"

"Déjenme contarles". Se hicieron bola otra vez para oír el secreto. Mas de repente se oye un grito penetrante, "Amá, Amá, dice Apá que le vayas a dar de comer, que no te tardes, tiene mucha hambre, ¡Amá!"

"Válganos, y no tengo nada que darle al viejo". Apuradísima, dice,

"Raymon, Raymon, dame una pieza de pan francés y un bote de frijoles, y apúntemelos. Hasta ese se me olvidó". La cuñada, todavía con lágrimas en los ojos, y riéndose, salió corriendo de la tiendita con la comida para su esposo.

"Pero no se le olvida el chisme de la cuñada", repeló Correo.

Estas mujeres hacían recorte de todos, y la que encabezaba no era otra más que Correo. La tiendita presenciaba toda clase de discusiones sobre enfermedades, pero el tópico predilecto era el del mal sobrepuesto, o es decir la brujería, el cual era interminable.

"Te digo, Chana, que dice la viejita Rosita que lo tiene pero bien embrujado. Rosita dice que ella no miente. Cuando trabajaba con Nena, fíjate, por eso dejó el trabajo, que ella misma, Rosita misma, recibía los sobres de polvos y que Nena se los daba a su marido en la cara de Rosita, ¡en el desayuno del pobre hombre! ¿Qué no te has fijado cómo está la pobre garra de marido? ¡Todo trasijado y pellejudo!"

El pobre marido igual que su mujer no se metían con alma creada, como dije en antes, y todas las viejas chismosas los traían en enjuagues. Y si acaso se rejuveneció la cara, también las fuerzas, porque cuando ya todo el barrio estaba en oscuras, las ventanas de la casa de Nena estaban alumbradas, ella planchando uniformes para entregarlos temprano en la mañana. El marido también no faltaba al trabajo, y él nunca hacía convite en los sábados. Trabajaba en una imprenta.

Los cuentos que se oían en la tiendita eran fantásticos.

Medio barrio ponía apodos y sobrenombres al otro medio. Chana era una mujer gorda y con ojos semejantes a los de toro, grandes, con pestañas gruesas, sin inclinación ni torcedura, mas era buena alma. Chana tenía una hermana muy simpática y bonita de facciones, y por x razones no se había casado. Chana se impacientaba con su hermana.

"No sé, por qué no se casa Nena [otra Nena] yo le doy consejos, pero ya la ven, seria, no ve ni para un lado ni para otro. Me canso en decirle, 'No te aplomes, Nena, no seas miedosa y huraña, así nunca se consigue marido', pero como si le hablara a la pared".

"Chana, Nena es muy bonita muchacha, tal vez no quiera casarse".

"Ora, ¿qué mujer me dan que no quiera casarse? Yo no creo que no quiera casarse, a Nena lo que le pasa es que es muy tonta. Le digo que cuando salga a algún paseo, que salga como el que sale a torear, saleroso y altivo, luciéndose". Chana se paraba en medio de la tiendita y echaba los hombros gordos atrás y llena de vanidad daba pasos de coqueta; realmente nos daba risa de verla. Luego decía, con postura de una española que va a salir bailando, "Que salga como toro en plaza". Se le bautizó como "Toro en Plaza". La Chana se murió y la hermana de Nena se fue de monja.

El pulso de la tiendita se precipitaba y se bajaba con las pláticas que a menudo la gente relataba. Es con diversión que nos acordamos del caso de un vecino joven recién casado. Pancho vivía en frente de la tiendita, con los suegros y su mujer. Le nació la primera niña, y como es natural para todo mejicano, siempre esperan el primer hijo que sea varón. Se sentía lastimado y por lo consiguiente de mal humor. No saludaba a los vecinos por días. Pronto se llegó la segunda espera. Otra vez Pancho esperaba un hijo, mas no fue así. Fue otra niña y nos dábamos cuenta porque llegaba a la tiendita y no saludaba. Lo hacíamos repelar y le picábamos, preguntándole, "¿Qué fue, Pancho?" Contestaba, voz ronca, y mal encarado, "Otra vieja".

Así pasó, la primera, segunda, tercera, cuarta y quinta, cinco niñas, y para él todas eran "viejas". Su mujer era finísima persona, sumisa, y estaba dedicada a su familia de niñas, las cuales eran amables y muy hermosas muchachas. Las vestía de lo mejor que podía en los domingos y mandaba a Pancho a que las llevara a misa.

Pancho no fue a trabajar por una semana. Esperaba a la zancuda por sexta vez y terco todavía que "sería un hijo". Esa mañana, fue muy temprano a la tiendita, cosa rarísima que fuera a esa hora, pero la mañana estaba hermosa y parecía que se sentía la atmosfera con mucha alegría. Cuando entró Pancho, ya no esperó que le preguntáramos qué había sido, sino con una cara sonriente y llena de orgullo y júbilo, dijo muy claro, "Ahora sí tengo un hijo, Raymon. Es hombre, está tan bonito, quisiera que todo el mundo lo viera". La sonrisa y el gozo de este hombre le dio un cambio notable; ya no era el de enantes, fastidiado y de semblante agresivo. Todos compartimos de esta felicidad. No fue el primer hombrecito; su esposa tuvo dos más. Ea una familia muy bonita; sus hijas crecieron muy hermosas todas. Así corrían los años, ya de subida y ya de bajada.

Pasaba el tiempo y la Gran Depresión seguía en su apogeo. Todavía el trabajo estaba escaso, y por lo consiguiente la tiendita sufría grandes apuros y luego venían los aprietos. Las alas del corazón sufrían caídas que al parecer no se recobraría, mas no dejábamos que se desanimara, y pensábamos cómo darle aliento.

Mi esposo consiguió unos agentes de anuncios, para que, en los días de fiestas especialmente, la adornaran con papeles de China. Cubrían las ventanas con listones de colores y se presentaban los productos atractivamente. Y así ya ponía la tiendita otra cara más alegre.

Tratando de fiestas, en particular la de Navidad, el negocio era triste. Las festividades dejaban a los pobres padres sin un centavo, y como decía mi madre, "Quedaban más arrancados que la manga de un chaleco".

No pagaban las cuentas, y decían, "La tiendita que se espere". Se apretaban el cinto, mas no dejaban a sus hijos sin juguetes. Se repetían estas cosas año con año, y fiesta con fiesta.

Y mientras, pensábamos que la predicción de los amigos se cumpliría. Luego no faltaba quién la alegrara y le diera esperanzas de vida, y vida abundante. Esto no era fácil, soportaba tanto sacrificio y privación. Los hombres padres de familias, pese a todo, pasaban meses sin recibir sueldo seguro. Y cuando nosotros nos sentíamos inquietos por el negocio malo de la tiendita, ya llegaba algún cliente que nos contaba alguna novedad, como cuando encontraban trabajo ya fuera hijo o esposo. Nos alegrábamos por este acontecimiento, tan sencillo, al parecer. Así se pasaban los días y los años intranquilos y de vez en cuando animados.

Recuerdo de un caso de una negrita a quien conocimos con el nombre de Katie. Vivía a cuatro cuadras rectas de la tiendita y se decía que tenía más de cien años, y no es de dudarse. Las uñas de las manos y de los pies me daban achinamiento del cuerpo cuando las miraba. Las de las manos parecían zarpas viejas y de un color plomizo y muy ásperas. ¡Jamás había visto tal cosa! Esta negrita era muy abusionera. Llegaba y se paraba enfrente o en medio de la tiendita, veía para los lados, luego cerraba los ojos y empezaba a decir, "Aquí no hay espíritus malos. Es casa buena". Era lo único que le podía entender en su letanía y en sus invocaciones. Al principio causaba temor y más cuando traía la cabeza amarrada con una garra roja chillante; realmente daba la apariencia de bruja.

Seguido iba a la tiendita a comprar diez centavos de queso amarillo, porque allí estaba muy sabroso y blandito. Si llegaba cansada, se lo comía sentada en frente de una de las ventanas, las cuales tenían marcos anchos y servían de asientos, y nos sentábamos muy a gusto.

En una de sus conversaciones, relataba que cuando era niña de cuatro años, el presidente Lincoln dio la libertad a todos los negros esclavos. En donde ella trabajaba su tarea era de ser compañera de la hijita del amo de la casa. La hijita tenía ocho años, y Katie tenía que hacer todo lo que la niña le dijera. En una ocasión la niña le dio de azotes y cuando el padre se dio cuenta, castigó a la hijita, diciéndole que ya no sería compañera de ella y ya no se permitía azotar a los negros esclavos, porque ya eran libres. La hijita se sintió frustrada al no poder hacer lo que aprendió siempre, azotar y flagelar a los esclavos cuando le placía. Después de su libertad, Katie quedó en la casa del amo con su madre, hasta que quedó huérfana. La veían bien, decía, mas nunca aprendió a leer ni a escribir. A los doce años fue a vivir con otra familia quien la enseñó el arte de adivinar, además de lo que ella ya sabía, el cual era de hechicera. Nunca se supo que ella causara un mal a alguien, ni de poner enfermedad a alguna persona. Tenía fama en la vecindad, pero de bruja. Notaban el número de personas que la visitaban para que les dijera la suerte, o algo que querían saber.

En una ocasión, la negrita Katie enfermó, y me mandó pedir que le llevara su mandado acostumbrado, el cual yo sabía. Por primera vez crucé el marco de su puerta. La cerca estaba bien atrancada, mas la pude abrir. Entré, rodeando tinas de agua limpia, según ella, para que no entraran espíritus malos a su casa.

Katie estaba acostada en una tarima que parecía obra maestra de lo que quedó de la antigüedad. El interior de la vivienda daba la apariencia de un museo de antiguallas. En una alacena, rara y vieja, había botellas, vasijas, y vasos que contenían menjurjes de diferentes colores y frascos con substancias de polvos en varios matices también. Parecían cenizas o carbones. Admiración me causó, pues los frascos, botellas y vasijas y otros objectos estaban bien colocados y limpios, pese a que la casa tenía piso de tierra y las ventanas con vidrios rotos y empañados. El techo era de vigas de madera, ya negra con descuido aparte del humo, y de donde pendían cortinas de telarañas, de viga en viga y de pared a pared.

Katie tomaba su alimento, una especie de harina de maíz, lleván- doselo a la boca con los dedos, largos y zarpeados. Yo ansiaba por salir rápidamente, mas ella me detenía hablándome, no sé de qué. Al salir de la vivienda extraña, me llevé mi buen susto. Durante el tiempo que permanecía dentro, no había oído ningún ruido, única- mente el que hacía Katie, el de murmurar, y cuando llegué al marco de la puerta, saltaron cuatro gatos negros maullando. Retrocedí, y vi a Katie sentada en su cama, con sonrisa de diversión, por el miedo repentino que me causaron los gatos. Y al verla riéndose toda desmolada, exponiendo una boca de caverna y una lengua inmensa roja, pensé, y dije, "Patas ¿pa´ qué las quiero?" ¡Y arranqué de allí y no volví jamás! Ella sí visitaba la tiendita seguido.

Pasaban los años y con ellos crecía la tiendita, y también nuestra familia se aumentaba, y naturalmente se aumentaba el trabajo. Nuestro afán fue de darle gusto a los clientes, aparte de venderles los mejores productos que teníamos. Insistíamos con todo el corazón en tener éxito. ¿Qué otra cosa podíamos hacer? ¡Nuestros únicos planes eran para la tiendita! Planes de tenerla siempre limpia, acomodando todo en orden y la mercancía nueva fresca y buena. Parecía fácil esperar a que viniera alguien, y a veces a que pasara algo, mas era difícil.

Aprendimos que aparte de tener esperanzas, era importante y necesario que hiciéramos otras cosas; nos podíamos aburrir con la vida monótona y lenta. Mi esposo ideaba para atraer más negocio. Ideó de tener en la tiendita "punchboards", que eran rifas en una tablita con números. Esto causó novedad, porque el primero fue un guajolote, pavo o "turkey", como le quieran decir. Recuerdo y me causa diversión cuando el primer Día de Gracias, "Thanksgiving Day", de la tiendita, se estrenó este punchboard, y era de cinco centavos el número (ponchada) y el que se sacara el número premiado se llevaría el guajolote. Tal vez mi esposo no sabía de aves para azar, pero tenía al pobre cócono colgado en medio de la tiendita, el cual causaba muchísima atención. Los chamacos mandaban a las madres a que poncharan un número, y en los domingos ellos tenían un "nickel" y ponchaban también su número. El total fue $2.50, el cual era un negocio magnífico, y más cuando se trataba de centavos. Me causa risa ahora, porque el cócono era una triste ave, flaca, larga y colgada en donde todos lo vieran. Me parece, como dicen los muchachos, "una puntada" grande.

Un día llegó Rubén muy contento y sonriente, preguntando, "Raymon, ya se llega el cumpleaños de la niña. ¿Qué no vas a tener un 'party'? Yo te ayudo si quieres".

"Sí, Rubén, pero no quiero que te pelees, y le digas a la gente que come mucho o a qué van. Aunque te diré que no tendremos mucho que comer, pero a ver qué hago". Rubén y yo nos entendíamos a perfección y si él me decía algo, él ya entendía que yo no divulgaba nada, y si yo le decía algo, entendido estaba que lo hacía, y lo guardaba, aunque con enojo y refunfuñón pero me respetaba y me daba atención. También se me pasó que no dijera a nadie del "party" y fue y lo anunció por todo el barrio. ¡Ya se imaginarán cuánta gente llegó a la fiesta! Fue una cosa fantástica.

Para sostener la estimación de los clientes, vecinos-no-clientes, amistades y desconocidos, a propósito, nos preguntaban, "¿Van a tener party para la niña?" y estábamos obligados a invitarlos. Primeramente, invitamos a los niños para la fiesta de la niña, que cumplía dos años. Vinieron tías, abuelas, primos, vecinos y conocidos de los vecinos, y los que no sabían, se iban con los invitados. Gracias, pues, gozábamos de un patio muy amplio, de tierra suelta y un poco de zacate. Los convidados no veían esto, sino lo que les regalaría de refrescos. Las abuelas no se avergonzaban porque traían a sus nietos, porque eran ellos invitados por otras vecinas, y decían con gusto, "Aquí venimos al chocolatito, sabemos que lo sirve muy sabroso". (Todavía tengo fama del chocolate.) Esta era y fue la única fiesta del barrio; acudían todos como si hubiera sido una familia. Reinaba la alegría. Pasábamos en veces apuros, porque no siempre contábamos con tanta gente, y más cuando teníamos que comprar cantidad.

Los chicos venían a romper la piñata y los adultos, al chocolate. Los chicos de diez para arriba se peleaban por los dulces o por los "balloons" que salían de la piñata. Esta fiesta la esperaban todos los vecinos cada año, pues era una fiesta de mucha alegría y de gozo.

Repito, para nosotros era un problema disponer de tanto refresco para todos los invitados. Con anticipación mi esposo buscaba baratas de dulces; en ese tiempo, recuerden que el azúcar estaba racionado, y era difícil conseguir dulces buenos, lo mismo con nieve y chocolate. De todas maneras, cumplíamos, y sentíamos de corazón una felicidad poder hacer esta fiesta cada año. Pasaron los años y recuerdo cuando nuestros hijos ya iban a la escuela, en una ocasión invitaron cada uno a los compañeros de sus respectivos salones, sin contar con nosotros. Pensamos y pensamos, hasta que optamos en rentar un camión de la ciudad, para que llevara a más de setenta y cinco alumnos de la escuela a un parque.

Allí tenían su "birthday party" cada año, y nomás una fiesta hacíamos al año. ¡Qué hubiera sido si hubiéramos celebrado en la casa! ¡Se hubiera caído! Después, no era problema los refrescos, el problema era en donde acomodarlos. El camión hacia más de dos viajes. ¡Qué alegría había!

Les daré una relación breve de un suceso que nos parecía muy curioso; aun todavía, pasan más de treinta años, y nos recordamos con nostalgia de esta persona. Nuestra casa necesitaba una pintada por el interior. Pensábamos poder conseguir a alguna persona quien hiciera el trabajo, primero en la sala grande, y luego ocuparlo en pintar la tiendita, que ya también necesitaba una mano.

Dos cuadras de distancia de la tiendita, vivía un hombre llamado José. José estaba mucho muy necesitado, y queríamos ayudarlo. Tenía un familión de siete hijos e hijas. Su mujer tenía ideas ilusorias, pues ella no debería salir a comprar a la tienda; era bajo su dignidad y mandaba a sus hijos a comprar lo más indispensable para tan numerosa familia. Así es que, marido y mujer hacían una pareja sin igual.

José era hombre honrado y bueno, y muy atento. Saludaba siempre y se detenía en su paso, se quitaba su sombrero, el cual estaba cubierto de cal y pintura, y de ribete, desgarrado. José era pintor y no parecía tener prisa ninguna. Mi esposo lo solicitó para hacer el trabajo, mas siendo los recursos cortos, deseábamos saber el costo.

Una tarde José fue a ver la sala. Mi esposo pensó que al verla José podía decirle el costo. Lejos de esto, José entró a la sala y mi esposo detrás de él. José contemplaba el cielo y las paredes, y andaba alrededor, calladamente.

"Don José, ¿cuánto me cobra por pintarme esta sala?"

José parecía que no tenía oídos, sin embargo, sus intenciones eran de trabajar, mas su manera de contratar negocios era rara. Al fin de darle tanta vuelta a la sala, ya mi esposo estaba borracho, como los caballos del malacate, y mi esposo detrás de él. "¿Cuánto, don José?" José no respondía. "Mire, don José, únicamente quiero que me encale o pinte esta sala, es todo. ¿Cuánto me cobra?" Sordo, José.

Seguía contemplando con calma el cielo y las paredes, ¿para qué? No sabemos todavía. Luego, se paró en medio de la sala, hablando en un tono extraordinario. Sus palabras acompañadas de ademanes flotantes, como si estuviera actuando un papel ilusionaría.

"Don Manuel". Él pausaba, miraba, no sé qué, luego decía con una expresión imaginaria de grandeza, "Mire, don Manuel, lo que quedaría muy hermoso en esta sala enorme y amplia sería un pintado estilo Luis de Catorce". Nos quedamos en amén. ¿Cuál sería ese estilo? Solo José sabía. Además, la sala era larga y pelona de decoraciones. Se impacientó mi esposo, y le preguntó, "Don José, únicamente quiero que pinte de cal o calsomina esta sala. ¿Puede hacerlo?"

"Don Manuel, como no, ¡es mi trabajo!" Se sonreía con buena gana. "Don Manuel, esta sala quedaría hermosamente presentada con una pintura jaspeada a colores pastel, ya que no quiere el estilo Luis de Catorce".

José seguía con sus palabras elocuentes y movimientos de brazos "Sería una belleza de admiración". Hablaba con franqueza y seguridad, mas no llegaba a un acuerdo de trabajo ni de cuentas.

Patéticamente notamos que no sería posible que José hiciera el trabajo, por más sencillo que fuera. Salió José, y todavía seguía con su estilo Luis de Catorce. Unos días después, el borrachito de enfrente de la tiendita, don Antonio, fue y se arregló con el negocio y en uno de sus días raros de sano, pintó la sala como la queríamos, en un solo día.

En los siguientes años la tiendita se lucía en estrenar. Primeramente, se le dio una pintura; ¡ya puso otra cara! Luego instalamos un teléfono, el cual no solo era para la tiendita, sino de toda la vecindad, día y noche. "Présteme el teléfono", para doctor, para conversaciones con amistades, parientes y varios, y de ribete, ¡¡para ordenar provisiones a otras tiendas de abarrotes!! Era el colmo. Parece cosa increíble, pero así fue.

Después del teléfono, se quitó el tabique. Se amplió el local y lo surtimos con más mercancías, según eran necesarias. También le compramos a la tiendita una hielera grande para los refrescos y un refrigerador para la nieve. La tiendita lucía con orgullo y satisfacción, un refrigerador moderno y elegante para toda clase de carnes. Años después se instaló un aparato de aire acondicionado. La tiendita ya había llegado a calidad de responsabilidad y madurez.

Llegó una mujer anglo al barrio y frecuentaba a la tiendita. Al principio únicamente llegaba a tomarse una Coca-Cola, diariamente, en tiempo de frío y calor. Elizabeth, al parecer, mostraba orgullo, mas ya cuando nos conocimos bien, no era así. Por medio de conversaciones y cambios de opiniones, llegamos a ser buenas amigas. Elizabeth tenía crédito en la tiendita y pagaba con puntualidad. Después llevó a su madre, su hermana y cuñado, también su esposo, y fuimos y somos muy buenos amigos. Hasta la presente, nos comunicamos por carta seguido.

Con el pasar de los años, un día llegó Elizabeth a la tiendita bañada en lágrimas. Ella siempre se guardaba discreta en asuntos familiares, mas me sentí que ella tenía confianza la suficiente para confiarme sus problemas y sentimientos. Su hermana, quien hacía corto tiempo había fallecido, le dejó a su cargo el niño único, para que ella lo criara.

El niño tenía únicamente escasos dos años. Elizabeth adoraba al niño siendo que ella no tenía hijos. El padre del niño, una persona excelente y astuto, consintió también en dejarle el niño a su tía, mas no dijeron o no llegaron a un acuerdo cuánto tiempo lo cuidaría la tía. El hombre, padre del niño, muy trabajador, no sabía del cuidado de niños, así me dijo él a mí.

En este día, Elizabeth no podía contener las lágrimas. Me dijo que su cuñado pensaba casarse. Detrás de Elizabeth, entró la madre de ella, viejecita muy sabia. En esto me estaba Elizabeth diciendo.

"Mrs. González, yo sé que el niño no es mío, pero lo quiero tanto que no sé qué haré si se lo lleva su padre". Y más lloraba.

La madre de Elizabeth, con calma y abrazando a su hija, me dijo, "Mrs. González, yo sabía y todos sabemos que algún día, George se casaría. Él no sabe de cocina, ni de casa, menos de niños. Le he dicho que yo, por mi parte, no me disgusto si él se casa. Pero Elizabeth no quiere escucharme, mírala cómo se pone, y ya tiene días así". La madre hablaba con naturaleza y sin agitarse.

"Mrs. González, tú sabes más que nadie cómo quiero a este niño, y ¿si se lo lleva su padre? ¿Qué hago yo?" Se mostraba muy emocionada.

"Elizabeth, yo estoy segurísima de que George no se lleva al niño. Ya tiene mucho tiempo con ustedes", yo les di corta opinión.

Mandó llamar al padre del niño, el esposo de Elizabeth, y él les dijo, "Yo no quiero llevarme al niño, quédense con él. Además, tengo otro trabajo fuera de la ciudad, y puedo venir a ver al niño cuando menos cada mes".

"Pero ¿qué si tu esposa quiere que tú te lo lleves?" Elizabeth quería estar segura.

"No, Libby", como George le decía, "ustedes lo conocen mejor que yo".

Pasaron intranquilos años, y el niño creció a un joven muy

simpático, pelo blondo y ojos azules como los de su madre. Cuando
Junior cumplió los quince años, tal vez, él notaba el temor de la tía,
de que él fuera a escoger irse con su padre y madrasta, los cuales
visitaban seguido a Elizabeth. Junior le quitó la duda para siempre.

"Mrs. González, ¿sabes qué dijo Junior?" Llena de alegría, llegó
a la tiendita un día, y me dijo, "'Tía, yo sé que siempre te molestas
cuando viene mi padre y madrasta a visitarnos. ¿Piensas que yo me
voy con ellos, ¿no? Yo te digo, tía, que yo me quedaré al lado tuyo y mi
tío y mi abuela, hasta que ustedes quieran. No conozco otra madre
más que tú. Los quiero a todos, pero a ti, como una madre'". Qué alegría sentía esta mujer contándome sus sentimientos. Esta vez lloraba,
pero sus lágrimas eran de gozo y dicha.

Elizabeth y su esposo se fueron a vivir a otra ciudad y también
el niño y la abuela. El joven Junior es un profesionista ingeniero, y
adora a su tía y la demás familia. Aquel niño con ojos azules y pelo
amarillo no parecía que aprendería algo. La tía me contaba antes
que se fueran que había veces que ella y su madre lo tenían que vestir
para que fuera a la escuela, pues era muy despacioso, igual que el
padre. Mas yo la animaba y le decía que no siempre eran así los niños,
que tuviera paciencia. Cuando él se graduó del colegio, me mandó la
primera invitación. Yo le mandé un regalito a él y una carta a su tía.

Me escribió ella y me decía, "No sabes cuántas veces he pensado en
ti, y a Junior le pongo el ejemplo de tus hijos, a los cuales él conoce
bien. Ahora me siento más dichosa porque ya él terminó su colegio.
Seguido nos acordamos de ustedes. 'Para mí la tiendita era como mi
casa', decía Junior. Y para todos nosotros también".

Así corrían los años, y como se dice, tiempos traen tiempos.

Estalló la Segunda Guerra Mundial, del día 7 de diciembre de 1941.
La tiendita se tornó en un cuartel general. Los clientes, especialmente las pobres madres que tenían hijos de diecisiete y dieciocho
años de edad, llegaban con grande aflicción, buscando el consuelo y

ánimo. Había en el barrio varias familias que tenían un gran número de hombres jóvenes. En realidad, no había familia que no tuviera hermanos, hijos, familiares de edades para ir a la guerra.

La tiendita ya no escuchaba chismes ni sarcasmos, ni picoteos de las comadreras. Ahora eran llantos, quejas y lágrimas, después pesares por la ausencia de sus hijos.

Entre los que fueron a prestar sus servicios a las fuerzas armadas fueron muchos de algunos que conocemos por medio de esta relación, como los nietos de Chalía, los hijos de Felisa, uno de los hijos de Correo, los del sastre, los del borrachito pintor, los tres hijos de la que se rejuveneció, Nena, y también los de la cuñada. También dos de los hijos de la viuda que vivía enseguida de Correo. Uno de ellos fue a la marina, y ya no lo conocíamos cuando volvió; era otra persona diferente, del cual su familia se llenaba de orgullo y gozo cuando vino a verlos. Otro fue el hijo mayor de Toro en Plaza, y sin olvidarnos del padre que trabajaba en el banco, quien era su hijo Jotinche. Y muchos otros más, como tres de los "sapos" y muchos más de los "tepocates". Todos muchachos buenos y pacíficos.

En esta época, recuerdo de un suceso del cual todavía nos recordamos cuando vemos al hijo de Correo, y él junto con nosotros hacemos finos recuerdos de esos tiempos. Cuando empezó la guerra en Europa, empezó también la persecución de los que favorecían a algunas de las naciones enemigas, siendo una de estas Italia. Recordarán que en algunos casos de familias, ya fueren alemanes o italianos, eran investigados y vigilados en sus acciones.

Pues un día escuchamos una algazara fuera de la tiendita. Todas las voces parecían hablar a la vez, y con curiosidad fui a la puerta a investigar. Sin más, entraron todos a la tienda, y el que hacía frente era Jotinche. Llevaba en sus labios desdeñosos una sonrisa de burla, y silencio, no habló.

"¿Qué es esto?" pregunté a un señor desconocido, pero muy vestido.

Entonces Rubén contestó, "Raymon, estos señores dicen que vienen del FBI y buscan a una persona llamada 'Mussolini'". Rubén sabía perfectamente bien quien era, pero quiso hacer "pedo" (dispensando la palabra), como todos ellos decían.

Correo tenía un hijo, y en una ocasión lo llevó a que le hicieran corte de pelo. Cuando volvieron de la peluquería, lo llevó a la tiendita y me dice, muy animada, "Mire, ¿a quién cree que se parece?"

Estaba en la tiendita Felisa y otras dos personas. Lo vieron y al mismo tiempo dijeron, "Oiga, ¿se parece en el peinado a Mussolini?"

"De veras que sí, muchísimo", dijo Felisa.

"Eso mismo digo yo, todo se parece a Mussolini. Lo bueno es que Mussolini está en Italia, si no, dijeran que era su hijo". Nos reímos de lo que decía Correo, y le volvió a alisar el pelo y le hizo el pico a un lado, y el niño, que tendría unos diez u once años, se lucía en esto.

Los agentes de FBI me preguntaron si conocíamos a alguien por ese nombre. Rubén se quedó serio; era muy mustio. Bajó la vista y le conocía que sé en ese momento estaba lleno de gozo y placer. Esperaba.

"Aquí en el barrio vive una persona con ese nombre", contesté yo, y pensé, "A ver hasta dónde llega este juego".

"Pedrito, anda y dile a Mussolini que venga a la tiendita, le voy a dar un dulce".

Corriendo salió Pedrito a hablarle a Mussolini. Todos esperábamos con sobresalto; la mayoría de los presentes sabían quién era Mussolini.

Al rato entró Correo y su hijo. Los agentes los vieron entrar, mas no sabían ni pensaban quienes eran.

"¿Qué quieren con Mussolini?" preguntó Correo.

"Estos señores quieren saber si alguien se llama Mussolini", anunció Rubén.

Correo tomó al niño de la mano y les dijo, "Este es Mussolini, pero ese no es su nombre, Mussolini es su sobrenombre". Le alisó su pelo y le hizo el piquito para un lado, y les dice, "¿Él no tiene parecido al hijo a Mussolini?'"

Los muchachos y la gente ya amontonada en la tiendita se rieron y los agentes se pusieron sus sombreros, me dieron las gracias. Se retiraron de mal talante, sin chistar ni una sola palabra más.

Cuando se acabó la algazara y se fueron las gentes, Mussolini se devolvió y me gritó, "Deme mi dulce. Dijo Pedrito que me daría dulce".

Mañana y tarde, era un tropel que hacía vibrar la tiendita. Ya teníamos dos empleadas en la tienda, junto con mi hija y mis dos hijos gemelos. Los gemelos, aparte de su trabajo en la tienda, tenían una ruta de periódicos en la mañana y en la tarde. Querían ellos guardar bastante dinero para ir al colegio. Ya tenían catorce años, un año menor que el hijo de Correo, "Mussolini". Mi esposo y yo abríamos la tiendita a las cinco y media de la mañana, para recibir el pan, leche y otra mercancía. Las empleadas llegaban hasta las ocho y media, ya para cuando llegaban, los muchachos del barrio se habían ido a la escuela. Quedaban únicamente los adultos y chiquillos que no iban a la escuela. Por unos momentos gozábamos de tranquilidad.

Más tarde llegaban las madres con sus letanías de lamentaciones. Ya una que se llevaban a su hijo, y otra al nieto o amigo, novio o hermano. No pasaba día sin que nos diéramos cuenta de alguien que se iría a pelear. Las escuchábamos y nos compadecíamos de ellas, mas también deseábamos que se terminara pronto, pues teníamos dos de quien dispusiera el ejército.

Los muchachos iban a la tiendita a platicarnos y decirnos que pronto los llamarían también a ellos. Les dábamos consejos que no se olvidaran de sus padres. Entre pláticas les hice una promesa, que todo aquel muchacho quien fuera a la guerra y se despedía de mí volvería con vida. Ya se imaginan cuántos muchachos fueron; unos los llevaban sus madres, otros sus tías, abuelas y amigos. Les diré que todos volvieron con vida, a Dios gracias. ¡Volvieron a la tiendita a darme las gracias porque estaban seguros de volver, pues yo les había dicho!

Uno de estos muchachos que le tocó ir al servicio primero fue uno de los nietos de Chalía. No quiso que lo fueran a despedir a la estación. Llegó a la tiendita muy triste, casi en lágrimas, temprano en la mañana. Lo conocíamos desde niño, y fue él que se llevó los dulces. De por sí, era medio tartamudo, y apenas me dijo, "Ya me voy, Raymon", con los ojos viendo al suelo e inquieto.

"Anda con Dios, que Él y sus ángeles velen por ti, y volverás con vida". Salió lentamente con su morral al hombro. Parecía cargar algo pesado. Su angustia me llegaba al corazón.

Parecía que la escasez se aumentaba. El gobierno federal se esforzaba en que todo hombre tuviera trabajo. Cuando se declaró la guerra, no quedaba hombre desocupado. Se establecieron fábricas, como nunca se había visto, por todo el país. La fábrica que sobresalía a todas era la de armas. Mujeres y hombres como enjambres se veían en camiones y camionetas ir a sus trabajos. La tiendita la traíamos a remolque y la guerra seguía en su pudor.

De noche la tiendita descansaba de las preocupaciones. Mas nuestra familia seguía ocupada dentro de la casa. El gobierno había racionado muchas cosas, y se necesitaban estampillas para comprar y vender mercancías. Había estampillas rojas, verdes y azules. Las estampillas que recogíamos en la tiendita, las teníamos que pegar en una hoja de papel, preparada para este propósito, para poder nosotros comprar. Sin estampillas no podíamos comprar cosas tan necesarias como azúcar y sus productos afines, grasas y aceites y sus productos, y también la ropa, pero lo que más se escaseó fueron los zapatos.

Otra memorable fecha, agosto 6, 1945, cuando estalló la bomba atómica en Hiroshima, otra aglomeración se juntó en la tiendita. La gente esperaba y necesitaban que les diéramos contestación a sus preguntas, pues sabían que nuestros deseos siempre fueron para darles consuelo y ayuda moral, en todo tiempo que necesitaran.

"Raymon, díganos qué es una bomba atómica. ¿No la echaron en donde está mi hijo?" Realmente nos daba compasión de más que nada, las madres con sus pesares y tristezas por sus hijos en los campos de guerra.

Escudriñábamos los periódicos americanos, y también revistas de todas clases, para darnos cuenta qué era una bomba atómica. Jamás, pero jamás, habíamos oído de átomos y menos de esas bombas, pese a que ya se sabía de átomos desde hacía más o menos veinte siglos [*sic*]. Si los periódicos o revistas no decían mucho del uso de la energía atómica, acudía a las enciclopedias para explicarles qué eran las bombas atómicas.

Fue una alegría grandísima cuando, a los pocos días, nos informaron que las paces estaban en tratado. La tiendita participaba de las tristezas de los clientes cuando se iban los muchachos del barrio, y gozaba de las alegrías cuando volvían con vida. Ninguno del barrio quedó en el campo de batalla; todos volvieron a sus hogares y a sus familias.

Durante los años de guerra, las comadreras ya no criticaban ni hacían chismes como antes. Correo, quien tanto quería a su hijo, me imagino al igual de otras madres, muy de madrugada salía a misa a confesarse y comulgar. También hacía vigilias porque volviera su hijo, el cual volvió en cuerpo y alma, bueno y sano. Gracias al Todopoderoso.

La tiendita de nuevo se tornó en "headquarters" cuando uno de los muchachos del barrio volvía de la guerra. Había abrazos, lágrimas y recuerdos de cuando eran niños y las travesuras que hacían, y de los dulces que compraban. Mas notaban que todavía había escasez de ellos por escasez del azúcar. Uno de ellos se acordaba que cuando no tenía centavos para comprar dulces, me decía, "Raymon, ¿quiero fiarte dulces? Te pago el día que le paguen a mi papá". Y el día que recibía el pago el padre, puntualmente iba a pagarme. ¡Él me preguntaba por qué no le había dicho por que lo llamaron así!

"Mira, ¿por qué crees que te decían el Cabezón? Porque no querías escuchar. ¿Te acuerdas cuando me dijiste que a tu papá le habían salido otros dientes? Y te dije que no podía, que solamente a los niños les salía dentadura, y te fuiste llorando, y decías, 'A mi papá sí le salieron, ¡él me los enseñó!'"

"Pero ¿cómo te pude decir eso, Raymon?" preguntaba Cabezón.

Cada mes llegaban uno o dos muchachos. Al ratito empezaban a llegar las invitaciones de matrimonios. Ahí me tienen a mí, haciéndoles bizcochos, cakes u otras galletas para las recepciones o para los "showers". Teníamos cariño para todos los vecinos y sus hijos. Al cabo del año o poco más, traían a sus hijitos a que los conociéramos. Luego, ahí va otro regalito, para los hijitos o nietecitos.

No se me debe de pasar contarles cuando regresó Jotinche. La casa en donde ellos vivían, la vendieron, y fueron a vivir lejos de nosotros.

Cuando se vio llegar a la tiendita y estacionarse un carro, flamante, todo mundo fue a ver quién era; no se conocía el que llegó. Rubén no era aquel de ropa pobre y mal ajustada, sino portaba un traje de un joven bien educado y de buen gusto. Le preguntábamos un retrete de detalles. "¿Qué hacías en la guerra, no nos digas que estabas en el frente peleando?"

Era el mismo que cuando estaba chamaco. "¿Yo, Raymon, peleando?"

Se las recargaba, ¡pero recargaba con garbo y mucho salero, que había servido como secretario de un general en Alemania! Sí, fue cierto. El mostraba seguridad y confianza en él mismo. Ya no tenía la actitud de un agresivo, y para todos eran cariños y sonrisas. En el ejército aprendió taquimecanografía, y hasta la presente, todavía hace este trabajo en la oficina.

"¿Qué pasó con el Cabezón, en dónde están los sapos?"

"¿Todavía no se te quita la costumbre de bautizar?" Era Correo.

Ya nos caíamos muertos, entre Correo y Rubén, abrazos fuertes, y rodaron lágrimas rechonchas como ella. ¡Qué contentamiento había en la tiendita! Ya no había sospecha ni crítica; tampoco había rencor. Había recuerdos, y más que todo la reconciliación, fue lo más bonito, y le daba al lugar un aire de felicidad y tranquilidad. Así iban acabando los años.

Era notable lo que había cambiado Jotinche, y era para su bien. Desarrolló una personalidad que atraía, instantáneamente. El traje de pantalón crema con rayas finas, color café, y una camisa azul claro y una corbata haciéndole juego. Zapatos en dos tonos, todo hacía verse que casaban bien.

"Rubén, ¿no te has casado?" preguntó Correo.

"¡Qué les cuento! ¡Ya por poco me casaba con una rusa! ¡Una mujer como no había visto en mi vida!"

"Cómo eres zalamero, Rubén", le dije.

"Pues, no lo crean. En una de las fiestas que dio el general, más bien era un banquete, pero qué banquete, fue en donde la conocí".

Cuando platicaba, los ojos se le hacían más grandes, y se notaban más grandes por los gestos y ademanes que acompañaban a la plática. Él se daba cuenta que yo sabía por qué se expresaba animadamente y con tanto ademán. Era con un propósito de llamar la atención, así era Rubén. ¡Quién nos hubiera dicho! ¿Quién hubiera, siquiera, pensado que cambiaría como ninguno de los que volvieron de la guerra?

Rubén, en llamar la atención, no había cambiado, y dudo que cambie. Para mí, él no podía fingir ni ocultarse, porque así era su carácter; yo lo comprendía y callaba. Él sabía. Cuando estuvo en Alemania me escribía cada mes o cada dos meses. Llegó aquí, fue a trabajar y me apuntó como referencia de carácter, y siempre le di buena recomendación. Nos quedamos mudos y leles cuando se despidió.

Los pitidos agudos de la locomotora terminaron el alegre ensueño de tan inolvidable recuerdo. Volví del letargo. Las maquinarias gigantes volvieron a sus tareas ruidosas y aturdecedoras. Me causó un dolor punzante, el tenerme que separar de aquel lugar.

El nombre de la tiendita está gravado en la memoria de los amigos quienes la conocieron a través de los años. Lugares como la tiendita pasaron al olvido o al recuerdo, y en donde hay recuerdo, se revive la vida. La tiendita se fue fuera de nuestras vidas, mas conservamos la memoria de ella, detalladamente.

Seguido me maravillo como aprendí de los clientes, vecinos y amigos de la tiendita. Recuerdos y conversaciones de ella nunca terminan.

Este no es relato de profundos problemas. Aquí se observó y se anotó la vida ordinaria, pobre y natural. No hay nada excepcional. Todo lo que pasó en la tiendita llenaría un libro y aún más. Los acontecimientos son verídicos, mas los nombres, algunos cambiados.

Nadie sabe en donde está la tiendita enterrada. Mis ojos están húmedos. Me despido de LA TIENDITA. Te dejo tranquila en tu tumba.

My Little Store

The supermarket was huge! Multicolored ads attracted my attention. The lines of shelves were filled with cans of different foods. How I admired the grandeur of this store. Its modern, brightly colored posters presented certain products as real dishes of appetizing foods enticing one to buy and taste them. How everything had changed!

When I entered, I had courage and confidence, but when I greeted the employees, they responded in a forced manner. I felt snubbed and forgot part of what I wanted to buy. I pushed my basket slowly, but people were in a hurry; guided by their eagerness, they grabbed cans or boxes and just threw them into their baskets. They looked like robots (auto-powered machines in human form), disinterested and cold. Basket bumped against basket in the push to get out quickly. I stared at all this with amazement.

No one knew me here, and there was no one to talk to. The loud sounds of cans and jars falling into the baskets, and the cash registers ringing up purchases, was overpowering. Then I approached the cashier to pay, it was the same, not a smile or goodbye, much less a *thank you*. It made me shiver! How strange this environment was!

The rush of people carried me like a stream of water in the sand. The employees frantically carried out the shopping bags and customers hurried behind them. There was no time to talk or thank them. Maybe they imagined that this was taking up time. I didn't understand! How complicated. The workers, neat and combed, were apparently very competent, but they were indifferent.

I left behind everything huge and large; I was lost in that immensity. I got in my car. I started off aimlessly. I felt discouraged. Sadness choked me up. Suddenly I realized where I was headed: To La Tiendita. What joy I felt. I wanted to give it one last visit. The joy was fleeting, because the place where La Tiendita had existed was covered with a mountain of dirt and buried beneath the monstrous highway. I wanted to bury myself under that mountain and feel the nostalgia for the joy that I felt when I lived in La Tiendita.

The giant machines had moved the dirt and dumped it in that place with so many memories. The frightening cranes with their huge chains made deafening noises. On the other side of the highway, the train made long sad howls, and my sadness increased, because the place was already deserted and gloomy. The houses of our friends, customers, and neighbors were no longer there. The gardens, along with the broken-down fences, were also gone.

As the sudden movement ceased, I began to reflect. The train passed and the machinery and cranes came to rest. Then there was silence. What a joy I felt! Through my mind passed events from my dreams. I started to unearth La Tiendita!

Going through the parade of years, I am intrigued by that life spent in La Tiendita. Family lives, close friendships, and more than anything, neighbors, customers, and noncustomers, whom we hold dear with all our hearts. There was something in those days that united us all, and that was the lack of jobs, the poverty, and the anxiety because of the lack of money. We looked after each other to share joys and sorrows. From our pains, anguish, and difficulties, we learned to get along together. For my husband, my family, and me, school taught us and gave us the maturity to cross over the borders more easily when there were new ones to cross.

La Tiendita was born in those years of uneasiness and insecurity. When it first opened its eyes, it was in a poor, mistrusted, and unknown neighborhood, but we expected a lot from that big, dilapidated, feeble house.

Our hope in overcoming the scarcity was La Tiendita, and we had confidence that it would not let us down. What if La Tiendita could speak? It would tell us, perhaps, and rightly so, "What a large suit you ordered for me—perhaps I'll die before I can finally fit into it and wear it for the first time!" But I would answer with pride and satisfaction: "You fit into it well. A larger one was ordered for you and you grew until you filled it from all angles, side to side and up and down." Well, La Tiendita became La Tienda, *the* store in the neighborhood.

To fill that big house, we went all over the city in search of furnishings. Some of my husband's friends had closed their grocery stores, so we were able to get showcases, counters, a refrigerator, and a scale and, as a bonus, they gave us the wooden shelves. As those storekeepers would say, "Why do we want them any longer? They aren't useful anymore."

We paid $50 for the furnishings, and it was necessary to spend the small amount of capital that we had left to buy the food items and necessities. We invested another $50 in groceries and asked for credit in the same amount.

When our friends found out that we were opening a store, they came to see the new place. "Do you really intend to open a grocery store?"

"We already started it, look," we calmly replied.

Stubborn and doubtful, they continued: "Don't you know they're closing ten grocery stores a month here in the city?"

"No, we didn't know."

They continued impatiently with us: "You know nothing about groceries; you're really crazy!" And they warned us, "Don't you realize there is a depression?"

We certainly didn't know anything about the grocery business or about the Depression. We only realized that work was extremely limited and difficult to find. My husband was one of the first to lose his job, but he had learned the job of a clerk working in a store owned by a Jewish family. This made us think we should do something, and we thought about a little store.

La Tiendita's opening was on July 4, 1934, which my mother said was a good omen. Damnit, the people didn't even remember the little store. Not even the flies showed up that day. The next day a neighbor asked us, "Why didn't you all go to Washington Park? The sandwiches and sodas were really good, we had a great time. Everything they gave us was free, ice cream, candy, and cookies!"

Who was ever going to remember the poor Tiendita?

Later they told us, "Hey, Raymon, if you only knew how great it was at the park yesterday. We really had a ball; we ate everything they gave us. Just imagine we got watermelon, cantaloupe, and sodas, and we ate until we were stuffed." Our friend Ofelia was all sunburned from the July sun but happy that she had gone to the celebration for the Fourth.

"Hey, and we popped firecrackers until they ran out," she went on happily. But she didn't buy a thing from the store.

We thought about what friends had told us, and even more, we went to great lengths so that La Tiendita would be a success, despite the difficulties. It was necessary for us to persist so the store could survive, because the life of La Tiendita was life for all of us.

We also thought about how we could attract customers. To the few who came, we offered what we had with smiles and encouragement, and we showed goodwill to both young and old.

My husband devised a way to have more business. He called the boys from the neighborhood and said, "Boys, I'll play you at checkers, what do you say?"

They answered excitedly, "Sure Don Manuel, just don't try and cheat us."

Soon the boys were showing up in greater numbers.

"Guys, I'm going to play fair and square." My husband let them win, of course, without the kids knowing it. What they won was a piece of candy, and at best a soda.

The next day the parents came to Don Manuel. "Don Manuel, will you give me credit? What do you say? I'll pay you when I get paid." We gave them credit. Almost everyone paid; we had to go collect from one or another, but they paid.

La Tiendita kept the secrets, tribulations, joys, and complaints of the people who frequented it. One of the first clients of the store was El Chorty. They called him that because he was short—very, very short, but hardworking and thrifty. Chorty worked at the the railroad roundhouse, the place where locomotives were serviced, which was located one block south of La Tiendita. He cleaned up the tracks and rail yards. By five in the morning, he was already working. He wore loose fitting denim pants, and a cap that came down to his neck. He always went around with a wheelbarrow full of stones and sticks that he collected while cleaning.

He went to the store to cool off and always showed affection for my one-year-old daughter. "Do you want me to dance with the bottle?" he asked her with a cheerful smile. The little girl would nod her head. Chorty took off his cap, smoothed his hair back, and put an empty milk bottle on his head, and with one hand at his waist and another fluttering like a wing, danced with the bottle. In no time you could hear, "Boys, boys, Chorty is dancing with the bottle!"

The boys ran around with excitement, hoping that, from one moment to the next, the bottle would crash on the floor. It was quite a sensation to see the man put the bottle on his head and dance without it falling off.

Chorty's coworkers liked him a lot. He was very responsible and never stopped working. The most curious thing about this man was that, after all those years, and after he had already retired, he would still go early to clean the train tracks. His coworkers, who were all Anglos, would say, "Chorty, go home. You don't work anymore." He just laughed, and the next day there he was early in the morning at work.

One day he came to La Tiendita and said, "Ma'am, could you please fill out these papers for me, they are in English, and I don't know what they want me to do." He told me what had happened.

Chorty and his wife went for a walk to Mexico and chose to take along a collection of gold coins, American and Mexican. When they returned, the immigration service confiscated them. No one knew about this collection but he had been collecting them for years. Gold coins and anything else of gold was forbidden, and even having them was considered contraband. The federal government had stopped the circulation of gold, but Chorty didn't realize it because he couldn't read or write in English or in Spanish. I wrote letters for him and filled out the forms to get his coins back, but he never saw them again. Chorty didn't complain.

One early morning, when La Tiendita had just recently opened, my husband had his back to the counters of candy, cookies, and other goodies, when out of the corner of his eye he saw a boy running out. My husband followed him. The boy was carrying fistfuls of candy. My husband went to his mother, who said, "I don't have time for gossip. Go see his Grandma; she has him very spoiled, see what she does."

"Pepino took some candy from the showcase, Chalía, and his

mother says to tell you." My husband said it as a joke, so Chalía took it that way, saying, "Damn kids. Look, don Manuel, the next time they do this, tell me. I'll pay you. Damn little devils."

The boy didn't take much, but it could get worse if we didn't put a stop to it. This never happened again, because they were a good family and until this day we have a good friendship with all of them.

Chalía, the grandmother, was one of our first customers. She was lame, but she was in good health. God keep her in his bosom, she was very frank. She would say, "You don't have the sago pudding I like. Order it and I'll buy it. I really like this tiendita." She was also the one who gave us our first big order. It was always a joy to wait on her and talk to her.

Chalía was our first customer/friend, and she was the last one. We had already shut down La Tiendita because the Highway Commission bought it to make way for the freeway that would pass through there. It was to be one of the largest highways ever seen in El Paso. Chalía would call us on the phone (by then, we had the luxury of owning one) and tell us, "Ramoncita, I want a little can of those green beans you had and a little can of chicken broth, but they had better be good. You know, no one but you knows what I like." We would buy it for her in another store. Chalía had more than five grandchildren and the same number of great-grandchildren. She and her husband were already very old, and their grandchildren understood her.

"That old woman is really annoying. It seems like everyone is at her beck and call," Felisa would say—with a gesture of great disgust—when she met Chalía in La Tiendita.

"Don't you get tired of her?" Felisa would say insistently. We smiled. She would keep it up and we had to say something. "Look, Felisa, there is a saying that goes, 'Mind your business or get out of the business.'" And we would take the conversation as a joke. Then we talked about something else and she left, calmed down and in good spirits.

Felisa was a very tall woman and very thin, so she looked bony.

She had five children and a grumpy husband. Everything seemed wrong to him, so we never got into a conversation. Even though he was old, his own family did not please him and he never set foot in La Tiendita. His wife, Felisa, used to go to La Tiendita to clear away the bad times he gave her. He always bought the groceries and she bought what the husband forgot [at La Tiendita]. Over the years Felisa acquired credit in La Tiendita and bought quite a lot, because the family became so large.

Her children went to La Tiendita so we could help them with their schoolwork, math and grammar. The parents did not understand a bit of English and were impatient with them, so Felisa sent them over to me. I was qualified to help with their studies; I had graduated from El Paso High School. Eventually, they didn't come crying because of the parents' scolding; they showed up happy when they needed help. When the neighbors found out about it, they sent their children to me for help.

After one Christmas Day, Felisa arrived at La Tiendita very sad and said, "Look what my son and daughter-in-law gave me." It was a pair of old-style shoes. "Couldn't they have given me anything better?" She threw them on the counter with contempt.

"Felisa, maybe they don't have enough for a better gift."

"Yes, they do, and they know what I want; it's the wife who bought these shoes, I'm sure. But don't even think I'm going to wear them; they are just so out of it." Felisa felt hurt. She really loved her son but not the daughter-in-law.

If LaTiendita was perhaps in need of business, there was no shortage of happy conversation, stories, and funny remarks. In those years we had time to waste, and therefore there was time to listen to complaints and concerns, not to mention gossip.

One winter night we heard loud knocks on the door of La Tiendita, and alarming cries. "Please open the door for me, Don Manuel, for your life's sake!" We ran and opened the door. It was one of the neighbors. We knew her well. She came in like a flash of lightning, terrified, her hair ruffled. She was trying to hide. Behind her another neighbor came in shouting angrily at her, "You devil, I'll catch up with you. Don't open it for her, don Manuel, don't let her in, that daughter of a so-and-so." She threw herself on top of the frightened woman to keep pulling at her, but my husband stopped her. They were tired; they had run for a few blocks.

They stared at each other, looking like dogs and cats, grunting and ready to grab each other and pull out each other's hair. My husband said to them, "Calm down, girls. You all have children, you'd better quit fighting. Stop acting like that, just look at yourselves. Don't let your children see you like this. Later it will be embarrassing to tell them what happened."

They calmed down, and after hearing some other advice, they left one by one; they didn't dare to go out together. We knew them for many years, and their husbands also. They stayed married to the same husbands and had more children, and apparently they were very happy. That was the way we learned about human nature.

As in every barrio and neighborhood, there were always boys and girls. In this barrio there were a lot of them, and if I were to make a list of all of the known neighbors, I would have to write a book. I will mention the most unforgettable and outstanding events of some of them.

Rubén, the one with the nickname Jotinche (little gay boy), was only ten years old and a very precocious boy. He had huge eyes and abundant wavy hair. His face was round, with thick, scornful lips. He was clever and quick to observe, find out, and it goes without saying, give nicknames to everyone! He helped me take care of my daughter, walking her in her stroller while I busied myself with other chores and when my husband was outside the store. This boy had a lot of self-esteem, so he was very honest. He was incapable of taking anything from the store, and I had every confidence in him.

Since it was summer when we opened the store, Rubén spent hours talking or giving details about all of the neighbors who lived in the neighborhood. There was a large family living there who were all very short in stature, so he gave them the name *tepocates* (tadpoles). They also were very dark skinned and went en masse to play outside. There were other kids. They lived in the house next door to Chalía. They had slumped shoulders and he called them *los sapos* (the toads). The more we insisted that he not give nicknames, the more he did so. Later we became accustomed to these names, and they were even accepted, even the one given to himself, Jotinche.

One afternoon he brought his sisters so I could meet them. They had very pretty faces, but their legs. What legs! *Zambas* (bowlegged) wasn't even saying enough—it seemed like they had been raised mounted on horseback. Rubén also told me that his father worked in the Banco de Juárez. This was heard by one of the neighbors, whose nickname was Correo del Bravo (the Bravo Mail). Juárez is a sister city of El Paso, Texas. Every day Jotinche's father went on the trolley to work, but we never knew what his job was. He was a good man; he had only the one defect, which was liking wine.

Correo del Bravo was the name of one of the Mexican newspapers, and that's why the name Correo was given to the neighbor! She brought the "news," so as not to call it gossip. Rubén and Correo had a bad opinion of each other; they were suspicious of each other, and we, just to be mean, said they were in competition.

Correo was stumpy and plump, with large clear eyes that gave malicious glances. She had two children and a lazy husband; she called him *huevón* (lazy bum) when she was upset with him, and said he had calluses on his butt. He was always just reading newspapers and magazines and sarcastically said that he lived off his "private means."

Certainly, this man was never known to have had a job, just the one called *parranda* (partying).

I could tell when Correo had some gossip. She bit her nails until she reached the flesh and always went around with bloody fingers—even more so when she couldn't spill the beans. She rented three or more apartments to live off and support her family. She did all of the cleaning and painted, cleaned out all the sewers, and planted her garden. She had two or more cages of birds, and still had time to find out about the lives of others. To me she was amazing.

Most of the neighbors rented one or two rooms to help themselves out. The houses were old, with several rooms, and the dwellers got along with as little as possible so that they could pay rent, water, light, and gas, or oil; most people had oil stoves.

The neighbors who lived across the street, on the other side of Correo, rented to three different people. This family consisted of eight children, who were orphans without a father. The mother worked to support them. We also gave her credit, and she paid her debts. Despite this large family, she still rented two rooms.

Jotinche's parents, besides their three remaining children, had to rent an extra room to a girl who called herself an artist and played the piano. She taught Jotinche to play some pieces of music, very simple ones, of course. He also learned two or three dances from her. The one he learned best was "La carioca." He danced it very well.

Chalía didn't rent, but her son and all of his family lived there. The *sapos* lived in the house next door. This family was numerous, but a compadre, his wife, and son lived there, too. Farther down there was a family whose father was not known for any vices, except that of working. The wife was heard frequently wanting to rent a room, but he wouldn't let her because, as he said, "We don't need to rent. I work and my family does not lack for anything." And he never did rent rooms.

During those years, there were almost no families who didn't rent one or two rooms, because if the head of the house didn't have a job, it was a disgrace. And if a mother with a family and no husband didn't have work, they would die of hunger. No one we knew how those who had no work wound up in such a state. They tried to do the best they could, as did the mother of those who lived next door to Correo. She had a fifteen-year-old daughter, very beautiful and witty, according to Correo.

"You mean you didn't know that my nextdoor neighbor married her daughter off to the gringo who owns the filling station?" she said.

We were all really flustered.

"But that old man could be her grandfather," said Chalía's daughter-in-law.

"Maybe she'll marry the other one off to the Arab who owns the clothing store."

"No one knows what is in the sack except the one who carries it."

If we had seen these comments from another point of view, we would have understood what this family was suffering through. The eight-year-old girl did not go to school in order to take care of the other children, who always looked skinny and filthy. On top of that, they were always fighting. After the eldest daughter got married, their troubles were somewhat alleviated. The son-in-law was good to his wife's family. All the little in-laws helped work at the gas station, and the man must not have been so old, since his wife had children from him, and to the regret of some neighbors, the little kiddies were light skinned and good looking.

It was not easy for people to rent rooms from their homes as they tried to make a living. They struggled to get along with the tenants, who frequently took advantage of renters' kindness.

That reminds me of Elena, a really fine person and, as the saying goes, "a good soul." She didn't seem to know about anger. One day she went to La Tiendita, very distressed and discouraged, and she confessed to me: "Raymon, fancy this, the tenant I have, you already know her, is alone, and because I had pity on her I rented her the largest room. She didn't have a refrigerator and my son gave me one, brand new, for Christmas. Again, I felt sorry for her, and so I let her place her fresh milk that they brought from a ranch in there. The milk from the store went bad quickly. It was brought to her from a ranch every other day. "Raymon, do you think I'm unfair?" Then, as the last straw, she brought in another sister to live with her because the sister's daughter could not stand her at home anymore. Without telling me, she also brought her food to my refrigerator, took out my food, and put theirs in. Do you think this is fair?" Elena told me this very deliberately.

I did not know how to answer this kind and helpful woman. The tenant, along with the sisters (she had a third one), was known to be deceitful and *holier than thou*. They were really bad; they did not need to rent a room from this poor woman because one of them had a big house that they rented to go live in one room that had no refrigerator or heater.

Elena's son realized what these old women were doing and threw them out. But they did not leave until they gave Elena a good piece of their minds, and to top it off, they robbed her of things she had lent them while they were living in the room. She suffered a lot because of those people.

One day Correo entered La Tiendita very smugly and with a mischievous smile, and said, "Hey." She always started her conversation like that. "Listen, Raymon, I hear that Jotinche says his dad works at the Banco de Juárez. He really likes to exaggerate things; he's just like his mother! He's just a floor sweeper in the bank!" She burst out laughing, making La Tiendita shake. It seemed that the laughter had called Rubén, or he had already been keeping an eye on her. Finally, the two of them confronted each other face to face; Jotinche did not even blink. Rubén's anger was very apparent, and in that moment he wasn't afraid of a fighting bull. I suppose that he suspected Correo of spreading gossip about his father, that he worked in the bank. Without saying a word and in a very bad mood, he parked himself in La Tiendita until Correo left with a smile and a look like a coyote.

The following Saturday afternoon, Jotinche came in hurriedly, trying to hide. Behind him, one of Felisa's sons, who was very spoiled and always looking for trouble, stopped at the door and shouted at him to provoke him.

"Jotinche, go help your father, he's coming and walking like a drunk snake, and he's dropping all the tortillas on the sidewalk. Hurry up." This explosion set off a firecracker in Rubén. His eyes were popping and sparking, and he answered, "What are you scared of, Cabezón (pigheaded, stubborn)? I don't see you helping yours when he gets drunk, and you have to hold him up to get him into your house. Eh? And he drops his beer bottles, heh? Heh?"

Cabezón slammed the door to La Tiendita, as if the poor ramshackle door owed him something, but he did not answer. The pointed remark hit him right where it might hurt the most. Rubén was a real devil when fighting with words, because with fists he was a runner. Cabezón was a big crybaby. With tears and snot hanging down, he left filled with anger.

Rubén was embarrassed by the mockery of his father and hid behind the oil tank until he noticed his father passing by. Silent and moody, he slowly left the store.

The fathers of the neighborhood were—some more, some less—given to drink. On Saturday afternoons, they formed a parade; some because they had money to get drunk with and others because they liked to follow the crowd. They walked in the middle of the street, on the sidewalks, talking nonsense and a half. The curious affair that caused so much amusement to the whole neighborhood was that, when someone would raise his hand to curse or make eloquent imaginary speeches, they couldn't stand up and fell to the ground. No one helped them up, so they went along on their hands and knees or however they could until they got on their feet by themselves.

Among these drunkards who made their pilgrimages every Saturday was a tailor with five children, a very happy lime spreader, and another lime spreader who boasted of being a painter, a daily drunkard, and to top it off, a lazy bum, as his wife used to call him. Another was a dandy who could be seen with pencils behind his ears, in his shirt pockets, and in the chest pocket of his coat, but he didn't even know how to write his name. When, according to him, the drinks would go to his head, it was never the beer but the wine that caused it. Anyway, he wobbled along and, no matter how hard he tried, kept crashing against the walls and fences of the houses. It was truly a treat we witnessed on Saturday afternoons.

We must give honorable mention to Correo del Bravo's husband. He didn't join the parade but rather partied for days, and the whole neighborhood noticed when he returned. His flip-flops, trousers, and other belongings were scattered in front of his house, but Correo didn't say a word about any of this. And Jotinche said, "Huh, we don't spread the word about that," mocking with impudent joy.

Rubén was always waiting for his little chance for revenge. He suffered from an immoderate estimation of himself. He felt offended and sought satisfaction from his offense. The hour of revenge arrived.

"Hey, Raymon, didn't you know that Correo's husband was a smuggler?" he said.

I was so surprised that it made me dizzy.

I didn't answer, and with satirical laughter, he subtly continued, "I know you didn't know anything about this; there's more if you want. He was also in jail, and they were going to deport him."

I really didn't know about this matter, and of course there was no reason to comment. Rubén felt a certain joy in the piece of gossip.

A few days passed and he returned to La Tiendita. I noticed that he was in a good mood and thought to give him some advice. Without mentioning names or cases, I told him that he should treat his father well and respect him.

Without hesitation he replied, rather he refueled, "I, I, should help my dad when he comes drunk down the street?!!" He was haughty and continued with disdain, "Huh, never. I'd rather not eat tortillas. Let Judas take him. He doesn't want to stop his drinking habit, so let him fall, I don't care." He left in a rage.

La Tiendita was taking its first baby steps forward. Business was picking up. However, the sales consisted of small change, but my mother told me, "Step by step one climbs the ladder." That was the way that time was; things didn't cost much, but there was nothing to buy them with.

There was plenty of time to spare, but there was nothing to do. Jobs were scarce. The employment offices were packed with people. They were even lining up outside, and lines were endless. Groups of men could be seen on the corners, hoping to be hired.

Years went by with labor shortages until the federal government found a way to employ men and women in need. People accepted any kind of work, even if it was not based on their abilities.

This reminds me of an American lady who had been a manager of a loan company; I worked with her in the office as her secretary. When the Depression arrived, they closed the office, even though it was one of the most prestigious in the state.

Four blocks from our store, toward the west, the government opened an office to solicit workers. This American lady had to pass by La Tiendita to get to that office. One of the times she passed by, she came in to drink a soda and we recognized each other and we talked. Through her tears she told me the situation she was in without work. "I now live alone. My mother, whom you know, went to live with another sister and I don't have a house or a job. Where do you think they sent me to work, these miserable people? In a factory where I separate rags, old clothing, and other things that I really don't want to mention. Since I can work as an accountant, I could have another job at a higher level. I now work with Blacks, Filipinos, Mexicans, drunkards, drug addicts, and I don't know who else!" She was crying inconsolably. "Well, I need the salary, although it's really a pittance, but what can I do, I have to live."

I felt sorry for my boss of eight years ago. That's how the times were.

There were parents of families who got only two or three days of work, and they were glad to have those days; even though the salary was small, it was a sure salary. The women at home made it last by saving as much as they could and buying their supplies on a daily basis. In all truth, there wasn't enough money to buy for a week.

At that time, we could buy something with a penny, like candy— but big pieces of candy like licorice, which came in strips a yard long. They lasted as long as a lollipop that you could suck on for a whole day. A penny bought cornbread or a piece of gingerbread in the shape of a pig, and they were so tasty. They certainly don't make them the same now. With three cents one could buy a can of milk, or on sale, two cans for five cents. Loaves of French bread, hot, for three cents. And they were bought at La Tiendita at five in the morning. Fresh milk with cream on the top for five cents a pint. It's for this reason that I say the sales at La Tiendita were for pennies.

Speaking of pennies, I remember a very old Black lady who was very, very fat, the poor thing. She made great efforts just to walk; even though she lived half a block from La Tiendita, she took a long time to get there. Day after day she came to the store to buy a loaf of French bread or two pieces of sweet bread and a small can of milk. When I gave her the change, she always gave my daughter, whom I carried in my arms, a penny and patted her on the head, on her shiny black hair.

Every human being has some fetishism, or superstition, and I was no exception. It was said that a gift given by Black people was good luck, and naturally we all believe in good luck. The pennies the Black lady gave to my little girl were kept in a can. Maybe it was luck, but when my daughter turned one, I had enough to buy her an insurance policy that would pay her $500 at the age of twenty, which she received.

The unfortunate Black woman lived alone and perhaps suffered from some illness, because it was really difficult for her to walk. The boys in the neighborhood ran when she approached, but she never mistreated them. She always said hello and smiled, but no one would answer. It was a remarkable thing—when she patted my child on her head, her voice was subtle and sweet, and with her old hands and fingers, wrinkled and ashen, she smoothed her silky hair. In return the little girl gave her a smile of innocence and sweetness. The Black woman died alone in the room she rented, and she was found two or three days later.

There were days when the gossipers all got together at the same time; they seemed to tell each other beforehand. Stories about fights, needs, sorrows, joys, and, not to mention, just plain gossiping, were the high point in the store. If we could have passed a tape recorder around, all the stories heard in this tiendita would cause funny comments today and would be seen as witty, really.

On this day they brought along sharp scissors. The one who was the butt of everything was a neighbor who never bothered a living soul and was very hardworking and very charitable. Her sister-in-law was the one who started the "cutting session." Very excitedly, she told those in La Tiendita, who at the time were going to buy things to make the meal, "Girls (they were a bunch of old women), what can I tell you, Nena went to get a makeover!"

A bomb exploded in the ears of the tongue waggers, who were hungry for a piece of gossip. "What are you saying?" they asked at the same time, and they got together in a big circle, like football players when they get together to come up with their next play. So these women had a huddle, and even more when it was all about Nena, the sister-in-law of the one telling the story.

"Look, she has bruises on her forehead and behind her ears. I tell you this and I almost don't believe it, but she doesn't have even one wrinkle on her face. Wait, wait, the poor girl hasn't gone outside for anything—it's been six months now—because the bruises don't want to disappear."

The laughter and comments made La Tiendita's windows tremble, and they could be heard a block away. "Hey, tell them how Nena dresses!" one said to the sister-in-law.

"If you could just see her!" She put her hands on her head but couldn't tell them because she couldn't contain her laughter, and the others laughed along with her. She calmed down and continued. "Look, she puts on a bathrobe, but really expensive, purple, long, then she ties on a yellow ribbon, canary yellow, eh, in her hair. Listen, listen, Cleopatra style." That made San Antonito laugh, said a neighbor. Their tears flowed with laughter, and the confusion continued, because they all wanted to give their opinion or ask something.

"Wait, that's not all. She also puts on yellow and black slippers with yellow ribbons attached."

Imagine the sister-in-law with her hand in the air and another at her waist, her eyes dilated, looking at the ground, walking around the store, which had plenty of space. More laughter and applause. It was a spectacle like I had never seen in my life.

"Hey, hey, don't they say she has her poor husband bewitched?"

"Let me tell you."

They drew close together again to hear the secret. Suddenly there was a piercing cry. "Mom, Mom, Dad says for you to go feed him. Don't be long, he's very hungry, Mom!"

"Oh, my goodness, and I have nothing to give my old man." In a big hurry, she said, "Raymon, Raymon, give me a loaf of French bread and a can of beans and put them on the tab. I even forgot about him." The sister-in-law, still with tears in her eyes and laughing, ran out of La Tiendita with food for her husband.

"But she doesn't forget the gossip about her sister-in-law," grumbled Correo.

These women sliced up everyone, and the one who led them was none other than Correo. La Tiendita was a witness to all sorts of discussions about diseases, but the favorite topic was that of overlapping evil, or witchcraft, which was endless.

"I tell you, Chana, the old lady Rosita says she really has him bewitched. Rosita says she doesn't lie. When she worked with Nena, you see, that's why she quit her job. Rosita, herself, received the envelopes with the powder and Nena gave them to her husband right in front of Rosita, in the breakfast of the poor man! What, haven't you noticed how her poor husband is like a rag doll? All bony and skinny!"

The poor husband, like his wife, didn't bother a living soul, as I said before, and all of the old gossipers put them through the rinse cycle. And if her face was rejuvenated, also her strength, because when the whole neighborhood was dark, the windows of Nena's house were lit up; she was ironing uniforms to deliver early in the morning. The husband didn't miss work either, and he never partied on Saturdays. He worked at a printing shop. The stories that were heard in La Tiendita were fantastic.

Half the barrio put nicknames and monikers on the other half. Chana was a fat woman with bull-like eyes, big, with thick eyelashes, but she was a good soul. Chana had a very nice sister with a pretty face, and for unknown reasons, she had not married. Chana would get impatient with her sister.

"I don't know why Nena (another Nena) doesn't get married. I give her advice, but you see her there, she's very serious, she doesn't look to one side or the other. I get tired of saying, 'Don't be so serious, Nena, don't be afraid and unsociable, you'll never get a husband that way, but it's as if I were talking to the wall.'"

"Chana, Nena is a very pretty girl, but she may not want to get married."

"Well, what woman doesn't want to get married? I don't think she doesn't want to get married. What's up with Nena is that she's very foolish. I tell her that when she goes out for a walk, she should go out like a bullfighter, captivating and cocky, showing off." Chana stood in the middle of the store and threw her fat shoulders back. Filled with vanity, she walked like a flirtatious woman. She really gave us a laugh just to see her. Then she said, striking a pose like a Spaniard who is coming out to dance, "Let her go out like a bull in a bullring." She was given the nickname of Bull in in the Bullring. Chana died, and her sister Nena went off to be a nun.

The pulse of La Tiendita quickened and fell with the stories that people would tell. It's fun to remember the case of a young, recently married neighbor. Pancho lived across the street from La Tiendita with his in-laws and his wife. When his first daughter was born, as is common for Mexicans, they had hoped the first child would be a boy. He felt hurt and was in a bad mood. He would not greet neighbors for days. Soon the second child arrived. Pancho was hoping for a boy again, but it didn't turn out that way. It was another girl. We knew because he came to La Tiendita and did not say hello. We made him grumble and goaded him by asking, "What was it, Pancho?" He answered, with a gruff voice and a gloomy face, "Another *skirt.*"

And it happened the same for the first, second, third, fourth, and fifth—five girls, and for him they were all "skirts." His wife was a very fine person, submissive and dedicated to her family of girls, who were kind and very beautiful. She dressed them the best she could on Sundays and sent Pancho to take them to Mass.

Pancho didn't go to work for a week; he was waiting for the stork for the sixth time, and he stubbornly said it would be a son. That morning he went to La Tiendita very early. It was strange that he would go at that hour, but the morning was beautiful, and it seemed that the atmosphere felt joyful. When Pancho came in, he didn't wait for us to ask him what it had been. With a smiling face and full of pride and jubilation, he said clearly, "Now, I do have a son, Raymon. It's a boy, he is so beautiful, I want everyone to see him." The smile and the joy of this man was a remarkable change. He was no longer the man from before, with an annoying and aggressive look. We all shared this happiness. He was not the only boy; his wife had two more. It was a very beautiful family. And so the years went by, some up and some down.

Time passed by and the Depression was still in full swing. Jobs were still scarce, and therefore La Tiendita had great problems. The wings of its heart suffered failures that seemed like it wouldn't recover from. But we didn't let it become discouraged; we thought about ways to give it some spirit.

My husband hired some advertising agents.

On holidays, especially, they would decorate the store with crepe paper. They covered the windows with colored ribbons and presented the products more attractively. So La Tiendita was already putting on a more cheerful face.

Dealing with holidays, and Christmas in particular, the business was sad. The festivities lef poor parents without a cent and, as my mother used to say, "They are poorer than church mice." They didn't pay the bills, and they said, "Let La Tiendita wait." They tightened their belts, but they didn't leave their children without toys. These things were repeated year after year, holiday after holiday.

Meanwhile, we were thinking our friends' prediction would be fulfilled, although there were those [friends] who would bring it joy and hope for life, an abundant life. This was not easy, for La Tiendita endured so much sacrifice and deprivation. The fathers with families, however, spent months without a steady salary. When we were worried about La Tiendita's bad business, a customer would come by and tell us some news, like when a child or a husband found work.

We were happy for that event, seemingly so simple. This was how the days went by, the years of restlessness and occasionally of excitement.

I remember the case of a Black woman we knew by the name of Katie. She lived four blocks straight down from La Tiendita, and it was said that she was more than a hundred years old. There was no doubt about it. Her fingernails and toenails gave me goosebumps when I looked at them. Her fingernails looked like old claws and were a leaden color, very rough. I had never seen such a thing! This woman was very superstitious. She would come and stand in front of or in the middle of La Tiendita, look both ways, and close her eyes, saying, "There are no evil spirits here. It's a good house." It was the only thing I could understand in her litany and prayers.

At first it made me afraid, and even more so when she had her head tied up with a gaudy red rag; then she really gave the appearance of a witch. She went often to La Tiendita to buy ten cents' worth of yellow cheese, because it was very tasty and soft. If she arrived tired, she ate it sitting in front of one of the windows with wide frames that served as seats. We could sit there very much at ease.

In one of her conversations, she recounted that when she was four years old, President Lincoln gave freedom to all Black slaves. Her job was to be a companion to the master of the house's daughter. The little girl was eight years old, and Katie had to do everything the girl told her to. On one occasion the girl gave her a whipping, and when the father found out he punished the child and told her she would no longer be Katie's companion; beating the Black slaves was no longer allowed, because they were already free. The daughter felt frustrated that she couldn't do what she had learned, to beat and whip the slaves whenever she felt like it. After getting her freedom, Katie remained in the master's house with her mother until she was orphaned. They thought well of her, she said, but she never learned to read or write. At the age of twelve she went to live with another family who taught her the art of fortune telling. She already knew how to be a sorceress. She was never known to bring harm or illness to anyone. She had a reputation in the neighborhood as a witch. Everyone noticed the number of people who visited so that she could tell their fortune or something they wanted to know.

On one occasion Katie became ill. She had someone ask me to bring her usual order, which I was familiar with. For the first time, I crossed the threshold of her house. The gate was well locked, but I managed to open it. I went in, walking around tubs of clean water, which she said were there so evil spirits couldn't enter her house.

Katie was lying on a platform that looked like a masterpiece from another age. The interior of the house gave the appearance of a museum of antiques. There were bottles, pots, and glasses containing different colored mixtures and jars with powdered substances of various shades. They looked like ashes or coals. I was amazed, because the vessels and other objects were well placed and clean, although the house had a dirt floor and windows with broken and opaque glass. The ceiling was of wooden beams, blackened from neglect, as well as from smoke. Curtains of cobwebs hung from beam to beam and wall to wall.

Katie ate her food, a kind of cornmeal, lifting it to her mouth with long fingers covered with mud. I wanted to leave quickly, but she stopped me and talked to me. I don't know about what. When I left the strange house, I was scared. During the time I had been inside I hadn't heard a single noise, except for Katie's murmuring, and when I reached the threshold four meowing black cats jumped out. I stepped back and saw Katie sitting on her bed, with a smile of amusement because of the sudden scare the cats gave me. When she laughed, I saw that she had no teeth, which exposed a cavernous mouth and a huge red tongue. I thought, "Feet, do your stuff," and got out of there. I never came back. But she visited La Tiendita often.

The years passed and with them La Tiendita grew. Our family also increased, and naturally the work did too. Our aim was to please our customers, as well as to sell them the best products we had. We persisted with all our heart in order to be successful. What else could we do? Our only plans were for La Tiendita! Plans to have it always clean, accommodating, everything in order, and with new, fresh, good merchandise. It may have seemed easy, just waiting for someone to come, and sometimes for something to happen, but it was hard.

We learned that besides having hope, it was important and necessary to do other things. We could get bored with a monotonous and slow life. My husband had an idea to attract more business. He thought of having punchboards in La Tiendita, raffles on a small board with numbers. This was taken as good news, because the first thing raffled was a turkey. I remember, and it amuses me, when the punchboard made its first appearance on the store's first Thanksgiving Day. It was five cents a number (punch), and the one who chose the winning number won the turkey. Perhaps my husband didn't know about roasting birds, but he had the poor turkey hanging in the middle of La Tiendita. This attracted a great deal of attention. The young kids sent their mothers to punch a number, and on Sundays when they had a nickel they punched their number too. The total was $2.50, which was a great deal, and even more when it came in pennies. It makes me laugh now, because the turkey was a sad-looking bird, skinny, long, and hung up where everyone could see it. It seems to me, as the kids say, "a big hit."

One day Rubén came in very happy and smiling, and said, "Raymon, your daughter's birthday is coming up. Aren't you going to have a party? I'll help if you want."

"Yes, Rubén, but I don't want you to start a fight and tell people that they eat a lot or or ask why they are coming. I'll tell you that we won't have much to eat. I'll see what I can do."

Rubén and I understood each other perfectly. If he told me something he understood that I wouldn't divulge anything, and if I said something to him, he kept it secret. Even though he was angry and grumpy, he respected me and paid attention to me.

I forgot to tell him not to tell anyone about the party, and he went and announced it all over the neighborhood, so you can imagine how many people came! It was a fantastic thing.

Our customers, "neighbors-not-customers," friends, and strangers—on purpose–would ask, "Are you going to have a party for your daughter?" In order to sustain their esteem, we were obliged to invite them. First, we invited the children to the party of our daughter, who was going to be two, then the aunts, grandmothers, cousins, neighbors, and acquaintances of the neighbors. Those we didn't even know showed up; they came with the guests.

Thank goodness we had a large patio with loose soil and a little grass. The guests did not see that but rather saw what we would give them for refreshments. The grandmothers were not embarrassed when they brought their grandchildren, because they were invited by other neighbors, and said with gusto, "We come here for the *chocolatito*. We know it's delicious how you serve it." (I still have a reputation for my chocolate.) This would be the only party in the neighborhood; they all came as if it had been a family. Joy reigned. At times we were a bit worried because we didn't always count on so many people, and even more so when we had to buy large quantities.

The young kids came to break the piñata, and the adults came for the chocolate. The older kids, from ten on up, would fight for the candy or balloons that came out of the piñata. Every year all the neighbors waited for this party, because it was a celebration of much good cheer and joy. I repeat, it was a problem for us to have so much refreshment for the guests. In advance my husband would go looking for cheap candy. Remember, at that time sugar was rationed, and it was difficult to get good candy; the same with ice cream and chocolate. In any case we always came through, and in our hearts, we were happy to be able to make this celebration every year. Years passed and I remember that one year when our children were going to school they invited each one of their classmates from their respective classrooms without telling us. We thought and thought, and decided to rent a bus from the city to take more than seventy-five students from school to a park.

They had their birthday party there every year, and we did just one party a year. What would it have been like if we celebrated at home? It would have tumbled down! There was no problem with the refreshments, except where to put them. The bus would make more than two trips. What joy there was!

I'll give you a brief account of an event that seems very funny even now, more than thirty years later. We remember it with nostalgia because of this person. Our house needed a paint job on the interior. We thought we could get somebody to do the large living room first, and then we could hire him to paint La Tiendita.

Two blocks from the store lived a man named José. He was very, very needy, and we wanted to help him out. He had a large family of seven sons and daughters. His wife had illusory ideas and thought she shouldn't buy from La Tiendita, that it was beneath her dignity, so she ordered her children to buy the most indispensable things for such a large family. That's right, that husband and wife made an unparalleled couple.

José was an honest, good man, and very attentive. He always said hello and stopped to take off his hat, which was covered with lime and paint, and to top it off, was torn. He was a painter and seemed never to be in a hurry. My husband asked him to do the job, but since our resources were scant we wanted to know the cost.

One afternoon José came to see the living room so he could tell us the cost. My husband thought that when he saw it, José would know what to charge. Far from it. He entered the room with my husband behind him, looked at the ceiling and walls, and walked about silently.

"Don José, how much will you charge me to paint this living room?"

José seemed to have no ears. His intentions were to work, but his way of making a business deal was strange. After walking around the room many times, my husband was dizzy, like the horses on a horse-powered winch, and my husband was right behind him.

"How much, don José?"

José did not respond.

"Look, don José, I just want you to whitewash or paint this room for me, that's all. How much will you charge me?"

José turned a deaf ear. He was still gazing calmly at the ceiling and the walls, but what for? We still don't know. Then he stood in the middle of the room and spoke in an extraordinary tone. His words were accompanied by floating gestures, as if he were acting out an imaginary role.

"Don Manuel," he said. He paused, looked at—I don't know what, and continued with an expression of imaginary grandeur, "Look. Don Manuel, what would be very beautiful in this large and spacious room would be a paint job in the style of Luis the Fourteenth. We stared in amazement. What that style would be, only José knew. In addition, the room was long and devoid of decorations. My husband became impatient and said, "Don José, I just want you to paint this room. Can you do it?"

"Don Manuel, of course—that's my job!" José smiled with good-will. "This room would look beautiful with a textured, pastel-colored paint job, since you don't want the Luis the Fourteenth style."

José continued with his eloquent words and arm movements. "It would be beautiful to behold." He spoke frankly and assuredly, but we didn't come to an agreement on the job or the price.

We pathetically noted that it would not be possible for José to do the job, however simple. He left, and he still went on about the style of Luis the Fourteenth. A few days later the drunk who lived across the street from the store, don Antonio, made arrangements for the job and, in one of his rare days of sobriety, painted the room like we wanted it in only one day.

In the following years the shop started looking brand new. First it was given a paint job, now it looked completely different. Then we installed a telephone, which was not only for La Tiendita but for the whole neighborhood, day and night—" Lend me the telephone"— for the doctor, for conversations with friends, relatives, and others, and to top it off, to order supplies from other grocery stores! That was the last straw. It seems an incredible thing, but that's the way it was.

After the phone, the dividing wall was removed. The premises were expanded, and we stocked it with more merchandise, as needed. We also bought a big refrigerator for the soft drinks and a refrigerator for the ice cream. La Tiendita shone with pride and satisfaction, with a modern and elegant refrigerator for all kinds of meats. Years later an air conditioner was installed; the store had already reached a level of responsibility and maturity.

An Anglo woman named Elizabeth moved into the neighborhood one day, and went by La Tiendita. At first, she only came to drink a Coke every day, in times of cold and heat. She seemed to be proud, but when we got to know each other well, it was not like that. Through conversations and exchanges of opinion, we became good friends. Elizabeth had credit at the store and paid on time. She brought her mother, her sister, brother-in-law, and her husband, and we were and are very good friends; even now we often communicate by mail.

After years passed, one day Elizabeth came to La Tiendita in tears. She was always discreet about family matters, but I felt that she had enough confidence to confide her problems and feelings with me. Her sister, who had recently died, left her only child with Elizabeth to care for and raise the child. The boy was barely two years old. Elizabeth adored him because she had no children. The child's father, an excellent and clever person, also consented to leave the child with his aunt, but they did not say, nor did they agree on, how long the aunt would take care of him. The father, a very hard worker, told me he did not know about taking care of children.

On that day Elizabeth could not contain her tears. She told me that her brother-in-law was planning on getting married. Behind Elizabeth, her mother, a very wise old lady came in. At that time Elizabeth was saying to me, "Mrs. González, I know the boy is not mine, but I love him so much that I don't know what I'll do if his father takes him away." And she cried even more. While hugging her daughter, Elizabeth's mother calmly told me, "Mrs. González, I knew, we all knew, that one day George would get married. He does not know about cooking, or housekeeping, and much less about children. I have told him that as far as I'm concerned, I won't get upset if he gets married, but Elizabeth doesn't want to listen to me, just look how she gets, and she's been like this for days." The mother spoke naturally and without getting emotional.

"Mrs. González, you know more than anyone, how I love this child, and if his father takes him, what do I do?" Elizabeth was very emotional.

"I'm sure George won't take the child. He has been with you for a long time," I said.

Elizabeth's husband sent for the boy's father, who said, "I don't want to take the boy away. You keep him. Besides, I have another job out of town, and I can come and see the child at least every month."

"But what if your wife wants you to take him with you?" Elizabeth wanted to be sure.

"No, Libby," as George said, "you know him better than I do."

Restless years passed, and the boy grew up to be a very nice young man with blond hair and blue eyes like his mother's. When Junior turned fifteen, he might have been aware of his aunt's fear that he would choose to go with his father and stepmother, who often visited Elizabeth. But he took away that doubt forever.

"Mrs. González, do you know what Junior said?" Elizabeth said one day when she arrived at the store. "'Auntie, I know you are always upset when my father and stepmother come to visit, aren't you? I tell you, Aunt, that I will stay by your side, by my uncle's, and my grandmother's, as long as you want. I don't know any mother other than you. I love you all, but you, like a mother.'" What joy this woman felt while telling me her feelings. This time she was crying tears were of joy and happiness.

Elizabeth and her husband went to live in another city, along with the boy and his grandmother. Junior is now an engineer and loves his aunt and the rest of the family. That boy with blue eyes and yellow hair didn't seem that he would learn anything. His aunt told me before they left that there were times when she and her mother had to dress him to go to school, because he was very slow, just like the father, but I encouraged her and told her he would not always be a child. She must have patience. When he graduated from high school, he sent me the first invitation. I sent him a gift and a letter to his aunt.

She wrote to me and said, "You don't know how many times I have thought of you, and I have given your children, whom he knows well, as an example for Junior. Now I am happier because he finished his university schooling. We often remember you all. "For me the store was like my home," Junior would say. "And for all of us, too."

Thus, the years ran by, and as the saying goes, "times bring times."

World War II broke out on that historic morning of December 7, 1941. La Tiendita became a headquarters. Customers, especially the poor mothers who had children seventeen and eighteen years old, came with great anguish seeking comfort and encouragement. Several families in the neighborhood had a large number of young men; in fact, there was no family who didn't have brothers, children, and relatives old enough to go to war.

La Tiendita no longer listened to gossip or sarcasm, nor to the mourning of the *comadres*. Now there were tears, complaints, and crying, and afterward regret because of the absence of their children.

Among those who went to serve in the armed forces were many we knew through this relationship, such as the grandchildren of Chalía, the children of Felisa, one of the children of Correo, those of the tailor, those of the drunken painter, the three children of Nena, the one who had the makeover, and those of her sister-in-law. Also, two of the widow's children who lived next door to Correo. One went into the navy. We didn't recognize him when he returned; he was another person, and his family was filled with pride and joy when he came to see them. Another was the eldest son of Toro en Plaza, and we can't forget the father who worked in the bank, whose son was Jotinche. And many more: three of the *sapos* and many more of the *tepocates*. All good and peace-loving boys.

During this time, an event occurred that we still remember when we see the son of Correo—he, along with us, has great memories of those times. When the war began in Europe, the persecution of those who came from some of the enemy nations also began, one of these being Italy. You will remember that in some cases, families—whether German or Italian—were investigated and monitored in their actions.

Well, one day we heard voices outside La Tiendita. All the voices seemed to speak at once and, being curious, I went to the door to investigate. Just then everyone came into La Tiendita, led by Jotinche. He had a mocking smile on his contemptuous lips. And he became silent, he didn't speak at all.

"What is this?" I asked a man I didn't know who was very well dressed.

Rubén replied, "Raymon, these gentlemen say that they come

from the FBI and are looking for a person called Mussolini." Rubén knew perfectly well who he was, but he wanted to "make a stink."

Correo had a son, and on one occasion she took him to have his hair cut. When they returned from the barber shop, she took him to La Tiendita and said to me, very excited, "Look, who do you think he looks like?"

Felisa and other people looked at him and said, all at the same time, "Hey, he looks like Mussolini with this hairstyle."

"That's really true," Felisa said.

"That's what I say, he looks like Mussolini in everything. The good thing is that Mussolini is in Italy, but one could say he was his son." We laughed at what Correo said. Correo smoothed her son's hair down again and moved his widow's peak to one side, and the boy, who was about ten or eleven years old, put on a good show with all this.

FBI agents asked me if we knew anyone by that name. Rubén became very serious, very sly. He looked down. I knew him well, and I know at that moment he was full of joy. He was waiting.

"Here in the neighborhood, there is a person with that name," I answered, and thought, let's see how far this game goes. "Pedrito, go and tell Mussolini to come to La Tiendita. I'll give him a candy."

Pedrito ran out to get Mussolini. We all were waiting a bit fearfully; most of those who were there knew who Mussolini was. In a short while Correo came back with her son. The agents saw them enter but didn't know or even imagine who they were.

"What do you want with Musolini?" Correo asked.

"These guys want to know if anyone here is named Mussolini," announced Rubén.

Correo grabbed the boy by the hand and said, "This is Mussolini, but that's not his name. Mussolini is his nickname." She smoothed his hair back and moved his little widow's peak to one side, and said, "Well, doesn't my son look like Mussolini?"

The boys and the people already crowded in La Tiendita laughed, and the agents put on their hats, thanked me, and left in a bad mood, without saying one more word. When the commotion was over and the people left, Mussolini turned around and shouted to me, "Give me my candy. Pedrito said you would give me a candy."

Morning and afternoon, there was a big crowd that made La Tiendita shake. We already had two employees in the store, along with my daughter and my twin sons. The twins, apart from their work in the store, had a paper route in the morning and afternoon. They wanted to save enough money for college. They were already fourteen years old, one year younger than Correo's son Mussolini. My husband and I opened La Tiendita at 5:30 in the morning to receive the bread, milk, and other merchandise. The employees wouldn't arrive until 8:30, and by then the kids from the neighborhood had gone to school. There were only adults and little children who didn't go to school yet at home. For a few moments we enjoyed peace and quiet.

Later the mothers arrived with their litanies of lamentations. One whose son was being taken away [to the war] was already there, and others whose grandson or friend, boyfriend or brother had gone. Not a day went by when we didn't hear about someone who was going to fight. We listened and sympathized with them, but we also wanted for this to be over soon because two of our own had been drafted by the army.

The boys came by La Tiendita to tell us that they would soon be called up too. We gave them advice to remember their parents. During these talks I made them a promise, that every boy who went off to war and said goodbye to me would come back alive. You can imagine how many boys came by. Some brought their mothers with them, others their aunts, grandmothers, and friends. I'll tell you that they all came back alive, thank God. They returned to La Tiendita to thank me because they were sure they would return, just as I had told them. One of Chalía's grandchildren went into the service first.

He didn't want them to tell him goodbye at the station. He arrived at La Tiendita very sad, almost in tears, early in the morning. We knew him as a young child; he was the one who took the candy. As it was, he had trouble with stuttering, and he could barely say, "I'm leaving, Raymon," with his eyes toward the ground and anxious.

"Go with God, may he and his angels watch over you, and you will come back alive," I said.

He walked slowly out with his duffel bag on his shoulder. He seemed to be carrying something heavy. His anguish touched my heart.

It seemed that the shortages were driven away. The federal government was making an effort so that all men could have a job. When war was declared, no man was left unemployed. Factories, the likes of which had never been seen, were set up all over the country. The factories that excelled were the ones making weapons. Swarms of women and men were seen in trucks and vans, going to their jobs. We still had La Tiendita in tow, and the war still continued in its shame.

At night, the store rested from its worries. But our family was still busy inside the house. The government had rationed many things, and stamps were needed to buy and sell merchandise. There were red, green, and blue ones. The stamps we collected at La Tiendita had to be pasted on a sheet of paper prepared for that purpose. Without stamps we couldn't buy necessities like sugar and its related products, fats and oils and their byproducts, and clothing. Shoes were the scarcest.

Another memorable date was August 6, 1945, when the atomic bomb exploded in Hiroshima. Another crowd gathered at La Tiendita. People waited for us to answer their questions. They knew our desire was to give them comfort and moral help whenever they needed them.

"Raymon, tell us, what is an atomic bomb. Did they drop it where my son is?" We really felt compassion for, above all, the mothers with their sorrows for their sons in the battlefield.

We scanned through American newspapers and magazines of all kinds to find out what an atomic bomb was. Never, but never, had we heard of atoms and even less about those bombs, despite the fact that scientists had known about atoms for more or less twenty centuries [*sic*]. Newspapers and magazines didn't say much about atomic energy. I went to the encyclopedias to explain to our customers what atomic bombs were.

It was a great joy when a few days later we were informed that a peace treaty was in effect. La Tiendita joined in customers' sadness when the boys left the neighborhood and rejoiced when they returned alive. None from the neighborhood remained behind on the battlefield. They all returned to their homes and families.

During the war years, the comrades no longer criticized or gossiped like before. Correo, who loved her son so much, I imagine like the other mothers, went to Mass early in the morning to confess and take communion. She also kept vigils for her son's return, which he did in body and soul, safe and sound. Thanks be to the Almighty.

La Tiendita again became a headquarters when one of the boys from the neighborhood returned from the war. There were hugs, tears, and memories of when they were children, the pranks they pulled, and the candies they bought. But they noticed the candy was still scarce because of the sugar shortage. When he did not have pennies to buy any, Cabezón said, "Raymon, can I have candy on credit? I'll pay you the day they pay my dad." And on the day the father received his salary, he punctually paid me. He asked me why I hadn't told him why they called him that.

"Look, why do you think they called you Cabezón? Because you didn't want to listen. Do you remember when you told me your dad had grown new teeth? And I told you that couldn't happen, that only children grow new teeth, and you left crying. You said, 'My father did grow new ones, he showed them to me!'"

"But how could I have told you that, Raymon?" Cabezón asked.

Each month one or two boys returned. Within a short time, invitations to weddings began to arrive. And there you have me, making them sugar cookies, cakes, or other cookies for the receptions or showers. We had a fondness for all the neighbors and their children. After a year or a little more, they brought in their little children so we could see them. Then there goes another little gift, for the little children or grandchildren.

I can't let the opportunity pass to tell you about Jotinche's return. His family sold their house and moved far away from us. When a brand-new car was seen pulling up to La Tiendita, everyone went to see who it was. We didn't recognize the driver. Rubén used to wear old, poorly fitting clothes, but now he was wearing the suit of a well-mannered and tasteful young man. We questioned him about a load of details. "What did you do in the war? Don't tell us that you were on the front fighting?"

He was the same as when he was a kid, saying, "Me, Raymon, fighting?" He was really laying it on thick, with a lot of style and charm, that he had served as secretary to a general in Germany! Yes, it was true. He showed himself to be self-assured and confident. He no longer had the attitude of an aggressive person, and he had affection and smiles for everyone. In the army he had learned shorthand and typing, and to this day he still does that work in his job.

"What happened to Cabezón, where are the *sapos*?"

"You still haven't lost the practice of giving nicknames?" It was Correo.

We almost keeled over. Between Correo and Rubén, there were hugs and tears rolling down their cheeks, chubby like hers. What happiness there was in La Tiendita! There was no longer suspicion, nor criticism, nor grudges. There were memories, and most of all reconciliation. That was the most beautiful part, and it gave the place an air of happiness and tranquility. This was how the years were winding down.

It was remarkable how Jotinche had changed, and it was all for his betterment. He had developed a personality that attracted instantly. His suit came with cream-colored trousers in thin brown stripes, a light blue shirt, and a matching tie. His two-toned shoes made everything go well together.

"Rubén, haven't you married?" asked Correo.

"What can I tell you, I almost married a Russian woman! Such a woman as I had never seen in my life!"

"You are really a flatterer, Rubén," I told him.

"Well, don't you believe it. At one of the parties the general gave, it was more of a banquet, but what a banquet. That was where I met her."

When he talked, his eyes grew larger, and they looked bigger because of the gestures and body language that accompanied his speech. He realized that I knew why he expressed himself in an animated way. It was to attract attention. That was what Rubén was like. Who could have told us! Who would even have thought that he would change so much more than the others who returned from the war?

In attracting attention, Rubén had not changed, and I doubt he will. For me, he could not pretend or hide, because that was his character. I understood that and kept quiet. He knew. When he was in Germany, he wrote me every month, or every other month. He came here, went to work, and put me down as a character reference. I always gave him a good recommendation. We remained speechless and stunned when he said goodbye.

The shrill blasts of the locomotive whistle ended this joyful reverie. I woke from my daydream. The giant machines returned to their deafening tasks. Having to leave that place caused me a sharp pain.

The name La Tiendita is engraved in the memory of the friends who knew her through the years. Places like La Tiendita pass on to oblivion or into our memory, and where there is memory, life is revived....The store went away from our lives, but we retain the memory of it in great detail.

I am often amazed at how much I learned from La Tiendita's customers, neighbors, and friends. Memories and conversations about her never end.

This is not an account of profound problems. Here the ordinary, poor, and natural life was observed and recorded. There is nothing exceptional. Everything that happened in La Tiendita would fill a book and more. The events are true, but some names have been changed.

No one knows where La Tiendita is buried. My eyes are wet. I say farewell to LA TIENDITA. I will leave you peacefully in your grave.

Barrio Literacy: Doña Ramona's Poems and Fables for Children

It is in the hearts of children that stories bloom, flourish, and take flight.

—UNKNOWN

It was August 1993. I had just returned with my mother from a month-long stay in Puebla, Mexico for a language immersion course. While I was in Mexico, my Spanish, although my first language at childhood, had improved with writing and speaking it every day. These travels added to my education as I entered my senior year at the University of Texas at El Paso, with a minor in Spanish language. Through my experiences abroad I was inspired to write my thoughts in a journal and even sketch out poetry and prose. I brought home a notebook full of writing that I wanted to share with my grandmother.

A few weeks after arriving home, I settled back in the small apartment with doña Ramona. One afternoon, seeing my grandmother sitting alone, I thought, "Here's the perfect moment to share my work." I pulled my travel journal from my *bolsa* and turned to the page with the poem I had written. This was my first full poem in Spanish, titled "La caída del sol." Though it was in draft form, I beamed with pride.

I shuffled quietly into the dining room where my grandmother was playing solitaire and asked, in a hushed voice, if I could read her my poem. "Abuela, ¿puedo leerte mi poema?"

Without hesitation she answered, "Seguro que sí. Siéntate". (Sure, have a seat.) She put down her cards and gave me her attention. To listen more intently, she closed her eyes, rested her chin on the curve of her cane, and leaned into the direction of my voice. It was late afternoon, rays of afternoon summer sun streaming into the space where we sat. I cleared my throat and began to read: "El sol se está admirando en su espejo, el mar, / Y le pregunta, 'Espejo, espejo, ¿quién es el más poderoso de toda la tierra?'" (The sun is admiring himself in his mirror, the sea, / And he asks it, "Mirror, mirror, who is the mightiest in all the land?") With my chest out and chin up, I read the remainder of the poem in my best Spanish.

My grandmother sat quietly for a moment. I hung on to her response, anticipating her critique. No criticism or correction came. She merely asked to hear it again. "Léelo otra vez," she asked. Beaming, I started again. During that moment, I was naive about her rich literary past. I did not know that she was a poet, nor did I know then that she had also written a poem in Spanish about the sun. After my second reading, she offered me some suggestions and nodded in approval. Not adding much more she said, "¡Bien hecho!"

Through the act of writing poetry, poets offer a window into their souls. A constellation of words, the crucible of a moment, a poem reveals the immediate truth of an event or the depth of an emotion. Poetry can serve several purposes at once. It can be a simple act of word play, a radical act of protest, or the claiming of an identity. My grandmother's poetry—a mere two of the forty-two poems and seventeen cuadros she wrote—is included here. The samples in this book reveal that, as a writer, she gazed at the stars and dreamed and contemplated the everyday routine of activity and learning. Looking at her collection of poetry, we see that González often used unique literary techniques such as writing in the voice of a child or writing to children in the voice of an adult.

With a focus on children, my grandmother's writing reveals that she was speaking to the future: *los niños de su barrio.* In her own way, she was creating a form of barrio literacy, which I define as the expression of one's community reality of the barrio, grounded in the use of the people's language across a variety of genres. González's barrio literacy, which she communicated through her poems and fables, passes on the joy of words and their power as they are read. She displayed her word craft through a variety of genres—short stories, memoirs, poems, cuadros, and fables—that represented her interpretation of barrio literacy.

González fully understood the power of words to create worlds. In her early years in Chihuahuita, she was one of some three thousand children from the barrio who did not attend school due to lack of city resources. In her writing, she expressed the emptiness of not attending school and the lifelong disadvantage it brought. She perceived, then, literacy and poetics as a path to overcoming life's difficulties. A worldview emerges in her poems that values the good of every day and every moment. The poems written in the voice of a child, such as "El espejo" (The Mirror), "Una cartita" (A Little Letter), "Juegos" (Games), and "Ilusiones," recall her childhood and express feelings of love, fear, confusion, sadness, and joy. Other poems, such as "Como siempre" (As Always), "Las horas del día" (The Hours of the Day), and "Joyas" (Jewelry), teach children how to manage their emotions, as well as how to manage their days in school. These poems, when read together, reflect the ways González thought and wrote about inviting children to learn about themselves and their culture.

González also wrote fables—eighteen in total—that follow the theme of writing for children. Fables have been told for centuries in many cultures, including Mexican culture and folklore, to teach children morals and character. Aesop is the most famous author of fables; other writers renowned for their fables are Ambrose Bierce, Rudyard Kipling, and Hans Christian Andersen. Fables carry three distinct attributes: the characters are animals or objects that act like humans; they illustrate a moral lesson; and they are brief. With Mexican culture grounded in oral traditions, the fable plays an integral part of a child's learning to listen and tell stories. After hearing several fables as a child and reading the Latin American fables in Horacio Quiroga's 1918 *Cuentos de la selva* (Stories of the jungle), doña Ramona wrote in this genre with zest. Additionally, having read writers such as eighteenth-century poet and essayist Tomás de Iriarte, she quoted some of his writings as morals for her fables. In "Los abejones" (The Bumblebees) she writes, "¿Cuantos pasar por sabios han querido / Con citar a los muertos que lo han sido? / ¡Y que pomposamente los citan! / Mas yo pregunto,¿Acaso los imitan?" (How many have wanted to pass themselves off as wise men / By quoting the dead who have been so? / And how pompously they quote them! / But I ask, Do they imitate them?) Noting her tendency to quote literary writers, we see that she wrote fables in a style that started with the moral and imagined a story around it. Titles include "La golondrina profetisa" (The Swallow Prophetess), "La riza es contagiosa" (Laughter Is Contagious), and "El monochango vanidoso" (The Vain Monkey).

González took pride in being an avid reader. Her bookshelves held the works a wide net of literary influences, among them Pablo Neruda, Horacio Quiroga, Tomás de Iriarte, Ambrose Bierce, Gabriela Mistral, and Frank Herbert. Given this, it is no surprise that she pursued the craft of writing poetry and fables. She wrote each genre in Spanish, her mother tongue, perpetuating the melody of that beautiful Romance language. To her reader, she would no doubt say, "Este es el idioma de mi pueblo, comunidad, y antepasados. Apréndelo. Léelo". (This is the language of my people, community, and ancestors. Learn it. Read it.)

```
                        El Sol

        Es la hora en que el Sol entra en el jardín. El Sol
baña a las plantas y flores con su luz brillante.
        La niña linda, mira al cielo azul, luego llega al jar-
dín oloroso a perfumados claveles y rosas.
        La rosa espera al Sol. Se pone encantada y abre sus ojas
encarnadas. Parece oirla cantar cuando el Sol está con ella.
        !Qué fragancia derraman los jasmines! cuando el rocío
los riega con su frescura y el sol los besa!
        Las mariposas afanosas chupan el néctar de las blancas
margaritas y de los azules mantos en las enredaderas. Las
flores gozosas ofrecen su zumo azucarado porque saben el buen
fin que tendrán.
        Las plantas floridas del jardín se muestran al Sol, ba-
ñadas de gozo.
        Corren pronto, así arriba, arriba las enredaderas, las
madreselvas, las azucenas, las margaritas, los lirios y otras
más flores. Abren sus copas azules, rosadas, moradas y blan-
cas para ser acariciadas por el rocío y el Sol. !Qué flores
tan bellas!...Florece el jardín con el Sol frente a mi ventana.
        Así, también, a ti niña,
                        El Sol te baña,....
                                El rocío te acaricia..
        Y el viento te besa.
```

Original text of "El Sol."

THE SUN[1]

It is the hour in which the Sun enters the garden. The Sun bathes
    plants and flowers with
its glistening light.
The pretty girl looks at the blue sky, then arrives at the garden
    which smells of perfumed carnations and roses.
The rose waits for the Sun, becomes enchanted and opens its red
    petals. It seems to hear her singing when the Sun is with her.

What fragrance do the jasmines pour out when the dew sprinkles
    them with its freshness and the sun kisses them?
Busy butterflies suck nectar from white daisies and from blue
    morning glories on vines. Joyful flowers offer their sugary juice
    because they know the good purpose it will serve.
The flowering plants in the garden bathed in joy show themselves
    to the Sun.
The vines, honeysuckles, lilies, daisies, iris and other flowers
    run quickly upward. They open their blue, pink, purple and
    white blossoms to be caressed by the dew and the Sun. What
    beautiful flowers! The garden blooms with the Sun in front of
    your window.
    So, too, you little girl...
      The Sun bathes you...
        The dew caresses you...
    And the wind kisses you.

EL VUELO[2]

Madre, ¡qué dulce arrullo en tus brazos!
¡Pálpo un tierno sentimiento de encanto!
Oígo el suave murmullo
de un inefable y misterioso canto.

Después...siento que algo me llama,
me desprendo de la cuna,
los consejos de calma, más de
los de urgencia, te asombran.

Te dejo un hueco profundo,
Madre, hoy tiro el vuelo al mundo,
sólo sé que un fuego extraño
me apresura en pos de un ser nuevo.

Viene el amor silencio y distinto,
como un canto fugitivo que me
eleva y me desciende a no sé dónde.
Siento me eleva a un nivel de cariño más alto.

THE FLIGHT

Mother, what a sweet lullaby in your arms!
I feel a tender sensation of captivation!
I hear the soft murmur of a deep
and mysterious song.

After... I feel something calling me,
I abandon my cradle,
the calm advice, more than
those of urgency astonish you.

I leave for you a deep, empty space,
Mother, today I ascend and fly into the world,
I only know that a strange passion
hastens me in search of a new being.

Love comes silent and clear,
like a runaway song that elevates me
and thrusts me downward to I know not where.
I feel that it elevates me to a higher level of love.

EL PÁJARO ZENZONTLE Y EL CONDE[3]

En un árbol frondoso entre otros arbustos y perfumadas flores, se paraba un pájaro zenzontle. El zenzontle cogitaba con garbo su canto melodioso y agradable al oído.

Un conde muy rico pasaba y se quedó escuchando el canto del ave. Admirado y embelesado, siguió escuchando al pájaro zenzontle, y no pudo más que expresar su halago. Dijo al pájaro, "Qué hermoso cantas; parece un canto celestial". Se mostraba risueño y contento su semblante.

El zenzontle siguió cantando su melodía pura y armoniosa. Él se sentía orgulloso de su canto en esta mañana tan clara y apacible.

El conde aún más embelesado escuchaba el canto. Otra vez dijo al pájaro, "¿Oye, por qué no abandonas este rústico y tosco nido? Tu tierna canción suena en vano y no la oye nadie, nomás tus aves compañeras".

Continuaba su canto sonoro el pájaro, despreocupadamente.

Paciente y tiernamente exponía su admiración el conde rico, diciendo, "Aquí estás triste, el sol te molesta con su calor ardiente, el aire se lleva tu hermosa melodía. Tú, ave cantadora, no naciste para un lugar áspero y sin vista".

El pájaro no escucha nada, continúa su canto.

El conde quiere posesionar al hermoso pájaro zenzontle y su canto tan dulce. Le habla con más ternura. "Ave encantadora, vente a mi hogar suntuoso y magnífico y ahí tendrás una jaula de oro y comerás de los mejores manjares entre caricias y tus cantos. Sería una cosa deliciosa y tus cantos más sonoros".

De tanto oír al conde, decidió mejor sería contestar a su buen admirador y prudentemente contesta: "Mil gracias, señor Conde, agradezco la oferta, pero no la acepto. Es mi humilde idea que vale más mi ambiente tranquilo aquí en el campo entre mis queridos compañeros. Es donde más libre vuelo que en palacio".

El conde se entristeció.

El zenzontle le dice, "Perdón, señor Conde, yo sé de los primores y delicias en palacio, pero aquí quiero estar con alegría entre mil flores y más que nada, aquí tengo yo mi libertad.

"La libertad es un tesoro.

Perder la libertad? ... Ni en jaula de oro!"

The Mockingbird and the Count

In a leafy tree among other bushes and perfumed flowers, a mockingbird stood. The mockingbird reflected cunningly upon his melodious singing which was pleasant to the ear.

A very rich count passed by and listened to the song of the bird. Astonished and enraptured, he continued to listen to the mockingbird and could not help but express his praise. He said to the bird, "How beautifully you sing, it seems to be a celestial song." His face was smiling and happy.

The mockingbird continued singing his pure and harmonious melody. He felt proud of his singing on this clear and peaceful morning.

The count, even more enthralled, listened to the song. Again, he said to the bird, "Hey there, why don't you leave this rustic, crude nest? Your tender song rings out in vain and no one hears it, just your fellow birds."

The bird continued his clarion song nonchalantly.

Patiently and tenderly the rich count expressed his admiration, saying; "Here you are sad, the sun bothers you with its burning heat, the air carries your beautiful melody away. You, my songbird, were not born for such a crude place without a view."

The count wants to take possession of the beautiful bird and his sweet song. He speaks to him with more tenderness. "Charming bird, come to my sumptuous and magnificent home and there you will have a golden cage and you will eat the best delicacies between caresses and your songs! It would be a delicious thing and your songs even more sonorous."

After hearing so much from the count, he decided that it would be best to answer his good admirer and prudently he answers, "Thank you very much, Mr. Conde, I am grateful for the offer, but I don't accept it. It is my humble idea that my peaceful environment is worth more here in the country among my dear companions. It is where I fly more freely, than in a palace."

The count became sad.

The mockingbird says to him, "Excuse me, Lord Count, I know of the finery and delights in the palace, but I want to be here joyfully among a thousand flowers. And more than anything, here I have my freedom."

Freedom is a treasure.

Give up freedom?... Not even in a golden cage!

Notes

Foreword

1. Sosa, Clark, and Speed 2020.
2. Enoch and Ramírez 2019.

Introduction

1. I often refer to Ramona with the cultural honorific *doña*, an elevated form for Mrs. or Madam, to represent the way her family and community considered her.
2. Ramirez 2001, 9.
3. Ramona González's writings included in this book are published for the first time. Her complete collection, with English translations, consists of forty-seven poems, ten short stories (some as long as forty pages), four creative nonfiction pieces, thirty-five fables, seventeen cuadros, and two hundred pages of dichos, or sayings, collected from the people of her barrio. The original documents, along with translations of the entire collection, are accessible through the Recovering the US Hispanic

Literary Heritage Digital Collections under the Ramona Gonzalez Papers. González's writings are open to the public, fulfilling one part of her dream of openly sharing her work.

4. Each of these Chicano authors won the Quinto Sol award for work published in the literary journal *El Grito*. Tomás Rivera won in 1971 for... *y no se lo tragó la tierra*; Rudolfo Anaya won in 1972 for *Bless Me, Ultima*; Rolando Hinojosa won in 1973 for *Estampas del valle y otras obras*; and Estela Portillo Trambley won in 1975 for the short story collection *Rain of Scorpions and Other Writings*.

5. González, Ramona n.d.a. The poem is presented here in translation from the original Spanish.

6. Quiñones 2016, 339.

7. Castillo and Córdoba 2002, 7, 29.

8. Cherrie Moraga and Gloria Anzaldúa are both well-known Chicana authors who began publishing in the early 1980s with their coedited work, *This Bridge Called My Back: Writings by Radical Women of Color*. They are known for bringing a more radical slant to the Chicana perspective through their writing and activism.

9. Marshall 2021, www.nytimes.com/2021/03/26/books/amanda -gorman-hill-we-climb-translation.html.

Memorias ancestrales/*Ancestral Rememberings*

1. De León 1997; 2015.

2. Orozco 2020; Ruiz 2008 [1998]; Roberson 2022; Boswell 2019.

3. Marchino 2011, 79.

4. Guerra 2016. Accessed June 10, 2021. https://savingplaces.org /press-center/media-resources/el-pasos-chihuahuita-and-el-segundo-barrio -neighborhoods-named-to-national-trusts-2016-11-most-endangered-list #.YPiZSruSm70.

5. Quintana 1975, 1.

6. Sandra Devereaux 1976, 92.

Un cuento de cuentos/*A Story of Stories*

1. *El Grito* 1975. Accessed July 27, 2021. https://opendoor .northwestern.edu/archive/items/show/378.

2. *Aztlán* began as a small Chicano journal in 1970 at the University of California, Los Angeles, and is still a premier journal in Chicanx studies. The 1968 bilingual journal *El Grito del Norte*, based in Española,

New Mexico, initially focused on social issues of the Black movement but expanded to cover the Chicano movement and then Native American communities and other minority groups. The 1973 journal *Encuentro Femenil*, originally *Hijas de Cuauhtémoc*, is considered the first Chicana literary journal. It was founded by Anna Nieto-Gómez, who suffered backlash from her stance on Chicana politics.

3. We do not have documentation of the publication but know this from family oral history.

4. Translating *dichos* offers a layer of complexity. Like idiomic phrases, they cannot be translated literally because they are culturally based, and what is common in one culture may be uncommon or even unknown in another. Here I have given close equivalents in English of the *dichos*.

5. González, Ramona n.d.h.

6. Ramona González Papers. González's poems can be found in the online exhibit sponsored by the US Hispanic Recovery Project.

7. Birth certificate Número 205 of Maria Ascensión Rodríguez. Hidalgo de Parral, Chihuahua, April 6, 1869.

8. Ruiz 2008 [1998], 18–47.

9. Hernández 2013.

10. The historic Santa Fe International Bridge was built in 1892, and was originally a wooden structure. It served as a prominent entry point for people and goods coming in and out of the United States and Mexico.

11. Ettinger 2002.

12. Romo 2005, 234–53.

13. *El Paso Herald* 1906." www.newspapers.com/image/41444272.

14. González, Ramona n.d.b. "Chamaca's Dilemma" is a forty-nine-page story written by González about a mysterious murder she witnessed as a young girl in Chihuahuita. In the story, she provides various details of the barrio. *Chamaca* is slang for "young girl."

15. Aoy School was founded in 1887 by Olives Villanueva Aoy, who was born in Mahon, Menorca, Spain, in 1823. He traveled throughout Mexico, lived with the Maya people, and later traveled to Utah and converted to Mormonism. He arrived in El Paso after years of travel and started an *escuelita*, a small school that served the growing number of Spanish-speaking children of Segundo Barrio and Chihuahuita. The school is still in operation today.

16. Juárez 2014. http://lincolnparkcc.org/history.

17. González, Ramona n.d., "Lincoln Park School." http://usldhrecovery.uh.edu/items/show/3117.

18. Hernández 2013.

19. González, Ramona n.d.g.

20. Wright 2020 [1976].

21. Hernández 2017.

22. Hernández. 2016.

23. Cub Reporter 1917. www.newspapers.com/image/432899173/
?terms=Peggy%20Hull&match=1.

24. *México de afuera* is an ideology that emerged among immigrants
who fled the Mexican Revolution, and asserts that Mexico and its culture,
language, literature, and customs are felt more strongly away from Mexico.

25. The historic Mormon chapel is located at 3625 Douglas Street in El
Paso, Texas.

26. The Relief Society is the women's organization of the Mormon
Church.

27. Rosicrucian beliefs are a combination of Christian gnosticism and
Jewish mysticism with a belief that its members possess a secret ancient
wisdom.

28. Hernandez 2016, 5.

29. *El Mestizo* 1973.

30. Quintana 1975, 1.

31. Blea 1992, 9.

32. González, Ramona 1973, 22–41.

33. López 2010, 184.

34. Blea 1992, 17.

35. Cutler 2014, 262–94.

36. Portillo Trambley 1993.

37. Portillo Trambley 1993, 5–6.

38. One afternoon while clearing out old office and research papers,
I discovered this letter tucked between two folders. To this day, I do not
know how this important document became wedged in my personal
papers.

39. Quintana 1975, 1.

40. Cutler 2014, 277.

Chihuahuita, el barrio de mi corazón

1. *El Paso Daily Herald* 1896.

2. Since fall 2022, Chihuahuita has again become a center point for
immigrants. Thousands of immigrants from Venezuela, Nicaragua, and

Colombia have fled to the border area just yards from Chihuahuita's streets.

3. "Historic El Paso" n.d.

4. González, Ramona 1972b.

5. Campobello 1988.

6. González, Ramona n.d.c.

7. Kabalen de Bichara 2013, 22.

8. Garza-Falcón 1998.

9. González 1973, 22-41.

10. All five stories can be found online at *Open Door Archive*, https://opendoor.northwestern.edu/archive/ items/show/378.

11. Ramona González 2017.

12. Slater 1914a. https://texashistory.unt.edu/ark:/67531/metapth138143/m1/4.

13. Slater 1914b. https://texashistory.unt.edu/ark:/67531/metapth138221/m1/6.

14. Slater 1915. www.newspapers.com/image/80073713.

15. Moat 1917. www.newspapers.com/image/81023922.

16. Moat 1917.

17. Romo n.d.

18. *Vox News* 2019. www.youtube.com/watch?v=tkD6QfeRil8.

19. *El Paso Morning Times* 1917. https://texashistory.unt.edu/ark:/67531/metapth198630/m1/1/?q=Auburn-Haired%20Amazon%20at%20Santa%20Fe%20Street%20Bridge%20Leads%20Feminine%20Outbreak.

20. Feit, Stettler, and Bell 2018.

21. Pina 2017, 43-75.

22. *El Paso Morning Times* 1909. https://texashistory.unt.edu/ark:/67531/metapth581919.

23. *El Paso Times* 1913. www.newspapers.com/image/432902004.

24. González, Ramona 1972a.

25. Possible reference to Duranguito and Sunset Heights.

26. Ibid.

27. González, Ramona n.d.i.

28. Pusey 1977. www.newspapers.com/image/435267915.

29. Viescas 1979. www.newspapers.com/image/435904195.

30. Viescas 1979

31. Viescas 1979

32. Viescas 1979

Cuentos del barrio/*Stories from the Barrio, Part I*

1. Stern 1991, 200.
2. Stern 1991, 201.
3. Slater 1914. www.newspapers.com/image/81014995.
4. González, Ramona n.d.j.

González Grocery, el alma del barrio

1. Forgey 1999. www.washingtonpost.com/archive/lifestyle/1999/09
/25/the-corner-store-at-the-intersection-of-memory-and-time/9b4b9024
-cba7-4d1c-af10-e1a05bde1679.
2. Haider 2020.
3. McKay n.d. Accessed February 20, 2022. www.tshaonline.org
/handbook/entries/mexican-americans-and-repatriation.
4. Chávez Leyva 1995, 63–77.
5. Hernandez 2017, Part I."
6. Balderrama and Rodríguez 1995, 53.
7. Balderrama and Rodríguez 1995, 53.
8. *Bangor Daily News* 1931. www.newspapers.com/image/665771669/

Barrio Literacy: Doña Ramona's Poems and Fables for Children

1. González, Ramona n.d.e.
2. González, Ramona n.d.f.
3. González, Ramona n.d.d.

Works Cited

Anaya, Rudolfo. 1972. *Bless Me, Ultima.* Berkeley: TQS Publications.

Balderrama, Francisco E., and Raymond Rodríguez. 1995. *Decade of Betrayal: Mexican Repatriation in the 1930s.* Albuquerque: University of New Mexico Press.

Bangor Daily News. 1931. "Deportation of Aliens," August 1, 1931. www .newspapers.com/image/665771669/

Blea, Irene. 1992. *La Chicana and the Intersection of Race, Class, and Gender.* New York: Praeger.

Boswell, Angela. 2019. *Women in Texas History.* College Station: Texas A&M University Press.

Campobello, Nellie. 1988. *Cartucho and My Mother's Hands.* Translated by Doris Meyer and Irene Matthews. Austin: University of Texas Press.

Castillo, Debra A., and María Socorro Tabuenca Córdoba. 2002. *Writing from La Frontera: Border Women.* Minneapolis: University of Minnesota Press.

"Historic El Paso County Population: 1850–Present." n.d. "Historic El Paso County Population: 1850–Present." Compiled by County Information Program, Texas Association of Counties (website). Accessed August 4, 2021. https://txcip.org/tac/census/hist.php?FIPS=48141.

Cub Reporter. 1917. "From Kansas Cornfield to Paris, Via Denver, Hawaii, El Paso and Columbus, N.M., Being Something of the Life History of Miss 'Peggy' Hull, Times Staff Correspondent in France." *El Paso Morning Times*, August 19, 1917.

Cutler, John Alba. 2014. "Quinto Sol, Chicano/a Literature, and the Long March through Institutions." *American Literary History* 26, no. 2:262–94.

De León, Arnoldo. 1997. *The Tejano Community, 1836–1900*. Dallas: Southern Methodist University Press.

De León, Arnoldo. 2015. *Tejano West Texas*. College Station: Texas A&M Press.

Devereaux, Sandra G. 1976. "Mrs. Ramona Rodríguez González: 'The Best of Two Traditions.'" In *Worthy Mothers of Texas, 1776–1976*, edited by the Texas Mothers Committee, 92. Belton, TX: Texas Mothers Committee.

El Mestizo. 1973. "Farah strikers, Chicano group, march in El Paso." November 1973.

El Paso Daily Herald. 1896. "Shindy at the Bridge." December 22, 1896.

El Paso Herald. 1906. "Poor People are Suffering from the Cold." January 10, 1906.

El Paso Morning Times. 1909. "Taft and Díaz Make History for Two Great Nations." October 17, 1909. University of North Texas Libraries, Portal to Texas History.

El Paso Morning Times. 1917. "Auburn-Haired Amazon at Santa Fe Street Bridge Leads Feminine Outbreak." January 29, 1917.

El Paso Times. 1913. "Americans Murdered by Mexicans." August 26, 1913.

Enoch, Jessica, and Cristina Devereaux Ramírez. 2019. *Mestiza Rhetorics: An Anthology of Mexicana Activism in Spanish Language Press, 1875–1922.* Carbondale: Southern Illinois University Press.

Ettinger, Patrick. 2002. *Tenacious Immigrants: Crossing the Border, 1880–1930.* Pass of the North Heritage Corridor, El Paso, Texas.

Feit, Rachel, Heather Stettler, and Cherise Bell. 2018. *El Paso del Norte: A Cultural Landscape History of the Oñate Crossing on the Camino Real de*

Tierra Adentro, 1598–1983, Ciudad Juárez, Mexico and El Paso, Texas, USA. Austin: AmaTerra Environmental, Inc.

Forgey, Benjamin. 1999. "The Corner Store: At the Intersection of Memory and Time." *Washington Post*, September 25, 1999.

Garza-Falcón, Leticia. 1998. *Gente Decente: A Borderlands Response to the Rhetoric of Dominance.* Austin: University of Texas Press.

González, Ismael, Manuel González, Norma G. Hernández, and Sandra Devereaux. 2016. "Second-Generation González Sibling Interview." Interview by Cristina D. Ramírez, October 16, 2016, Audio, 1:48:27. Ramírez personal archive.

González, Ramona. 1972. "El Barrio Chihuahuita, 1972." In the Ramona González Papers. https://usldhrecovery.uh.edu/exhibits/show/the-ramona-gonzalez-papers/item/3044

González, Ramona. 1972. "Historia y cuentos de Doña Ramona: Adiós, barrio Chihuahuita 1972." In the Ramona González Papers. https://usldhrecovery.uh.edu/items/show/3025

González, Ramona. 1973. "'El tesoro enterrado' and other stories." In *Chicanas en la literatura y el arte*, a special edition of *El Grito*, year VII, book 1 (January), edited by Estela Portillo, 22–41. Open Door Archive: Northwestern University. https://opendoor.northwestern.edu/archive/items/show/378.

González, Ramona. n.d.a. "A la niña." In the Ramona González Papers. http://usldhrecovery.uh.edu/items/show/3020.

González, Ramona. n.d.b. "Chamaca's Dilemma." In the Ramona González Papers. http://usldhrecovery.uh.edu/exhibits/show/the-ramona-gonzalez-papers/item/3051.

González, Ramona. n.d.c. "Cuentos: el patio, el compadre, el borracho y la maceta." In the Ramona González Papers. http://usldhrecovery.uh.edu/items/show/3068.

González, Ramona. n.d.d. "El pajaro zensontle y el conde." In the Ramona González Papers. https://usldhrecovery.uh.edu/exhibits/show/the-ramona-gonzalez-papers/item/3136.

González, Ramona. n.d.e. "El sol." In the Ramona González Papers. http://usldhrecovery.uh.edu/items/show/3184.

González, Ramona. n.d.f. "El vuelo." In the Ramona González Papers. http://usldhrecovery.uh.edu/items/show/3211.

González, Ramona. n.d.g. "Lincoln Park School." In the Ramona González Papers. http://usldhrecovery.uh.edu/items/show/3117.

González, Ramona. n.d.h. "Los libros." In the Ramona González Papers. http://usldhrecovery.uh.edu/items/show/3115.

González, Ramona. n.d.i. "1910 Episode." In the Ramona González Papers. https://usldhrecovery.uh.edu/exhibits/show/the-ramona-gonzalez -papers/item/3017.

González, Ramona. n.d.j. "Por vida de estas santas cruces, yo viví en estos barrios." In the Ramona González Papers. http://usldhrecovery.uh.edu /items/show/3155

Guerra, Juvenio. 2016. "El Paso's Chihuahuita and El Segundo Barrio Neighborhoods Named to National Trust's 2016 11 Most Endangered List." National Trust for Historic Preservation. Accessed July 3, 2021. https://savingplaces.org/press-center/media-resources/el-pasos -chihuahuita-and-el-segundo-barrio-neighborhoods-named-to-national -trusts-2016-11-most-endangered-list#YpQSPO7MKUl.

Haider, Arwa. 2020. "A Cultural History of the Beloved Corner Shop." BBC, March 25, 2020. www.bbc.com/culture/article/20200325 -a-cultural-history-of-the-beloved-corner-shop.

Hernández, Norma G. 2013. "Our Story: Then and Now, Los González Rodríguez." Unpublished manuscript.

Hernández, Norma G. 2016. "The Distaff History of the Family: II, Ascención and Ramona." Unpublished manuscript.

Hernández, Norma G. 2017. "Second-Generation González Sibling Interview: Norma Hernández." Interviewed by Cristina D. Ramírez, December 8. Audio, 1:05:29. Ramirez personal archive.

Juárez, Miguel. 2014. "The Rich History of an El Paso landmark." *Lincoln Park: El Paso's Chicano Park* (website). Accessed July 14, 2021. http:// lincolnparkcc.org/history.

Kabalen de Bichara, Donna. 2013. *Telling Border Life Stories: Four Mexican American Women Writers.* College Station: Texas A&M University Press.

Leyva, Yolanda Chávez. 1995. "'Faithful Hard-Working Mexican Hands': Mexicana Workers During the Great Depression." *Perspectives in Mexican American Studies* 5: 63–77.

López, Dennis. 2010. "Good-Bye Revolution—Hello Cultural Mystique: Quinto Sol Publications and Chicano Literary Nationalism." *Melus* 35, no. 3: 183–210.

Marchino, Lois A. 2011. "They Gave Us Their Words: El Paso Women Writers," in *Grace and Gumption: The Women of El Paso,* edited by Marcia Hatfield Daudistel, 79–94. Fort Worth: Texas Christian University Press.

Marshall, Alex. 2021. "Amanda Gorman's Poetry United Critics. It's Dividing Translators." *New York Times,* March 26, 2021.

McKay, Robert R. 1989. "Mexican Americans and Repatriation." *Texas State Historical Association Handbook of Tejano History.* Accessed February 20, 2022. www.tshaonline.org/ handbook/entries/ mexican-americans-and-repatriation.

Metz, Leon. 2008. *Border: The US–Mexico Line.* Fort Worth: Texas Christian University Press.

Moat, Esther Kendall. 1917. "Enforced Baths for Chihuahuita Inhabitants Fail to Make a Strong Appeal to the Victims Not Jubilant Over Clean-up." *El Paso Herald.* Oct. 16, 1917.

Mora, Pat. 1993. *Nepantla: Essays from the Land in the Middle.* Albuquerque: University of New Mexico Press.

Mora, Pat. 1995 *Agua santa / Holy water.* Boston: Beacon Press.

Orozco, Cynthia. 2020. *Agent of Change: Adela Sloss-Vento, Mexican American Civil Rights Activist and Texas Feminist.* Austin: University of Texas Press.

Paredes, Américo. 1958. *"With His Pistol in His Hand": A Border Ballad and Its Hero.* Austin: University of Texas Press.

Paredes, Américo, and Richard Bauman. 1993. *Folklore and Culture on the Texas–Mexican Border.* Austin: Center for Mexican American Studies, University of Texas at Austin.

Pina, Michael. 2017. "The Archaic, Historical, and Mythicized Dimensions of Aztlán," in *Aztlán: Essays on the Chicano Homeland,* edited by Rudolfo Anaya, Francisco A. Lomelí, and Enrique R. Lamadrid, 43–75. Albuquerque: University of New Mexico Press.

Portillo Trambley, Estela. 1993. *Rain of Scorpions and Other Writings.* Tempe: Bilingual Press/Editorial Bilingüe.

Pusey, Allen. 1977. "Chihuahuita: Forgotten But Not Gone." *El Paso Times,* June 19, 1977.

Quintana, Joe. 1975. "One of 10 Top Texas Mothers Ramona González
   Inspires Love." *El Paso Times,* November 14, 1975.
Quiñones, Sandra. 2016. "(Re)braiding to Tell: Using Trenzas as a
   Metaphorical-Analytical Tool in Qualitative Research." *International
   Journal of Qualitative Studies in Education* 29, 3: 338–58.
Ramírez, Cristina. 2001. "Abuela, sí estás aquí." *Border Senses* 3 (Fall):9.
Ramona González Papers, The. 1960–1975. Recovering the US Hispanic
   Literary Heritage Digital Collections (database). See González entries
   above for web locations of specific documents. https://usldhrecovery.uh
   .edu/collections/show/22
Rios-C., Herminio, "Quinto Sol editor letter." In Ramona González Papers.
   Accessed April 5, 2024, http://usldhrecovery.uh.edu/items/show/3165.
Rivera, Tomás. 1992. *And the Earth Did Not Devour Him.* First electronic
   edition. *Latino Literature.* Houston: Arte Público Press.
Roberson, Susan L. 2022. *Women across Time / Mujeres a Través del Tiempo:
   Sixteen Influential South Texas Women.* College Station: Texas A&M
   University Press.
Romo, David Dorado. n.d. "This Day in History." January 28, 1917: The
   Bath Riots. *Zinn Education Project: Teaching People's History* (website). www
   .zinnedproject.org/news/tdih/bath-riots.
Romo, David Dorado. 2005. *Ringside Seat to a Revolution: An Underground
   Cultural History of El Paso and Juárez, 1893–1923.* El Paso: Cinco Puntos
   Press.
Ruiz, Vicki L. 2008 [1998]. *From Out of the Shadows: Mexican Women in
   Twentieth-Century America.* Oxford: Oxford University Press.
Slater, H. D. 1914a. "The Chance El Paso Has Longed For." *El Paso Herald,*
   May 25, 1914, University of North Texas Libraries, Portal to Texas
   History.
Slater, H. D. 1914b "Destruction That Means Progress." *El Paso Herald,*
   August 22, 1914. University of North Texas Libraries, Portal to Texas
   History.
Slater, H. D. 1915. "Just the Truth—That's All." *El Paso Herald,* February 4,
   1915, University of North Texas Libraries, Portal to Texas History.
Sosa, Kathey, Ellen Riojas Clark, and Jennifer Speed, eds. 2020.
   *Revolutionary Women of Texas and Mexico: Portraits of Soldaderas, Saints, and
   Subversives.* San Antonio: Maverick Books.

Stern, Jerome. 1991. *Making Shapely Fiction*. New York: W. W. Norton.

Timmons, W. H. 1990. *El Paso: A Borderlands History*. El Paso: Texas Western Press.

Turner, Virginia. 1994. "Rich History: Writer wants to bring Chihuahuita to forefront." *El Paso Herald Post*, 1994.

Valdéz, Diana Washington. 2016. "Supermarket makes history in South El Paso." *El Paso Times*, February 26, 2016.

Viescas, Carol. 1979. "Senora's memories mirror Chihuahuita passages." *El Paso Times*, August 12, 1979.

Vox News. 2019. "The dark history of 'gasoline baths' at the border," July 29, 2019.

Wright, Bill. 2020 [1976]. "Tigua Indians." Texas State Historical Association (website). Accessed April 4, 2024. https://www.tshaonline .org/handbook/entries/tigua-indians.

Archives Consulted

Border Heritage Center, El Paso Public Library

C. L. Sonnichsen Special Collections, University of Texas at El Paso

El Paso High School Alumni Association Archives, El Paso High School

El Paso County Historical Society, Burgess House, El Paso, Texas

Library of Congress

Newspapers.com, operated by Ancestry

Nettie Lee Benson Latin American Collection, University of Texas at Austin

Portal to Texas History

Texas State Library and Archives Commission

Image Credits

González family photo archive: pages 8, 36, 71, 193, 199
Ramona González Papers, Recovering the US Hispanic Literary Heritage
    Digital Collections: pages 9, 25, 32, 60, 283
Courtesy of the Library of Congress, LC-D418-30155: page 40
Courtesy of the El Paso Library Border Heritage Center: pages 41, 187
Courtesy of the Texas State Library and Archives Commission: page 4
Courtesy of the El Paso High School Library Archives: page 50
Courtesy of Open-Source, Northwestern University: page 58

Acknowledgments

An extensive community of family, friends, and colleagues helped bring this book to fruition. Without the support of Trinity University Press, this recovery effort of my grandmother doña Ramona González's collection of writings might have languished. A heartfelt thank you goes to my parents, Sandra (González) Devereaux and Dr. Neil J. Devereaux. After Rodolfo and Norma Hernández delivered doña Ramona's writings to our family, my parents held the vegetable box full of my grandmother's writings in safekeeping for several years. My father helped digitize my grandmother's writings and also did the translations. My mother and father steadfastly encouraged me to follow this path and furnished information to every question I had about the chronology of my grandmother's life.

Genealogical work, including recovery of family correspondence and documents, cannot be written without the robust participation and engagement of the wider family. I also wish to thank my tía Norma González Hernández; tíos Manuel González (1937–2017) and Ismael González (1937-2023); and my mother, Sandra González Devereaux. Their insights into the family history during several interviews helped fill the gaps in my knowledge of events. I also thank my cousins Xochitl Chafino and Raquel Hernández. They supported this project completely, held faith in me, and believed that our grandmother left her work to be recovered from within her family. They believed that I was doña Ramona's messenger.

I thank Alex Ramírez for *always believing* in this project from the moment my family uncovered the writings. *Sí se puede.* I am also grateful to Stu Hunter Williams for our lively conversations about the project, and his numerous reviews and edits of my manuscript.

Several friends and colleagues also provided input on the manuscript. Special thanks are owed to Anita August, Chris Hamel-Brown, Fred Kiefer, and Grace Wetzel. I also want to thank Norma Elia Cantú for writing the Foreword. Yes, Ramoncita's name coming to you was magic.

I also wish to thank the College of Social and Behavioral Sciences at the University of Arizona for a research-fellow grant to help fund this project at its earliest stages. Gratitude is also owed to Recovering the US Hispanic Literary Heritage Digital Collections at the University of Houston, which generously awarded a Mellon Humanities Research Grant that allowed these writings to be made accessible through its online exhibit. I owe countless thank yous to the University of Texas at Austin and the Nettie Lee Benson Latin American Collection for archiving the full collection of the Ramona González Papers. Thank you, Daniel Arbino, head of collection development, for working with our family to secure these documents at the Benson Collection.

Further, publication of this book was made possible with donations from the Department of English and the Provost's Author's Support Fund at the University of Arizona, the El Paso High School Alumni Association, and my family—Norma G. Hernandez, Ruben Devereaux, my parents, Neil and Sandra Devereaux, and my uncle, Ismael González.

CRISTINA DEVEREAUX RAMÍREZ is Professor of English in Rhetoric, Composition, and the Teaching of English and Head of the Department of English at the University of Arizona. She is the author of *Occupying Our Space: The Mestiza Rhetorics of Mexican Women Journalists and Activists, 1887–1942*, which won the 2016 Winifred Bryan Horner Outstanding Book Prize, and coeditor with Jessica Enoch of *Mestiza Rhetorics: An Anthology of Mexicana Activism in the Spanish Language Press, 1875–1922*. Ramírez teaches graduate level archival research and professional writing and mentors students in the US and Mexico. She lives in Tucson, Arizona, and travels frequently to Mexico for research and collaborations.

www.ingramcontent.com/pod-product-compliance
Lightning Source LLC
Chambersburg PA
CBHW020842020726
47497CB00005B/1219